The

MIDNIGHT
WITCH

The
MIDNIGHT
WITCH

Paula Brackston

THOMAS DUNNE BOOKS
ST. MARTIN'S GRIFFIN
NEW YORK

Thomas Dunne Books.
An imprint of St. Martin's Press.

THE MIDNIGHT WITCH. Copyright © 2014 by Paula Brackston. All rights
reserved. Printed in the United States of America. For information,
address St. Martin's Press, 175 Fifth Avenue, New York, N.Y. 10010.

www.thomasdunnebooks.com
www.stmartins.com

The Library of Congress has cataloged the hardcover edition as follows:

Brackston, Paula.
    The Midnight witch / Paula Brackston. — First Edition.
        pages   cm.
    ISBN 978-1-250-00608-0 (hardcover)
    ISBN 978-1-250-02296-7 (e-book)
        1. Witches—Fiction.   2. Fantasy fiction.   3. England—
Fiction   I. Title.
    PR6102.R325M53 2014
    823'.92—dc23

                                            2013033245

        ISBN 978-1-250-06329-8 (trade paperback)

St. Martin's Griffin books may be purchased for educational, business, or pro-
motional use. For information on bulk purchases, please contact the Macmillan
Corporate and Premium Sales Department at 1-800-221-7945, extension 5442,
or write to specialmarkets@macmillan.com.

First St. Martin's Griffin Edition: March 2015

        10 9 8 7 6 5 4 3 2 1

For Andrea - *može da uvek bude šećer i krem za kafu.*

The
MIDNIGHT
WITCH

1.

The dead are seldom silent.

They have their stories to tell and their gift of foresight to share. All that is required for them to be heard is that someone be willing to listen. I have been listening to the dead all my life, and they never clamor more loudly for my attention than at a funeral. This is in part due to proximity, of course. Here I stand, beside an open grave, somber in black, quiet, watching, waiting, pain constricting my chest more tightly than the stays of my corset, and all around me souls stir. But they must wait. Wait to be called. Now is not the time. I know they are eager to speak to me, and I value their trust in me, but wait they must.

It is always important, what the dead have to say. At least, they consider it so. As if departing this world has conferred upon their every single utterance a dignity, a value, that was not present while they trod the ground instead of sleeping beneath it. There are times their insistence and their self-importance tire me, I admit. Times such as now, when I am far too consumed by grief to want to hear them. Even so, I can never forget, *must* never forget that sometimes their words are indeed of great value. Necromancers through the ages have known this; we have learned to listen to their bold prophecies and their whispered warnings. What would the genteel lords and ladies assembled here today think, I wonder, if they knew that among them now are those who summon spirits from the past to divine the future? What would they think of me if I were to tell them I am most at ease in a catacomb, or sitting in a graveyard cloaked in darkness, talking softly with those who have crossed the Rubicon and dwell in the Land of Night? That I find comfort and solace in the companionship of the dead, as my ancestors did before me? What would they say if I told them I have always harbored a secret fondness for coffins? There is something about their sleek lines, the rich tones of the burred walnut, the gleam of the brass fittings, the comforting thought of a place of rest and safety, that appeals to me.

Now, though, as I watch my father's coffin being lowered into its grave, no amount of admiration for its workmanship can distract me from the loneliness I feel. My father was not an openly affectionate man—most thought him rather cold and aloof—but he loved me, and now he is gone. At twenty-one I should be excited about the future. Instead I feel only the sadness of loss, and the weight of duty upon my shoulders. My brother will inherit the role of duke and all that goes with it, but I am heir to my father's other title. A position that bestowed upon him both immense power and fearsome responsibility. And now it is my turn. I am to become the new Head Witch of the Lazarus Coven.

As I stand at the graveside I let my gaze sweep over the gathered mourners. Hundreds have turned out to pay their last respects to the late duke, but only a handful among us know that the coffin which is the current focus of attention, and which is now being lowered into the damp, dark earth, is, in point of fact, empty. The August sunshine has warmed the soil so that its musky scent drifts up from the open grave. To me the aroma is familiar and stirring. It smells of long ago, of ages past, of loved ones moved from this world to the next, of death and rebirth, of rot and regeneration. As the smell fills my nostrils I identify the presence of cleansing worms and busy beetles, and under it all, from nearby newly filled graves, the subtle beginnings of sweet decay. I am not the only one to detect the presence of disintegration. From the branches of a majestic cedar comes the agitated cawing of sharp-beaked rooks.

The heat of the summer afternoon is starting to tell on many of the mourners. The pool of black the gathered company presents seems to ripple as women sway unsteadily in their heavy gowns, their restricting corsets robbing them of much of what little air there is. Here and there fans are worked listlessly. The men fare no better beneath their top hats, and some pluck at their starched collars. The relentlessly high temperatures of this summer of 1913 are not conducive to comfort for anyone dressed for a society funeral. Even the gleaming black carriage horses, despite standing in the shade of an ancient yew tree, fidget, causing the blackened ostrich plumes on their bridles to shudder and flutter in the inappropriately cheerful sunshine.

I feel my mother's grip on my arm tighten. Her gloved fingers dig into the night-black crape of my sleeve. She looks worryingly frail.

"Mama?" I whisper as close to her ear as her elaborately veiled hat will allow. "Mama, are you quite well?"

"Oh, Lilith, my dear. I do feel a little faint."

The dowager duchess teeters alarmingly.

"Freddie!" I hiss at my brother, who stands only a few paces off but wears an expression that places him in another world entirely. "Freddie, for heaven's sake, help Mama."

"What? Yes, yes, of course. Now then, Mama. Steady as she goes." He smiles weakly, slipping his arm around our mother's tiny waist. "Not long now," he murmurs. "Soon be over," he adds, as much to himself as anyone else.

I take in the pale couple that comprise my family and wonder if I am equal to the task of looking after them. They need me to be strong. To take Father's place. But how can I? How can I? My mother's very existence has been defined by her husband for such a long time. She was a duchess for so many years, and now she must alter her view of herself, of her position, to become Lady Annabel. She finds this modern, fast-changing world confusing and illogical, and overhanging us all is the possibility of war. She is adrift, and I must be her safe haven. It is so typical of Mama that she insisted on such a grand and lengthy funeral. She has overseen every detail—from the number and variety of lilies, to the breed of the carriage horses, and the funereal livery of the footmen. I understand that she is sure in her mind that she knows precisely what her beloved Robert would have wanted. She believes it is expected of her as the duke's widow to carry out his wishes. However keenly she feels her grief, she will not let it show. However lost she knows herself to be, she will present a small point of stoic dignity at the center of the cortege. Only those closest to her will be aware of how much she is suffering. I know the truth of it. My mother is burying not simply an adored spouse, but the greater part of herself. Freddie and I will go into the world and have lives of our own; she will remain in privileged purgatory, from now until the moment of her own death, no longer duchess, no longer wife, no longer with a purpose of place around which she can shape her existence.

And Freddie. Freddie has singular problems which require singular remedies. Perhaps he can be persuaded to move out to our country estate in Radnorshire, far away from the destructive temptations on offer in the city. It would be a solution of sorts. But how will I succeed where even Father failed? Freddie knows what he would be giving up if he went back to Radnor Hall. I fear he would as soon jump into Father's grave.

That brother of yours will bring you to ruin!

Who is that? Who speaks to me unbidden, uncalled, unsummoned? What spirit would venture to do such a thing? Who is there?

One who watches you, Daughter of the Night. One who knows you, and your worthless brother, better than you know yourselves.

I must close my mind to this unwelcome, unfamiliar voice! Despite the relentless heat of the day I feel a sudden chill. Spirits may become restless, may long to communicate, but still they wait to be called. I will not listen. Not now. Now it is the living who need me. Freddie, perhaps, most of all.

Watching him as he attempts to support Mama he appears almost as insubstantial as she does. His skin has about it a transparency that seems to reveal the vulnerability underneath. Tiny beads of sweat glisten on his brow. He leans heavily on his cane, as if he cannot bear his own weight, let alone that of anyone else.

I remember the first time Father brought us here, Freddie and me. It was gone midnight, and the house was quiet. He came to the nursery, and told Nanny to get us up and dressed. I could have been no more than nine years old, so Freddie must have been seven. It was certainly strange, to be roused from our beds in the dark hours, and to leave in the carriage with only our father. I recall Nanny's anxious face watching at the window as we left. Did she know? I wonder. Did she know about Father? Did she know where he was taking us?

He had the driver park the carriage at the gate to the cemetery, and then led us through the narrow paths between the graves. He walked quickly, and Freddie and I had to trot and scamper to keep up. I remember feeling a little excited at such a mysterious outing, but I was not afraid. My poor baby brother, however, was so dreadfully scared. By the time we reached our destination—this very spot—he was crying quite loudly, so that Father had to scold him and insist that he be quiet. We stood still then, among the tombs and statuary, letting the dark settle about us. I heard an owl screech, and several bats flitted past, their wing beats causing the warm summer air to stir against my face. Father said nothing, gave us no instructions, told us not a thing about what was expected of us. He merely had us stand silently among the dead, wrapped in the night. Freddie fidgeted the whole time, stifling his sobs as best he could. But I was quite content. I felt . . . at home.

I take Mama's arm once more and hold on firmly. The vicar presses slowly on with the service, his voice flat and monotonous, like a distant bell, weathered and cracked, echoing the dying heartbeats of the man whose body we commit to the earth, and whose soul we commend to God. Except that his body is absent, and his soul will linger a while yet.

Beside a mournful statue of an angel, sheltering in the relative coolness of its winged shadow, and at some remove from the main company attending the duke's funeral, Nicholas Stricklend, permanent private secretary to the minister for Foreign Affairs, waits and watches. He has no desire to engage in small talk with others in attendance. Nor does he wish to give his condolences to the chief mourners. He wants merely to observe. To witness the interment. To assure himself that the leader of the Lazarus Coven is indeed dead and gone, once and for all, no longer occupying that privileged position of power and influence.

A squirrel scampers by close to where Stricklend stands. The quick movement of its claws on the dust-dry ground scuffs up fallen pine needles, some of which land on the senior ranking civil servant's spotless shoes. He regards the needles with distaste. Their presence offends him. He does not consider himself unrealistic in his expectations of life; he is aware that perfection, however sincerely strived for, is often unattainable. However, it is his habit to aim for nothing less, so that even when his attempts fall short, a high standard is maintained. What he finds irksome almost beyond endurance is the way in which the actions of others on occasion cause his cherished ideal to be compromised. Focusing on his shoes he exhales firmly, directing his breath effortlessly, as if it were within everyone's capabilities, the distance to his feet so that the pine needles are blown away as on a zephyr, and his shoes regain their matchless shine. The squirrel, sensing danger, freezes. Its face registers first fear and then pain, as it drops to the ground. After one small gasp it is stilled forever. The nearby rooks fall silent.

Stricklend returns his attention to the family of the recently deceased duke. He met Lord Robert's widow several times when she was still the duchess of Radnor. No doubt she would remember him, just as she would remember all her guests. She would naturally value her reputation as an excellent hostess but now, even so soon after the duke's passing, she appears to Stricklend diminished. Her husband's illness had been protracted and his death prepared for, but still the shock of it shows. Though her face might be veiled, her demeanor, her deportment, her seeming lack of substance are plainly visible. On her right, her son, Frederick, presents a picture of almost equal frailty. The young man is tall and good-looking, with the family's black hair and fine, aristocratic features, but he is painfully thin, and there is a restlessness about him that gives him away. Stricklend doubts the youth will make a good duke. He will not come close to filling his father's shoes.

The person who is of real interest to him, however, is the slim figure to the left of the dowager duchess. Lady Lilith Montgomery, only daughter and eldest child of the late Lord Robert Montgomery, sixth duke of Radnor, wears her striking beauty casually yet with dignity. She does not flaunt the head-turning loveliness with which she has been blessed any more than she would flaunt her position of privilege as the daughter, and now sister, of a duke. There is about her an air of seriousness. An earnestness. A self-contained strength, that Stricklend finds both admirable and attractive. He witnessed her coming out into society through the summer with careful attention. But it is not her feminine attributes that matter to him. Nor her social standing. What is of concern to him, what he is keenly interested in, is her ability to take on the mantle of Head Witch in her father's place. Only time will tell if she is up to the task. If she is not, it will be a bad day for the Lazarus Coven. A very bad day indeed. It will also be a singularly good day for Nicholas Stricklend.

🕷

Despite the weight of his valise, the bulk of his knapsack of artist's materials, and the awkward legginess of the easel he carries on his shoulder, Bram Cardale traverses the cemetery with a vigorous step. Being tall and strong means his luggage is less burdensome for him than it might have been for others, added to which a sense of purpose lends energy to his stride. He is glad of the shortcut, for he has walked a mile or more already, but he could happily travel until sunset, for today he begins his new life. Behind him lie burned bridges, disregarded offers of secure employment, and the comfort and stability of his family home. Ahead lies nothing certain, save that he is to lodge with the renowned and feted sculptor, Richard Mangan, and he is, at last, to attempt to become the painter he believes himself capable of being. Such a leap of faith shocked his parents. His father took it particularly badly.

"But, lad, you've a position waiting for you at the factory. You'd throw it all up to . . . to what? Paint pictures?"

"It's what I was meant to do, Father."

"All of a sudden our life, what we do, that's not good enough for you?"

"I don't expect you to understand."

"You're right about that."

"Can't you be pleased for me?"

"Pleased you're going off on the rim of your hat to live in a house of adulterers and heaven knows who else instead of taking your place here, where you belong? Oh, aye, I'm certain to be pleased about that."

Bram had not attempted to win his father round to the idea of his chosen future. He had dried his mother's tears and promised to write. There had been a moment, when she had looked deep into him in the way only she could, when he had faltered. She had touched his cheek with such tenderness, such concern . . . but if he did not go now he feared he would remain forever living a half-life, his talent, his art, his need to create, stifled and smothered. He could not tolerate such an existence. True, there could be no guarantees of success, and he might end up alone in London, a failed nobody, his talent exposed as an illusion. He risked one manner of madness if he went, and another, a slower more tortuous insanity, if he stayed. He had caught the evening train from Sheffield that very night. Guilt dogged his footsteps, but with each passing mile his certainty that he was doing the right thing grew.

The energy of London, the vibrant hum of the place, the sheer scale, all speak to him of possibilities and of freedom. He could not paint properly while still living under his father's shadow, living a provincial life, where he was hampered by his family's expectations of him. He knows he is acting selfishly, but if he must paint—and it seems he is driven by some irresistible force to do so—he must find a place and a company conducive to artistic expression and endeavor. He had written to Richard Mangan scarce hoping for a response, so when he was invited to take rooms in his house he knew it was an opportunity he could not pass up. Here was his chance to give vent to his ambition.

As he approaches the halfway point on the path to the east gate of the graveyard, Bram is struck by the number of mourners attending a burial. Large funerals are not uncommon in Sheffield but he has witnessed nothing of this kind before. He pauses in his journey, sliding his easel to the ground for a moment. He can make out several funeral carriages, all drawn by very fine horses, each black as coal, and draped in heavy velvet. The hearse itself might no longer be in attendance, but the remaining conveyances are no less impressive or flamboyantly liveried. Each has painted on its doors and embroidered on the drapery of the horses the emblem of a dragonfly, delicate and slim, its body shimmering green. Mourners stand a dozen rows deep, at least two hundred of them. Close to the grave the chief mourners look to Bram to present a touchingly small family. The young woman wears a broad hat with a long spotted veil, but he can discern elegant deportment and fine features even so. And a graceful, slender neck, the only part of her not swathed in black. Bram finds the whiteness of this small, exposed area of flesh somehow startling. Erotic, almost. A shaft of sunlight cuts through the branches of the lone cedar tree to illuminate the trio at the graveside, so that the fabric of their clothes, though cellar-black, reflects the light with such brilliance that the glare causes him to squint.

He wonders at once how he would paint such a phenomenon, how he would capture on canvas the strength of that light in the midst of such gloom. A familiar excitement stirs within him at the idea of the challenge. His pulse quickens. Images flash through his mind, light upon dark, dark upon light, blocks of color and bold brush strokes. In that moment of inspiration all is possible. He drops his luggage to the ground and scrabbles in his knapsack, pulling out board and paper, digging deeper for dusty shards of charcoal. He supports the board with one arm, pinning the paper to it with his fingers at the top. In his right hand he grasps the charcoal and turns to stand facing the scene he wishes to capture. He is in the full glare of the sun, and can feel perspiration beading his brow, dampening his hair. His hat offers more heat than shade, so he pushes it from his head, letting it lie where it falls on the parched ground. He frowns against the glare of the blank page, hesitating only a moment before beginning to sketch. A passing couple comment sharply on his inappropriate behavior. He is immune to their criticism. He knows he is witness to the grief of strangers, and he knows his actions could be seen as callous or disrespectful. The small part of him that still pays heed to such conventions, however, is stamped down by the urgency of his desire to depict what he sees, to immortalize that moment. It is not merely the juxtaposition of shapes, of sunlight and shadow, of patterns and elegant lines he wishes to show. Nor is he interested in recording a comment on society and its cherished traditions. It is the very essence of his subjects he strives to transpose to his picture.

To show what cannot be seen one must first represent what can be seen, he tells himself.

His mind works as swiftly as his hand as he draws. Deft, energetic marks begin to fill the paper.

It is my lot to spend my life in pursuit of the impossible. To reveal what is hidden. But am I able? Am I equal to the task?

He continues to work even as he feels his head spin with the heat of the day and the intensity of his concentration. Even as curious onlookers pause to peer over his shoulder. He works on, seeking to show the brilliance of life in the midst of a ceremony for the dead. Even as the vicar closes his good book. Even as the beautiful, slender girl beside the open grave raises her head and finds herself to be beneath his fervent gaze.

2.

It is nearly four o'clock by the time the funeral cortege leaves the cemetery. I am relieved the service and burial are over, but I do not relish the idea of what lies ahead. Mama spent many teary hours instructing Mrs. Jessop, the housekeeper, and Withers, the butler, on precisely what will be required when those invited back to the house after the funeral arrive.

All serving staff are to wear their mourning livery for the event, and those working below stairs will sport black armbands. There is to be a buffet of grand proportions, and the house dressed and presented in somber but dignified style. The food will be light, and refreshing. The heat will no doubt have already sapped the strength and wilted the nerves of those attending, so iced tea will be offered, along with lemonade and sherry. Withers will have selected a reasonable burgundy for those who felt the need of it, and whiskey, of course, for the men. Deliveries of lilies and black ribbon arrived almost hourly throughout the morning. Secretly, I wish we could have had a simple gathering. I favor the modern trend for a paring down of the traditional trappings and trimmings of a society funeral. But I understood my mother's need to throw herself into her role as widow, and to do this one last act as lady of the house. For now, at least, she has the diversion of being occupied to lessen her grief.

After slow progress through the busy streets the driver at last draws up in front of what has been the London home of the

Montgomery family for generations. Number One Fitzroy Square stands four stories tall, its broad white frontage separated from the world by gleaming, black iron railings. Wide steps lead up to the columned portico which frames the heavy black door. The brass door furniture and bell pull have been polished to a deep shine and only ever touched by gloved hands. The square is formed by four streets of such houses, all striking in their symmetry, their snowy facades, and their pleasing classical proportions. In the middle of the square there is a large private garden, ringed by a fence of railings which match those in front of the houses. Each household is in possession of a key so that they might enter and enjoy the lavishly planted gardens, with their walnut and chestnut trees, their shady walks and flower-filled beds. The foliage of the trees and the abundant shrubs provide a dignified yet pretty division between the houses on one side of the square and those opposite, and are so cleverly designed as to give the impression almost of a small slice of the countryside, transplanted to the heart of the city.

I feel my mood lighten a little, as it always does when coming home. I might have to graciously accept condolences from people I hardly know for several hours to come, but later, when the last guests have been helped into their carriages, I can, here, be myself.

Are you willing to listen to me yet, Lilith?

I feel my spine tingle as the same spirit I heard in the graveyard whispers in my ear once more. I am shocked. Shaken. No spirit has ever spoken to me in this way, without being called. I struggle to retain my composure. I will have to talk to this restless soul, that is certain. But not now, not here. My family needs me now. My non-witch family.

A young footman opens the door of the carriage and Withers, broad shouldered and dependable as ever, appears to offer his assistance to Lady Annabel. Freddie, enlivened no doubt by the prospect of a drink, has already sprung from the other side of the carriage and hurried round to help his mother.

"All right, Withers," he says, with jarring eagerness, "you can leave Lady Annabel to me. Come along now, Mama. Let's get you a nice glass of wine, shall we?"

"Don't be silly, Freddie, you know I never drink wine. Withers, is everything ready?"

"All just as you instructed, Lady Annabel."

"The flowers . . . they must be sprayed regularly. This dreadful heat . . ."

"I've put William to the task, my lady."

The dowager duchess halts her faltering forward progress and stares at Withers. For a moment she looks utterly lost.

"William?" she repeats in a small voice. "Do you know, I don't seem able to picture his face?"

I hurry to her side. "William Radley, Mama. The second footman, you remember?"

"Oh, yes. Yes of course. Fancy my forgetting. William Radley. How silly of me."

"You are exhausted, Mama," I say, taking her arm.

"And thirsty, shouldn't wonder," puts in Freddie.

I cast him a look that goes unnoticed as the two of us bear our mother up the steps and into the coolness of the house. Freddie is ready enough to offer help when it suits his purposes. It is not the sort of help I can ever allow myself to rely upon. There will always be Freddie's own needs behind any offer of assistance. I would be a fool to forget it.

Mama need not have worried; Mrs. Jessop and Withers have carried out her wishes to the letter. The hallway of Number One Fitzroy Square was built to impress, and impress it does. The careful Art Nouveau decor that my mother has so successfully embraced seems only enhanced by the vases of cream aromatic lilies, tied with black satin bows, which have been placed at considered random throughout. I find their perfume in the sultry heat almost overpowering and am aware of a burgeoning headache behind my eyes. Three immaculately turned-out servants hold trays bearing tall glasses.

I pause to speak to Withers, taking off my hat and handing it, with a nod, to my lady's maid, Violet.

"I shall sit with Mama in the morning room. Would you direct people to us there?"

"Yes, Lady Lilith."

"But have them shown to the dining room first. Everyone will be drained from standing in the sun for so long." I turn to speak to Freddie, but he has already divested himself of hat and cane, snatched up a glass of wine and is striding through the door to the study.

The morning room is blissfully shady, the sun having long gone off its tall windows. I encourage Mama to sit beside the fragrant bouquet of flowers which fills the hearth. I remain standing, the better to greet our guests. For over an hour the great and the good, mostly members of the aristocracy, some British, some having traveled from abroad, express their sympathy at the passing of the duke, and we graciously accept their condolences. My feet are soon aching and the pain in my brow has sharpened so that it is hard not to frown. It occurs to me that my mother and I are expected not only to hide our grief, to remain dignified and composed, whatever we are feeling, but we are also required to assist people we hardly know who stumble over their platitudes and condolences. It is incumbent on us, the hostesses and chief mourners, to put others at their ease, never mind our own inner turmoil. What use are offers of sympathy when they demand such effort of will and stoicism in return? This entire event, the food, the flowers, the manner in which one must conduct oneself, is for the benefit of people other than the family of the deceased. Who was it, I wonder, who decided that heartbroken relatives should host a party at the very moment all they wished for was to be left alone to grieve?

"Lilith." A low voice shakes me from my thoughts. "Lilith, I am so very sorry."

I turn to find Viscount Louis Harcourt striding into the room, his habitual confident step that of a man who knows his position in the world and is proud of it. He extends a hand, snatching up my own gloved one, kissing it briefly and holding it to him. "How very pale you look," he tells me, "and how very beautiful."

"Louis." I summon a small smile for him. After all, whatever the occasion, should not a girl be gladdened by the sight of her fiancé?

"Your father was a fine man. He will be greatly missed." He pauses and moves a little closer, so close that I can feel the warmth of him. I am tall, but still he has to stoop a little to speak in my ear. "If there is any way I can be of help . . . anything . . . you have only to ask. Darling Lily, you know that, don't you?" He reaches behind my ear. "Oh, how sweet," he says, opening his cupped hand in front of me to reveal a large butterfly. "Must have mistaken you for a flower."

"Louis, please, this is no time for party tricks."

"I only wanted to see my girl smile," he tells me.

I look at him levelly. If the thought flitted through my mind that I might mention to him the uncalled spirit I heard earlier, I quickly dismiss it. Would he even take such a thing seriously? His habit of using his magic at inappropriate moments is something I am accustomed to, as is the way he has of employing the sleight of hand of a music hall magician. I am aware, today, that there is more to it than a desire to amuse. He wishes to remind me that we share a special bond, because we are both born witches. As if I need reminding. It is one of the main reasons I have not resisted the match my parents always wanted for me. I think it comforted my father, in his last days, to know that I would marry into such a strong, wealthy, well-respected family. Louis and I grew up together. Our parents move in the same rarified social circle; his father and mine were, if not quite friends, then at least fellow Lazarus witches. The earl of Winchester always slightly resented my father's superior position in the coven. It was as if having to settle for a lower ranking in the aristocracy, being only an earl rather than a duke, made it rankle more that he must also defer to Father when in his witch's persona. My father did not count Louis's father as a personal friend, but they shared a mutual respect, born of an understanding of how the world works for singular families such as ours.

And, after all, my parents were not the only ones to regard Louis as a fine catch. Most of those here today know nothing of his coven membership; they simply see him as one of the most eligible bachelors in London. Dear Louis, I believe that is how he has always regarded himself. He knows how attractive he is, with his golden hair, bright blue eyes, and easy grace. He knows the effect he has on young women, knows how many mothers would have happily consented to him marrying their daughters. He exudes wealth and breeding effortlessly, with his fine features and twinkling eyes. I confess I find him attractive—it would be difficult to feel otherwise. And I am fond of him. But it is a fondness born of childhood acquaintance and many years of familiarity. There is something missing, at least for me. I believe he does love me, though I am not so naïve as to think his feelings for me would be the same if I were not the daughter of a duke, and heir to the title of Head Witch.

Is it foolish of me to hanker for some girlish notion of romantic love? Does such a thing even truly exist, I wonder.

After a few moments of giving me his rather intense attention, Louis moves on to express his sympathies to Mama and I slip away. I have no appetite, but remove myself to the dining room on the pretext of looking for something to eat. In fact, I merely wish to make sure all the guests are being properly looked after. None can leave until they have been fed and watered, and the sooner they all go, the happier I will be. The instant I form the thought I feel guilty. These people are, for the most part, here because my family matters to them. I should not be so ungrateful. I should not resent their presence. And yet, looking at such a quantity of glamorously turned-out men and women, who are at this moment busy helping themselves to a glass of this or a bite of that, it is hard to see them as genuinely sympathetic mourners, and easier to see them as partygoers, here to see and be seen, to show off their finery, to engage in tiresome one-upmanship or gossip.

I am spared pondering the matter further by the arrival of the earl of Winchester, Louis's father. As always his presence unsettles me. I know that he will be watching me closely, and that if he can find a way to remove me from my inherited place in the coven and put Louis in my stead, he will do so. Having me marry his son is surely the easiest path to power.

"My condolences, Lilith," he says. "Your father was a great man. His loss will be keenly felt by many."

"Lord Harcourt." As always with Louis's father, I find I am on my guard. Will this continue, I wonder, when I become his daughter-in-law?

"You have been left a very special legacy. Rest assured, should you find your inheritance . . . *burdensome* . . . there are those who would be only too happy to relieve you of it."

"And you would no doubt count yourself among them."

"Each of us must play to our own strengths, don't you think?"

"I have no intention of *playing* at anything. Now, if you'll excuse me . . ." I turn on my heel and walk briskly from the room. I will not, must not, let him see how anxious I am about taking up my father's position in the coven. Any sign of weakness would be seized upon. I can never afford to give him the slightest cause to claim I am not up to the task. Never. One day he and I will be of the same family, a family of which he is the head, but even then I will remain his superior in the coven. He makes no secret of how uneasily this sits with him. I will not allow him to bully me into deferring to him where coven matters are concerned, however much deference I will be required to show him in society.

It is a blessing to see my dear friend Charlotte Pilkington-Adams stepping lightly into the room. Dressed as always in the very latest fashion she somehow succeeds in making even funereal attire look becoming. The fabric of her gown is not the heavy crape Mama insisted we both clad ourselves in, but the lightest devore velvet, the cut of which allows her to move freely, while still softly enhancing her youthful curves. Though the outfit must be uncomfortably warm, she gives no outward sign of suffering any discomfort at all. Her abundant blond curls are pinned decorously beneath her hat, but still manage to peep out attractively. Charlotte's pretty face lights up at the sight of me, so that she has to quell her natural exuberance in order not to seem too cheerful for the occasion.

"Darling Lilith." We exchange kisses. "Such a horridly difficult day for you, and yet you look wonderful."

"And you are a very welcome drop of sunshine, Charlotte. Thank you for coming."

"Have you been endlessly cornered by bores? I would have rescued you sooner, but there is such a crush at your front door I could scarce get in."

"We've never been so popular. Funerals hold a morbid fascination for some, I suppose. And an opportunity to gossip."

"Your father was greatly admired. And people want to support you. Is there anything I can do?" She takes my hands in her own. "You must be utterly exhausted."

"You can keep the countess of Framley away from me. She's bound to make cutting remarks about Father not being laid to rest in a mausoleum."

"I should have thought that was his business and nobody else's. Silly old bat. Fear not, I shall keep a beady eye on her and intercept if she comes near. I notice Louis is here looking delicious as ever."

"Try to resist nibbling him," I tell her. "Cook has gone to some trouble to provide canapés and suchlike."

"Don't I know it! How is a girl supposed to keep her figure when you tempt us with such sinful treats?" She underlines her point by snatching up a tiny smoked-salmon mousse *en croute* from a passing silver tray. "In any case," she goes on, "I wouldn't dream of coming between the two of you. *The* most glamorous couple in London. How you do tease, keeping us all waiting for a wedding date."

"You'll have to suffer for a while yet, Charlotte. I'm not going to be rushed into anything."

"Hardly rushed. You've been engaged forever."

"We've been engaged for precisely a year. And now I am in mourning. I couldn't possibly start organizing a wedding. Even Mama would stop me, and you know how keen she is to see me settled as Viscountess Harcourt."

"As long as you're not planning to run off and join the movement for women's votes or something so energetically modern." She sighs. "I suppose you're right. I simply thought it would be such a lovely cheerful thing for you to have to think about, after these terrible few months. You will find yourself at something of a loose end now."

I have to remind myself often that dear, sweet Charlotte, whose friendship I value so highly, knows nothing of the Lazarus Coven, nothing of my own new role within it, nothing, in short, of the fact that her best friend is a witch. She has no idea what demands there will be upon my time and my thoughts now. She sees me as a young woman who wants nothing more than to be a bride and has no obligations other than those to her fiancé. How far that is from the truth. But I can never tell her. Just as I can never tell Mama. Must I always keep secrets from people I care for? Must I always hide the greater part of myself?

It is late in the evening by the time the last of the guests leave. Mama has already retired to bed. Freddie slipped away some hours earlier, to heaven knows where, to do heaven knows what. At last, with a slow summer dusk descending, I am free to climb the broad staircase to the sanctuary of my own room. I find my darling black cat, Iago, stretched out upon my bed.

"So this is where you've been hiding." I smile as I stroke his silky fur. The cat stretches farther, making himself an impossibly long and slender shape on the white bedspread. I lean down and kiss his sleek, black head, causing him to set up a rumbling purr. "You will miss Father, too, won't you, my little friend?" By way of an answer he gently nudges at my hand, his whiskers tickling my palm. I clearly recall the day, more than a decade ago, when my father presented me with him. He was not a kitten, but a young cat, not yet properly grown, thin and soft as a velvet scarf. The intense blackness of his fur the perfect foil for his vivid green eyes.

"Oh, Papa! He is splendid!" I cried, taking the cat from him at once. "And his eyes are nearly the same color as my own."

"His name is Iago," Father told me. "So that you will always remember that no one, however handsome, however clever, is to be trusted entirely."

I was familiar with Shakespeare's tale of jealousy and betrayal. The cunning character of Iago and his slippery treachery were etched into my young mind.

"But I trust you, Papa."

"A child is obliged to trust a parent. It is different when you have choice in the matter. Then it is up to your judgment."

It had seemed a curious thing to say, but then I was only a girl, how could I have understood? Now, now I understand very well. Indeed, the Lazarus creed has enforced the lesson daily since I turned thirteen. *Faith in Silence.* If you do not speak your secrets aloud, others will not have the chance to betray you with them. Keep the faith, and keep silent. It is what I have been trained to do all this time. It is something I am unlikely ever to forget.

Although my father had subtly and gently been preparing me to take over the role of Head Witch ever since I was born, it was only once I had been inducted into the coven that my instruction began in earnest. These sessions always took place at nighttime. Withers, though not a witch himself, was always complicit and helped make sure my absence from the house was not detected. Later, when I was old enough to warrant my own lady's maid, Father found Violet for me. It has been such a boon, all these years, to have someone in my everyday life who knows about the existence of the coven, and of my place within it. We attend coven meetings together, and if I need to go out on coven business I am accompanied by Violet. This system has served us well over the years. Were I to venture out unchaperoned, eyebrows would be raised and questions asked, not least by Mama. Fortunately, my mother is a sound sleeper, so that all those secret hours spent in the company of my Lazarus tutors went unnoticed by her, even if she did have cause, from time to time, to comment on my apparent tiredness, or the dark circles beneath my eyes.

However much I disliked the subterfuge involved, how I reveled in those hours I spent learning to become a fully-fledged Lazarus witch! It is our custom that several members of the coven should undertake to instruct a young witch. Some will have only a small part to play. This was the case with dear Lord Grimes, who introduced me to the ceremonial duties that are expected of a Head Witch. His role as Master of the Chalice is a somber and important one, but he is such a sweet man, and took such pains to make sure I was neither bored nor confused, that I quickly grasped the formal elements of my future role. There were others who listened to me recite the creeds and incantations, and still others who had me sing until I was word perfect with our songs of celebration and thanksgiving. Most of my tutoring fell to two people, and the first of these was, naturally, Father, who spent long hours hearing my defense of the functions and duties of the Lazarus Coven, challenging my assumptions, truly making me think hard about what was expected of me.

How often Father reminded me that it was all to ensure I was properly prepared to take over from him one day. And now that moment has come, and the Lazarus Coven is in my hands. I sit on the edge of the high bed and reach to the side of the head-board with its carvings of rose-briars, to pull the bell rope. Slipping off my shoes I wriggle my tired toes and sigh with relief that the worst part of the terrible day is over. I feel almost overcome with weariness suddenly. I was about to ring for Violet, but instead I decide to have a moment to myself. I feel a small shiver of excitement as I step over to the far wall and slide the little oil painting to one side to reveal the safe. I close my eyes and let my fingers spin the lock, muttering the words that release the combination that guards the precious items within. There is a faint clicking sound and the door springs open. Reaching in to take out the antique green leather case I find myself revived at the very thought of holding the wonderful stones in my hands. I settle at my dressing table and open the box. The Montgomery diamonds have been in the family for generations, and are famous even abroad. My mother wore them when she was first married to my father, but has always considered them too ostentatious. It was Father who suggested they be given to me on my eighteenth birthday. Mama was aghast at the idea to begin with, questioning how an unmarried woman could possibly wear such a necklace in public. But dear Papa, knowing the deeper significance of the gems to us—to me—insisted. He also insisted I be permitted to wear them when I came out into society, and so I have done, at many grand balls. Each time I feel the cool diamonds against my skin I sense a connection with my ancestors. Not merely the aristocratic family of the dukedom of Radnor, but my coven family. For the stones are a central part of the Lazarus Coven, as without them, the Elixir would be powerless. I cannot resist touching them. Their magic is strong. The low light of the bedroom is still sufficient to make them flash blue and green. They are in an unusual arrangement, linked together as if they were a cascading waterfall of ice, each diamond set into a fine holding of pure white platinum, hard and bright. As always, proximity to the stones revives me. Iago, who has little time for the importance of such things, jumps up onto my lap, purring loudly, putting himself firmly and furrily between myself and the object of my interest. The clock chimes the hour.

"You are right, puss. I must call Violet and get myself ready."

I put the necklace away, ring for my maid, and take my seat at the dressing table once more. I begin to remove the pins from my hair and am still doing so when Violet arrives on swift, silent feet, hurrying to take over.

"Please, my lady, let me," she says.

I willingly give myself up to my maid's care. I am certain I would look a fright without her help. My hair can look kempt and presentable, it is so very black and heavy, but only with proper attention and dressing. Left to my own devices, I would wear it in a ropelike plait, nothing more complicated. But certain things are expected of me, and a particular standard of turn out is the least of them. I close my eyes as Violet brushes my hair with long, rhythmic strokes. Is this how Iago feels when I stroke him? It is marvelous to be so comforted by such a simple thing.

"A sad day, my lady," says Violet. "And a long one."

"Would you tell everyone downstairs how much Mama appreciated all their hard work? She was very pleased; everything ran like clockwork."

"Thank you, my lady. I'll be sure to pass the duchess's kind words on."

"Not the duchess any longer, Violet. Just Lady Annabel now."

Violet pauses and says, "It will all take quite a bit of getting used to."

Her words end in a sob. Looking in the mirror I see the maid fighting back tears. I forget how much company I have in my grief. Poor Violet. It is small wonder she is so sad. She came to the house as a kitchen maid when she was only eleven, although her age was an estimate, as she was an orphan without a known birth-date. I always liked her. We are close in age, but, more than that, we share the coven as our family. She arrived at Fitzroy Square an orphan, and Father must have seen that there was something different about her. Something that was receptive to magic. With foresight typical of him, he encouraged the friendship between us. More than once Mama protested when she found Violet in the nursery with Freddie and me, but Father insisted we were helping train her as a maid. How much harder my duplicitous existence would have been, and would still be, without Violet.

When I became old enough to have a lady's maid of my own I requested her. We are as close as servant and mistress can be, and I know how much she had cared for my father. It is a measure of this closeness that I continue to call her by her first name, rather than her surname, as etiquette would normally require in the case of a lady's maid. I reach up and pat Violet's hand. In the silver-framed mirror in front of us, our eyes meet in the reflection. She has a pretty face, open and curious, with wide brown eyes and hair that curls of its own accord.

"Courage, Violet. You of all people know that he is not completely lost to us."

Violet nods tearfully and musters a brave smile.

"Take no notice of me, my lady," she says, busying herself with putting away the silver brush and tidying the hairpins. I know her well enough to understand that further sympathetic words will only bring on more tears.

I stand up so that she can unbutton my gown. The stiff silk is wearisomely heavy and I will be glad to be free of it. With the long row of buttons at the back unhooked, I am at last able to slip it forward over my shoulders and step out of it. Next Violet unties the laces of my corset. I am naturally slim, and have a long, slender waist, but fashion demands my stays be worn fiercely tight even so. It is a blessed relief to have them undone after such a long day. With the corset removed, I can step from my underskirt, and then pull my thin silk chemise over my head. I sit once more to tug off my stockings. My cotton petticoat feels wonderfully light and allows the gentle breeze of night air from the open window to refresh my skin. I hold up my arms so that Violet can help me into my crisp white nightdress, which I tie loosely at the neck. When I glance at the blackened pane between the undrawn curtains my own pale reflection gazes back

"Come," I say to Violet, "it is properly dark now. We must go."

"Yes, my lady." She fetches my velvet cape, helping me to drape it around my shoulders and fasten it with its elaborate gold clasp.

"Such a lovely green," she says.

"Dark as a pine forest, shimmering as a dragonfly's wing." I quote the words my father spoke on the day I first wore my witch's cloak. The night of my thirteenth birthday when I was initiated into the Lazarus Coven and my life changed forever.

Followed closely by Iago, we leave the bedroom, walk the length of the first floor hallway, and use a door at the far end which leads onto a steep wooden staircase. These stairs, though plain and worn, are not for servants or tradesmen, but for the sole use of the family of the house to gain direct, and discreet, access to the garden from the bedrooms. The narrow door at the bottom gives onto the lawns. Outside, night has fallen, still and warm after the sweltering day, and muted sounds of the bustle of the city beyond the high garden walls can be heard. A clear moon glows against the blue-black of the sky. I walk quickly down the little gravel path, Violet following briskly behind, on a short journey we have made together over the years hundreds of times.

We traverse the lower part of the grounds, which are mostly lawns and shrubs with lovingly tended rose beds. A short flight of steps takes us up to the terrace, which is shaded and sheltered by small fruit, walnut and magnolia trees. To the left of these stands the white-painted wooden summer house, with its pretty curved eaves and verandah. Iago knows precisely where we are going and bounds ahead to wait at the door. I take a key from the pocket of my cape and turn the lock. The interior of the summer house is just as might be expected, with striped deck chairs leaning against the walls, a folded parasol waiting in a corner, two trestle tables and a croquet set, all slightly worn and a touch shabby from many hours of use. This summer house, however, differs from its many cousins in one small detail. On the far wall, carefully designed to look like part of the weatherboard construction of the building, there is another door. I take a second key from my pocket and unlock this one. We slip through it, the cat darting ahead. I pause to make sure it is locked again behind us.

We stand for a moment in the almost total blackness of the space we have just entered. No city noises reach us here. I compose myself, taking a deep, sustaining breath, inhaling the faintly musty smell of the stairwell, feeling the cool air of it upon my face. I close my eyes, as I know Violet will be doing. It would not be seemly to rush the transition from the Outerworld to a place that is consecrated and sacred to the coven. A minute's reflection, a moment of stillness, a chance to master a racing heart, calm a ragged breath, or quiet a noisome mind. These are habits born of years of listening and watching, of learning and growing, of becoming a true and loyal member of the coven of Lazarus.

And the nearer I draw to the heart of our coven, the more at home I feel. How could I ever explain such a thing to one who has never experienced the joy of being a born witch? What would dear Charlotte make of it? Would she think me a monster?

When I open my eyes they have adjusted to the gloom, so that different levels of darkness present themselves. There is a faint line of paler darkness, from the windows of the summer house seeping in from around the door behind us. There is a chink of moonlight dropping from a tiny fissure in the stone roof above. And there is the coal black of the descent in front of us. Although I am familiar with every stair, every twist and turn, every uneven convolution of the descending steps, I will not venture farther without light. This is my sanctum. My coven. Mine. I will never approach cloaked in the dark. I will always, now, arrive in a glow of warm light. For the Head Witch of the Lazarus Coven is the bridge between day and night, between outer and inner, between life and death. Here, from this day on, I stand for the pulse of the living, even when I walk among the dead. I must always move in light, or risk being lost to the other side before my time.

"Light!" My voice echoes off the cold walls. "Light now!"

A short whooshing sound accompanies the flames which spring to life ahead of us. Heavy iron sconces hold thick torches at regular intervals along our route, all now burning brightly, flickering in the eddying air of the underground passage, casting dancing shadows all around. We move forward and downward, one hand holding up our hems, the other sliding lightly down the wall. There is no rail or rope to hold onto, but the damp stones beneath our fingers add at least the illusion of support during our steep descent. The staircase doubles back beneath the garden until we come to a long, low-ceilinged room which is directly under the house. Here the grimness of the stairwell is replaced by a certain amount of comfort. Thick rugs cover the floor, and maps and paintings relieve the dull gray of the stone walls. Around the room are low wooden benches with padded seats, as if in a somewhat expensively decorated waiting room, for indeed that is the function of the space. This antechamber is a place for gathering, for assembling, for collecting, before being admitted farther into the coven's sacred place of worship. There are several doors in each wall. Some, as in the case of the one I have just closed behind me, conceal staircases. One other—a grand double door, ornately embellished with an enormous green dragonfly, its body brightly enameled, its wings constructed from layers of finest spun silver—is the entrance to the main hall. A second, in a wall by itself, stands beneath a low lintel, solid and fortified with iron studs and wide strap hinges. Iago has sprinted down the stairs and now sits on a bench, idly washing his paws.

I turn to my maid and take her hands.

"Wait here for me."

"Are you sure, my lady?"

"I am sure."

"Then I will stay behind. But, if you need me . . ."

". . . I will call you."

Violet nods and gives a small smile of encouragement. I am not sure why I should feel so nervous. Is it excitement? No, something more. Fear, perhaps? I choose not to believe that. In truth, what is there to be frightened of? I have been preparing for this moment for so long. Father prepared me. I must believe I am ready. I summon my courage and move swiftly across the floor to place my palm against the low door.

"Open," I command, and the door swings slowly on its heavy hinges. I step inside. As I pass them, torches burst into flame, until at last the passageway broadens and I am standing in the wide and ancient space where the bodies of my forebears truly lie: the Montgomery catacombs. And there, in the center of the stone tiled floor, a tired smile playing on his dear, familiar face, his hands outstretched in greeting, stands my father.

Bram is not expected at Richard Mangan's house until nine o'clock, so he finds a table in a small restaurant in Marylebone. While he waits for his meal he takes out the sketches he made at the cemetery and pores over them, subjecting them to the scrutiny of his very harshest critic—himself.

Such poor imitations of what I saw. The strength and dignity of those mourners, that light . . . it is here and yet not. No. No. Wait, perhaps in this one? Yes! It is there. The spark of something. I must work on with this. Color. Color will bring it alive.

His food arrives and he reluctantly clears space on the table.

Am I wrong to believe I can do this? Will my new mentor assist me in revealing my talent, or will he simply reveal me to be a fraud?

He dines on what he fears might be his last steak for a considerable time, allowing for the little money he has brought with him, and then completes his journey to the address in Bloomsbury where the sculptor and his family live. He has been cautioned to expect, as Mangan had put it, "a fair amount of lassitude given and advantage taken where behavior, be it by adults or children, is concerned," along with the warning that neither his wife nor his mistress see the value in housework. As they keep no servants—a result of both principle and thrift—this, he has been told, leads to a degree of "dishevelment" in the household.

He finds the street without difficulty. It is at the very limit of the district, where smart, stucco-fronted houses give way to less grand constructions of London brick. At first glance, the house itself looks reasonably kempt. There is no front garden, just a few stone steps up to the door. The woodwork paint is peeling in places, but the building seems solid enough, and there are gaily patterned curtains at the open windows. The day is fading into twilight, and what appears to be oil lamps give a welcoming glow from the rooms at the front of the house. From these same rooms come sounds of music and shouting, so that Bram assumes some sort of party is in progress. He knocks on the door, and not surprisingly, it goes unanswered, so, finding it unlocked, he lets himself in.

Despite what he has been told, nothing could have prepared him for the mayhem which he finds inside. The air is thick with the smell of oil paint and turpentine, so strong it catches at the back of Bram's throat. The hallway itself has no lights, but is lit only by what lamplight falls through the doorways off it, or through what appears to be a large hole in the rear wall. There are pictures and mirrors aplenty, but no furniture, not a chair or a table, and nothing by way of hooks on which to hang a coat or hat. There are half-finished paintings propped against every wall, and wrapped lumps of stone, or smaller clay maquettes taking up space. The floor is of bare wood, which makes an excellent surface on which to ride bicycles, as three or possibly four (they move too quickly to tell) small children are demonstrating. Their shrieks of glee accompany some vigorous work on a piano in one of the adjoining rooms and the barking of a large, hairy, excitable, but mercifully friendly hound, which bounds about Bram as he attempts to set down his luggage.

A rosy-cheeked woman, who carries more weight than is flattering, appears in pursuit of two of the smaller children.

"Twins! Twins!" she calls after them as they speed away on a shared tricycle. "I have filled a bath for you. Come along now, do. We mustn't waste the hot water. Whatever would Pa say?"

The children seem not to care, but only pedal faster and giggle louder.

"Twins!" the woman wails at them as they disappear through the hole in the back wall and out, as far as Bram can tell, into the darkening garden. Noticing him at last, the woman brightens. "Oh! Are you he? The artist, is it you?"

"Well, yes, I am. It is." Bram snatches his hat from his head and is about to introduce himself properly but the woman spins on her heel and yells up the stairwell.

"Gudrun! Gudrun, he's here. Will you tell Perry? Gudrun, where are you?" she cries, chasing her words up the stairs.

Bram waits awkwardly in the hall while further chaos swirls around him. More children tear in one door and out of another. The dog decides they are more fun than he is and gives chase. Bram can hear raised adult voices on the floor above. A boy with startling red hair, aged about seven Bram guesses, comes to stand next to him. He stares up with a pale, serious face.

"Pa's gone out," he says.

"Oh, I see. Was that your mother? Mrs. Mangan?"

"No, and yes," says the boy. "She's not my mother. She is Mrs. Mangan."

"Ah."

"My name's Freedom," the boy tells him, and then points at various darting figures. "That's Honesty, Truth, and Purity. Those are the twins. Their names are Leo and Vincent, but mostly we just call them the twins."

"I'm Bram. Bram Cardale. I've come to stay here. I'm a painter."

The boy receives this information without a flicker of interest. *How many like me has he seen come and go,* Bram wonders. *How many hopefuls with their fragile talent and bright ambition?*

"Do you know when your father is expected home?" he asks.

The boy shrugs.

"Who can ever know for certain what Mangan will do?" says a voice on the stairs. A woman comes down, her hair the exact color and texture of the boy's, but worn long, loose and flowing about her shoulders. She is very tall and very beautiful, and her accent gives away German origins. Her skirt is loose and covered in paint, and the shape of her blouse suggests the absence of any sort of corset. She moves with fluid, graceful strides. "Mangan will do whatever Mangan wants to do whenever Mangan pleases," she says, coming to stand in front of Bram.

Now that she is close to him he can see there is oil paint on her face, too. She takes a slim cheroot from a silver case and puts it in her mouth. "Have you a light?" she asks.

"I'm afraid I don't smoke."

"Pity." She looks him up and down slowly. "Are you as strong as you look?"

Somewhat taken aback Bram says, "That's a difficult question to answer. How strong do you think I look?"

"Quite. Though you are pretty, too. Or you would be, if you weren't wearing those terrible clothes." She makes a despairing gesture at his outfit. "If you keep all those buttons done up in this heat you will surely die, Artist. Do you wish to die young?"

Bram does not know which slight, comment, or question to respond to first. Before he can think of a suitable response the apparition turns and calls up the stairs in her slow, deep voice. "Perry. Come down and meet our new pet artist."

Bram isn't sure he likes being described in such a way and thinks he has never met anyone so strange.

But then, he reminds himself, *this is London. This is an artist's home. People do things differently here. I must embrace such freedom, not shy away from it.*

Recalling reports of Mangan's private life, he takes the woman to be his famous mistress from Berlin, a successful painter in her own right. The smaller, plumper one, the boy has confirmed as the sculptor's wife. Freedom is clearly the mistress's child. As he hasn't noticed the vivid red hair on any of the others he assumes them to be Mangan's legitimate children.

Mrs. Mangan descends the stairs rather breathlessly, followed by a somewhat skinny young man with a kind face and sandy hair.

"Gudrun, there you are. Perry, you don't need a muffler, dear, it's such a warm night." She unwinds the scarf from around the young man's neck and pushes him gently toward the door. "Now hurry along, do, all of you. There's not a moment to lose."

Bram finds himself being steered out of the house.

"Where are we going?" he asks, his feet not yet recovered from all the walking he has done, and feeling his arrival has somehow not received the reaction he was hoping for.

Gudrun dips her hand into Perry's inside jacket pocket and removes a lighter. She lights her cheroot and replaces the lighter, letting her hand rest a moment on the lapel of the jacket as she does so. It is a small gesture, but one that strikes Bram as intensely intimate. All the more so because the young man does not take the slightest notice of her doing it. She inhales deeply, leaving her friend to answer Bram's question.

"Jane wants us to retrieve Mangan," he explains.

"Fetch!" says Gudrun through whirls of smoke. "Like we are the good little dogs."

"He went off in a frightful tizz, determined he was going to Mr. Chow Li's place."

"Mr. Chow Li?"

Perry's legs are fractionally shorter than those of Gudrun and Bram, so that he has to scamper to keep up.

"He has an opium den. It's quite famous, you know. Down by the river."

"Wouldn't it be quicker to take a cab?" Bram suggests.

Gudrun looks at him keenly.

"Are you rich, Artist?"

"No, I'm not."

"Then keep your money. You'll need it."

Perry laughs. "She's right. We've never a shilling between us, any of us. It's not that far to walk, really." Remembering his manners, as if they were some unpracticed skill, he sticks out his hand. "I'm Peregrine Smith, Mangan's assistant. Call me Perry, everyone does."

"That's what you think," says Gudrun cryptically.

"Bram Cardale." He shakes his hand. "Does he let you help? Really? With his sculptures, I mean?"

"Oh." Perry colors. "Hardly. I just help with . . . you know . . . things. Make myself useful. But I do dabble a bit. When I have time. Nothing in the same league as Mangan, goes without saying . . ."

"Then why bother saying it?" Gudrun lengthens her stride and puts some distance between herself and the men.

"Is she always this . . . difficult?" Bram asks.

"Oh no," says Perry, "sometimes she's much worse."

They laugh, and then fall to silence as they make their way through the teeming streets. They quickly leave the more salubrious area of the city and begin to wind between narrow rows of dingy little houses. The roads are, in many cases, nothing more than alleyways, and soon the summer stink of the river water drifts up from the Thames, guiding them toward Mr. Chow Li's dwelling.

3.

I have to resist the near overwhelming desire to throw myself into my father's arms. I know, of course, that he is walking in spirit, that his body lies in the gleaming coffin newly placed among our ancestors behind him, and that, however heartfelt his gesture, he cannot embrace me. I am not, as many others would have been, in the least bit alarmed or afraid to see my father's ghostly form standing in front of me. I understand the dangers and the benefits of calling on the dead to aid magic and to divine the future. It has always brought me great comfort to know my loved ones are reachable in this way, if they themselves are willing to be called. Even so, I have to prepare myself for the fact that I will miss Papa's physical embrace, and that it will take time to adjust to his nonmaterial presence. Standing here with him now I remember the first time I was called upon to fully summon a spirit on my own. It was a thrilling moment. The first time I not only heard but *saw* someone from the Land of Night. Saw them take shape in front of me. Watched them walk toward me. Spoke with them. Listened to them. All the time knowing they were there because I was a necromancer, and they had answered my call.

It is not a skill that comes to anyone on the first time of trying.

For weeks, Louis and I had been charged with perfecting the art of calling spirits to speak with us, without asking them to show themselves. As ever, Louis was bored with the mundane business of repetition and practice, and eager to move on to what he saw as necromancy proper.

"I mean to say, Lily, how many times are we expected to do this? I can call the voices at the drop of a hat. Your father knows that. So does Lord Grimes, and Druscilla. It's a waste of time, doing it again and again." He paced the floor of the antechamber restlessly.

My other teacher, to whom I owe any skill with magic that I might lay claim to at all, is the eldest senior witch of our coven, Druscilla Larkspur. Druscilla is a woman who has magic at the core of her bones. To stand next to her is to feel it. I wonder that non-witches are not disconcerted by the force that emanates from her, for they can have no understanding of what it is that makes her eyes shine and her skin glow, even though she has at the very least passed her ninetieth year. True, she looks in all other respects like an elderly woman, if rather tall and surprisingly straight backed, and though she carries a walking stick she appears never to need to trust any weight to it. She is very thin, and her face shows the struggles and cares that have afflicted her through life. Yet there is such a strength about her. She was a patient teacher, but loathed laziness, and would suffer neither pride nor false modesty in her students, so that each of us trod a fine line if we were not to incur her displeasure. She often conducted her sessions in total darkness, which was a test in itself.

I smiled at Louis. "Druscilla says practice is never a waste of time, not if you are striving for perfection."

"I don't think it's something one can be perfect at. It's not as if the spirits are all orderly, organized beings who do what they are told . . ."

"You are not supposed to *tell* them anything, not when you are calling . . ."

A noise from the doorway to the catacombs made us both jump.

We turned to find Father standing there, wearing an expression of barely contained irritation.

"I am glad to hear you have learned that much from your studies at least, Lilith," he said.

Somewhat stung, I answered, "I do my best, Papa."

"I hope so. Let's hear it, then. Let's see how much you both know, if you are so very *expert*." He spat out the final word, pointedly directing it at Louis. "Which of you can tell me the difference between 'calling' and 'summoning'?"

To his credit, Louis responded without a trace of rancor in his voice.

"A called spirit is requested to attend, invited to step into the Land of Day and commune with the living. A summoned spirit has no choice. If the necromancer is skillful, whoever he summons must at the very least speak with him. At best he must show himself, too, whether he wants to or not."

"And if the necromancer is lacking in skill? What might be the outcome then?"

"That would depend," said Louis, ignoring the intended slight, "on what sort of spirit was being summoned. If it is a Gentle Spirit, merely . . . reluctant, it might happen that no connection is made. If, however, it is a Dark Spirit, and vehemently resists the control of the necromancer, well, it might . . . cause difficulties."

My father raised his eyebrows eloquently.

"I mean to say," Louis pressed on, "the spirit might exert its own will upon the necromancer, or the gathering. He might cause harm." Even Louis could hear the inadequacy of his response. He fell silent.

Father walked into the room, pacing slowly as he spoke.

"A Dark Spirit incompetently summoned can wreak havoc. He can inflict actual pain and injury upon not only the inadequate necromancer, but also anyone present. More than this, he may refuse to return to the Land of Night and set out on a haunting.

This coven can only exist so long as its code of secrecy is observed."
He stopped close to Louis and looked at him sternly. "How long
do you imagine that could continue if recklessness allowed spirits
to flit hither and yon, terrifying people and muttering about being risen from the dead by members of the aristocracy?"

Louis opened his mouth to speak, but my father raised his hand
to silence him.

"What is more," he went on, "you have not touched upon the
other very real danger attendant on inexpertly performed summonings." He turned to me. "Well, Lilith, can you enlighten us?"

"Yes, Papa. The gravest outcome would be that a being from
the Darkness would take advantage of the rupture brought about
by the summoning . . ."

"The rupture in . . . ?"

". . . in the Rubicon. That is, in the divide between the Land of
Night, where the deceased dwell, and the Land of Day, where the
living tread the earth. The Darkness, as we know, contains those
souls who are not fit to inhabit either of the other realms."

"Such as?"

"Such as demons, warlocks, poltergeists, and many other creatures, most not human."

"So, Louis." My father sat on one of the tapestry-padded benches
that ran along the wall of the antechamber. His momentary anger had passed, and he looked at Louis with a face that was stern
but kind. "Would we want those sorts of beings abroad in the
Land of Day, do you suppose?"

"No, sir. No, we would not."

Father nodded. "And if you had any idea of how difficult it can
be to retrieve a demon once he has escaped it might give you pause.
You are both born witches, so have had the advantage of growing
up in families who have understood and nurtured your birthright to belong to the coven and learn our spellcraft. But Lazarus
witches are set apart, in that their main function is necromancy.

Working with spirits from the Land of Night is a skill that must be learned. And learned well. Never forget that." He paused, studying our faces and then suddenly slapped his knees with his palms and made his tone lighter. "Now, children, indulge your tutor. Give me the Lazarus creed, if you please. Loud enough to show you mean it, but without shouting, if you can manage that."

Louis and I exchanged brief grins. The scolding was over. Together we recited:

> *"Faith in Silence:*
> *To Protect the Great Secret,*
> *To Preserve it for those yet to come,*
> *To Honor those who have gone before us,*
> *To Spare the innocent."*

He nodded, and I swear I saw a smile tugging at the corners of his mouth, his eyes crinkling just the tiniest bit.

"Very good. Well now, let's not keep Druscilla waiting any longer. I believe she is hoping you will both succeed in fully summoning a spirit without any of the mishaps you are so clearly well-versed in. Go on, she's an old lady. Her time is more precious than most," he said, waving us toward the Great Chamber.

And now the spirit who stands before me, as clear and vibrant as any living being, is my own dear father.

"Daughter, my darling girl," he says softly, his voice, as is so often the case with the risen spirit, sounding thinner, lighter, less substantial than his corporeal one had been.

"Oh, Papa!" I must fight to control my tears.

"Hush now, this is not the time for weeping. We both knew this day would come. And, as you see, I am still here, am I not?"

I shake my head, digging my fingernails into my palms to force myself not to crumble. "But . . . Father. . . ."

"I know. There are . . . adjustments to be made."

"And to step into your shoes, as Head Witch . . . will I command the respect that the leader of a coven should do?"

"You will, Lilith. In time. I grant you, it is unusual for a girl scarcely twenty-one to take on such a role. Unusual, but not unheard of. Think of all those who have stood where you now stand, doubting themselves just as you doubt yourself."

"But what if I fail?"

"You will not fail," he tells me. "Look at me, child."

I do as he asks, my mouth firm with determination, but my eyes, I fear, giving away my deep anxiety.

"You will not fail because you *must* not fail. You understand, don't you, Lilith?"

"Yes."

Father nods slowly. "You are my daughter. You have studied hard and long for this honor. I know that you are equal to the task, my dear. And you know that you do not face what lies ahead on your own. You have the support of the coven, Lord Grimes and Druscilla in particular. And of course you have my counsel, my guidance, always."

"Yes, Papa." I have to be strong, not only to live up to his expectations. There is so much at stake. I force myself to take a steadying breath and stand tall. "I will not disappoint you. I promise."

"Have all the arrangements been made for the inauguration?"

"They have, as you instructed, and as coven law dictates. Precisely one full month from the stopping of your heart, at the pinnacle of the night, we will convene here. Word has been sent out."

"Good, good. It will be a proud day for me, daughter." He smiles at me and then gestures toward a low bench. "Now, sit with me, and amuse me with details of the day. I want to know how quickly the earl of Winchester told you he would happily take over this onerous responsibility from you, how many times the countess of Framley called you a lamb, and how much of my second best claret was sacrificed to the occasion."

Feeling the weight lift from my shoulders and the joy of my father's companionship lift my mood, I sit beside him and we chat amiably about the day's events. I consider telling him about the unknown spirit who spoke to me unbidden earlier, but hours have passed and there has been no recurrence. Perhaps I was merely overwrought. Grief, heat, and concern for my family allowing my mind to play tricks. Father and I have enjoyed fewer than ten brief minutes together before the silver bell in the corner of the chamber rings, blunted echoes of its clear notes reverberating off the low ceiling and dense walls of the cavernous space.

I spring to my feet.

"Withers! Something is wrong."

"You must go."

"So soon, Papa? I had wanted so much to stay with you longer tonight."

"We will have time again. You are needed. Go now," he says, gently but firmly, and as he speaks he moves silently backward into the shadows until the gloom swallows him entirely.

Hastening back to the house, Violet and Iago at my side, I meet our trusty butler in the hallway.

"Forgive me for disturbing you, Lady Lilith, but this has just been delivered." He holds out a note.

Taking it from him, I immediately recognize the curious hand of Mr. Chow Li.

FM he ailing. Better you come get.

My heart drops. Today of all days. But then, why not today? I am not the only one who has just inherited duty and responsibility. I am not the only one mourning Father's passing.

"We shall need a cab, Withers."

"I have one already waiting outside, my lady."

"Then we should go quickly."

"I have taken the liberty of asking Mrs. Jessop to prepare a daybed in the library, my lady. It may be we are not able to . . . encourage His Grace up the stairs."

I am shocked to hear my brother referred to by his new title. Something else I shall have to come to terms with. Like it or not, things have changed forever, and now, however poorly suited he is for the role, it is Freddie who is the duke of Radnor.

Nicholas Stricklend finds he often does his best work in the hours of darkness, when there are fewer people likely to interrupt his thoughts. Whitehall is, of necessity, a place of bustle and busyness, with so very many civil servants doing their best to manage the politicians who pass through their tender care. It was to avoid the mainstream of this mayhem that he secured himself a suite of offices, and of rooms, indeed, in the newly built Admiralty Arch which spans Pall Mall on the southwest corner of Trafalgar Square. Competition for such a prestigious workplace had been fierce, but Stricklend had never been less than completely certain that he would get what he wanted. His private accommodation is on the top floor, to the rear of the main arch, at its center, so that the windows look directly up Pall Mall and give a clear view of Buckingham Palace. He selected offices on the floor below, with windows at the front, allowing him to overlook the roofs of Downing Street, and the spires of the Houses of Parliament. Never has a building been so perfectly constructed, he believes, to demonstrate the point of power in the land: the confluence of monarchy and state. The royal family to the west, solid, ancient, and privileged. The government to the east, thrusting, dangerous, and clever. Both built upon the labor of the masses. Both kept in their fortunate positions by the love of those same beasts of burden.

Both served, or ruled, depending on your view, by the cunning of those who bridged the gap, much as the Marble Arch does, between the two worlds. Where birthright meets public mandate, in the tension of that connection, stand invisible men who are able to manipulate both to further their own aims. Stricklend is just such a man. Ordinarily, of course, the petty desires of these Machiavellian figures are not of great importance to anyone but themselves. The rise of a civil servant through the ranks, the acquisition of a grace and favor property, the opportunity to make money on the stock market, or mingle with aristocrats on their country estates, none of these things make the slightest difference to the man following his plow, or the schoolboy reciting his tables. National security remains secure. The order of things will continue unchallenged. Ordinarily. But Stricklend is not ordinary, and neither are his plans.

He chose to furnish his suite in a spartan, businesslike fashion. The broad mahogany desk, shipped in from Singapore and weighing nearly as much as the four stout men who had delivered it, reflects, in both its stature and its orderliness, the workings of its owner's mind. It is in perfect scale with the room it occupies, and yet it projects its own special importance, gravitas, and power. Its top is covered with tooled green leather, bordered with gold leaf, on which sit, in regimented lines, a spotless blotter, a heavy crystal inkwell, three fountain pens, and two evenly sharpened pencils. There is no eraser, for Stricklend will never have need of one. He is of the opinion that a thing done properly is a thing done perfectly, and will therefore require no correction. To the left-hand side of the blotter, placed at a right angle to the edge of the desk, a plain black telephone is positioned precisely at a comfortable arm's length from the Windsor chair upon which no one, but no one, other than Stricklend is ever permitted to sit.

The desk faces the door, to meet squarely anyone who deigns

to come through it. The window behind, and the inspirational view it provides, are for contemplating only when standing up. The evening finds the permanent private secretary in pensive mood. Having satisfied himself that the sixth duke of Radnor is indeed dead, he has now to decide how, and when, he should engineer a meeting with his successor. Whether or not having a woman as head of the Lazarus Coven will prove an added complication to his plans is not yet clear. The Sentinels had been about to make their move when the late duke had fallen ill. Everything has been put on hold. The death of the Head Witch has changed things, of that there is no doubt. Precisely how, and to the advantage of whom, remains to be seen.

These solitary deliberations are interrupted by the arrival of Elias Fordingbridge. The clerk is no more than five foot four, but still feels the compunction to stoop, as if he were much taller, or as if he were simply trying to avoid appearing in any way above himself. He steps across the threshold with his customary partially sideways gait, again as if he wishes to present himself as taking up even less of the world than he actually does, however slight his place in it actually is.

"My apologies for disturbing you, Mr. Stricklend, sir," says Fordingbridge, fixing his gaze on the floor so that there will be no chance he might look his superior in the eye, "but I thought you would want to see this." He proffers a copy of the evening paper, folded neatly to show a report on the bottom left corner of the front page.

Stricklend takes it from him. The headline reads:

SIXTH DUKE OF RADNOR BURIED TODAY

Stricklend purses his lips. It is an article of minor importance, on the face of it. A small story to fill a small place in the late edition of the London paper. Except that he knows what, in reality, the death of the duke means. And he knows that Fordingbridge knows. What bothers him now, what causes him to furrow his brow and drop the paper onto his desk, is just how careful his clerk has been to keep what he knows from anyone else. It strikes him that folding a newspaper to highlight a particular story, and hurrying along public corridors with it with all too apparent eagerness bordering on excitement, does not demonstrate an awareness of how vital, how crucial, discretion and secrecy are to the success of certain plans. He sighs. It is clear to him that diligence and caution are lessons the pathetic little amanuensis needs to be taught over and over again.

"From where did you obtain this newspaper, Fordingbridge?" he inquires, his voice, as always, soft, his words considered.

"From a stand outside the main entrance, Mr. Stricklend, sir."

"A stand outside the main entrance. I see. And how many people, do you think, observed you making your purchase?"

"Well, sir, the street was still busy, but I don't suppose many were interested in my actions. Sir." The clerk clasps his hands in front of him and begins to look increasingly uneasy.

"You don't suppose . . . no, Fordingbridge, that is, I fear, a major part of the problem, your not supposing. You see, I imagine you took no trouble supposing how many people might also observe you noticing the article at the bottom of the page, and that they might have registered your interest in this piece, and that they might have become aware of the haste with which you sought to bring this news to my attention, suggesting that the article was, therefore, of no small interest . . . to me. Do you see where this might be leading us, Fordingbridge? Do you?"

The look of terror in Fordingbridge's eyes suggests that he knows exactly where this might be leading them, and it is somewhere he wishes with all his being not to go.

"Oh, Mr. Stricklend, sir, I promise you, I was careful, truly, I was," he whines, clasping and unclasping his hands, bending his feeble body even farther forward so that he is almost bowing before his master.

"But not careful enough," says Stricklend. "I think you would agree, wouldn't you, Fordingbridge? Or are you going to stand there and compound your stupidity by questioning my judgment on the matter, hmm?"

"Oh! No, sir, please . . ."

An expression of tedium passes over Stricklend's face as he sends the Suffering Spell across the room. He finds it tiresome in the extreme that he has to so frequently admonish his servant and remind him of what will happen if he fails in his duties.

He watches as Fordingbridge endures his punishment and decides that, if nothing else, the wretched creature is learning to accept painful penalties as his due. He does not cry out when the skin on his hands starts to bubble and bulge but rather stares at them, almost fascinated to witness his own torment. It is only when the agony inflicted by the phantom burrowing worms reaches the tender areas of his neck and his face that he emits a pitiful, high, whining noise. Stricklend judges the point has been made and reverses the spell. Fordingbridge gasps, taking some moments to regain his composure. When he has done so he swallows hard.

"Well?" Stricklend asks. "Have you nothing to say to me?"

"Thank you, master!" he splutters. "Thank you."

The permanent private secretary nods, satisfied, and dismisses his clerk with a wave of his hand.

4·

I allow Withers to help me from the hansom cab and instruct the driver to wait for us. He is predictably reluctant to linger in such a street, but a few extra coins persuade him it is worth the risk. In fact the place I ask him to halt is some way from Mr. Chow Li's house. Shame enough that a stranger should be involved in recovering my brother at all. There is no necessity for him to see the actual premises. Or its clientele.

We make our way through the filth of the narrow alleys as hastily as we are able. The district of Bluegate Fields falls considerably short of the bucolic image conjured up by its name. The houses lean against each other like so many listing tombstones. Some are terraced rows with mean windows, but most are single story, little more than shacks, with swaybacked and makeshift roofs, and doors that open directly onto the muck and muddle of the unlit passageways and streets. As we draw closer to the river there are also tall, dark brick buildings, some as high as four floors, built as warehouses for merchandise brought up and down the Thames. Such is the gloom, that had Withers not had the foresight, born of experience, to bring a lamp, our progress would have been both halting and hazardous. Drunken men and women lurch from the shadows, calling abuse or suggesting ways in which they might assist one another. I pay them no heed but stride on, lifting my cape to avoid the worst of the mire. Withers is a large man, and his size and purposeful step go some way to warding off unwanted attention. I know, however, that the fact we are able to pass unmolested is due mainly to the guardian presence I summoned to accompany us. The protection I receive from the spirits who answered my call for help is not visible, not to those who are not witches. Should a witch be walking in Bluegate Fields this night, however, and happen to glance in the direction of the slender woman in the deep green cloak with her sturdy butler, they would clearly see the three long-dead soldiers marching, swords drawn, at my side. They would notice their feathered hats and short, silk-lined capes which marked them out as Royalists fallen in a war over two centuries earlier. And they would have registered the fierce and determined expressions which told of their loyalty to the young witch they now serve. The ordinary folk who reside alongside Mr. Chow Li see none of this. It is not what they *see* that makes them keep their distance and let us pass, it is what they *feel*. An indescribable sense that something stands between themselves and the curiously out of place woman in their midst. Something bold and dangerous. Something they had best keep away from.

We will stay close, mistress. Have no fear.

Thank you, my loyal Cavaliers.

As we approach the familiar red door we find the alleyway blocked by a small gathering of agitated people. The commotion appears to center around a ferocious-looking man with a wild beard and even wilder eyes. As I draw closer I recognize him. I glance at Withers, but can see that he is not as familiar with the outlandish creature as I. It is none other than the artist, Richard Mangan, one of our more colorful coven members. He is clearly drunk, and to let him see me now, to have him talk to me in such a state, would be risky indeed. It is an accepted rule of being a Lazarus witch that, when one unexpectedly encounters another in the Outerworld, we take great care not to reveal that we are acquainted unless we have previously been introduced to one another in society. To do so would raise many awkward questions. I am not surprised to see him in his cups, but I am surprised to find him here. Can it be that he, like my brother, is in thrall to the pernicious substance on offer in this place? I pull my hood a little lower over my face and turn slightly into the shadows.

Withers comments, "Not the usual behavior of one of Mr. Chow Li's customers, my lady."

"Indeed not."

For the most part, those who frequent the Chinaman's establishment arrive in minor states of agitation or deep despair, and whatever their private torment, leave at least quietly. While the artist is clearly being asked to leave, and encouraged to do so by his friends, he is doing it with considerable noise.

"A man is only as good as his word!" he rages. "If, then, a man's word will not be taken as good, not even by one who knows him, what should we make of him? Of either of the fellows?" The bear of a man reels as he rants, his arms flinging wide, one hand clutching an empty brandy bottle. "I offered my promise of payment by the week's end, but I was not believed! Not trusted!"

A slight man with light brown hair makes a feeble attempt to calm his friend, but to no effect.

"I will not be silenced!" bellows the inebriated Mangan. "My honor is at stake! I will defend myself as I must!"

A slender woman with striking red hair flowing loose almost to her waist puts a hand on his arm and says something I cannot catch. For a moment it looks as if her words might have struck home, but then the Mangan begins to argue the point with her.

I grow tired of waiting and turn to the nearest of the troublemaker's acquaintances.

"Would you kindly tell your friend to allow us to pass?"

The young man looks as if he is surprised to be asked such a thing. Even in the patchy lamplight I can see he has a strikingly handsome face and dark, dark eyes. It occurs to me that I have seen him before, though I am unable to say when or where. When he speaks his voice is deep but gentle, almost hard to discern above the general din of what is going on around us. His slight accent suggests he is not a Londoner, but heralds from the north of the country.

"I'm sorry," he says. "We are doing our best to persuade him to come with us."

Mangan increases the volume of his protestations.

"It seems your best is not sufficient."

"I'm afraid he is a little the worse for wear," says the young man.

"You are pointing out the obvious. Better you and your friends had not thought to come here with him in such a state."

At this the man appears to bridle a little, though I cannot imagine anyone in the habit of using what Mr. Chow Li provides is in a position to defend extreme behavior, his own or anyone else's. He is prevented from responding by being summoned by the red-haired woman, who demands his assistance in grappling with the artist as he staggers about. With a great deal of struggle and more noisy complaint from the drunkard, the party lurch and sway up the narrow alley. I watch them go, wondering, not for the first time, how apparently well-spoken and educated people come to find themselves prepared to stoop to such a condition. I also make a note to speak with this errant witch, discreetly, next time we meet in the coven. Such behavior is unacceptable.

Stepping forward I knock smartly on the red door, which is quickly opened by a diminutive Chinese woman who, to my knowledge, has never uttered a word of English. I understand her to be a relative of the proprietor, rather than his wife. As soon as Withers follows me over the threshold the door is bolted behind us. Once again I stand in the darkness, but this time the stairs in front of me climb steeply upward, and are of worn and splintered wood. Mr. Chow Li's property had, in an earlier incarnation, been used to store and distribute grain. All that remains of such industry is the thick coating of dust which clings to everything, including the stale air in the stairwell. The ground floor seems abandoned, and the first, from what I can discern, contains the living quarters for the owner and what family he has. Visitors are compelled to climb to the second floor, where the stairs open into a long, low-ceilinged room which spans the length and breadth of the building. A powerful fug of smoke, a singular smell, sweet and sickly, and the odor of warm bodies assails me as I enter the fetid space. On either side, the room is lined with low beds against the wall, some with curtains drawn about them, others open to view, exposing the slumbering occupants. There is little light, save for two lanterns hanging in the center of the room. Beneath these sits Mr. Chow Li, cross-legged, his walnut face scrunched in concentration as he prepares another pipe. He is sitting amid the paraphernalia of his trade—small dishes and pans, a little stove, and a selection of plain pipes set about him. His assistant, another Chinese woman of indeterminate age, wordlessly hands him this package and that spoon, seeming to know exactly what it is the old man requires at the precise moment he needs it. Becoming aware of the presence of his visitors, he looks up from his work and his features are transformed by a grin of convincing sincerity.

"Ah! Lovely Lady!" He springs lightly to his brocade-slippered feet and hurries forward to greet us. "Pleasure always to have Lovely Lady come Chow Li's home," he gushes. I hear a gruff snort of derision behind me from Withers, who does nothing to conceal his contempt for the opium master.

"I received your message." I have no desire to enter into pleasantries or small talk with the man, today of all days. "Please take me to my brother."

"Ah, Mr. Freddie not good this night. I told him 'Too much wine! Too much wine!' But he say, 'Oh, no matter, Mr. Chow

Li,' and he say he bury his father today. 'Be kind to me,' he say. Ah! Very sad. So Mr. Chow Li give him what he want.''

"And your 'kindness' has made him ill," I say curtly. A kindness that can be bought easily enough for the right amount of money.

Impervious to my anger, the old man scuttles ahead, beckoning, leading us to the far end of the room. I do my best to ignore the recumbent figures I pass. I feel as if to breathe here is almost an intimate act, as if I were sharing something forbidden and low with these unknown men and women. The large windows on the river side of the building are open, but the night is so close, so steamy, that there is no fresh air to relieve the thickness of the atmosphere in the den. I have been forced to retrieve my brother from one of these very beds on numerous occasions, and each time I have left the property feeling sick and lethargic, my mind dulled and my will sapped. What must it be like to smoke one of Mr. Chow Li's pipes? How can I hope to pull my brother back from the clutches of something so tenacious and overwhelming?

Freddie is sprawled on his back on a low couch in the corner of the room. The sight of him so stricken makes my heart lurch. Each time I witness him in such a state my reaction is the same. It is as if I am seeing him dead. I lean over and grip his shoulder, shaking him gently.

"Freddie. Freddie, it's me, Lilith. Can you hear me?"

His response is a low groan. I feel his brow and am shocked to find him running with sweat. I take the lamp from Withers and hold it over the grubby cot. Even in the unnatural light I can see that Freddie's skin is almost green, his lips blue-tinged, and his pulse, throbbing in his forehead, dangerously slow.

"How long has he been like this?" I demand of Mr. Chow Li.

"Mr. Chow Li send message. Very busy here today . . ."

"How long?"

A stiff shrug is all the answer he gives.

"Quickly, Withers, help me raise him."

Together we haul Freddie up off the bed. As always, I am thankful for my butler's strength. I know he hates having to come to such a place, but he is fiercely loyal, and he adored Freddie as a small boy, teaching him card tricks when Nanny was not looking, and even letting him slide down the laundry chute on occasion. I know it pains him to see that same playful boy grown into such a lost young man. We will take him home, making certain Mama does not see him in so disturbing a state, and I will summon the gentlest healing spirits to come and help me ease his suffering as the hateful poppy loosens its grip upon him. I will mop his brow, and murmur soothing spells and soft words, and watch as he suffers once again. And I will be there, steadfast and calm, in the difficult days when he returns properly to reality.

Mr. Chow Li hastens to clear a path for us as we navigate the room. The stairs are too narrow for me to be able to help Withers, so that he is compelled to lift Freddie and carry him, like a babe in arms, with painful care and slow progress, down the dusty staircase. At the door, I round on the bobbing Chinaman.

"It seems to me," I say, "that you have no shortage of custom. Is it too much to ask that the next time my brother appears on your doorstep you turn him away?"

"Ah, Lovely Lady. If Mr. Chow Li say no, Freddie go some other place. Maybe someplace bad."

The irony of this reasoning leaves me open-mouthed. I want to shout at the odious man, to make him admit the harm in which he is complicit. But, the sad truth is, I know him to be right. At least if Freddie comes here I know where to find him. I pray to the spirits that I do not come one day to recover only his body.

Once we are safely returned home, and Freddie is sleeping soundly on the daybed Mrs. Jessop has prepared for him, I return to my room. Violet has waited up for me, but I send her to bed. There is little of the night left and I am too disturbed in my mind to sleep. Instead I sit on the padded window seat, leaning my head against the cool glass and gazing out across the slumbering square. The first indications of dawn are beginning to lighten the horizon, but the streetlights of the city still glow brightly against the gloomy background. The trees in the garden of the square are still nothing more than a tangle of darkness behind the iron railings.

Iago, sensitive as ever to my mood, springs onto my lap, where he curls up, closes his eyes, and settles to purring softly. His presence is indeed a comfort, for just now I feel I have a mountain to climb, and despite Father's assurances that I will have help from him and from the coven, I know in truth I must scale it alone. Freddie seems utterly beyond my reach at times. I believe I am all that anchors him to what is safe and good in our lives. Am I sufficient? He, too, must live beneath the burden of a secret, and he is so ill equipped to cope with what knowledge he has of the coven. I know Father worried that he would speak to the wrong people, when he was not in control of his mind or his tongue. That he would say things that, once said, could not be taken back, and that might threaten the secrecy that protects the Lazarus witches and the duties we are charged with. What would my father have done to control him had he become a danger to us? I wonder. How far would he have gone to silence his own son? It was always made clear to me that I was a witch first, and a daughter, sister, or even wife, only after that. The coven must come first. Always. No matter the personal sacrifice. Will it fall to me, one day, to sacrifice Freddie for the good of the coven? Could I?

Both Father and Druscilla spent many hours explaining to me the importance of what it is we do in the coven. Druscilla, in particular, strove to make me understand what was at stake.

"I know about the dangers of summonings going wrong," I told her one day, while we sat in the darkened chamber, "and I can see that there are risks that something might escape the Darkness, but, well, aside from that, I don't see how what we do is dangerous. I mean, we gain insight from the spirits we talk to. And they tell us of things that are going to happen, or warn us about people who might do us harm. How can that hurt anyone? And why should not others want to talk to the spirits, too?"

Druscilla sighed. I could not see her shake her head, but was becoming accustomed to conversing with her without being able to watch her. My other senses were heightened, so that I not only heard the minute movement, but sensed it, too, in a way that I could not have done a few months before. And I sensed her slight disappointment in me, too. Disappointment at the fact that I had not yet grasped such important points. It was all there, in that tiny, hidden gesture. When she spoke, however, there was no note of frustration in her voice, rather a sincere wish to help me understand.

"While the Lazarus Coven practice Elemental Necromancy," she explained once again for me, "which wakens only the souls of the dead, there are those who choose the dark path of Infernal Necromancy. These people are followers of the First Sentinel, a disbanded and discredited coven who, centuries ago, regularly reanimated corpses and caused the dead to walk. Such practices have long been outlawed, and their followers disgraced and banned from either joining or forming a new coven. But ambition is a fearsome thing, and all witches have heard tales of the Sentinels, a mysterious clan who wait and watch and long for the moment when they might pry the Great Secret from the Lazarus Coven and return to their gruesome and amoral work."

"Gruesome and amoral? What could they wish to do that is so terrible?" I asked.

"Child, can you not imagine how wrongly such skills could be used? Leaving aside, for the moment, the repugnance of wantonly raising the dead, whether they wished it or no, using them cruelly, holding them hostage to the need to be sustained as revenant beings without, perhaps, revealing to them the means for doing this . . . Apart from that, there is the question of how other covens, or other necromancers who are not witches, how they might use the Great Secret."

"But, Druscilla . . . even you do not know what it is."

"I do not. That is information only the Head Witch has. This is precisely to protect it from the likes of the Sentinels. I do not need to know all the information to know that such power in the wrong hands would be ill-used. I trust the spirits. I trust the teachings of the coven. I trust the Head Witch. And all of these tell me that with the Great Secret comes an even greater responsibility, and that should the wicked have it in their hold, tremendous suffering could be caused."

She waited for me to respond to this, and when I said nothing—for what could I say?—she added, "You need to acquire an understanding of faith, Lilith. Faith is not built on knowledge. Faith requires no proof. No evidence. No explanation. Faith is entirely a matter of trust and belief. We cannot *know,* we can only *believe.*"

I believe. I trust. I have faith, and I will keep it in silence. Whatever that requires of me. Yet even as I form these crucial points in my head I find I am distracted by another thought. Something altogether unexpected. Or rather, some*one.* After all the turmoil of the night, following as it did from such a testing day, through all the conflicting concerns that now occupy my mind, comes the faint but clear image of a strong, lithe figure, a strikingly good-looking face, and a pair of dark, dark eyes. I shake the picture from my head, tutting at my own foolishness for recalling a stranger, so briefly met, who I am unlikely to ever encounter again.

Bram stands in the center of the shabby space that is his new home and takes a long, reviving breath. The forty-eight hours since his arrival at the Mangan home have passed in a dizzying blur of domestic drama, unfamiliar faces, and noisy children. Mercifully, Jane Mangan does not allow any of her offspring up to his attic rooms. He briefly thought this was a sign of some respect for his privacy, or to let him work in peace. He liked that notion; that his art was sufficiently valued by others in the house that they thought he should not be disturbed. It didn't take him long to realize, however, that the real reason the children are forbidden to venture beyond the second floor is the perilous state of the stairs. They are old and wooden and worm-ridden, and suffering greatly from neglect, as is most of the house, so that to tread them without caution is to risk serious injury. Only the previous evening he was hurrying to reach his garret before the spluttering candle in his hand burned out and had stepped onto a stair that simply was no longer there. His foot disappeared through the hole, and his leg up to the thigh. He had to struggle in deep darkness for some time before he was able to free himself. His shin is still sharply painful. At least he has managed to beg two oil lamps from Perry, who agreed that candles were not sufficient. The house has not been fitted with electricity, and there is no money to pay for gas, so, as Perry put it, "It's every man for himself when it comes to light. Or heat. Or food, for that matter." Which doesn't seem to Bram to be the spirit of communal living he had expected.

What surpasses his expectations, however, is the accommodation he has been allocated. So long as one navigates the stairs with care, the rooms at the top of the climb reward the effort. The floorboards here are rotten in two places, and he has already positioned furniture above them to prevent disaster. For the most part, though, the floor is sound. The room runs the width of the house and has windows at both front and back. These are dormers, set into the sloping rafters, and not particularly generous, but the fact that there are many of them allows ample light in the day, perfect for painting by. Gaps in the tiles admit further pools of sunshine, as well as welcome air. Indeed, were there not so many openings, the room in the roof would be unbearably hot and stuffy in the heat wave.

Something shall have to be done about them before winter, he thinks, *else I shall freeze.*

He has moved the dusty bed to the far wall and unpacked his few clothes and personal belongings into the tallboy to one side of it. There is a low trestle table, which will serve very well for his artist's materials, two scruffy armchairs, a full-length mirror, a washstand with jug and bowl, a chamber pot, a tin cupboard with mesh door (in which he is able to store food safe from mice), and a hat stand. Being so sparsely furnished makes the attic singularly suitable for his purposes. It will make a better studio than it will living quarters, but he prefers it that way. It feels workmanlike. Professional. Gives a clear indication of where his priorities lie. He sets up his easel so that the north light will fall upon the canvas it holds and whatever he is painting, and stands back to admire his new domain. It is not hard to imagine what his parents would make of his chosen home. He knows his mother would be appalled at the lack of hygiene, the dangerous stairs, and the general dilapidation of the place. His father, on the other hand, would be aghast at the rowdiness of the children, Gudrun's manner of dress, and what he would no doubt deem the corrupting morals of the Mangans themselves.

Looking at the pristine blank canvas in front of him, Bram is overwhelmed by the urge to begin, to actually paint. He has been so taken up by the mundane business of settling in, and so distracted by those he now shares a house with, his attempts to start work have been frustrated.

But what to paint? I have no sitter, no subject. Except perhaps . . .

He hurries over to his stock of paper and pulls out the sketches he made in the graveyard. It pains him to see how inadequate they are, but they are all he has. Looking at them now he can clearly recall the mood of the scene, the sharp shadows, the glare of the sun, the angle of the girl's jaw as she turned her head away.

And those eyes. The second time fate placed her before me, when she stood outside that shabby house in Bluegate Fields, those eyes shone with such an intensity of color, her skin appeared so pale . . .

He finds a pin and secures the sketches to the wall behind his easel. Next he takes up tubes of oil paints and selects a limited palette—burned umber, raw sienna, lamp black, chalk white, cadmium yellow—colors he knows will assist him in finding the drama of what he saw.

If only I knew who she was, oh how much better to be able to have her sit for me! Surely the funeral will be among the notices reported somewhere? I could search for her. But why would she agree to so much as speak to me? She found me at an opium den, with a raving drunkard. I fear if she remembers me at all it will not be with high regard.

When he saw the woman outside Mr. Chow Li's house he recognized her at once as the same woman he had seen standing at the graveside in the cemetery that morning. The woman he had felt so compelled to draw. She had taken off her hat and veil and replaced them with a cape and hood, but there was no mistaking her. Bram was shocked to think of her frequenting such an establishment. Could such an elegant, apparently wealthy, well-spoken woman, a woman of unmistakable presence and poise, could she really lie among the dead-eyed clientele he had seen at the place? It made no sense to him.

She is too special for such habits. Too . . . powerful, somehow.

He surprises himself with the thought, but the more he recalls her, the more he knows he is right. There was a curious strength about her. There was something uncommon in her green eyes when she held his gaze.

What color were they exactly? Viridian? Emerald? How I would love to paint them from life; to see her here, in front of me. A man could surrender all his will to eyes such as those.

He is brought back from his memory of that night by the sound of Jane Mangan calling his name. He goes to the door and peers down the dark staircase.

"Ah, there you are." She stands on the bend in the stairs on the second floor, a child on her hip, seemingly able to get around the house in the gloom without anything more than the small storm lantern she raises aloft. "We are about to eat. Mangan wondered if you'd like to join us for supper. Do say you will. Nothing fancy, you understand. Just a simple stew."

Bram hesitates. Oil paint glistens on the palette in his hand. The canvas still stands maddeningly empty. He is on the point of refusing, of letting himself be ruled by his passion, of losing himself in the act of creation once again. But he is only two days here, and Jane is so good and so gentle. She reminds him of his mother, and he cannot bring himself to snub her.

"I'll come right down," says Bram, immediately conscious he has nothing to contribute to the meal. This is the first time he has been invited to dine with the family. Indeed, it is the first time he has been aware of them having a meal. For the most part the children seem to graze, or dash past nibbling some bread or fruit. How the adults sustain themselves he isn't sure. He has bought some cheese and bread which he keeps in his room, along with a few tins of this and that, though mostly he has so far not felt troubled to eat much. It has been too hot, and he has been too busy settling into his studio to bother. Quantities of tea and some shortbread have kept him going. At least there is no requirement for him to dress for dinner.

Downstairs there is a sense of happy family muddle, children and adults all squeezed around the kitchen table, dog wagging and barking for tidbits, Jane ladling a carrot-heavy stew into an assortment of bowls.

"Twins," Jane pauses in her dishing-out, "put George in the garden, do. He's making such a frightful racket."

As the small boys drag the dog out one turns to Bram to explain, "We named him after the king!"

Gudrun shrugs and puts in, "Mangan enjoys giving orders to a monarch."

"Join us, Bram from Yorkshire!" Mangan beckons to him. "Do not linger upon the threshold or the hungry hordes will devour your meal."

"There is a little meat in the stew," Jane assures him, "though I'm afraid it is very much brother-where-art-thou, rather than brother-don't-push."

Bram takes his place on a wobbly stool next to Freedom.

How curiously they live. All these mouths to feed, and so little to feed them with. And yet they take me in, an additional burden. I must prove myself different. I must make my way, under the guidance of this strange man, and repay them for their kindness. For their faith in me.

The heat of the day has not yet penetrated the thick walls of Number One Fitzroy Square, so the temperature in the morning room is pleasant enough. I sit with Mama after breakfast attempting to encourage her to arrange activities beyond the house, but she is resistant even to the idea of a walk in Regent's Park. I try to tempt her with the idea of the rose gardens, but she says it is too late for roses, and she does not wish to see them faded and dying. Since the duke's funeral she has become increasingly listless, and I fear for her health. I wish my skills as a witch extended to some manner of healing that might ease her suffering, but the fact is, there is no magic in the world that can banish the pain of grieving.

Withers knocks and opens the door.

"Viscount Harcourt has arrived, my lady," he informs Mama.

"Show him in, Withers," she tells him, at last showing a modicum of interest. Indeed, my marriage is perhaps the only subject for which she has any enthusiasm, it seems.

Louis brings his customary energy and sense of purpose with him into the room. He greets us with easy charm and succeeds in eliciting a smile from my mother. Fifteen minutes of pointless chat and Mama's determination to turn every minute of the conversation around to who is marrying whom, are more than I can stand.

"It is too lovely a day to be indoors," I say, rising again. "Louis, would you like to sit awhile in the garden?"

"If Lady Annabel can be persuaded to join us," he answers with convincing sincerity.

As if my mother would ruin this opportunity for you to speak to me alone. I think not.

"Oh, no." Mama, suddenly the frail dowager duchess, sinks a little deeper into the cushions of the sofa. "I shall be quite content to remain here in the cool. You two young things go out. Run along now, I insist," she says, waving us away.

Outside the air still retains a morning freshness, though the sun is bright and the sky a cloudless stretch of blue above us. In the rigorously tended flower beds lilies and pinks bloom quietly and sweetly, but the sunshine sets the orange petals of the tiger lilies alight and causes the blue of the giant ceanothus on the south wall to sing. I lead Louis along the narrow gravel path, up the broad stone steps, past the little pond and its trickling fountain, and up to the paved corner with wrought-iron table and chairs. Someone has had the foresight to open the sun parasol, so that a pool of shade covers the seating area. Iago is stretched out on the warm stones, luxuriating in the sunshine. I stoop to stroke him as I pass, his gleaming fur almost too hot to touch comfortably.

"You foolish puss," I tell him, "you'll cook yourself." I choose a chair in the shade and sit down. Louis takes the seat next to me. My eye is caught by the small rose bed to the left of the table. Mama was right, it is late for roses. Most blooms are starting to wither, petals crisping in the heat. Father would have had words with the gardener for not seeing to them sooner. No one wants to look at death while they sip their lemonade. No one save a necromancer, maybe. Who else can see the beauty in decay?

I glance at Louis and know that he would understand. There is, indeed, an intimacy to be found in the company of another witch that is inevitably absent when I am with a non-witch. I know Louis would have me believe that only a witch could ever truly understand another witch. And the viscount is a very fine witch indeed, and has grown into a necromancer worthy of respect. And he is my friend, and I do feel in need of a friend just now.

"Well, Lilith, I am astonished to find myself sitting alone with you, and at your own instigation," says Louis, his bright blue eyes laughing. "Should I be encouraged?"

"I could not endure another word on the subject of weddings."

"Lady Annabel is somewhat single-minded on the topic."

"With Father gone, marrying me off has become her chief concern."

"And she does enjoy it so. Why not humor her? Marry me before the month is out and make your dear mother happy."

"Charmingly put, Louis."

"I've tried charm"—he shakes his head—"waste of time on you, Lily, you deflect my best attempts as if you were clad in armor."

"I can't possibly agree to some huge society wedding while we are in mourning."

"There is nothing to stop us naming a day, a date that reflects a respectable pause, of course, but at least it would be a date. A fixed point. Something for us all to look forward to."

"I really can't think of weddings, not now. I have new responsibilities. New challenges I must rise to."

"You will make an excellent Head Witch. I know it."

I look quickly about me. I am uncomfortable even saying the words to myself in private, let alone somewhere where they might be overheard.

Louis takes my hands in his.

"Darling Lily. You don't have to do this alone. I will support you in every way possible, if only you'll let me. You must know that." He looks at me with disarming affection. I believe he is fond of me, that his interest in me extends beyond pleasing his father. Beyond even simple desire. Is it love, then? Is that what he feels? Why can I not feel it for him?

"Thank you, Louis. I do value your friendship, and, of course, I too look forward to the day when we can be married. But the coven must come first now." I smile back at him, but it is a guarded, polite smile, and he knows it. I withdraw my hands. "You will attend the inauguration, won't you?" I ask him.

"Nothing would keep me away. Are you nervous?"

"About the ceremony? No. About stepping into the role my father played so well? I'd be lying if I said I wasn't daunted."

"You will be magnificent. And wise."

I shake my head. Louis grins. "You agreed to marry me one day," he says. "Best dashed demonstration of wisdom I ever saw."

This time my smile is warmer. "I will need a friend, Louis."

"You have one, right here at your side. Always."

I am about to say something more on the matter when I am distracted by the sound of whispering, which grows to shouting. The noise is so unexpected and so forceful it shocks me, blotting out all other sounds. I put my hands over my ears as the voice grows louder, more insistent. I recognize the echoey, distant, reedy quality of the speech of the dead. I am accustomed to listening to them, of course, but this is different. This is not one of the familiar spirits who have become friends to me over the years. Nor is it a spirit I have called or summoned. This voice belongs to another, a soul who is somehow more disturbed, and who is shouting, demanding my attention in a disturbing manner. As the volume increases and the words become clearer I recognize the speaker as the same one who came uncalled into my thoughts at

Father's funeral. The spirit is saying, no, *shouting* my name, over and over, the sound booming in my mind so that with a gasp I throw my hands over my ears in a futile attempt to shut it out.

"Lilith?" Louis is becoming concerned. "What is it? Tell me what is wrong."

I shake my head, as much to try to clear it as to indicate to him that I cannot speak. My mind is filled with the ever-increasing bellowing of my own name. I have never been so assailed by the voice of a spirit.

Stop! Stop! "Stop!" I cry aloud.

Louis kneels before me, putting his hands on mine, at a loss as to how to help, anxious to ease my distress.

There is nothing he can do. Abruptly, the shouting ceases. All that remains is a buzzing echo in my mind. I meet Louis's troubled eyes as he searches my face for answers.

"It's all right," I tell him, though in truth I am still shaking. "There was a voice, a spirit, very loud, very . . . strong."

"But you didn't call anyone?"

"No. I did not." I am unable to clearly understand what has just taken place, but the message delivered in such a startling way by the unwelcome spirit is clear. I am a witch who calls herself skilled in necromancy, a person who summons the dead to help me when I wish. Only this time, the dead are summoning me.

5.

Bram has visited several artists' ateliers, some belonging to paint-
ers, others the workplaces of sculptors, but he has never in his
life seen anything like Mangan's studio. The space must have orig-
inally consisted of a large room at the rear of the house. A wall
has been roughly knocked down to extend it into an adjoining
room. This in turn has had its doors and far wall removed so that
both spaces now run into the rather rickety conservatory that
clings, spiderlike, to the back of the building.

"Light! Light, my young friend," Mangan explains, waving an
expansive arm at the devastation wrought upon the old house.
"An artist cannot work without it. Art cannot thrive in the darkness. What is comfort, what is convention, what is property next
to the value of the aesthetic? All must be subjugated to art. There
can be no half measures."

*This man is incapable of any action which is not extreme, Bram thinks.
His opinions, his politics, his personal life, even the way he moves and
speaks—all are extreme. Is it any wonder he produces such radical work?
But which came first? Does the man shape the nature of what he creates,
or does it shape him? If I stay here long enough will I, too, become
extreme? Will being in his company draw from me further my own obses-
sive nature, so that I, too, am consumed by my art? Such an existence
can only be a short step away for me. Would I produce my best work this
way, or would I merely lose stability further?*

Mangan's chosen medium is stone. Huge chunks of pale

limestone hewn from the quarries at Portland sit heavily on the groaning floorboards. Here and there is evidence of shoring up of the level below, with stout props visible through gaps, installed to reinforce the floor and prevent the stone disappearing into the cellars. Two pieces of natural rock are untouched, a third shows marks and gouges and other signs of the early stages of work. Another has been extensively chiseled to reveal the lumpen, rough form of a reclining woman. At the conservatory end of the studio are several smaller sculptures, all at different stages of development, all bearing Mangan's distinctive style—angular, bold, with planes that catch the light and hollows which harbor secret shadows. While Mangan revels in showing his new protégé his work, Perry labors away preparing stone and sharpening tools in one of the darker corners of the space. He smiles over at Bram reassuringly.

When does he ever get to do his own work? I wonder. Is everyone so in thrall to Mangan that they allow themselves to be . . . absorbed by him and by his art? I must not let that happen to me. I must guard against it.

Bram is still weary from scant sleep. After sharing a meal with the family, he retired to his room and set about working on his first painting in his new home. He had started with such high hopes, applying paint to canvas boldly, confidently, joyously. But as the hours progressed, so the image in front of him seemed to slip away. What he saw on the canvas fell woefully short of what he was aiming for. Exasperated, he dipped a rag in turpentine and scrubbed away the failed picture. He took a breath, steadied himself, and began again. Two more hours passed in a futile attempt to make something of the sketches from which he was working, to reproduce the energy and the drama of what he remembered. But to no avail. He worked on, into the night. Discarding and starting over. Again and again. Each time with equal determination but dwindling faith in his own ability.

Now, today, he must start afresh. Renew his belief in himself.

He steps forward and touches one of the pieces of stone Mangan has selected for his sculpture. The surface is surprisingly warm beneath his fingers. When he lifts his hand again a fine layer of dust coats his skin. The same gritty film that covers everything, and everyone, in the studio.

"So, Bram from Yorkshire." Mangan comes to stand beside him, momentarily and unexpectedly still. "What do you think of my work?"

"What do *I* think?" Bram is taken aback. He is in the presence of genius, here to learn from a master, and he, an inexperienced, unknown painter, is being asked his opinion of the great man's work.

"Don't be coy." Mangan resumes striding about the room, snatching up this hammer or that chisel, gesticulating as he goes. "I surround myself with artists because I wish to be challenged, to be tested. Assail me with your criticisms. Beat me with your ridicule. Such wounds as you inflict will serve only to strengthen my resolve, I promise you." He turns his intense gaze onto Bram, searching his face for honesty.

"Well, I . . ."

"Come, come!"

Bram studies the sculpted stone in front of him. It is sufficiently representational to be clearly seen as a figure, a female, but the norm has been exaggerated, twisted, stretched, to extreme limits. Limbs would start perfectly formed, the sensuous curve of a shoulder leading into an upper arm, say, and then flatten and meld back into the rock, as if the base material will not fully release it. The face has no features, but the line of the jaw and the pale, broad brow are exquisitely and lovingly rendered.

"I think . . . I think this is quite extraordinary," he says at last, letting his palm rest on the figure's knee. "I think it breathtakingly bold, and modern . . ."

"Yes, yes, yes, exactly what art critics have been saying about

my pieces for years. But how does it affect you? You are an artist—
what does it make you *feel*?"

Bram has never been asked such a question. His mother might
guess at any inner turmoil her son was experiencing, but she would
not expect him to speak of it. And his father would place no importance whatsoever on feelings.

*It frightens me, his work. I find it disturbing. But how can I tell him
that? And why does it make me feel that way? I believe it has to do with
a fear of my own ungovernable desire to produce art, and that it might
lead me to become as wild as he. Would that matter? What would I
sacrifice?*

"It makes me feel . . . insignificant," he offers.

He can tell at once that his answer disappoints. Mangan sighs
and turns away.

"Never mind," he says. "You are new here. It was not fair of
me, perhaps . . ."

*What was he expecting? What was he looking for? I am being
stupid—if I want his approval surely the way to find it is through my
own work.*

"I hope you will be brutally honest when you assess what I produce," he says.

"You have begun?" Mangan asks. "You have something to
show me?"

"Only sketches." He feels panic at the thought of revealing such
unformed, unfinished jottings, which are all that remain of his
abortive efforts to make something of the funeral drawings. "I
had hoped to present you with a finished work. Indeed," he adds,
a little more brightly than he intended, "I have my canvas waiting. I mean to start this very afternoon."

"Excellent! And who is to be your model?"

"Ah. I . . ." He knows that nothing but working from life will
satisfy the great man. Inspiration strikes. "I was hoping to ask
Gudrun if she would sit for me," he says.

"Gudrun? Not possible, I fear. She has taken her boy to have his teeth attended to."

"Oh." *Now I feel ridiculous. A portrait painter with no one to paint.*

"My advice to you is to take yourself out into this seething city, my friend. Put yourself among the people. There you will find something that moves you."

"You think so?"

"I do not doubt it. A true artist—for such I intend to consider you to be, unless or until you prove me wrong, Bram from Yorkshire, which I sincerely hope you do not—a true artist sees with a different eye to other mortals. You will find the gems among the rubble. Something will speak to you." He pauses, then adds with a shrug, "A muse may take a little longer to unearth."

Or it may be I have already found her. Found and lost again in the same few days. I will search for her, that beauty possessed of such strange strength. I will find her. I must.

The night of the inauguration is unhelpfully hot and humid. I am unable to stop myself fidgeting restlessly as Violet helps me with my hair and makeup. I must look my best. Elegant, well-groomed, serene, and if possible older than my twenty-one years. I feel hopelessly young and insignificant, and not nearly up to the honor which is about to be bestowed upon me. Iago jumps onto my lap and sets up a comforting purr, but even the feel of his silky fur beneath my fingers does little to settle my nerves.

"Easy for you to be so calm," I tell him. "All you have to do is watch."

"Will he be allowed in for the ceremony, my lady?" Violet asks as she carefully pins back front sections of my hair. Earlier she washed it and put lemon juice in the rinsing water, so that it is pleasingly glossy now.

"He certainly will. What's the point of being Head Witch if

you can't decide a few important things?" It is a feeble attempt at a joke, but it lightens the tense moment a little.

"Shall we give him a ribbon to wear?"

"I don't think he'd tolerate one, would you, Iago?" I scratch behind his ear and the purring increases in speed and volume. I, on the other hand, have no choice in how I am to present myself. I stand up and move to the full-length mirror, turning slowly to take in how I look. It is customary for the nominee at an inauguration to be clad in something simple and plain. I selected a cream linen sleeveless shift that skims what curves I have modestly, stopping just above my ankles. The slim silhouette makes me look even taller than usual. There are two slits in the side seams up to my knees to enable me to walk, and, crucially, to kneel easily. I feel frighteningly exposed, with no corset, no underwear, and so little material between myself and what will be a considerable gathering of people, all with their critical gaze focused upon me. Still, there were small mercies to be considered. A century earlier I would have been required to attend naked. At least I do not have to suffer that humiliation. I will feel vulnerable enough as it is.

I know there are those who disapprove of my becoming the leader of the coven. It is inevitable, given such a large collection of strong-willed, powerful people, that there should be rivalries and voices of dissent. I also know, however, that most will accept that the position is my right. The Lazarus Coven has always followed the system of inherited rule. One day my eldest child will succeed me. If I ever find anyone I wish to marry. I wear no jewelry and will remain barefoot throughout the ceremony. Aside from being secured back from my face, my hair is loose. I can't help thinking of my initiation. I was just thirteen when I presented myself, similarly attired, to be accepted into the coven. But on that occasion there was only my father, Violet, and a handful of coven members to witness me taking my vows. And no one had any expectations of me. How differently they might have re-garded me if we had known then that dear Papa was not to walk this earth many more years.

Glancing at the gold clock on the mantelpiece I see that it is already midnight, the most potent time of night for Lazarus witches, so that all our most important events are timed to start to coincide with the mesonoxian hour. The coven will be assem-bled in the secret chamber beneath Number One Fitzroy Square. There will be hushed voices, tension growing as they wait for their new Head Witch to arrive. Not until the first hour of the full night is past its first half can I appear. Then, and only then, will the time be right for the successor to the Head of the Coven who now dwells in the Land of Night, to put herself forward.

The minutes crawl by. I close my eyes and steady myself with an incantation asking for strength. The ancient words are so fa-miliar to me, learned over many years of diligent study, and I find their exotic sounds reassuring. I have been preparing for this mo-ment for so long. My father prepared me. I will not fail him.

Do you truly believe yourself to be worthy of the title your father held?

Who is this? Who speaks to me uncalled?

The shock of hearing the unwelcome spirit again, tonight of all nights, sends chills through me. I still my mind and quiet my thoughts. If I give any outward sign of my distress, Violet does not notice it.

You are wrong to put your faith in a few prayers, a handful of dusty words, and scribblings, Daughter of the Night. You dabble with forces be-yond your imagining.

Leave me! I will not converse with one who violates my thoughts in such a way. One who is too cowardly to identify himself.

At this the spirit laughs. It is a mirthless, guttural sound. I shake my head and open my eyes. Iago jumps from the chair and winds himself around my ankles, his fur tickling my bare skin. He meows loudly, sensing some unseen disturbance. Mercifully, the spirit falls silent. I try to put from me the notion that he is with me still. That he will be with me throughout the inauguration. How frequently does he listen to my thoughts? I wonder. Is he, in fact, with me always?

Looking up I am startled to see Violet has put on her mask and her cape. Of course I knew that everyone present would be masked. Everyone other than me. Even so, it is a shock to see my trusted friend and maid hidden and disguised, here in my own bedroom. The wearing of masks is deemed necessary to reinforce the coven's creed of secrecy. For we guard a secret so powerful, so wonderful, and so terrible, that no person is greater than its keeping. I force myself to concentrate on what I must do now, and not to be distracted by listening for the return of the spirit who appears to dog my steps.

"My lady." Violet's speech is distorted by her mask, which has been specifically designed to prevent individual voices being recognizable. "It is time to go."

"Has Withers seen to it that no one will see us leave the house?" It would not do to have a servant catch sight of the two of us so outlandishly attired crossing the lawns and disappearing into the summer house.

"He treated everyone downstairs to wine with their supper, my lady. Strong wine. They will all be fast asleep by now."

As will Mama and Freddie, for much the same reason, though I strengthened their wine with a Sleeping Spell.

Taking no lamp, but being guided by the moonlight, we leave the house and follow the path to the rear of the garden, Iago trotting on silent paws beside us. When we reach the stone staircase that descends and twists so steeply, I speak the words that make the torches burst into life. A low murmur of voices can be heard drifting up toward us and the cool air that would fill the subterranean space on any other day has been replaced by an unpleasant warmth generated by the presence of so many heavily robed people. Or rather, not people at all, but witches. Every last one of them. So much spellcraft, so much skill, so much magic, all gathered in one place this night. All gathered for me.

When we reach the antechamber I pause, taking three long steadying breaths. I must not let my nervousness show. Not now, not here. The great double doors, with their striking embellishment of the giant Montgomery dragonfly glittering in the torchlight, stand closed, waiting. As custom demands, I stay still and silent, using nothing but my own will and my capacity for magic to slowly alert the coven to my presence. At length, the chamber on the other side of the doors falls into silence, too, save for approaching footsteps. There is a jarring clunk as the lock and handle are turned, and the doors slowly open. On the threshold stands a stout figure dressed in a robe of fiery reds and oranges, worked in exquisite needlepoint to cover the brocade that swings from his broad shoulders. He leans heavily on the ancient oak staff that he holds in his left hand. However contorted his voice might be, however much his mask obscures his face, there can be no mistaking the sturdy physique and arthritic gait of Lord Grimes, Master of the Chalice, stalwart friend of the late duke, and skillful necromancer. The sight of him calms me a little. I know I can rely on his unquestioning support, now and in the years ahead. He greets me with a low, if rather stiff bow, before stepping aside, indicating the chamber with a sweep of his arm.

"Enter and welcome, child," he says.

I step forward, my heart beating loudly. I am aware of Violet slipping into the chamber behind me to take up her place in the ranks. A dash of darkness to my right gives away Iago's entrance. The Great Chamber boasts a higher roof than the catacomb it adjoins. The curved ceiling could have given the feeling of a cave, but such is the extent of the decoration that it is impossible to think of it as such. The brick and stone from which it was constructed have been plastered and painted the Prussian blue of a

Nordic summer night sky. The joins of the rafters which crisscross it are studded with carved bosses, painted in rich colors, each depicting the symbols of a coven family—the Montgomery dragonfly, the Harcourt viper, the Grimes owl, and so on.

I have never seen the chamber so full of people. Robed figures line the walls on all sides, forming many long rows. There are so many witches present that the intricate carvings in the paneling of those walls are almost entirely obscured. The silence in which my observers view me is oppressive, yet I had expected it. Secrecy and silence. How well we are drilled in these tenets. How much of a habit they become, so that people of the Outerworld often think us cold or reserved. Even though space is scarce with so many in attendance, all present respect the sacred circle at the center of the chamber, so that the crowd holds itself at a dutiful distance from the painted floor. I stop when I come to the edge of the outer ring.

Many covens, I understand, use a pentacle as their holy space, but the Lazarus Coven have always favored the circle, symbolizing as it does a continuation, a life without end. The rim is of pure gold, layer upon layer of leaf painstakingly applied to the stone floor until it gleams and shimmers, priceless and fabulous, marking the limit of where one might tread without purpose or invitation. Inside the ring of gold is a broad swath of silver, to signify the beauty of the night and the influence of the moon in a witch's spellcasting. The main part of the circle, which is a good twenty paces across, is split into halves, the uppermost one containing an image of the sun in a cloudless sky, the lower the black of night with moon and stars. The two are separated by a winding red river, known as the Rubicon. The coven adopted this symbol some centuries after they came into existence, when they had been searching for an image to signify the narrow but crucial division between day and night. Between life and death. The ancient Roman river from which it took its name was red because of the soil beneath it. The pigment on the chamber floor, however, the dark red which is regularly and solemnly renewed and replenished, is colored by blood.

The Master of the Chalice walks past me and takes up his position beside the high altar. The instruments of magic and ceremonial objects sit in their places upon the silver-threaded silk that covers the altar, the precious gold chalice most prominent among them. There is also a beautiful statue of Hekate, queen of all witches and our guardian when we are spellcasting. The Master of the Chalice bangs his staff three times on the stone floor, the dull sound rebounding off the high ceiling.

"We come to witness to the inauguration of the new Head Witch of the Lazarus Coven. The nominee stands before us, unadorned and revealed. What is your given name?"

"Lady Lilith Montgomery, daughter of His Grace, Lord Robert Montgomery, the sixth duke of Radnor," I answer, struggling to keep a tremor out of my voice.

"By what right do you lay claim to the title of Head Witch?"

"The right of my bloodline, being the eldest child of the last Head Witch, whose coven name was Brightstar."

"What is to be your coven name, daughter of Brightstar?"

I hesitate. Up to this point I was too young to take a coven name, and so have used my given name, but as Head Witch this will not serve. All leaders of the Lazarus Coven must have coven names, and they are important. I have agonized over my choice for many sleepless nights since my father's death. A witch's name must mean something, must signify some quality or strength or aspect of that person's nature that is important and special to them. For a Head Witch it is imperative the name fit, or it will not be respected. *I* will not be respected. I raise my chin and force my voice to ring out clear and strong.

"I will be called Morningstar," I declare.

There is a collective intake of breath among the coven members, like the shocked gasp of a wounded giant. It is a response I un-derstand.

The Master of the Chalice is driven to question me on my choice.

"Why have you selected such a name?" he demands. "You must have known this would be a contentious decision, child. Explain yourself."

Slowly I turn on the spot where I stand so that my answer is directed at all of the assembled company. I must show that I am not afraid of any of them.

"I know that there are those among you who believe this name is synonymous with Lucifer, and so hold that it is another name for the devil. But I believe it stands for the star that is bright enough to shine in the daytime, to outshine even the sun. The star that in this way links the night with the day, as it is visible in both. For me this is the perfect symbol for the position of Head Witch of the Lazarus Coven, standing as I must between life and death, holding the hand of the living while communing with the dead. What could better represent my role? And if the name could be taken to refer to one who fell from the light into the darkness, might that not serve as a warning to others? A warning against pride and ambition beyond the good of the coven?"

There is a great deal of whispering among the witches, whis-pering that grows gradually louder and more forceful until the Master of the Chalice is compelled to strike the floor with his staff again to restore order and quiet.

"It is the prerogative of the nominee to select their own name," he reminds the dissenters. "We will proceed. The candidate will step into the sacred circle."

Silence falls once more as I move forward with a stride show-ing more confidence than I feel. Out of the corner of my eye I glimpse Iago sitting beneath the altar, watching my every move. I will him not to trot over to me. His presence is barely tolerated as it is. Such a show of disrespect would surely have him thrown out. And his presence comforts me. He reminds me of my father's faith in me.

A female witch detaches herself from the group and comes to stand next to the Master of the Chalice. In a clear, high soprano, she begins a sweet song of worship. At the end of the verse the whole company joins in, raising their voices, which are curiously twisted through their masks, to ask the spirits to look favorably upon their potential new leader. I am not permitted to sing, but allow the music to feed my courage, to remind me that I am not alone, and that there are many present who will support me. When the piece is completed the Master of the Chalice bids a minor witch strike the heavy brass gong at the end of the altar six times, signifying the beginning of the hour of questioning.

Now I will be tested. But I am ready. For the next sixty minutes my fellow witches are permitted to question me on all aspects of leadership of the Lazarus Coven. I am asked about points of sacred law, or rituals and rites, of spellcraft and magic. I am compelled to explain how I see the role of the Head Witch and what I hope to achieve. It is an exhausting process, and by the end of it I feel drained and relieved that it is over.

The gong is struck once again, marking the finish of the questioning. The Master of the Chalice nods slowly at me, and though I cannot see his face I am certain he is smiling, pleased with how I have withstood the questioning. There remain only a few formalities before he can bestow my new title upon me.

"If there is one who would challenge the nominee's suitability to lead the Coven of Lazarus let him voice his doubts now, or forever hold his silence," he says.

"I challenge!"

There are shocked cries. People turn to see who it is who has spoken. The Master of the Chalice leans heavily on his staff and when he speaks his voice shakes with amazement.

"From where does the challenge come? Step forward. Show yourself!"

There is a shuffling among those standing to the left of the altar and a slim, male figure, dressed in a robe of heavy purple velvet, plain, but beautifully cut, moves forward to stand alone.

My pulse is racing. I have never heard of anyone challenging a nominee during an inauguration. The asking for a challenger to declare him- or herself is a tradition, a formality. I doubt anyone present has ever heard of such a thing actually being done. Who is it? Who would seek to shame me like this?

"I demand to know the identity of my challenger!"

The figure in purple shakes his head. "I am not obliged to give it. My anonymity is protected, it is not forfeit simply because I challenge your suitability for the position of Head Witch. Am I not correct, Master of the Chalice?"

I try to imagine what his voice would be like without the obscuring mask. Is it familiar? Do I know this man? The coven is so large, even I do not know everyone in it, and yet it could be someone I know well. There is no way to tell.

"It is the challenger's right to conceal his identity if he so wishes," confirms the Master of the Chalice, his words a little breathless now.

"Coward!" comes the cry from the back of the room. "To hide behind a mask and yet publicly doubt the nominee in such a way is cowardice. He should have the courage to reveal himself!"

A murmur of agreement rolls around the room, but the witch merely gives a little bow.

"Forgive me, brother witch," he says, "I prefer to challenge anonymously. I believe it will be fairer and more effective."

Why? Why would that be the case? I must know who he is.

"You must give the reason for your challenge," the Master of the Chalice tells him.

"Let us hear it!" a witch in a sage-green robe demands. I know her slender shape and erect bearing so well I am certain it is Druscilla. "Lady Lilith is a fine and rightful candidate. What possible challenge can be made?"

There are shouts of "Aye!" and "Shame!" and "Speak out!"

The challenger holds up his hands. "The nominee's brother, the seventh duke of Radnor, is a man controlled by his desire for opium."

"What of it?" shouts an agitated witch in the back row. "She is not responsible for the shortcomings of her brother."

"Responsible, no. But where one family member has a significant weakness of will, is it not fair to suppose another might be similarly afflicted?"

Druscilla speaks up again. "A fondness for the milk of the poppy is not an inherited condition. The nominee's father, Spirits keep him, showed no signs of any such predilection."

"That may be so," says the purple witch, clearly not in the least rattled by the vehement responses to his challenge, "but I still say there is a risk. The nominee is young. Who can say how her character will develop, or what lurking flaws may later reveal themselves? Her brother does not simply sip poppy milk to ease a malady, he frequents a nefarious opium den, a place where people go to lose their wits. His mind will become permanently enfeebled if he continues in this way. His sister is no doubt dutiful and devoted—he is a duke now, after all. Who knows in what ways his weakness might compromise the family and leave her vulnerable? And vulnerable people do desperate things to protect themselves. They are open to blackmail, to name but one possibility. How safe would the coven be with such a dangerous flaw so close to the seat of power? Does the nominee deny his habit?"

All eyes turn back to me. I keep my voice as level as I am able. How can this be happening?

"It is true, my brother is troubled, and yes, he does smoke opium on occasion."

"On occasion!" my challenger scoffs. "You understate the case somewhat, I believe. Could it be that you do not consider such behavior reprehensible? Perhaps you are tempted, already, to try it yourself."

There are shouts and gasps from the company, but this time not all of them seem to be dismissing the challenger's words. Doubt has crept into the room and is worming its way into the minds of many present. I will lose their support. They must not see me try to run from his accusations. I turn squarely to face the stranger who would rob me of my inheritance.

"I will respond to the challenge," I declare, and the room falls into uproar. Some witches shake their fists at the challenger, others shake their heads and swear oaths beneath their breath. Arguments break out for and against. One witch makes a lunge for the accuser and has to be restrained and ejected from the chamber. I understood their reaction to what I have said. By agreeing to respond to the challenge I have given the purple witch the right to observe my response, a Proof of Worth, it is called, a task I must complete to demonstrate to all my suitability for the post.

The Master of the Chalice bangs his staff on the stone floor repeatedly until at last the turmoil subsides. All present are familiar with the theory of a challenge and of worth being proved, but I doubt many have thought what it would be like to witness such a challenge undertaken. Formality decrees that the Master of the Chalice set out the obligations.

"There is only one way the nominee might show Proof of Worth. It is written thus: 'Whosoever is challenged, let her summon a demon.'"

A nervous hush descends. I have heard of demonic calling being practiced, but have never seen it done, let alone done it myself. What my father told me, what my studies informed me, was that it is dangerous, unpredictable, and difficult to summon a creature of the Darkness. If a witch succeeded, they might not be able to control it, let alone return it to its rightful place again.

From somewhere deep within myself, some reserve of strength I did not know I possess, I muster a smile and a semblance of calmness. I will face the challenge. I will select a task. I will perform it to the best of my ability, and I will, once and for all, banish all doubts anyone might have about my worthiness.

"Master of the Chalice," I say, "I will answer my challenger. I will demonstrate Proof of Worth. I will summon a demon."

A new aroma now permeates the chamber, faint at first, but growing stronger and unmistakable: the smell of fear. There is a fidgeting of feet, and one or two witches make as if to quit the room. Another witch speaks out.

"Let no one leave! The doors must remain barred for the duration of the task. Whatever happens, we are a coven, we support a nominee in her bid for leadership. She is doing only what is required of her. We will not abandon her to suffer the consequences of a law we have all ourselves sworn oaths to. We are a part of this madness. Let us remain."

There are generally noises of agreement, and a subtle rearranging of the positions held in the room. Those doubting my ability to successfully execute such a dangerous task melt farther into the background. My supporters come to the fore to stand firm and stalwart on the edge of the circle. I am heartened to see so many of them are willing to aid me. Or do they think they will be required to save us all from whatever dreadful being I call from the Darkness? Are they, too, convinced I will fail?

I become aware of a figure standing in the shadows to the right of the door. It is Papa! Whether or not others can see him I am unable to tell. It does not matter. What matters is that he has come. He is here, lending me the strength of his spirit presence.

"I believe I am permitted someone to assist me," I say.

"That is correct," the Master of the Chalice agrees. "Will a volunteer step forward?"

For a few dreadful seconds it seems no one would offer to help, but then I see Violet threading her way through the company until she stands at the edge of the circle. I smile at my dear maid, immensely grateful for her courage and loyalty.

"Are you certain you wish to do this? You know I cannot guarantee your safety."

"Yes, my la . . ." Violet recalls where, and who, she is, and resists the habit of years in addressing me. "I am certain."

Now that I am in the circle and about to spellcast I should not leave it until the task is complete, so it will fall to Violet to fetch me the things I need. I search my mind, sifting through the hours of reading and years of instruction I underwent with Father's help.

Demon Calling: the summoning of a creature from the Darkness for use against an adversary or as Proof of Worth. But what will I need? I'm sure I can recall the words, but I must remember every item. To omit something could prove catastrophic.

"Bring me the Witch's Coffer, a vial of bone dust, and a burning candle."

Violet does as I ask. I sense the excitement mounting among those watching. However scared they might be, this is a rare chance to witness a piece of magic most of them have never seen before, and most would never themselves dare try.

The coffer is an ancient wooden box with a hinged lid about the size of a hamper. I set it down within the daytime half of the circle. The worn, polished wood feels cool beneath my fingers as I lift the lid. I select the Maygor's Silver Thread, a soft, glittering rope the thickness of a plait of hair but considerably heavier. It is wound in a coil and is a little under ten paces long. I was allowed to use it in my lessons twice before, but never for Demon Calling. I loop the rope over my arm and close the box. Next, I pick up the candle and move to the center of the space where I tip it, so that hot wax drips onto the floor. I move slowly clockwise, creating a circle about two paces across, which encompasses a small area of both day and night, bisected by the red Rubicon. As I mark out this inner circle I speak the words I dredge from my memory, hearing my father's voice as I do so, as if he were whispering them into my ear.

"In the name of Lazarus I cast this circle, that it be a gateway to the Darkness. I stand in the sacred space of our coven, safe and strong. None shall come that are not called. None shall go that are not sent."

I put down the stub of the candle and take up the vial of bone dust. Removing the stopper I lean over and sprinkle the fine gray powder over the area I have drawn. When this is done I look to Violet again and give a firm nod. She knows what is required of her, and begins to chant in a soft, low voice, the incantation for protection. She might never have been a part of such strong magic, but every witch knows this chant, and knows that the more it is used during spellcasting the more it shields those present from the forces of the Darkness. For a long minute she chants alone, then, tentatively at first, other witches join in, then more, until the chamber buzzes and thrums to the low voices as they utter the sacred and powerful words over and over again.

I touch the rope on my arm.

"Maygor's Silver Thread, gift from our revered ancestor, awaken and do my bidding," I say, before blowing gently on the delicate glistening strands. Within seconds the rope begins to shine brightly until it seems to pulse almost with a life of its own. I can feel the strength of the magic inside it as it slips a little tighter around my arm so that I feel as if a serpent is embracing me. I raise my arms slowly and am about to begin the calling when I notice my father's spirit restlessly shaking his head.

He's trying to stop me. Does he think I cannot do this? Is he afraid for me? No, I know he believes in me. Wait. I have forgotten something, that's it! He's trying to tell me there is something missing from the circle. But what? The rope, the candle wax, the bone dust . . . Ah! The Book of Divine Wisdom! Yes, of course, I should have it beside me.

I reach out a hand toward Violet. "There is one more item I need. Bring me the Book of Divine Wisdom." As she fetches what I require I fancy I hear more than one sigh of relief among the gathered witches. They are powerless to interfere. Even though they knew I was doing something wrong, they could not speak out. If things go badly they will not help me. I must do this alone. Alone save for Father.

I glance toward where he stands and see his spirit is still and calm once more.

Placing the book by my feet on the edge of the wax circle I raise both my arms.

"As it is written in the words of the ancients, as my brothers and sisters have done before me, in the name of Lazarus I summon a demon creature! Let it hear me and come from the Darkness, passing through river of blood twixt day and night. Let it step into the circle. By the might of Solomon's wisdom, and Maygor's magic, and the strength of the coven, I summon you, Demon! Hear me now!"

As my voice rises I drop my hands, causing the silver rope to slide down my arm. Catching the end in my hand I let it unravel, snapping it back fast so that it cracks like a whip. A whip that twists and turns, driven by the magic energy in which it is steeped.

"Hear me, Demon!" I call once more, cracking the rope again, and again, and again. The witches continued their chanting, louder and stronger. I pace around the wax circle, calling to the demon, lashing the floor with the silver rope, my eyes fixed on the center of the wax loop. At last the colors within it, the painted images, begin to shiver and shift, and then to blur. They appear to melt, leaking into one another until there is nothing but a gray-brown miasma. And through it something—something dark, and oily, and terrible—begins to emerge. One three-fingered hand, sharp with talons, shoots up from the abyss. Then another. The chanting in the room falters. There is a powerful stench of burning, and of some acrid substance that stings throats and causes eyes to smart. The creature continues to claw its way up from the depths, writhing and struggling as it does so. At the sight of its hairless, bulbous head most of the chanting ceases and several witches cry out in horror. I am transfixed by the slimy shape that is making its painful way from the Darkness. It's happening! Dear Spirits, I called a demon and one has come!

After what seems like an age of agony, the thing is revealed, crouched low in the inner circle, its yellow eyes narrow as it casts about, bewildered and furious. It is the size of a large hound, but without a single hair on its body, which is instead covered in a glutinous substance that drips about it, singeing the floor where it lands. It opens its slack mouth and lets out a hideous wailing noise. All chanting has stopped now. Witches back away in fear, and it is only that fear that keeps them rooted to the spot rather than fleeing from the chamber. I know it is up to me to control the beast. I must keep it in the circle at all costs. I stride around the perimeter, cracking the silver rope, calling to the demon.

"I am Morningstar, heiress to the title of Head Witch of the Lazarus Coven and you will obey me and only me."

The demon answers with a low growl and lets its weight fall back on its haunches. At first it looks as if it might be sitting, submitting to my commands. But then, to my horror, I realize it is crouching, ready to spring.

"Stay back, Demon!" I am shouting at it now. If it leaves the circle I will lose what little control I have!

The demon turns its head, looking this way and that. It takes a shambling step forward, its broad foot crossing the wax of the small circle. It flinches, lifting its foot quickly, as if irritated, more than frightened. With a quick hop it leaps into the main circle, where it throws back its head and bares its teeth at me. If it senses how terrified I am we are lost. Fighting the impulse to run, I force myself to take a pace toward the creature. Surprised, or perhaps a little perplexed, it lowers its head and slides a fraction away from me. I take another step.

"Hear me, Demon. You were summoned by me, and so you will return to the Darkness at my bidding."

The creature growls again but keeps low and retreats a little farther. It turns its gaze from me and begins to look around the chamber, shifting its weight from one back foot to another. It is in this instant that I realize what it is about to do. Spirits save us, it's going to jump out. It wants to escape. It wants its freedom!

You foolish girl! Did you truly consider yourself able to control a demon?

No! Not now, not here! Leave me!

I must not allow the spirit to draw my attention. I must not let my concentration waver for a second. I open my mouth to command the demon to return to the Darkness, but it is too late.

The beast springs out of the sacred circle, and in one bound is at the back of the chamber. Witches scream and scatter in all directions as the terrible thing moves among them. I draw back my arm and flick out the Silver Thread. My first throw falls short. The demon begins to advance on two terrified witches who are cowering against the paneling. I try again, and this time the end of the rope finds its target and wraps itself tightly around the creature's wrist. I brace myself, clinging on to the other end with both hands. The demon howls in rage, struggling to try and rid itself of the tether, but it is held there with magic centuries old. All it can do is lean its weight against its bond, so that I am pulled off my feet and begin to be dragged across the stones. I must not leave the circle! I will have only a tiny part of my magic outside it.

Again I hear the unholy sound of the haunting spirit's laughter echoing through my mind.

He is winning, Daughter of the Night. You will fail!

No. No! I will not!

My bare feet give me no purchase, and the linen of my shift tears as I am hauled toward the outer rim. I try to recite further words from the Book of Divine Wisdom, to focus my will, to do anything that might make me stronger, but I am being pulled inexorably out of the safety of the circle. One of the witches tries to open the door, causing several others to cry out and two more to bar his way.

"It must not escape the chamber!" one yells.

As my skin is scraped raw against the rough stones I notice my challenger still standing by the altar, seemingly unaffected by the horror that is unfolding at his behest. He does not attempt to protect himself, nor to help me, as some of the other witches are now doing. But their efforts are ineffectual. They have no time to spell-cast, no instruments of magic to hand, no circle of protection. All they can do is try to frighten and bully the demon into going backward. One even strikes it with his cane, but the wood breaks to splinters. The demon clutches at the Silver Thread with its free hand and yanks hard, reeling me in as if I were a floundering fish on dry land. It is too strong!

He is toying with you. You will be defeated, Lazarus child.

I ignore the cruel voice in my head. I know I have only seconds left before the situation becomes completely out of control. Seconds before all my father taught me, all I have worked for, perhaps even the existence of the coven itself, would be for nothing. How can I let it happen? How could I bring this terrible being into the world only for it to break out, unfettered and free, able to do whatever dreadful things its evil soul might crave? I cannot let this happen. I will not! I close my eyes and let myself go limp. I hear a wail from behind me and cries of despair.

"She has given up! Look! She is finished!" someone shouts.

The demon, too, seems to believe his tormentor is beaten. For just a moment it relaxes its grip on the rope and pauses in its efforts to haul me out of the circle. I use that moment. I consider asking the spirits for help. I could call on my guardians, my protectors, who have shielded me so many times when I have ventured into dangerous places looking for Freddie. My loyal Cavaliers, they would fight bravely for me. But no. It is I who am challenged. I must complete the task myself. In one fluid movement I spring to my feet, my eyes open, fixed on the demon.

"I am daughter of Brightstar. I am of the Coven of Lazarus, and I will command you, Demon. You do not belong here, and you must return to the Darkness." So saying I swing around and run, full tilt toward the steaming fissure at the center of the circle. Fearing I will be swallowed up by it myself, the Master of the Chalice cries out a warning, but I am committed to my course. Behind me the demon, caught off guard, falls onto its side and is dragged back toward the circle. I leap into the air, bounding over the entrance to the pit, hauling hard on the Silver Thread as I do so. It seems as if I might succeed, but the demon is not finished yet. As it skitters past Violet it flings out a gnarled hand and grasps her ankle. Violet screams as the demon's contact on her bare flesh burns her skin. The effect of the extra weight at the end of the rope is to halt me midleap, so that I drop abruptly, falling short of firm ground. I land with my upper body and arms on the daytime half of the circle, but my legs dangle into the foul-smelling opening in the floor. I can feel the heat from the depths singeing my bare feet. I find myself struggling wildly. Violet continues to scream. The Master of the Chalice has grabbed her and is using his considerable weight to prevent the demon from dragging her away, but its grip on her ankle does not loosen. As I fight to drag myself up from the pit, I notice my challenger remains unmoved by our plight, not even attempting to help Violet. Anger spurs me on. I twist the Silver Thread twice around my wrist. I am free from the hole now and able to reach the vial of bone dust, which I snatch up and hurl at the demon. The glass smashes against its chest, the fine powder spreading out in a cloud over its body. The creature roars and writhes, and releases its hold on Violet. Standing up, I pull hard on the rope, swinging the demon across the stones and toward the pit.

But the beast is not finished yet. It musters its strength and makes another lunge at Violet, grabbing hold of her hair. It regards me for the briefest of moments, its yellow eyes latching onto my gaze so that I see my own anguish reflected there. From the assembled company come one or two bursts of magic in an attempt to free my poor maid, even though whoever sends them knows they are breaking coven rules to intervene. However well-meant, their efforts are futile. Violet wails and struggles to free herself, but now the demon wraps his other arm around her neck and shuffles toward the opening in the ground.

"No!" I shout. "Let her go!" I lean my weight against that of the demon, but cannot hope to stop its progress now. Violet shrieks and the creature, seeming to tire of her, coolly, heartlessly, twists her head in his arm. The sound of her slender neck snapping is unbearably clear.

"Violet!"

There is a second, an instant in time which seems to stand still, where the beast teeters on the brink of the abyss. In that moment I am overwhelmed with sadness for my lost friend, with rage at the awful creature. And then it falls, taking Violet's body with it. And as it falls the rope becomes taut again so that I am yanked toward the hole after it, the Silver Thread still wound tightly around my wrist.

I know I should let go, but the need to hold on to Violet, to bring her back, is instinctive and defies the logic of the situation.

From behind me, I hear the Master of the Chalice call out in desperation, "Release the thread's hold, child!"

"I cannot! Violet!" I scream, even as I am dragged farther across the floor, my own grasp on the slender rope slipping as sweat coats my palms.

"You must!" Lord Grimes insists.

Suddenly I am aware of someone standing in the circle with me. It is Druscilla. She raises her hand and calls in a clear, firm voice, "Maygor, release!" In less than a heartbeat the rope slips from my arm, dropping to the ground, dull and inert, a simple cord once more.

I lie where I have fallen, gasping, my toes at the very edge of the pit, my breath ragged, fear and exertion causing my body to tremble. My shift is in shreds, and my legs bloodied from being scraped by the stone floor. Slowly I climb to my feet. As I watch, the hole within the wax circle closes over and seals itself. I raise my head, letting my gaze sweep over the shocked witches around me. Violet is gone. The demon that I summoned snuffed out her life as if she were nothing. My sorrow, my guilt, my horror at what I have allowed to happen render me speechless. At last I feel Druscilla's cool hand on my shoulder.

"You must claim your title, Lilith."

"I cannot! I have failed. Poor, dear Violet . . ."

". . . loved you. She would not wish you to falter now. You passed the Proof of Worth."

"I let Violet die!"

"There is more at stake here than one life, do you not see that?" she snaps. "You summoned a demon and returned it to the Darkness as required. Claim your title now, or everything will have been for nothing. The Lazarus Coven must have its leader, and that must be you!"

I struggle to make sense of what she is saying, of what has happened. How can I claim to have succeeded when I let Violet die? How can I?

You are right to doubt yourself, Daughter of the Night. You have failed, just as all the Lazarus witches will fail.

No! I cannot help Violet now, but she must not have died in vain. I will do my duty. I will be what I was born to be.

Slowly, painfully, I get to my feet. I let my gaze sweep the room, and I force my voice to be as clear and steady as I am able to make it.

"I am Morningstar," I say, "true heiress to the title of Head Witch of the Lazarus Coven, and I claim my birthright!"

6.

The night is cloud-laden and black, the hour too late for revelers or workers to be abroad, too early even for the milk float or fish carts. Sitting at my window, watching the stillness of the city in the late hour, I go over the events of the night before last in my mind. I have scarce managed to sleep since the ceremony, and am finding it hard to think clearly. I glance back into my empty bedroom. Only two days ago, Violet would have been with me. How horribly alone I feel, and how heavy is the weight of the guilt I carry. I should have saved her. I could have saved her, I'm sure of it, had not the wicked spirit distracted and taunted me so. I allowed him to divert my attention at the crucial moment. Violet paid for my mistake with her life. I will never forgive myself.

To compound my failing, I have had to lie about her disappearance. I have concocted a story about her running off in the night with a mystery lover. Mama believes me, saying she always knew a foundling would prove unreliable and be given to curious behavior. Withers knows the truth, and he has yet again proved his loyalty to my father, and therefore to me, by doing his best to convince the other servants that he knew of Violet's secret liaisons. It seems it is not enough that I watched her die, but I must also besmirch her reputation.

I glance down at my legs, grateful that my heavy black skirts so completely cover the scrapes and cuts I sustained in my battle with the creature in the chamber. I recall the relief I felt when the beautiful Robe of Office was finally placed about my shoulders. The Master of the Chalice had called for a cheer of assent and the assembled witches had responded loudly and with fervor. But how could I feel any happiness? It was all I could do not to weep through the remainder of the ceremony.

I had proven myself, Druscilla told me. That one of our number had lost their life in the doing of it did not, she insisted, constitute a failure. I am the rightful Head Witch. My doubters cannot argue against that anymore. I must put my personal feelings aside, for the good of the coven.

As Nicholas Stricklend sits by the window of his top-floor apartment in Admiralty Arch he observes how the twilight suffuses the palace at the top of Pall Mall with a rosy glow, altering it slowly from white to palest pink. Within an hour the late summer sun will have dipped beyond the horizon to the west of the city, and a flat, colorless tone will descend, to be quickly chased away by the many lamps which line the Mall, and the cheerful gleam of modern electric lights that will shine out from the windows of the Georgian facade. Prettiness rarely catches Stricklend's attention. What interests him more is the transformation. The fleeting change in character Buckingham Palace undergoes, whether it wants to or not, the whole process controlled by celestial movements and atmospheric conditions, and influenced very little by man, be he king or commoner. For Stricklend's whole purpose in life is control. Either fighting it, or imposing it, on his own behalf, or that of others. Behind him Westminster is being put to bed, and a peacetime government will snooze the night away safely. In front of him the glittering world of royalty will continue to exert its influence, its privileges and favors, its snubs and slights, throughout the evening.

There comes a tentative tap at the door, which is then cautiously opened by Fordingbridge.

"So sorry to disturb you, sir, but you have a visitor," says the clerk, who is no more comfortable in the presence of his employer in the secretary's private rooms than he is in his offices one floor below.

Stricklend shifts minutely on the leather Chesterfield. He knows who the caller will be. He also knows he will refuse to reveal his identity to Fordingbridge. It is hard to pass up the opportunity to make the little worm work for his supper.

"And who, pray, might this *visitor* be?" he asks.

"Forgive me, sir, but he refuses to give a name." The clerk squirms and clasps his hands in front of him.

"Tell me, Fordingbridge, am I in the habit of admitting anonymous callers?"

"Why no, sir. But, well, the gentleman is quite insistent that you will want to see him. I did not want to refuse him, and risk causing offense . . ." Here his voice peters out.

For form's sake, Stricklend asks, "And what does this mysterious stranger look like?"

"It is very hard to say, sir, for he is wearing dark glasses and, well, what I believe to be false whiskers."

"Whiskers, you say?"

"Indeed, sir. A full set."

Stricklend enjoys the pause in which he likes to think he can actually hear Fordingbridge's heart pounding, despite the size of the room and the distance between them. At last, tiring of the pretense he says, "The gentleman is expected. He has a preference, let us say, for privacy. You may show him in."

Relief flooding his face, the clerk backs out of the door on silent feet. A moment later the caller, precisely as Fordingbridge described him, steps into the room, and without waiting to be asked, takes a seat in a red leather winged chair opposite Stricklend. If the clerk had given the impression the man's appearance might be in any way comical this is definitely not the case. He is dressed in expensive evening attire of top hat, tails, and a cape, using the finest silks and tailoring. His beard and mustache are abundant, but not so outlandish as to be immediately thought false. Stricklend is impressed, and suspects that had he passed his fellow Sentinel in the street, he himself would not have recognized the man who has come to be such a useful player in the push against the Lazarus Coven.

The younger man's expression is inscrutable.

"Your servant is irritatingly loyal," he says. "I thought for a moment that he might actually turn me away."

Stricklend shakes his head. "His fear of doing the wrong thing surpasses all other impulses within him," he assures his caller.

"A toothless guard dog, then."

"I have very good teeth of my own."

"I don't doubt it."

"He assembles a passable gin. Can I offer you one?"

"Thank you, no. I have an appointment shortly."

Stricklend raises his eyebrows. "I am fortunate you could fit me into your hectic list of engagements."

"Our business is important, but will be brief. I'm certain you will agree there is little to discuss beyond confirming the facts at this point."

"Indeed. And what interesting facts they are. Your identity, I must assume, is still a secret; your infiltration of the Lazarus Coven an ongoing success? Good. I found your report on the occasion quite illuminating."

"The outcome was not one for which we might have hoped."

"On the contrary."

The visitor frowns at Stricklend. "Surely our aim had been to prevent the Montgomery girl from succeeding her father."

"That would, indeed, have been a helpful result."

"Instead she has shown herself to be a capable witch, no doubt garnering plaudits from many present, and winning over any doubters. I fail to see how such a conclusion to the challenge can be advantageous for our purposes."

"Lady Lilith is the late duke's daughter, after all. It was unlikely that she would fail the task given her."

"You expected her to be triumphant?" The young man gives a snort. "Then I must question the wisdom of having the challenge set in the first place. All that has been achieved is to show the wretched girl in a favorable light, to strengthen her position, in fact. There is much at stake here, Stricklend. What game are you playing?"

Stricklend pauses before answering. He does not care for his visitor's tone. He does not care to have his wisdom called into question. In truth, he does not care for the man sitting opposite him. He finds him peevish and uncooperative and a little too ready to point out the failings of others in an attempt to puff up his own importance. A habit Stricklend considers a sign of weakness, and an indication a person cannot, ultimately, be trusted. He makes a silent promise to himself that, when the moment presents itself, he will find a way to rid himself of this particular ally. One less dagger lurking in the shadows, he reasons, is one more threat to his master's plan removed.

"Believe me," he says at last, "I am not a man who plays games. Had the young witch failed the challenge the Lazarus Coven would, I grant you, have been thrown into disarray, a situation we might well have taken advantage of. But, in that event, there would be no guarantee her replacement would fit better with the wishes of the Sentinels. I am quite fond of the adage, 'Better the devil you know.' At least now we are informed of precisely whom we are dealing with. The girl has courage and not a little talent in the art of conjuring. The summoning of a demon is no easy matter."

The visitor shakes his head. "The summoning is simple enough. It is controlling what answers the call that requires skill."

"And the new Head Witch equipped herself admirably on that score, by your own account."

"One of the minor witches was taken by the demon. There was a certain amount of panic and chaos."

"Things could have been much worse."

"They very nearly were."

"My dear man, is that the memory of fear I detect?" Stricklend rarely smiles, and when he does so it is not a pretty sight.

The visitor shifts in his seat, tapping his cane on the polished floorboards with ill-masked agitation. "You were not there," he says pointedly.

"To my regret. I should have liked to have witnessed the young woman at work. As it is I shall have to make do with your report. Which I'm sure is both accurate and thorough."

"There is little I can add to it. Lilith Montgomery was shaken by the loss of the young witch, but she behaved as was expected. The inauguration was completed. The Robe of Office conferred. The vows taken. The Lazarus Coven has its new Head Witch. She was convincing in her composure, despite what had happened." He takes out his pocket watch and checks the time. "If the girl is, as you insist, a worthy successor to her father, she will guard the Elixir with as much fervor as he did, and no doubt frustrate our plans at every turn if . . ."

". . . if the Sentinels do not see to it that this time, things are different. That this time, the Coven of Lazarus is, once and for all, put to the sword." Stricklend examines the fingernails of his left hand closely. "Do not lose sleep over what you saw the girl overcome in that chamber," he says. "She may have proved herself to be a witch of note, but I intend to see to it that the most memorable thing about her tenure is that she is recorded as being the very last witch of Fitzroy Square."

Two days later I find myself speeding toward Mangan's house. I am in Charlotte's carriage, as I accompany her on her first appointment with him. She is understandably excited at the prospect of meeting the famous artist and being sculpted by him, and she chatters on happily, requiring little from me by way of reply. I stare out at the streets. This time they are bustling with people. Ordinary people living their ordinary lives, going about their business. I find I envy them the apparent simplicity of their existence.

I become aware that Charlotte has stopped speaking and is looking at me intently.

"I'm sorry, Charlotte, what did you say?"

"My goodness, Lily, you are a thousand miles away this morning. Are you quite well?"

"Just a little tired," I tell her, and for the hundredth time I experience the sadness of keeping such secrets from my dear friend. "I slept badly."

"Hardly surprising. You must have all sorts of things racing around in your head, poor you. And all of it to do without your own lady's maid. Fancy Violet bolting like that. And the way simply everyone over the age of thirty insists on droning on about war being around the corner. I mean to say, what are we supposed to do about it? And of course you must miss your papa dreadfully. And I know how you worry about your mama and Freddie. And the constant wondering about when to marry Louis . . ."

Despite myself, I cannot help laughing. "Charlotte, you are incorrigible."

"No point beating about the bush. The man's utterly in love with you, and you make such a lovely couple. A wedding would cheer us all up, you know it would."

"Have you been talking to my mother?"

"Oh, Lily, you know how I long to help you organize your big day. Any excuse to dress up," she says, reaching over to squeeze my hand. Her words are flippant, but I know she is only trying to be cheerful, to tease me out of my melancholy.

"My family is in mourning," I remind her. "If we did set a date it would have to be months, perhaps years from now."

"Well, it seems a silly waste of time to me, your not starting your lives together. You have so much in common," Charlotte points out. "Both fabulously wealthy, irritatingly good-looking, impeccable pedigrees . . ."

"Charlotte, I'm not a racehorse."

"You know what I mean. You are so well suited."

We are both witches, I add silently to myself. I know this is the main reason my father wanted me to marry Louis. He, of all people, knew how hard it was to have such a secret casting a shadow over a marriage. With a non-witch for a husband I would never truly be able to be myself. To be totally honest. To let my guard down. And now I have the mystery challenger to think about. Someone wanted to see me fail. How can I concern myself with weddings at the moment? But, of course, I cannot make this point to Charlotte.

"Oh, look, Lily, this must be the place!" she cries, leaning out of the carriage window for a better view of the unremarkable brick town house.

We step from the carriage into dazzling sunshine, which dances prettily off Charlotte's becoming, slender dress, making the pale blue shimmer. I feel suddenly drab and unattractive in my some-what old-fashioned black gown.

"Come along, Lily." Charlotte takes my arm and all but drags me up the steps to the house. "I can't wait to meet the famous Richard Mangan! They say he has a beard like a Russian tsar and a growl like a grizzly bear."

"Both of which sound insufferably hot to me."

"Now, now. No gloom. Not today. Let's try and be merry just for a short time, shall we?"

I manage to smile and nod but am unsure that I will succeed in being convincingly merry. Finding the front door open we step inside. The hallway is cool and dark, with not a sign of anyone to receive us. I have to remind myself that Charlotte believes this to be the first time I have ever set foot in the house, or ever encountered any of its occupants.

"Hello?" Charlotte sings out. "Hello, anybody there?"

We venture farther in, navigating the gloomy space, walking around discarded shoes and toys. Sounds of chiseling emanate from the back of the house.

"His studio must be that way," says Charlotte, forging ahead.

"Shouldn't we wait for someone? We can't just barge in," I tell her, trying to act as I would if it were true this was my first visit to the place.

"Of course we can. This is an artist's house. Things work differently here, you'll see." She strides on. With a sigh, I follow. We clamber over assorted boxes and heaps of unknowable objects until the hallway opens out through a gaping hole in the wall and we step into the studio itself. Charlotte gives a little gasp as she takes in the scene. I am shocked, too. Charlotte is doing her utmost not to stare at the very beautiful and very naked model reclining on a table on the far side of the room. The sculptor stands, hammer and chisel in hand, entirely absorbed in working a likeness of the woman's form into the rough lump of stone in front of him.

The model returns our bashful glances with an expression that shows not the merest hint of embarrassment, and she makes no effort to cover herself up. Instead she says in a rather bored voice, "Mangan, you have visitors."

I recognize her now as the woman I saw with Mangan outside

the opium den. I remember that glorious red hair and her German accent.

With difficulty, Mangan forces himself to turn from his work. He frowns at us so fiercely I half expect him to start ranting and raving again, but I know that however great his reputation for wild living, he takes his work seriously, and is not drunk today.

Charlotte finds her voice and steps forward, hand extended. "Mr. Mangan . . ." she begins.

"Mangan will suffice. I want none of your 'Mister,' thank you."

"Oh." She tries again. "Charlotte Pilkington-Adams. We . . . I . . . have an appointment. Do you recall?" When he changes his expression to one of blankness she goes on. "The commission? You agreed you would undertake a sculpture of myself. For my parents."

"Ah yes!" He is at once animated, throwing his tools to the ground to clasp and shake Charlotte's hand. "The society beauty, delivering herself into my rough hands." Charlotte blushes a little at this but is not given the chance to speak. "You are brave, child, as well as deliciously innocent and fresh." He lets his fingers rest lightly on first her hair and then her cheek before gently turning her face a little to the side, the better to examine it in the light. "You have about you the look of the perfect maid, untouched save by God's hand. Delightful!" he booms, causing Charlotte to jump. "You understand I rarely accept commissions."

"Indeed, it is so good of you . . ."

"But when I saw you, when we were introduced—where was it? Some wretched ball or other Gudrun had dragged me to."

Behind him the model stirs slowly, sitting up and pulling a diaphanous robe about her. "It was the Asquiths' summer ball, Mangan."

"I barely remember it."

"Why would you?" she says. "You were very drunk."

"Yet I remember this face. Yes." He takes Charlotte's chin in both hands now, his eyes alight with inspiration. "I remember knowing I must work with this face."

Fighting his mesmerizing gaze, Charlotte mutters, "This is my good friend, Lady Lilith Montgomery."

Mangan plays his part well. He turns to me as if only just noticing my presence and steps forward, studying me closely.

"And another beauty," he says, apparently to himself. "Oh, a very different manner of harmony in these features. Such strength. Such . . . elegance."

Now I feel like a racehorse again. And how I dislike the duplicity, the lies that our secret identities compel us to live out.

"And you have no desire to be immortalized in stone?" he asks me suddenly.

"I don't believe I would like immortality," I reply. "Nor do I find the medium of stone appealing."

Charlotte shoots me a look. Even the model seems surprised by such a statement. Mangan is stunned into a moment's silence before letting out a bellow of laughter.

"Boldness in a young woman—a rare thing!" he declares.

"But honesty is not, I hope."

"I'm sure Lilith did not mean to give offense." Charlotte gently attempts to smooth things over.

"Are you?" Mangan asks, throwing me a covert wink, so that I have to resist my own urge to smile. "I am not so certain. But"—he waves his arms in an expansive gesture—"she is your friend, sweet child. You know her better than I. Now, come, let me show you some more of my work. And we will arrange a time for sketches. If I am to sculpt this innocent visage I must explore its every detail. I must know it. Gudrun!" he barks. "Must our guests die of thirst in this house?"

She shrugs. "If they did you would no doubt pick up your hammer and let their corpses be your models."

"Morbid woman! Go and find Jane. She will care that our guests are properly looked after if you do not."

"Jane has gone out, with the children. You sent them out because they were making too much noise."

He grunts. "Families are both a blessing and a curse. Still, you may yet discover the kitchen if you look hard enough."

Scowling at the way in which she is dismissed, Gudrun flounces from the studio, the chiffon of her gown billowing as she moves, exposing her body shamelessly. On leaving she passes a tall man in the doorway. He emerges from the darkness of the hall and I recognize him at once—for his face has often come unbidden to my mind since we first met—and I recall our conversation outside the house of Mr. Chow Li. His striking appearance is not easily forgotten.

Mangan, who has ushered Charlotte into the part of the studio that is mostly under glass, calls back. "Bram! Come in. Come and meet these divine women. I mean to have them both model for me, though the dark one is reluctant. See what you can do to persuade her, why don't you?"

At least he has the good grace to look uncomfortable at such an introduction. Though perhaps he is merely ill at ease because he knows I am aware of the sort of place he chooses to frequent.

"I am very pleased to meet you," he says a little stiffly, and gives an awkward nod of the head that isn't quite a bow, before changing his mind and offering me his hand. It is clear to me he has no more grasp of the topsy-turvy conventions of an artist's home than the rest of us. I shake his hand.

"We have already met," I remind him. "Or had you forgotten?"

"I would have to be blind or stupid or both to have forgotten you," he says, and then adds, "but on that occasion we were not introduced."

"It was hardly a place for formalities."

"You know it well?"

I try not to let my discomfort show on my face. "Of necessity. I am compelled to go there on occasion to collect my . . . a family member who . . ."

"I see," Bram cuts in. "I am sorry to hear that."

"Sorry that my relative is so afflicted, or sorry that I do not share your love of such a destructive pastime?"

He flinches as if I have struck him. With a glance in Mangan's direction, and lowering his voice slightly he says, "There are those who suffer lapses in character from time to time. Perhaps it is unkind to judge them."

"Indeed." I refuse to be won over by his argument. "And yet to see a friend in such a state and to encourage them . . ."

"Encourage?"

"Have you not considered that a person already in thrall to the dreadful substance might find it easier to abstain if those he kept company with did so also?" Even though I know Mangan's indulgence in opium is an infrequent and small thing, less so than his drinking, indeed, I cannot let the thing rest. It distresses me that this apparently well-mannered and intelligent young man should think Mr. Chow Li's a worthwhile place to visit at all. I hear myself being unkind, intolerant, unreasonable, even, but I cannot stop myself. Why should it matter what this stranger does or thinks or feels?

"My abstinence has no bearing on my mentor's actions, I assure you."

"Do you know that? Have you tried even to modify your own behavior?"

Bram opens his mouth to respond but says nothing. The silence between us grows.

He has no answer to that. Spirits save us, how I detest what the drug does to people. Good, clever, gifted people, ruined. I do not trust myself to discuss it further. I'm here for Charlotte, I must not spoil things for her. Mangan has his dissolute moments, but he is a decent, caring man beneath the image of outlandish genius. I do not know this other artist well enough to assume the same is true of him.

At last Mangan's voice shatters the uncomfortable moment. "Cease your dithering, man, and come here. Cast your eyes upon this delicious example of young womanhood. How would you paint her, Bram, tell me that? How would you capture that essence of the ingénue, eh?"

I follow Bram as he answers Mangan's summons. I walk in the cool of his shadow. His shirtsleeves are rolled up to reveal strong forearms which are splattered with paint, and he moves with an easy gait. He wears his hair longer than most men of my acquaintance, and has about him the sense of someone breaking free of their fetters. I find conflicting thoughts chasing through my mind. I have no time for wastrels and hedonists, and yet there is something undeniably attractive about this man. Something beyond his dark good looks and lithe body. Something more.

When we find her, Charlotte is glowing with excitement. She grabs hold of my arm and whispers urgently in my ear.

"Isn't Mangan simply marvelous? I can't wait for him to begin work. Imagine, little me being transformed into art by *him!*"

"I find it hard to believe your parents agreed to this. Have they met Mr. Mangan?"

"Oh yes, at the Asquiths' do. Though they've never been here of course." She laughs gaily. "Mama would faint away at the sight of Gudrun, though I think Pa would become a regular visitor if he knew what went on here."

"Better not tell him, then."

"I shan't. This will be my place to come where I can shake off all silly convention and etiquette, just for a few hours. Oh, Lilith, it's going to be such fun!"

Mangan throws an arm around Bram's shoulders. "I am to undertake a rare commission of Miss . . ."

"Charlotte. Please, call me Charlotte."

". . . You should paint her while she sits for me. What do you think to that idea?"

Bram smiles, and I am irritated to find myself responding to the warmth in his face, the sincerity of the gesture.

"I'd love to paint you, Charlotte. If you don't mind."

"Mind? Heavens, no! I'd be delighted. A portrait as well as a sculpture in stone! Are you famous yet? Oh, never mind, I'm sure you will be soon. When can we begin? My engagement diary is practically empty, I swear. There is nothing to do this time of year."

"Charlotte," I feel obliged to be the voice of caution, "don't you think you should consult your father first? About the painting, I mean. After all, they only agreed you might sit for Mr. Mangan . . ."

The sculptor gives another loud guffaw. "You've nothing to fear from Bram, I promise you. A man of unquestionable integrity. I'd call him a gentleman if I didn't consider the name an insult. A fine fellow, solid and honest as the day is long."

Mangan bustles Charlotte out into the garden to show her some of his larger works. Bram remains, his head tilted slightly to one side, as if waiting for something more from me.

"I'm sure I appear very . . . cautious to you," I say, finding myself uncomfortable beneath his gaze.

"Your friend will be quite safe here with us."

"Perhaps. Until you take it into your heads to have her accompany you on one of your . . . outings."

Bram's smile disappears completely, to be replaced by an expression somewhere between hurt and anger.

"I see you have already formed a very low opinion of me," he says.

"I have no opinion of you."

"That's not true. You think you know me, and you have judged me. Which is a pity," he goes on. "I would far rather you thought well of me. I'm not sure why it matters that you do, but it does."

For a moment I stare at him. It is so unlike me to be at a loss for words that I am thrown, disconcerted by what he has said, and by the way he is looking at me.

The front door of the house is flung open and a squealing gaggle of children charge down the hallway and into the studio.

"Pa! Pa! We are home!" cry what must surely be twins in unison as they belt past us, a large shaggy dog on their heels, and several more children, all equally vociferous in their search for their father. They roar out into the garden where Mangan can be heard greeting them happily. A flustered woman brings up the rear. She looks hot and out of breath but still finds a smile with which to greet me.

"Ah, you must be the lovely Pilkington-Adams girl I've heard so much about. Mangan is simply longing to sculpt you." She yanks her hat from her head and mops her damp brow with the back of her hand. "Where have those children got to? Freedom has ice cream all down his shirt front. The dog's eaten most of everybody else's and is bound to be sick any minute. Children!" she calls as she trails out after them. "Children, you are too sticky to go near your father. Come and be washed. Oh! Hello there, who are you?" she asks, clearly having got as far as Charlotte.

Bram steps toward the hall. "That was Jane, Mangan's wife," he explains. "She's chaotic and harassed, but she'd give you her last bowl of stew. Around here that means something. Try not to judge her too quickly." And without giving me a chance to reply he disappears into the dark depths of the house.

Jane marches back in from the garden dragging two small children with her.

"Bram gone? I was hoping he'd help me bathe George. Wretched dog has candyfloss in its fur as well as ice cream and Mangan won't allow it back in the house in such a state. Can't think why not, it's no stickier than his offspring. Leo, stop wriggling, do. You *will* be washed," she insists.

"Does he often do things like that? Help you give the dog a bath and . . . suchlike?"

"Oh, Bram is a sweetie. Couldn't wish for nicer. I know he looks very Byronesque, and he does have a tendency to brood if he's on his own too much, but we see to it he's kept sociable." She laughs. "A person does not have a choice in the matter in this house. He's only been with us a few weeks, but he gets on famously with everyone. And the children adore him." She shakes her head. "Do you know he had barely set foot in the door, his very first day in London, and I sent him off to retrieve Mangan from that dreadful Mr. Chow Li's clutches? Not that you'll know who I'm talking about. Vincent, if you try to bite your brother again there will be consequences." She strides onward, hauling her reluctant charges with her, but has not entirely vanished into the gloom of the hallway before she calls back over her shoulder. "That's a tremendously dear man, you know, and such a talented artist. A very rare bird indeed."

7.

Bram regards the portrait on the easel in front of him with deepening disappointment. He has been working on it for days, now. He had taken Mangan's advice and wandered the streets with his sketchbook, seeking inspiration. He has drawn scene after scene of the city: Oxford street shoppers, an overturned milk cart, a flower stall, the Thames at twilight. All interesting subjects, and good material to work with, but nothing that truly stirred him. He persuaded a chestnut seller to come to his studio and be painted, in the hope that a model would be more satisfying to paint directly, rather than working from sketches. The sitter had been patient and stoic, only mentioning once that, as he was still wearing his heavy coat and fingerless mittens, the studio was uncomfortably hot.

At the time Bram had been moderately pleased with the finished picture, but now, only a few days later, it fails to please.

There is a reasonable likeness and a convincing skin tone. The composition is satisfactory. The draftsmanship professional. There is, in fact, nothing technically wrong with the painting, it is just . . . dull. Dull and flat and lifeless. Where is the flair? The spark of life? The character in the features? The beauty? I can't show this to Mangan.

An image of Lilith's face, bold and graceful, springs up before his mind's eye. His joy at seeing her again, at discovering her identity, at knowing she is not lost to him, is tempered by her reaction to him. He recalls the way she spoke to him, the way she judged him, and the memory irks him anew. She was quick to label him as contemptuous, on scant evidence.

But then, had not I formed an instant opinion of her, too? And there was sorrow behind her words. Some personal pain.

He remembers she had said it was a relative who used Mr. Chow Li's services. He can only imagine how terrible it must be for her—for a woman like her—to have to go to such a place. It is a measure of her character that she would undertake such a mission. She cut a striking figure, tall and elegant in her hooded cape. A point of restrained glamor amid the gray, brutal surroundings of Bluegate Fields. When he was introduced to her in Mangan's studio he found himself awkward in her company. Disturbed by being so close to her. She has a presence that is not easily ignored. Later that same day, over black tea with no sugar, the children having eaten the last of it on bitter oranges from the leavings at Brewer Street market, Jane told him more about her. The daughter of a duke, born into one of the wealthiest families in London.

No use Bram from Yorkshire filling his head with thoughts of a member of the aristocracy.

He knows how these things work. He knows how society ladies like to amuse themselves with artists who are the talk of the town. And those artists are rarely too proud to undertake their commissions. Poverty has a way of taking the edge off principles. Hunger can blunt them altogether. Mangan is no different from the many creative men who have been required to bend their talents to suit the whim of a patron. Charlotte Pilkington-Adams's parents will pay handsomely for the sculpture. Bram will strive to produce a portrait of her in the hope they will decide to purchase it, too. The young woman would enjoy the thrill of being a muse for a short while, and then the dalliance would be over. Perhaps Lady Lilith would accompany her, if only to make certain her friend is not led into some nefarious habits. She would no doubt be polite and take a modest interest in the process. But then the artwork would be completed, and the acquaintance would be at an end.

And our paths would be unlikely ever to cross again.

The thought causes an unexpected tightness in his chest, which in turn makes him feel annoyed at his own foolishness. He snatches up a rag and dips it in turpentine. He hesitates for a moment, his hand hovering above the surface of the canvas. The acrid smell of the turpentine brings him to his senses. With mounting irritation he rubs at the canvas, watching with some morbid satisfaction as the image blurs, the colors melt, and the shapes lose their definition as he works to erase the dismal painting.

The heat of summer fades and the year falls quietly into autumn. I find my grief for my father is also undergoing subtle transformations. The disbelief at his passing, the numbness of the early days, the gnawing ache as I adjust to life without him—all these phases come and go in such a short space of time I am only able to see them clearly with the crystal vision of hindsight. Now, just a few months after his death, and after so many mutations, my grieving has settled into a constant undertow of sadness that tugs at my mood and my thoughts seemingly without respite. The sorrow wearies me.

What must it be like for poor Mama? I am young enough to have a future to travel toward, whereas she is propelled only by her past now. Nor does she have the comfort of knowing, as I do, that dear Father is never far from us.

I cherish the all too brief moments I have been able to spend in the company of my father's spirit. I was taught, many years ago, of the progression of the soul from the living world after a person dies. I understand that contact with a spirit in the Land of Night is easier, more vivid, more tangible almost, in those first precious weeks. Gradually the pull of the noncorporeal realm grows stronger, so that it is harder to keep that connection. And while it is possible to commune with the departed, the connection is increasingly distant, increasingly faint, increasingly tenuous.

As is my habit, once the household is abed for the night, I slip silently down the narrow wooden staircase and go out into the garden. The cool night soothes me. I am wearing a soft woolen shawl over my nightclothes and red brocade slippers, and my hair hangs in a heavy plait down my back. The night air has a freshness about it that suggests the first frost of the season might adorn the plants and lawns before morning. After such a long, airless summer in the city, I am glad of the shift in the weather. I follow the path past the now-bare magnolia tree and take a seat on the small patio in front of the summer house. From the other side of the walls that enclose the garden come sounds of London slumbering. A lone carriage makes its way around the square, the hoofbeats of the sprightly horse that pulls it dwindling as it heads east. Some ways off a dog barks a muffled warning. Through an open upstairs window of the neighboring residence drift the subsiding sobs of a new baby, shushed with a lullaby. I close my eyes. I often sit in the stillness of the night, relishing the peace, feeling the darkness easing my worries, letting my mind open and float as if in a waking dream. Father showed me that the dark was nothing to fear. It is what people imagine it hides that terrifies them. I know the shadows to be peopled with all manner of souls stepping through time, traveling lightly between this world and the next, either at their own bidding or while being summoned. This time, however, I feel apprehensive. Whereas ordinarily I am at ease calling the spirits to talk to me, I realize now that I am wary. Since the Dark Spirit began to stalk my mind and ambush my thoughts, I am loath to do anything that might reawaken him. If he is listening to me so much of the time, if he is so present, surely my communing with others from the Land of Night will provoke him into speaking once more.

Perhaps I should do just that. What manner of Lazarus witch am I if I allow such a spirit to make me a reluctant necromancer? Should I always step cautiously in fear of him? Might that not be the very thing the Sentinels want? No, better that I face him. Better that I make him see I will not be cowed. Not be frightened.

I set my feet flatly on the ground, place my hands in my lap, palms up, bow my head forward, eyes still closed, and allow my mind to quiet and settle. My breathing slows and deepens. My pulse steadies and lightens. Slowly the earthly sounds about me grow fainter and more distant until they seem to come from some far-off place and have nothing whatever to do with me. My lips move as I silently recite the common prayer for calling those who have passed on to the Land of Night. I repeat the arcane words, which are as familiar to me as the Christian prayers I was taught to say by my nanny before bed. The rhythm builds to a chant, over and over and over, until my mind has entered an altered, meditative state. At last I stop, sitting motionless, listening, waiting. Within seconds there comes the familiar chill of the cool, airless breath of the deceased upon my neck.

So close! Who is there? Who has answered my call?

There is no reply, but I know beyond doubt that I am no longer alone. The simple request has brought forth a spirit willing to talk with me. It is not my father, of that I am sure, for I spoke with him only last night in the crypt and the frequency of our meetings has begun to tire him. He would not come unless I specifically asked for him.

Who are you?

When this spirit speaks the words have no sounds as such, but feel as if they are laid, one by one, directly onto my consciousness. I understand this to be an indication that the person is very long dead. Decades at the least. Centuries, maybe. The language the deceased has chosen to communicate in is an ancient English, peppered with phrases of Latin. I sense the presence is male. I focus on what I am being told. Although the presence is strong the words are indistinct and somewhat muddled.

The challenger? Can you tell me about the challenger, Gentle Spirit?

More words form and drift through my mind, seemingly unconnected, snippets of what appear to be archaic ritual mantras or creeds. Words referring to power and strength. Words that tell of great sorrow to come.

Sorrow for whom?

The message remains unclear, though its tone, its strength of feeling, are unmistakable. And now, suddenly, I feel someone else close, someone threatening. And I know it is the Dark Spirit.

You look to the wrong people for help, Daughter of the Night.

Won't you tell me who you are? Why you haunt me? Who is making you do this?

Your pretense at interest in me beyond what threat I pose is a thin disguise. I know all Lazarus witches dissemble when it suits them. Such sly creatures, afraid to show their true selves.

If you think that, then surely you must wish to reveal your identity to me?

A movement in the shadows startles me, making my heart leap. I am not alone, and whoever is with me in the garden now is not a visiting spirit.

"Who's there?" I ask, my voice, though a whisper, sounding loud in the stillness that surrounds me. "Who is it?"

"Tis only I, darling sister," says Freddie, stepping onto the patio beside me. Here the moonlight falls unimpeded by trees or foliage so that, while not strongly illuminated, my brother is plainly visible.

"What are you doing out here at this hour?" I demand, more

abruptly than I had intended. My heart is still thudding from conversing with the Dark Spirit. However unnerving his presence, I need to challenge him, to show him I will not be threatened by him. To find out if he does truly act at the behest of the Sentinels. But now Freddie is here, and I must turn my attention to him.

"I might ask you the same question," he replies, lowering himself onto a chair. "But then, I know better than to inquire after your . . . curious nighttime activities. Father taught me well. If I was not good enough to join your merry little band, the very least I could do was to keep its existence a secret."

"It can't have been easy for you," I say, and I mean it. I myself hate the lies I have to tell to protect the coven. How much harder must such deceit be for one who feels excluded from it?

Freddie sighs and runs a hand through his sleek black hair. There are moments he so resembles Father. And yet, in truth, he is little like him. He looks heartbreakingly sad. And so very alone. What happened to that happy little boy who shared my childhood?

As if reading my thoughts, Freddie smiles suddenly. "Do you remember that very hot summer before I went off to Harrow? We spent every afternoon swimming in the lake."

I soften at the memory. "The minute we could escape from the appalling Mr. Carstairs. Oh! Was there ever a more boring tutor?"

"Papa thought he would make us serious."

"Mama thought his manners very fine, as I recall."

"Plain fact is, we'd seen off so many tutors, it was hard to find one who'd take us on."

"*You'd* seen them off. I was a ridiculously well-behaved child."

Freddie grins. "If it pleases you to think so I won't argue," he says. "Let's agree at least that you were a willing coconspirator in my adventures."

"I certainly remember counting those dragging hours until we could escape to the lake that summer. You built a swing so we could drop into the deep water."

"I was a particularly fine dropper, you'll allow that. Some spectacular backward flips."

"No one else could do it."

"I was the unchallenged king of the flip. Even our wretched cousins couldn't match me."

"Partly because you kept putting them off with well-timed shouts about their ludicrous bathing costumes."

"Well, they were ludicrous. They had only themselves to blame for presenting such easy targets."

I laugh lightly, surprising myself with the unfamiliar sound. It has been a long time since I have laughed.

"We used to have fun, Freddie, didn't we?"

He nods.

"It all seems an age ago," I say.

"We were children." He raises his hands in a gesture of hopeless acceptance. "And now we are adults and life is not allowed to be fun anymore."

"Oh, Freddie."

"I don't think I make a very good adult at all," he decided. "I should have stayed a child."

I lean forward and take his hand. To see him so beaten by life when he is barely nineteen years old pulls at my heart.

"You were so happy at Radnor Hall," I say, clearly picturing the bright-eyed boy he had been, scampering among the undulating gardens of our country estate, or urging his pony on at breakneck speed across the parkland, or climbing to the very top of the tallest tree in the orchard to reach the best apple. "Why don't you go back there? Just for a while," I race on as he slowly shakes his head. "Oh, think about it, Freddie, at least consider the idea."

"I would shrivel up and die there."

"But you love the place. You were so content there, so free . . ."

"I was a boy, Lil. I can't go back to being seven."

"You could shoot and hunt and fish. The air might put some color back in your cheeks."

He smiles at me ruefully now, gently taking his hand from mine. "You and I both know my devilishly fashionable pallor has nothing whatever to do with a want of fresh air."

"I can't stand seeing you so unhappy. And nor can Mama. After losing Papa, it distresses her to see you unwell. And of course she cannot know the cause."

"If you're trying to make me feel guilty you needn't bother. I already hate myself quite sufficiently, thank you."

"Freddie." I snatch up both his hands this time. "I really do believe going home to Radnor Hall could help. There are not so many . . . distractions there."

He gives a mirthless laugh. "Out of temptation's way, you mean. No Mr. Chow Li to tend to my needs."

"Perhaps it is too easy for you, living in London, too easy to . . ."

"My darling sister, I can assure you, nothing is easy for me."

In the silence that follows I search desperately for the right words, for the words that would make him listen to me. The small clouds that have been partly obscuring the bright moon part briefly, allowing pearly moonbeams to fall upon Freddie's face. The shadows beneath my brother's eyes deepen, so that I feel I am gazing into the empty sockets of a skull. The image is so powerful it makes me gasp. As if sharing my vision, the Dark Spirit speaks again.

Your brother does not belong in the Land of Day!

Be gone! My brother has nothing to do with you.

Freddie notices my change in mood.

"You are cold," he says. "Let's go in."

I try to remain in the moment with him, forcing myself to press him to go away. I will not let the wicked spirit come between me and my brother. "Is there nothing that would persuade you?"

"You don't know what you're asking. Really, you don't."

"But what is there for you here? Apart from . . . I mean . . . you haven't anybody to stay for . . ."

"That you disapprove of my friends comes as no surprise, Lil, but they *are* my friends. They . . . understand me."

"They use you." I cannot help speaking my mind. "I've seen how they take advantage of your good nature and your money."

"Am I so very loathsome? Can I only buy friendship?"

"That is not what I meant."

"Isn't it? What use am I to you? Or to Mama? Or to anyone? At least my friends value me, in their own unedifying way."

"We value you. I value you."

"You can't look at me without that dreadful pitying expression you seem to reserve solely for me. Do you know, it is precisely the way our dear late father used to look at me? Quite a legacy you have there, that disappointed look."

I feel the familiar exasperation a conversation with Freddie often brings about. Taking a breath, I try hard not to sound as despairing of him as I feel. At last I say, "I miss you, Freddie. I miss the brother I had."

"I'm sorry about that, sister dear, truly I am. To be honest, I quite miss me, too, sometimes. But there it is. The clock cannot be made to run backward. Time has shaped me into the person I am now, like it or not." He takes a silver cigarette case from his inside pocket and selects a small Russian cigar. He lights it and inhales deeply, filling the air with the smell of dark, treacly tobacco. "Being in mourning doesn't help a fellow, I must say. Doesn't help one bit. All this moping around, wearing black, having to turn down invitations endlessly."

"It's not for very long," I say, though in my heart I agree with him.

"Feels like an age already, and Mama is determined we suffer this purgatory for a whole year. A year! I shall lose what little there is of my mind. Only this morning I overheard the Lindsay-Brown girls discussing a fabulous ball being planned for March and when I asked why I had not been invited I was told there was no point as I would still be unable to accept. March, Lilith. That's next spring." He smokes energetically, and his left leg has begun to jiggle. The thought takes hold in my mind that Freddie might actually be right. Being in mourning means he has even less to do than usual. He could not be persuaded to take an interest in Parliament, and he is a social outcast, and will continue to be so for months yet, because of the death of our father. An idea comes to me.

"I will strike a bargain with you," I tell him. He raises an eyebrow and waits. "If you agree to spend the winter at Radnor Hall . . . no, hear me out." I hold up a hand to fend off his interruption. "If you leave London and return home for the next four months, I will see to it that Mama agrees to have us officially out of mourning in time for the ball in March."

"She'd never agree to it," he scoffs.

"She will. I promise."

He hesitates, clearly tempted by the idea.

"I'd have your word? I swear if you make me endure a winter of Radnorshire weather and all that dangerously fresh air for nothing I won't be responsible for my actions."

"If you go, and stay there, just until the end of February, I'll accompany you to the wretched ball myself." I watch his face closely. "Well? Do we have a deal, Your Grace?"

"Only if you promise never to call me that again. Makes me feel like a bally bishop," he says, laughing as I throw my arms around his neck.

8.

On this morning it occurs to Bram that his life has never contained so many women, and that those he encountered when he lived in Yorkshire were altogether more straightforward than the ones who now challenge him. He has tried, and failed, to paint two flower girls and a barmaid, with mixed success. One thought herself rendered plain, another objected to the color of her hair, and the third thought he had invited her to his studio for an entirely different purpose altogether. Then there is Gudrun, who has become even more prickly than is her habit since he rebuffed her advances. And now he is faced with painting Charlotte and must not fail, as he sorely needs the money he anticipates her delighted parents handing over for a pretty portrait.

But still his head is filled with thoughts of Lilith Montgomery. He might well have been able to keep his musings in check, had she not taken it upon herself to accompany Charlotte to each and every one of her sittings. This means that he is required to paint while Charlotte sits, or rather lies, semiclad in front of him, unable to hold a pose for more than a few seconds without fidgeting; Mangan, having produced some wild sketches, paces like a caged lion, gesticulating with hammer and chisel but getting very little in the way of actual sculpting done; Gudrun stomps in and out of the studio with, apparently, the sole intention of upsetting people; Perry dithers about proffering materials and tools and generally getting in the way; Jane fights a losing battle to keep the children, and George, either quiet or out of the house; and Lilith sits, still as a sphinx and quite as inscrutable, observing the chaotic proceedings with what Bram can only imagine to be disdain.

It isn't until she shifts slightly to return his gaze that he realizes he has been staring at her.

"Shouldn't you be looking at Charlotte?" she asks, with the faintest hint of a smile. "She is the one you're painting, after all."

Bram feels himself blushing like a schoolboy. He pointedly dabs at the palette of oil paints poised on his arm. He tries to think of a witty response, but there is too much noise around him, and too much confusion in his own mind. What is clear to him, by Lilith's manner and the few words she has spoken during these sittings, is that her opinion of him seems to have softened somewhat. He wonders what has brought this about. The first time he encountered her in the studio she had him down as a hopeless opium user, a bad friend, and a likely dangerous influence on Charlotte. Now she appears to be if not quite friendly, at least not openly hostile toward him.

And that matters to me, though it should not. Why would I care what she thinks? We can never be so much as friends. I would be a fool to think otherwise. Maybe I am a fool, then, for I cannot deny I am affected by her presence.

He attempts to concentrate on his painting. Charlotte is a glamorous beauty, who offers a decorative and elegant image to capture. Despite the noisy atmosphere of the studio, and the not inconsiderable distraction of having Lilith there, he is moderately pleased with his work.

Perry appears at his shoulder.

"Oh, I say, Bram. That is rather good."

"It is some way off being completed yet."

"Even so, you must be pleased. Has Mangan seen it?"

Bram shakes his head, glancing over at his mentor who is

working with ferocious determination on an area of stone that would, beneath his talented hand, evolve into Charlotte's chin. "I'm waiting for the right moment," he says.

Perry laughs and pats him on the back. "Courage, my friend! You know you won't be happy unless he is," he points out before hurrying off to answer his master's cry for the floor to be swept and the stone dampened.

To his surprise, Bram sees Lilith get up from her chair and come to stand in front of his easel.

"Can I see?" she asks, almost shyly. "Or would you rather I didn't? I don't want to trample on any delicate artistic sensibilities." There is no mockery in her tone, he thinks, rather a genuine wish not to offend.

"Your feet are far too elegant to do any trampling."

"Don't you believe it," she says. "When I was a child my elderly dancing instructor would hobble from the room after each session, claiming I had deliberately sought out his bunions."

"And had you?"

"On the whole I think I'd rather keep my distance from a bunion, wouldn't you?"

Bram smiles at her, and is so engrossed in studying her face he forgets she has asked something of him. After a long moment she raises her eyebrows.

"You have only to say if you don't want me to look at it until it's finished."

"What? Oh, the painting . . . I don't mind. You can look if you wish. In fact, I'd like you to."

"Really?"

"You are close to Charlotte. You will be able to see if I have captured her in the portrait. Success lies beyond a mere likeness, of course."

"Of course," she agrees, stepping round to stand beside him. She considers the picture intently, first leaning in as if to examine the minutest brush strokes, then moving back to view the over-all effect.

After a while Bram can stand her silence no longer.

"Please say something. With every passing second I am imag-ining a more damning critique."

"I'm really not qualified to offer a *critique*."

"You are a person looking at a portrait of someone dear to them. Your response will be valid, however unfavorable."

She turns to look at him now, subjecting him to the same rigorous scrutiny as she has the painting. "It really matters to you, doesn't it? What I think."

"Naturally, as I said, you are Charlotte's friend. And, no doubt, as a young lady of good . . . education, moving in society . . . well, you surely encounter many paintings. Many portraits. I expect you have, in fact, a perfectly well-developed sense of what is good art and what is not. As it were." Bram is horribly aware that he is rambling but is powerless to stop himself.

If she goes on standing so close to me and looking at me like that I shall have to kiss her. I've never wanted to kiss someone so much in my life. Now I'm being completely ridiculous.

"So, you see," he says, just a little too loudly, "your evaluation is indeed . . . worthwhile. Or will be, when you eventually de-cide to give it." He knows he should turn away from her, mix some paint, perhaps, work at a corner of the painting. Anything, rather than just stand there, watching her watching him. But he wants to look at her. He wants to drink in every available second of her.

At last she speaks, not for one instant taking her eyes from his. "I think Perry is right, it is rather good."

"Oh. Thank you," he says, but he is not, in truth, thinking about the painting anymore. He is thinking about how Lilith's eyes shine as she teases him. He is thinking about how clear and pale her skin is. He was thinking about how, even wearing black, she glows, somehow. He finds himself smiling at her, a broad, honest grin that he simply cannot hold back. And it is a smile that has very little to do with her appraisal of his picture. To his astonishment, and, were he to admit it, to his delight, she returns his smile with one of pulse-speeding loveliness.

Bram Cardale, he scolds himself silently, *what in God's name do you think you are doing?*

🕷

A minute before curtain up, Stricklend takes his seat in the front row of the balcony. He has timed his arrival with care. As a late-comer he would have drawn unwanted attention to himself, or even risked being kept out until the end of the first act. Had he arrived early, on the other hand, he might have been drawn into unwelcome conversation with someone in an adjoining seat. On the whole, experience has taught him, operagoers are a garrulous and sociable breed, given to striking up acquaintances based on a mutual liking for Wagner or Puccini, or a desire in common to participate in the activity of being an audience, and therefore responding to a performance as one amorphous whole. It would surprise no one who knows Nicholas Stricklend to hear that he does not share this taste for communal behavior. Indeed, on the occasions where a simple desire to experience sublime music compels him to purchase a ticket, he does so in spite of, not because of, his fellow devotees. He would much prefer an auditorium empty save for himself and those on stage. On this particular November night, however, it is not the program that has lured him from the pleasant solitude of his apartment. He is not a lover of Mozart, deeming his work to be irritatingly frivolous, in the main. And he finds a theater full of those who seek out such light entertainment to have a childish buzz and fidget about it that is as tiresome as it is distracting.

The orchestra plays well, and Figaro delivers his lines in a pleasing bass. Even so, the minutes pass slowly. Stricklend wants to wait for the story to be sufficiently underway that the audience will be giving it the greater part of their attention. If he waits too long, however, the call of the interval glass of champagne or light supper course will have them restless and looking about them, which would not suit his purposes. At what he decides is the perfect moment, Stricklend picks up his opera glasses and holds them to his eyes. They are his own, a pair he bought in Vienna some years ago, fashioned from pale silver, finely crafted, set in ivory, and with a silk cord attached so that they might be comfortably worn about the neck when not in use. Through the superior lenses, he can make out the youthful flush of Susanna's throat, and the thickly applied kohl around her lover's eyes. Opera singers, in his opinion, are best viewed from higher up and farther back. Slowly he moves the glasses and refocuses them on the figure sitting at the front of a private box to the right of the stage. He has an uninterrupted view of this particular box, which is why he selected his particular seat. The man framed in the ellipses of his glasses is evidently enjoying himself. He holds a large glass of red wine in one hand, and a sizeable cigar in the other. His eyes are unnaturally bright, suggesting his evening revelries began some time earlier, and that here is a man accustomed to partaking of the good things that life has to offer. His companions for the evening Stricklend recognizes as his wife, his brother and family, and one or two minor aristocrats whom he has presumably brought along to impress with the lavish way he entertains them and the erudition of his taste in music. Their expressions imply that good wine has gone some way to ensuring they will speak favorably of the evening, nevertheless. Stricklend wonders if they would be seen out with him if they knew him to be a practicing necromancer and a member of the Lazarus Coven. A senior witch, held in high esteem by his fellows. And a staunch supporter of the Montgomery household. It is this last fact that, to Stricklend's mind, renders him an unacceptable obstacle. One that must simply be removed, lest he stand in the way of what the Sentinels desire. What Stricklend himself desires, above all else.

Keeping the glasses trained on his intended victim, Stricklend takes a gentle hold of the silken cord with his left hand. The plaited slub feels pleasingly cool in the heat of the auditorium. Slowly he winds it around his hand, once, twice, gradually letting the cord tighten, taking up the slack so that the narrow rope starts to dig into the loose flesh between his thumb and forefinger. His lips move, silently forming the Suffering Spell he chose with such careful deliberation. As the ancient entreaties and curses fill his dry mouth, the man in the private box puts down his cigar and begins to pull at his starched collar, feebly at first, and then with increasing irritation. Soon he is tugging at his tie, releasing the neat white bow so that it falls into limp lines down his shirt front. His wife becomes aware something is wrong with her husband, and utters a small cry of alarm as she watches his wineglass fall to the ground and empty its contents into the dense wool carpet. The man staggers to his feet, one hand clawing at his throat, the other clutching the brass rail in front of him. Others in his party seek to come to his aid, clustering round uselessly, fanning him with their programs, calling for water, powerless to ease his distress. Stricklend can sense the man attempting to summon his powers as a witch to protect himself, but his actions come too little and too late.

And all the while the notes of Mozart's melodies drift about them like so much confetti caught up in a breeze.

Stricklend tightens the cord and moves on to the Stopping Spell he selected for the occasion. It is a relatively basic piece of magic, perhaps lacking something in elegance, but he has used it several times before, and it gives reliable, and crucially, swift results. As he continues to watch through his opera glasses, he pulls the cord still closer around his hand, aware of the veins beneath his skin constricting and interrupting the flow of blood, in much the same way the air is being squeezed out of the gasping man opposite him. The wife has become distraught and sets up a wail that even the orchestra cannot compete with. The second violins falter. The conductor is distracted and turns to follow their gaze, causing the percussion section to crash into one another. Susanna pales beneath her greasepaint. The man in the private box has insufficient breath left to make any noise at all, so that it is to the accompaniment of women's shrieks and a stalwart French horn that he finally pitches forward over the rail and plummets into the stalls.

As Bram approaches Number One Fitzroy Square the thrill of anticipation hastens his steps. When he had found the scarf pin belonging to Lilith on the floor of Mangan's studio he knew he had the perfect excuse for calling on her. He would return the silver pin with its green tourmaline stones set into the small dragonfly, claim he had been passing anyway, that it was no trouble, and so on, and so on. Despite his determination to see Lilith, he knows he will have to deal with those who might not regard him as a suitable caller.

I shall make certain not to be diverted by some overprotective servant. I shall insist on placing the pin in her hand and no other.

Perry bounds past Bram and pulls the iron bell handle confidently. When he heard of Bram's intention to visit the house he had insisted on accompanying him.

"Can't have you standing there all on your own. Don't want you to look predatory, seeking her out," he had said. "And besides, you'll probably think better of it at the last minute if I don't go with you."

The bell sounds deep within the house and the door is opened. A young butler peers out at them through suspicious eyes.

"Is Lady Lilith at home?" Bram inquires in his most confident voice.

"Is Her Ladyship expecting you, sir?"

"No. She is not. I have something to give to her. Something that belongs to her and was lost. I have come to return it."

The butler frowns. Perry springs forward, proffering his calling card.

"Peregrine Smith. Would you be good enough to tell Lady Lilith myself and Mr. Bram Cardale are here and hope very much she will receive us?"

The butler takes the card and, reluctantly it seems to Bram, admits them into the hallway. Perry lets out a low whistle and hops about examining portraits and objets d'art.

After what feels like an interminable wait, Lilith appears at the top of the stairs. Bram is aware of his pulse quickening, and his mouth becoming nervously dry at the sight of her. He cannot recall a woman ever having the effect upon him that Lilith does. She descends the stairs, her simple black dress showing off her tiny waist and accentuating how tall and slender she is. Her hair is secured in a loose bun today, which nestles in the nape of her long neck.

Remain calm, Bram tells himself. *If she only glimpses the strength of my desire for her she will more than likely be frightened off.*

"Mr. Cardale, Mr. Smith, what a pleasant surprise." She greets them formally, but warmly enough, Bram thinks. The butler remains a few paces off like a sturdy guard dog, on the alert for the first hint of trouble.

Bram offers the scarf pin to Lilith. "I found this," he states a little more bluntly than he had intended. "In Mangan's studio. You must have dropped it when you attended with Miss Pilkington-Adams. I . . . I wanted to return it to you. As quickly as possible. I thought you might be looking for it," he finishes.

He notices for the first time that there is still oil paint beneath his fingernails. He snatches his hands away.

Lilith smiles slowly. She turns the pin over. Light flashes off the gem-studded wings of the little dragonfly.

"Why, thank you," she says. "I had indeed missed it. I am fond of this pin—it was a present from my late father. It was so good of you to bother to deliver it to me in person."

"It looked . . . important. I thought it best not to entrust it to a messenger or post boy."

"And you brought a guard, in case some robber should try to wrest it from you?" she teases, nodding in Perry's direction. Perry grins and looks as if he might say something but Bram successfully silences him with a harsh stare. Lilith says, "I think the very least I can do after such diligence is to offer you tea. I'm afraid Mama is indisposed this morning and is staying in her room." She turns to the butler. "Radley, would you ask Cook for some of her splendid shortbread and a pot of Darjeeling?"

She leads her visitors through to the drawing room. Although winter is settling in now, there is still plenty of golden sunshine falling through the tall windows, which are framed by swags of silk and brocade of palest blue to match the eggshell walls.

"What a pretty room," Bram murmurs.

"Mama would be pleased to hear you say so. She prides herself on having an eye for decor, and took to the Art Nouveau movement wholeheartedly. Father was not particularly enamored of it. He said all the flowers made him want to sneeze, even if they were only painted or carved in wood."

"But she has shown restraint I think." He wanders about the room, taking in the Tiffany lamps and a fine Mackintosh table. Lilith follows him as he explores, while Perry takes a place in a window seat at the far end of the room.

"Oh!" Bram cannot help exclaiming, "That is a piece of Lalique, unless I am mistaken," he says, stopping next to an elegant vase of frosted glass with a fine pattern of leaves twisting up it.

"You have a good eye. Mama is particularly proud of that. Mrs. Jessop will insist on trying to put flowers in it, which sends my mother into a tirade about the beauty and value of the thing, and how it is not some lowly vessel in which to display chrysanthemums."

"Now I know you're teasing me—I don't believe a single humble chrysanthemum ever entered this house."

Lilith smiles, and it is all Bram can do not to tell her, then and there, how much she moves him. She is even more striking than his memory of her, which now seems pitifully inadequate. Looking at her he realizes it is not simply a question of beauty, of a fortuitously straight nose, or luminous skin, or dark eyes. There is something else. Some other quality that sets her apart. He cannot find a satisfactory way to explain it to himself.

A spark of energy? A glow? No, not that. A presence . . . I cannot put it into words.

She looks up at him and he is flustered to be caught, yet again, gazing at her. And in his agitation he moves his arm back slightly and his elbow nudges the Lalique. It is as if everything that happens next happens in a dreamlike haze of slowed motion. He sees Lilith's eyes widen. He catches sight of the vase slipping inevitably, irretrievably, off the edge of the table. He hears a gasp, though he cannot be sure who has uttered it. He snatches at the falling object, but grasps only air. It continues on its inexorable journey toward the floor, toward its certain ruin.

But the vase never reaches the ground.

It simply stops, in the air, as if suspended on an invisible thread.

Bram knows this to be impossible, but he also knows, beyond any doubt, that he is seeing it happen.

Lilith quickly reaches down and takes hold of the heavy piece of glass, returning it to its rightful place without for one second meeting Bram's astonished eye.

"Now," she says, in a voice that is far too matter-of-fact, "where has Radley got to with that tea?" She turns and walks briskly to a painting above the fireplace. "This will interest you, I think. See? This was painted by none other than Mr. Alma-Tadema. One of Mama's favorite artists. I think the orange of the girl's dress a little harsh, but it is effective in its setting, don't you think?"

She meets his gaze now, and he is surprised to see fear in her eyes. He could question her. He could turn the conversation back to the glassware, back to the minor miracle he has just witnessed. But he sees that she is willing him not to. Not now.

Very well, not now. But one day. One day we shall speak of it. For we must both own to seeing that same impossibility occur, if I am ever to unravel the mystery that is Lilith Montgomery.

9.

The instant I set foot inside the large Chelsea house I know that agreeing to accompany Charlotte to what she had promised me would be a "harmless soirée" was a mistake. In the hallway we are met by frantic ragtime music coming from a gramophone positioned at the foot of the stairs. Every available inch of space is taken up by people dancing, many still clutching their drinks, all to the accompaniment of shrieks of glee and raucous laughter. Some of the hemlines are higher than any I have seen before, and most of the dresses so flimsy and diaphanous as to be startlingly revealing. I feel horridly drab in my black gown with its modest neckline, corseted waist, full sleeves, and heavy skirts.

"Charlotte!" I hiss at her as a harassed maid takes my coat. "You promised me this would be a quiet affair. A handful of interesting people engaged in diverting conversation, I seem to recall you telling me. You said nothing about wild partying. Look at all these people!"

"It does look rather lively," she confesses. "Not to worry, Lily. No one here will know who you are. I told you, this is a chance for you to have a tiny bit of fun for once. Is that so terrible?" she asks, unwrapping the fur stole from her shoulders. "Oh! An ice sculpture. Look! It's a turkey. To celebrate the turkey trot, which I insist you dance later on. It's a scream. Isn't it all too wonderful? Now"—she takes my arm and leads me into the melée—"have a glass of champagne and stop looking so cross, or no one will dare speak to you."

We battle our way across the hall and into the drawing room, which has been cleared of furniture to make more room for dancing. It is a large room, with long windows, much like any other built at the same period, but it is unlike any I have stepped into before. Every surface—walls, ceiling, even the floor—is covered in the most intricate murals, all rendered in vivid colors and touched here and there with gilt. The scenes depicted are of medieval maidens and knights in armor, or fairylike creatures drifting through tangled forests. Or half-naked figures languishing among flowers. The effect is striking. I am sure the space would feel full of frantic life even if it were not full of revelers. And what revelers they are. Many are dressed in the most outlandish ways possible, as if each were trying to outdo the next. There is a preponderance of exotic fabrics and styles of clothing, with many of the women, and quite a few of the men, sporting bejeweled turbans.

"Mama would have a fit of the vapors if she knew I was here," I protest.

"I promise not to tell her. Oh, come *on*, Lily, darling, *do*." She squeezes my arm, her eyes beseeching. "I know you are officially still in mourning, but it's doing you no good, stuck in that big empty house all the time. You are beginning to look quite peaked, if you'll forgive my saying so. You will feel so much better for letting your hair down, just a teeny, weeny bit. Besides, there's no one here remotely connected, I promise. These are artists, writers, poets. Young people who are making their own way in a dazzling new world. Ooh, here, a glass of this will oil the wheels," she says, passing me a bubbling flute from a tray held perilously aloft by a nearby footman. She is immediately engaged in conversation, at some volume to rise above the noise, with a bright-eyed couple beside her.

I know I ought to leave now, turn my back on all this gaiety, and go home. And yet, I confess there is something very appealing about staying and allowing myself to be part of such freedom. I do not see a single familiar face among the partygoers, which means it is unlikely they will know my identity. Such anonymity is seductive. I find myself tapping my foot to the syncopated ragtime beat and a smile, unbidden and unexpected, visits my face. The atmosphere is quite intoxicating. I notice a portly young man doing his level best to master some frenzied new dance. I can't tell if he is executing the steps correctly, but he does look wonderfully silly, so that I cannot suppress a giggle. As I take a sip of champagne my elbow is jogged by a passing dancer, so that the bubbles fizz up my nose making me sneeze. I attempt to fish a handkerchief from my sleeve, but one miraculously appears in front of me. I am so busy sneezing it is a moment before I can properly open my eyes to see who holds it. Bram stands before me, grinning broadly.

"It's not called bubbly for nothing," he points out as I take the proffered square of cotton. "Though I would have thought you'd have had plenty of opportunity to master drinking the stuff."

I narrow my eyes at him. "Naturally. All aristocrats are weaned from mother's milk directly to Châteauneuf-du-Pape."

"That's what I'd heard."

"Being born in Yorkshire, I expect you went straight on to brown ale."

"Stout, actually," he corrects me, still smiling.

I hand him back his handkerchief, but he shakes his head.

"Keep it," he says. "That way I will have an excuse to call on you again to request its return."

"Is it a family heirloom, perhaps?"

He laughs openly at this. "It is good to see you out enjoying yourself. I don't think I have ever seen you so . . ." he searches for the right words, ". . . at ease."

"The music is hard to resist. And such a concentration of fun . . ." I attempt to wave my arm to indicate the packed room and energetic dancing couples, but there really isn't the space. "Have you come on your own?" I ask.

"With Mangan and Gudrun. Perry was invited, too, but he said he had an appointment. He's being very mysterious about it. Gudrun suspects a woman. She and Mangan are here somewhere, though I haven't spied either of them for over an hour."

"I can't wait to see Mr. Mangan dancing."

"Oh, it's very frightening. We try to dissuade him. With such a crowded dance floor there are bound to be casualties."

It is a revelation to me that I can be so relaxed in this man's company when at the same time he unsettles me so. I cannot help thinking of the Lalique vase. Of what I did. Of what he saw me do. He knows that I stopped the glass from shattering, that I halted its progress through the air. And I chose not to work a spell of forgetting on him, a fact that has disturbed me ever since. But it was a choice. Almost as if I wanted him to see. What has he made of it? I wonder. What has he told himself to explain the inexplicable? And will he challenge me about it? It would surely be better if I did not give him the opportunity to do so. But I have no wish to remove myself from him. It is, in fact, both surprising and a little thrilling to find that I am prepared to risk his questioning me in order to remain in his company. I take another sip of my champagne, aware that he is observing me closely. What would Louis make of me being here, allowing another man to scrutinize me so?

Charlotte comes bounding up to us, a lanky young man in tow.

"Oh, Lily, you've found Mr. Cardale—how perfectly splendid that you are here! I've just seen Mr. Mangan holding forth on the merits and demerits of the Impressionists. He's in the kitchen, fueled by a dangerous-looking punch. Oh, listen, the 'Maple Leaf Rag'! We can do the turkey trot to this! Come on, Spencer, we simply have to dance. You, too, Lily," she calls over her shoulder as she races into the fray.

Bram raises an eyebrow at me. "Have you ever . . . ?" he asks.

"I admit, I have not."

"Nor I."

We watch the gyrating dancers, limbs flailing, moving at some speed despite the restrictions of space and the very real danger of injury from other frenzied couples. The music is wonderfully fast and catchy.

"It does look rather fun," I say quietly.

Bram takes my glass from me and sets it down on the mantelpiece.

"Shall we?" he asks, holding out his hand to me.

"I have no idea of the steps," I warn him, putting my gloved fingers into his hand.

"If a turkey can manage them, I'm certain you and I will cope," he says.

I have always considered myself to be a reasonable dancer, but this is like nothing else I have ever attempted. Bram and I do our best to copy the footwork and arm movements of our fellow trotters, with increasing hysteria. A tiny woman in a beaded dress and glasses barrels into us at one point, and an enthusiastic young man treads heavily on Bram's left foot. Soon we are forced to hold onto one another if only to avoid injury. By the time the rag reaches its triumphant final notes we are quite helpless with laughter. As the music finishes a cheer goes up amid cries of "Again! Again!" Bram groans at the idea of repeating the exercise. The crowd becomes more and more vociferous, demanding the record be played over at once. Bram still has his arm protectively around my waist, and I find that I have no wish to step out of his casual embrace. At this moment, a rosy-cheeked woman flings herself from the chair she has been standing on into the arms of her beau. In doing so, she drops her cocktail glass, which smashes on the wooden floor. I glance at Bram. He returns my look, and I know he is thinking of another piece of glass. One which was saved from smashing. His expression grows pensive.

"Let's go outside. Somewhere quieter," he says. When I hesitate he takes hold of my hand. "Please."

I know I should refuse. I should stay in the safety of the noise and bustle of the party, where conversation is nigh on impossible. But I want to go with him. I want to. So I let him lead me through the throng, out of the drawing room, threading through the hectic people, across the hall, down the passageway to a door that opens onto the small walled garden at the back of the house. The night is still and the sky clear. The cool air is refreshing after the fug of the party, but cold. Bram takes off his jacket and, ignoring my protestations, slips it around my shoulders. I can feel the warmth of him held in its silk lining. We walk to a wrought-iron garden seat at the edge of the lawn. I find I cannot look at him now. I know what is coming. I should not be here, with him, waiting for questions I must not answer. What do I hope for? What is it that compels me to stay? I steal a glance at him. His expression now is one of thoughtfulness, as if he is struggling to frame the inquiry that I so dread. His dark eyes look almost sorrowful. His profile is exquisite; some might say too beautiful for a man. I am astonished to find that I *want* him to find a way to broach the matter of the falling vase. I *want* him to start the conversation that can only lead to one thing: my revealing my true identity to him. This realization fills me with panic. What am I thinking? All my years of being a Lazarus witch, of knowing how vital secrecy is to the protection of the coven—have they come to nothing? Here I am, ready to tell a man I scarcely know . . . tell him what? How, precisely, do I anticipate this dialogue proceeding? Am I to confess to using magic, and casually inform him that I am a witch who practices necromancy, and then we can return to the dancing? The champagne must be addling my mind!

"Lilith," he says softly, and the sound of his voice uttering my name stirs something in me. "The other day, when I visited you at your home . . . as I watched you . . . I saw . . ." He looks at me, searching my face, no doubt trying to read my expression. "You did something . . . wonderful."

I hold his gaze. I must know that he is being honest with me. "You weren't . . . frightened?" I ask.

"I was astonished."

I start to blush and look down at my feet. The grass is damp, and the light from the rear windows of the house catches the water droplets, making them shimmer in the darkness. How can I tell him? Where would I begin? It is too much. Too soon.

Would you trust this non-witch with all your deepest secrets, Daughter of the Night?

The Dark Spirit's unmistakable voice interrupts the intimate moment as if it were a bomb blast inside my skull.

Go away! Leave me alone!

I will go only when you have given me what is rightfully mine.

I don't know what you mean!

You do, Morningstar. If you want to be rid of me, if you ever want to be free, you will give it to me.

I leap to my feet, Bram's jacket slipping from my shoulders.

"Lilith?" Bram stands, taking my hand once again. "What is it? I shouldn't have pressed you on the subject. Forgive me."

He cannot begin to understand. You will never be able to explain to him how different you are.

I could! He would listen, I know it. He would try to understand.

That you talk to the dead? That you call them to you and walk with them? If he were to know the truth about you he would be repulsed. He would think you despicable.

"Lilith, please . . ."

"I have to go. I'm sorry. I . . ." I pull my hand from his and hurry back toward the house.

"Wait!"

Run, little witch, run away. A necromancer cannot pull one from the Outerworld into the circle, you know that. This man cannot help you.

I clutch at my head, trying to block out the spirit's voice, but I know it is futile. Bram runs after me, calling my name, but I know that the Dark Spirit is right. We are too different. The gulf is too wide.

Bram catches me up just as I reach the door to the house. He takes hold of my arm and spins me round.

"What is it, Lilith? Why are you so afraid of talking to me? Why do you shroud yourself in secrecy? I . . . I care about you. I promise you, there is nothing you could tell me that would make me feel differently about you."

I shake my head. "That is a rash promise," I tell him. "You do not understand. You cannot."

He pulls me closer. "Let me try," he says. For moment the warmth of him, his strength, almost undo me. How wonderful it would be to have him hold me like this often. To feel so wanted, so protected. And now it occurs to me that, in all the years I have known him, and for all his fondness for me, I have never felt this way about Louis. The thought unnerves me. My judgment is clouded. I must get away so that I can think clearly.

I raise my eyes to look at Bram as levelly and steadily as I can.

"If you care about me at all, then let me go," I say.

He hesitates, and I see how difficult it is for him to release me, to let me leave without explanation, without giving him hope that we might speak again. Slowly he lets his arms fall to his sides and takes a step back. Without another word I turn for the door.

"I will wait, Lilith," he calls after me softly. "When you are ready, I will listen," he says.

I do not trust myself to look back or to respond but hurry into the hall and ask the nearest maid to fetch my coat.

10.

"Isn't this simply divine, Lily? Don't you think? I must try it on. And so must you!" Charlotte claps her hands together with glee.

I agreed to accompany my friend to her appointment with her dressmaker, but have not come with the intention of buying anything for myself. It is, however, hard to resist the seductive charms of such a place as the House of Morell, Ladies Tailor, Court Dressmaker and Furrier. In truth, I am at sixes and sevens after the events of the party. I am still aghast at the vehement persistence of the Dark Spirit, and angry with myself for allowing it to so disturb me. I *must* take charge. I must learn to block him from my mind, to somehow rid myself of his presence. And then there is Bram. I came so very close to revealing the truth about myself to him. Even now, without champagne to embolden me, and removed from his company, I find the thought of him stirs me. Stirs me so that I feel both joy and guilt. For, after all, I am engaged to Louis. How quickly my life has become so complicated.

"Oh, say you will try something." Charlotte holds up the beautiful gown of peach silk and lace. "You would look wonderful in it. I know you would."

"Charlotte. I am still in mourning."

"Oh. Yes, how silly of me. But never mind, I'm sure Edith can find you something gorgeous in black."

"This is your appointment."

"Darling Lily, don't you long for new clothes?"

That makes me hesitate. I have never been a particularly keen follower of the latest fashions, unlike Charlotte. There always seems to be something more pressing to think about. But lately I have begun to feel dreadfully drab. I know in part it is due to the family's status of mourning, the endless black I must wear, the careful shunning of anything the least bit bright or showy, but it isn't only that. After last night, after spending time with Bram, I feel . . . different. The party, the way I was able to behave, to be . . . he moves in circles who live such freer lives than mine. I so want to be a part of it. With him. Not this somber, stiff daughter of a duke, always serious, in mourning, worrying about my family. How marvelous to live as Bram does, to follow a passion, not to care what others think. Not to be tied by what is expected. But then, was I not shown how impossible such freedom is for me? What better reminder could I have had than the relentless haunting by the Dark Spirit? I might be able, one day, to escape the fetters placed about me by my position in society; I will never be free of those bonds that tie me to the coven. My heritage as a witch comes at a price. It may be that my heart must pay that price.

Mrs. Morell appears with an assistant and both set about telling Charlotte how radiant she is looking and how the dress she has in her hand is the very thing for her complexion at this time of year. I gaze out through the window of the dress shop. The weather shows we are properly into winter now, with a heavy, dark sky that promises freezing rain or snow. The October gales have abated, but only to be replaced by a bone-chilling drop in temperature. Freddie has already written several times to complain of the inadequacy of the heating at Radnor Hall. He told me the fresh air was doing him no good at all as it was much too cold to venture out into it for more than ten minutes at a time. He spends most of his days huddled by the fire in the study and might as well be back at Fitzroy Square. I replied to remind him, yet again, of our deal, and to beg him to sit it out. I assured him the weather was no better in London, the streets were filthy after so much rain, and half the household staff have succumbed to chills and coughs. However bored and uncomfortable he is at our childhood home, he is safer there. I do not doubt that there is opium to be found somewhere in the vicinity, but no such place as Mr. Chow Li's exist. And now he will have to escape the ever-watchful Withers to go in search of it, for at last I have managed to bring about his traveling to Radnorshire to be with Freddie.

Mama took some persuading that our butler could be spared for such a long stint, and the real reason could not be revealed. It had required convincing her that Withers was in need of a change of scene and some time away from gritty London himself to get her to agree to let him go. Withers proved to be a fair actor when the part required a pitiful cough.

"Lilith, do come and look at this." Charlotte's voice draws me back into the warmth of the little shop. "Edith has found something exquisite in black. Oh, how ever could you resist?" She gestures enthusiastically at the garment Mrs. Morell is proffering. It is indeed lovely. I lean forward and touch the fine chiffon which is so soft it feels like melting snow beneath my fingers.

"From France," the proprietor explains. "Arrived this very morning."

The dress is cut so that it flows loosely, allowing for a corset, but not requiring the tiny waist that has been fashionable for so long. Instead, it has a higher waistline with a fine, beaded chiffon overskirt falling softly to the ankles over a silk paneled underskirt.

"Oh try it on!" Charlotte all but jumps up and down with excitement. "It will suit you perfectly, I know it will."

Would it really be so wrong? I wonder. To dress in something fine and new and pretty for once? Would Father think me frivolous, or would he want me to enjoy myself? However well I thought I had known him, it is difficult to be sure what view he would take.

An hour later I am quite breathless with laughter, and we have reduced the shop to giggly chaos, with gowns, stoles, shoes, and coats strewn across chaise, chair, and table alike.

"Charlotte," I tell her, "you are both a tonic and a bad influence."

"Oh, really, Lily, you can afford to update your wardrobe," she says, helping herself to more shortbread and dipping it in the tea Mrs. Morell's assistant has fetched for us.

"But three dresses," I protest.

"And a rather gorgeous winter coat, which you were sorely in need of, I have to tell you. When did you buy that poor old thing you insist on wearing?"

"It's a perfectly good coat, and not a bit worn-out yet." I do my best to sound as if I care, but already I am completely seduced by my new finest wool version, with its sleek cut and luxurious fur at the collar, cuff, and hem.

"All I'm saying is at least you won't look as if Queen Victoria were still on the throne next time you go out."

"I was beginning to feel a little drab."

"Mourning clothes can do that to a person. These lovely new things are glamorous, yes, but they are all entirely respectable and in keeping with your status, and don't let anyone tell you otherwise," she says, polishing off her biscuit and holding out her cup for more tea. She kicks off her shoes and tucks her feet up under her. I envy her her ability to be at ease wherever she is. "It's interesting," she goes on, "that you agreed at last to let me help you shop for something new."

"As you said, my wardrobe was a little . . . out of date. I don't want to look old-fashioned."

"Hmm. Perhaps."

"Perhaps?"

"Or perhaps there's another reason you want to stop dressing like someone's maiden aunt. Perhaps there's somebody you want to look your best for? Somebody new? Somebody devilishly handsome, rather charming, and obviously very keen on you? Name of Bram Cardale, artist recently arrived in the area?'

"I don't know what you're talking about," I say, trying to hide behind my teacup.

"Lilith Montgomery, you are a poor liar. I have known you far too long not to notice when there is a fresh sparkle about you. A dimpling little smile when we set off for Mangan's studio."

"Now you are talking nonsense."

"Oh, am I indeed? And did I imagine I saw you enjoying yourself hugely dancing with him last night, hmm?" She hesitates, and then adds, "Darling Lily, I shouldn't say it, and you may very well be cross with me, but I've never seen you look like that when you dance with Louis."

Much to my relief, Mrs. Morell arrives at that moment with a discreet cough, an offer to have the gowns and coat delivered, and the bill. I am spared further grilling on the subject of Bram as I have to attend to settling the account. All the same I cannot deny to myself that I have imagined how I might look to him in my new clothes. The dresses make me feel different. Younger. Freer. Would he see a difference in me? And what if he did? The plain fact is, Charlotte is right: I am different when I am with Bram. I am a version of myself I had not known existed. With Louis I am who I have always been. Is that the attraction? I wonder. Do I see in Bram the opportunity to escape the roles in which I have been cast?

And surely it is foolish fancy to think I can continue seeing Bram, anyway. Charlotte cannot have many more sittings left, and after that I will have no reason for visiting the studio. Am I merely trying to make myself feel better? To bolster my confidence by having him admire me? I came so close to confiding in him, to telling him everything. Was it the champagne and the dancing that made me drop my guard? I wonder. Or was it the man himself? It would have been a terrible mistake, I see that now, in the unforgiving light of day. It is ironic that the Dark Spirit may have done me a service by stopping me from speaking further. And yet here I am, like some giddy girl, wondering how Bram would like me in pretty new clothes. I might distract myself with Charlotte and a little shopping, but I know I will have to return to my duties. The Dark Spirit has made his next move by declaring he wants something from me. He can only mean the Lazarus Elixir. I can play at being a carefree young woman for only a short time, that is the truth of it.

Later, in the privacy of my own bedroom, I examine my purchases once again. I have promised to dine at home with Louis tonight, and Mama, without so much as looking in a single box, has insisted I wear one of my new dresses for his benefit. Alice helps me try them on again. One is far too dressy, intended for I know not what occasion, but definitely not dinner *à deux* with Louis. All are black, of course, but they are, each in their own ways, as far removed from the heavy, somber mourning clothes I have been encased in for so many months as it is possible to be. One is the fine chiffon French design Charlotte had demanded I try. I am glad she did. It makes me feel light when I put it on, insubstantial, almost. I still wear my corset beneath it, but Alice lets out the stays, so that I feel blissfully relaxed in it. I do not dare reveal to Mama the curious undergarments Charlotte cajoled me into getting. They are of ivory silk, something she informed me is known as a "teddy," with a matching slip. Wearing them is like being caressed by a cool breeze as I move. They feel daringly sensuous and modern. Mama, who has taken it upon herself to inspect my choice before I go down, is already in a state of agitation about what she considers the immodest length of the dress skirts, which skim my ankles, and the slender, sinuous cut of the dress.

"But, Mama, surely it is more modest to touch the body only here and there, rather than to push and pull it into some uncomfortable version of the shape I apparently should be, rather than the shape I actually am?"

"It's all very well for Charlotte to wear things like that, her family don't seem to give a second thought to such matters."

"Mama! You make them sound quite radical, when you know they are not. They merely allow their daughter to move with the times, that's all."

"Whereas I do not, I suppose?" She looks genuinely hurt.

"Surely I can wear something more appropriate for my age now . . . I am twenty-one, after all. I should dress like a woman of today."

"You should dress like a Montgomery—with dignity, not one of these wild girls who stands on pavements in short skirts to shout about votes for women, or some modern creature who cares not two hoots the impression she gives." She looks me up and down with a mixture of concern and pride. It shames me to think I am so capable of manipulating her, but I know precisely how to win the argument.

"People expect me to keep up with changing fashions, Mama. Louis expects it."

"Louis does?"

"Of course. You can't really believe a man like him would look twice at a girl he considered out of touch. He wants a wife he can be proud of. Someone on his arm who will impress."

My mother's face gives away her shifting priorities as they move from the good of the family name to the match she has her heart set on for her only daughter. She marshals her thoughts and makes a half-convincing attempt at nonchalance.

"I suppose you might wear that this evening. As you are to dine alone with Louis."

"Oh? Not too daring, then?"

"We don't want him thinking of us as provincial."

I smile at her. Only my dear mother could consider anyone might level such an accusation at us.

"I'm sure he will approve," I tell her, kissing her lightly on the forehead. She has lost what little weight she has carried since Father died, and appears not to fill out her paper-fine skin anymore. It pulls at my heartstrings to see her eyes brighten at the thought of what might be.

And so it is that I descend the stairs wearing the beautiful chiffon dress, feeling ridiculously glamorous for dinner with a friend I have, after all, known since childhood. For a moment I wish Freddie was here. He and Louis were close when younger. It saddens me to see even their long-standing friendship fade and falter in the face of Freddie's new lifestyle. I wonder how he is truly managing at Radnor Hall. I have persuaded various neighbors and distant relations to call on him, eager that he should have steadying company. But the months are long, the weather bad, the nights dark, and no doubt lonely. Withers would tell me if there were any undesirable visitors from London, but he cannot observe Freddie's every move, particularly if he goes off in his newly acquired motorcar, to heaven knows where.

Louis appears at the door of the study and smiles broadly at the sight of me.

"Lilith, you are a vision," he tells me.

"Careful who you say that to," I reply, coming to stand in front of him, not liking the idea that he might think I have dressed up for him, and so wanting to make light of his comment. "I've heard that seeing visions is considered a sign of insanity by some people."

"Then no doubt hearing voices is irrefutable proof, in which case you and I are both for the asylum," he says, still smiling. He offers me his arm and I take it, and together we go in to dinner.

Mama, who has claimed a headache and so is dining in her room, must have sent word to Cook not to stint. We are presented with a fine consommé, a fish course of Dover sole, with partridge and quince jelly to follow. The meal is rounded off with an exotic pineapple sorbet.

"Your dear mother keeps an excellent kitchen, and a very good cellar, too," he says, dabbing at his mouth with exaggerated pleasure. "And there was I, destined for sardines on a tray in my room. Could you think of anything more pathetic?"

"Louis, I doubt you have eaten a sardine since you were ten years old. And anyway, you knew perfectly well you would be invited to dine with us if you called late in the afternoon."

"Why, Lily, you make me sound so very . . . calculating." He adopts a ridiculously wounded expression.

"You are your father's son."

"Ouch!" he cries, clutching dramatically at his heart. "You have a vicious streak in you, Lilith Montgomery."

"You mean I choose not to simper at you, unlike most of the women you surround yourself with."

He smiles again, his best, most winning smile, and reaches for my hand across the table. "Surely that is the privilege of a fiancée. Anyhow, I'd rather suffer cruelty from you than any amount of simpering from someone else. And besides, it's fortunate I thought to drop in tonight, or that heavenly dress would have gone unseen."

"Perhaps," I say coolly, slowly withdrawing my hand. "Or perhaps I would have worn it anyway."

"At home with your mother?"

"Or out with somebody else."

"Somebody who?"

"Oh, Louis, don't tell me your little spies haven't informed you of my every move since Father died?"

"Spies? Lilith, my darling girl, now you have lost me."

I think about taking the subject further. I have noticed the movements in the shadows. My guardians have alerted me to uninvited presences, too, on several occasions. I had not planned to question Louis about it, and slip the reference in to our light conversation only to see how he will react. But I have learned nothing. He is too accomplished at masking his true reactions for me to be able to tell if he genuinely does not know what I am talking about. In fact, I suspect it is his father who set his minions to keeping an eye on me. And the earl of Winchester is not the sort of man who feels the need to keep his son informed of all his actions. I let the matter drop and make some flippant comment about it being more likely Mama is making sure I do not socialize with anyone beneath the rank of viscount, which makes Louis laugh.

He is good company, and I find myself relaxing with him for once. Somehow, now that we are on our own—save for the discreet footman who waits upon us—away from the somewhat overbearing wishes of my mother, and removed from the business of the coven, he is simply Louis: a person I have known most of my life. Someone who knows me better than even Charlotte. Someone who understands me in ways that a non-witch never could. The thought leads me to Bram. A sadness grips me, surprising me in its strength. How can I be so affected by the mere thought of a man I have known such a short time, a man hopelessly outside my social circle, and a man who is not a witch? But already I know the answer. Even Charlotte has noticed how I alter in his company, how I look forward to our visits to the studio. After all, hadn't my extravagance at Edith Morell's shop been really, truly, about him? And when I recall how I felt when he held me I know I have never, and will never, feel the same in Louis's arms.

"Lilith?"

I realize Louis is talking to me.

"I'm sorry, " I say. "I am rather tired tonight. Not very good company."

"Just then you looked as if you were somewhere else entirely."

"Did I?"

"Something is troubling you. What is it? You know I'll help if I can," he says, and I believe he means it.

"Oh, I've a lot to think about at the moment, that's all. You know how things are, trying to get Freddie to stay at Radnor Hall, Mama still not herself, my position . . . elsewhere," I add, glancing at the footman, who gives the impression of being made of stone, but is no doubt taking in every word.

Louis nods. "You will do marvelously well, I know you will."

"Time will tell, Louis," I reply. "Time will tell."

Nicholas Stricklend watches the retreating figure of Fordingbridge as he backs out of the room, shutting the door behind him. The day has been a long and testing one, taken up largely with trivial matters that are the everyday business of Whitehall, and they have tried Stricklend's patience. He crosses the room to the cabinet against the far wall, takes out a bottle of Armagnac, and pours himself a generous measure. Returning to his chair he sits and ruminates upon what being a Sentinel has meant to him. What it has won him. And what it has cost him.

Stricklend's childhood had followed a course traditional to many, in that he had been sent away to a prestigious boarding school at the age of seven. He had not found it easy to make friends, for he had no charm, no natural warmth, and no desire to ingratiate himself with boys he saw as almost always inferior to himself. He had shown some talent for boxing and for cricket, so that he had at least earned a grudging respect from his fellow pupils, if not their affection. He had also excelled at his studies, so that the masters viewed him as a satisfactory if rather unlikable student. He had kept to himself and eschewed clubs and social events wherever possible. It had seemed to him, he recalled, that he had in this way arrived at a method of making his school life tolerable, and he had hoped to move steadily toward achieving excellent passes in his exams and going on to university without mishap. But small boys grow into bigger boys, and these, he remembered with no small amount of bitterness, were less willing to accommodate someone who did not conform.

He had been thirteen the first time he had been singled out and set upon. Returning to the dormitory from the library late one evening he became aware he was being followed. He was not afraid; he knew his skills as a boxer, his height, and his strength would mean he could equip himself well in a fight if the need arose. What he did not, at that moment, understand, was that his persecutors were not so reckless as to risk personal injury. They had contrived to have about them a gang of followers, each more eager than the next to prove themselves to their leader. They pinned him to the ground, kneeling on his arms and holding his feet while blow after blow fell about his stomach, his face, his head. Then, when he was bleeding and dazed, they dragged him by his ankles the entire length of the corridor. He can still recall the feel of the boards beneath him as he was hauled along, his back snagging on a nail that was ever so slightly proud, causing a deep tear in his flesh and leaving a scar he carries still. They took him outside. It was December, and the ground was hard, the night clear, the mercury low. He was manhandled to his feet and bound to the leafless magnolia tree in the center of the quad. Stricklend had struggled against his bonds, but to no avail. The ringleader was called Hilton, a thickset boy with an unfortunately broad face and a prodigious growth of bristle on his chin. He leaned in close.

"Think you're better than the rest of us, don't you, Stricklend?

Well, guess what? You're not, see? Nothing special about you. No reason to give yourself airs. No title. No family to speak of. Precious little money. You come from nothing, and you'll go right back there when you leave this place, so you can just stop looking down that hoity-toity nose of yours at the rest of us. Hear me?"

Stricklend fought to open his eyes properly, but blood was congealing on the lids. He felt a loose tooth beneath his tongue. Tasted blood in his mouth. Felt pain in his stomach. From somewhere dark and distant he retrieved his voice.

"Hilton," he said, "do you know how incredibly ugly you are?"

The older boy scowled. He hesitated for only a moment before drawing back his fist and bringing it forward with angry force into Stricklend's face. Into the still of the night came the unmistakable sound of bone splintering. One of the more delicate boys vomited copiously onto his own feet.

"Not so pretty yourself, now, are you?" Hilton hissed into his ear before whistling at his troops and leading them off at a run.

Once alone, a curious peace descended upon Stricklend. He felt himself starting to drift, floating downward, ever downward. The sound of approaching footsteps halted his descent. Through one half-opened eye he saw what appeared to be a giant crow looming over him, its wings by its sides, its bright eyes peering at him in the moonlight. The crow shook its head and then untied the rope that held him to the tree. He fell forward and was caught not by some freakishly large feathered being, but by the strong arms of the junior Latin master, Mr. Reginald Ellis. Stricklend felt himself lifted and held tight, the master's gown wrapped about him. He was aware he was being carried into the school, but not, as he had expected, toward the dormitory, or to Matron's room to have his wounds tended. Instead Mr. Ellis took him up the narrow, winding stairs that led to his own quarters. Even in his confused condition Stricklend knew this was strange. Masters were forbidden to take pupils to their rooms. Lurid tales of teachers leaving under clouds of suspicion were well known in every school. Was that to be his fate now? he wondered. Was he to be taken advantage of? Defiled? After all that he had already endured?

Mr. Ellis sat him down in an armchair near the hearth and set about stoking up the fire. He fetched water and cloths and bathed Stricklend's wounds with detached care, rather than any prurient interest. He did so in silence, so that the only sounds in the small attic room were Stricklend's own occasional protestations of pain, and logs crackling in the fire. At last the blood was washed from his face and head, and soothing ointment had been applied to his many cuts and bruises. The Latin master stood back to contemplate the boy before him.

"Well, Stricklend, you are quite a mess, aren't you? Those cuts shouldn't scar too badly, but that nose of yours . . . hmm. Did a good job, whoever hit you. No"—he raised a hand—"I'd really rather you didn't name him. Though I can understand you wanting to. In fact, I'd wager you'd like to break his nose, too, wouldn't you?"

Stricklend nodded, painfully.

"Quite so. But you are unlikely to get the chance, I'd say, given the blindly loyal foot soldiers he no doubt surrounds himself with. No, I'm afraid you're not going to be allowed the satisfaction of using your boxing skills on the boy. Unjust, I know, but there it is."

Stricklend turned his head to stare into the flames. The truth of what Mr. Ellis was saying was every bit as painful as his injuries.

The Latin master sat down in the winged chair opposite and regarded Stricklend with his head to one side, as if weighing him up.

"You are a bright boy. Consistently top of your year. Should make Cambridge for mathematics, if that's what you want. Pity to see such intelligence treated so very badly." He leaned forward, fixing Stricklend with a bright-eyed gaze. "What if there *was* a way, another way, of getting your own back? Of teaching all those foolish thugs a lesson. Of ensuring that they never put a finger on you, so that your time here at Winthrop will pass smoothly and without fear of any such incident ever occurring again. What would you say, Stricklend? Might that be of interest to you, hmm?"

Stricklend forced himself to sit up a little straighter to show he was listening.

Mr. Ellis smiled. "I have noticed how you strive for perfection, Stricklend. How excellence is both your spur and your goal. I admire that. I know there are some who consider you . . . aloof. Never mind them. Let those who value popularity and the approval of their peers continue on their merry way. You, Stricklend, my boy, *you* have it in you to be something quite . . . different."

Now, as Stricklend sits in his prestigious office, sipping his expensive brandy, certain of his place in the world and his purpose in it, he still feels the importance of that moment in shaping his life. It was, it seems, destined that he should have been cast out and ridiculed in order to gain entry into an altogether more desirable society. He had, not surprisingly, never heard of the Sentinels. Never, previously, seen anything remarkable about the young teacher who had drilled him and the rest of his class in Latin verbs and challenged them to decline the same over and over, regardless of the hour or the wit of the boys, until they were word perfect. That pursuit of perfection should have alerted him to something, he now thinks. But how could he ever have imagined such things as Ellis was to teach him? How could he ever have dreamed of the power, and the purity of the power, that was to be given him by being taken into their fold?

He runs a finger down the line of his nose, tracing the kink where the bone had set askew and inflicted a lasting flaw in his own perfection, leaving him with a permanent memento of the beating that altered both his face and his future that night.

He stands and walks to the window. In the fading light of the late afternoon, the crowds below in Trafalgar Square exclaim at the prettiness of the fountains, throw food to the nodding pigeons, gaze up at the lofty statue of Nelson, or allow their children to scramble over the great lions at its base. He finds that their seeming ignorance of what is taking place in the world about them—their apparent carefree attitude, their ability to amuse themselves so simply when the order of things is about to come crashing down about their ears—he finds it builds within him a contempt for the masses. Pondering this thought, he admits to himself that, aside from the grudging respect he afforded his father, the only person he ever regarded with anything approaching warm affection was his tutor and mentor, the man who instructed him in the craft and skills of the Sentinels, that same young Latin master who had tended his wounds all those years ago and recognized something special in him, Mr. Reginald Ellis. Ellis had given generously of his time in training Stricklend. Over the remainder of his years at the school the two had met most nights, when all others were slumbering in their dormitories. Ellis had instructed his eager pupil in the history and knowledge of the Sentinels. He had coaxed from him the energy and strength that he had first noticed, along with the boy's keen intelligence and ability to focus, which so suited him to the art of sorcery. In Stricklend he found a student untroubled by conscience or favor, and one who quickly recognized the beauty of power, the purity of it. Stricklend had learned the Sentinels' belief that sorcerers and necromancers are made, not born, and that it is their unquestioning allegiance to the group that gives them their strength. He was told of the injustice that had brought about the downfall, centuries ago, when the Lazarus Coven, jealous of the Sentinels' talents and power, had taken the

Elixir and the Great Secret from them, under guise of protecting it, and claiming to be the only possible moral guardians of such dangerous magic. Stricklend soon came to see that regaining what was rightfully theirs was imperative for the society. As he progressed in his schooling, and as his natural flair for the tasks presented to him became obvious, he knew that he himself would be instrumental, after so many generations of waiting and hoping, in reclaiming the Elixir.

Stricklend had not known it at the time, but he had passed an important test in selecting a modest punishment for his tormentor at school. He had been content that the boy had suffered for his behavior, and that he would never bother him again. That was sufficient. This cold restraint had earned him praise from Mr. Ellis, who had assured him he would not only now be received into the Sentinels' society, but that membership of the elite would surely soon follow. Even he, though, might not have foretold that Stricklend would, ultimately, become the most powerful Sentinel of all. Or perhaps he had an inkling.

He had said, "At least I have the satisfaction of knowing that I have done my job, Stricklend. You will rise to greatness, and that will be a great day for the Sentinels, I am certain of it."

Recalling the conversation now, Stricklend fancies he had seen sadness in the Latin master's expression, despite his words. Had he known then? he wonders. Did he know what Stricklend would be asked to do to prove his unquestioning loyalty to the Sentinels on his induction? Did he guess on whom the Sentinels would require him to demonstrate his mastery of the Stopping Spell? He has played over in his mind, many times, the moment when he stood before his mentor, poised to take his life. Ellis had shown neither fear nor surprise, only a calm acceptance of his fate. Such was the man's *own* loyalty. How could Stricklend, in the face of such dignity and courage, how could he, then, not have done what was asked of him? Obedience without question. And he never did question. Never sought an explanation as to why he was instructed to kill his tutor, his guardian, his only friend. It was the defining event of his life, he knew that then. The instant the Stopping Spell halted Ellis's heart for good was the same instant Stricklend felt the pure power of such unswerving dedication. It was, and is, what drives him still.

11.

Bram wakes up to find himself on the floor of his room, still dressed. He rubs his eyes, scratches at the stubble on his chin, and stretches his aching limbs. The cold has awakened him, and his fingers are numb and colorless, save for smudges of charcoal and oil paint. He rubs his palms together briskly, blowing into them in an effort to restore some life. Scrambling to his feet he is confronted with the chaotic results of two days and nights of painting. Sketches litter the studio floor. Brushes and palettes and tubes of paint lie abandoned. Rags wet with turpentine sit in gray heaps, testament to the number of times he snatched them up to obliterate his work. To begin again. And again. He gets to his feet and forces himself to consider the four canvases propped against the wall. He feels his heart gallop. A familiar excitement grips him.

There is something, something there. Yes!

He hurries over to examine the pictures more closely. One is of the flower girl who sat for him some time ago. It shows her in profile, sitting next to her stall at the end of the day, most of the flowers sold, a few drooping blooms remaining. The girl's pose, her own coloring, her attitude, all seem to echo the wilting, forgotten flowers. It is as if she too is the overlooked one, not quite lovely enough to be chosen. The painting pleases him. It is the first work he has produced since arriving in London that makes him believe he *can* do what he came here to do. Can be what he intends being.

The three other paintings—all produced in these frenzied, sleepless hours, where he has not set foot outside his attic rooms, or spoken to anyone—all show the same glimpse of the hidden lives of the sitters. All show the same strength. At last he turns to the canvas on the easel. The blank, greasy canvas, where each attempt to capture Lilith seemed to take him further and further from the truth of her, so that in the end he wiped away his faltering efforts. The final thing he recalls before falling into an exhausted sleep on the bare boards was the sadness in her eyes as he erased them.

A slender ray of sunshine forces its way through the grimy skylight, making him squint. The clock on his bedside table says ten o'clock. Bram shakes his head, determination rousing him. He will not be defeated.

I will paint her. I must.

He pulls on his coat against the chill of the room. There is still water in the kettle, so he puts a match to the gas beneath it and sets about gathering fresh paint and brushes. His plans are interrupted by swift steps on the stairs, and Freedom appears in the doorway.

"Jane wants you," he says simply, before turning and disappearing into the gloom of the stairwell.

With a sigh, Bram turns out the gas burner and follows the boy, promising himself to return to his task at the first possible moment. He feels he has grown accustomed to the chaotic nature of life at home with the Mangans. Their excesses and eccentricities rarely shock him now, and he is so used to the noise and frenetic energy the children supply he misses it when they are out of the house. It comes as a surprise to him, then, to find that there is another level of Bedlamic wildness into which the household can be propelled, given certain circumstances, and one such is Mangan falling ill. Mangan has a heavy cold, though to hear him rail and moan anyone could be forgiven for thinking it at the very least influenza, or possibly some little-known tropical disease. From his bedroom come sounds of suffering and drama equaled only by the enthusiastic and noisy care he is given by his wife, his mistress, and his children. Jane comes striding from the room carrying a tray of dirty plates and glasses. Mangan's hoarse cries follow her onto the landing.

"Brandy under these circumstances must be considered a medicament, Jane. Surely you can see that?" His entreaties disintegrate into coughs.

Jane turns a wild-eyed, sleep-deprived face to Bram.

"Oh, dear Bram! Have you any brandy hidden in your little aerie? We've not a drop left in the house, and poor darling Mangan is suffering so."

"I'm sorry, Jane, I haven't any."

She looks on the point of dissolving into tears of exhaustion.

"No? I'm certain Perry will have none. Twins! Keep your noise down, do! Your pa has a dreadful headache as it is, without having to listen to children thundering up and down the stairs."

The twins charge past at dangerous speed. Freedom follows on more slowly. Bram has noticed the boy is his father's shadow, always watching quietly, taking in the great man's every word. With Mangan temporarily bedridden, the child looks bored and lost.

"Have you tried Gudrun?" Bram asks.

Jane tuts and lets her face show an uncharacteristic flash of anger. "All Gudrun has to offer is cigarettes and sex, neither of which Mangan needs nor wants at this moment. Boys! Do please avoid slamming what doors are left on their hinges!"

"I could go out and buy some brandy, if you like," Bram suggests.

Jane looks as if she might hug him, were she not still holding the tray.

"Would you? Oh, Bram, that is frightfully kind. Mangan will

pay you back, of course. He will insist," she says, vigor renewed as she squeezes past him and heads for the kitchen.

Bram realizes he has just agreed to spend the last few shillings he has to his name, and is certain he will never see them back again from his mentor, despite Jane's promises. And his painting will have to wait. He squashes down the rising resentment he experiences at this thought, and quickly fetches his hat and money. He hurries down to the front door. When he opens it he is astonished to find himself face-to-face with Lilith.

He smiles broadly, and then is suddenly acutely aware of his disheveled appearance; his crumpled clothes, uncombed hair, and unshaven face.

Lilith smiles prettily at the sight of his surprise, and he feels his heart lurch.

"You were not expected," he tells her. "Mangan is unwell. Jane sent word, or at least, she intended to . . ."

"No message arrived. Charlotte," she turns to call to her friend who is paying the driver of the motor cab, "did you receive a message about Mr. Mangan being ill?"

"What? No! Nothing serious, I hope?"

"The casual observer might think so, but no, a cold only."

"One would not imagine the great artist to be an easy patient."

"Indeed, he is not."

Charlotte joins Lilith on the front step. "Is there to be no sitting, then? Such a pity. Can we do anything to hasten poor Mr. Mangan's recovery?"

"I was on my way to purchase brandy."

"An excellent plan," comes Perry's voice from the hallway behind him. He is shrugging on his coat and wrapping a woolen scarf about his neck. "Good morning to you, Miss Pilkington-Adams, Lady Lilith," he says, lifting the hat he has only just set on his head.

Charlotte smiles at him. "Oh, no formalities and titles here, I beg of you. It is so tiresome. Charlotte is a perfectly serviceable name, and I do wish people would call me it. And my father always insists we drink brandy when we have colds. Even as children we had the wretched stuff spooned into us."

"Did it effect a cure?" Perry asks.

"None of us is able to recall!" Charlotte falls into tuneful laughter.

Bram sees this is his moment, his chance. A very small, very slight chance, but the only one he is ever likely to have.

She felt so close to me at that party. Can we find such intimacy again?

"Why don't we all go? The four of us, I mean. To the Soldiers' Arms on the corner of Cleveland Street. We can buy Mangan's brandy there. And to be certain it is of the very best quality we can test it ourselves first."

"Go to a public house?" Charlotte all but squeals.

"It is a respectable one," Bram assures her. "And it has a large fire we might sit by."

Perry rubs his hands together. "Ah, a cozy hearth, a glass of fortification, and excellent company. What could be better? What do you say, ladies? Will you join us?"

"Oh, Lilith, do let's!" Charlotte squeezes her friend's arm.

Lilith glances at Bram and he is sure he sees her blush. "Very well," she says quietly. "As there is to be no sitting . . . perhaps just for half an hour."

Perry steps forward and bows before Charlotte, offering her his arm. "Allow me to lead the way," he says. "Though of course I'm not the regular at the establishment that Bram is."

"Hey!" says Bram.

"You do seem to know a lot about the place," Lilith says.

"I've been there precisely twice," Bram tells her. He meets her eye and tries to read what he sees there.

She is happy to be in my company, at least, and not awkward after how our previous evening ended. I must take comfort from that. But I must not press her. Must not frighten her away again.

Charlotte and Perry set off down the pavement, leaning into the icy wind that has gotten up. Bram offers his arm to Lilith and feels a frisson of pleasure as she takes it. She is wearing a beautiful black woolen coat trimmed with thick fur, and a matching hat that suits her very well. As they walk along the street together he is certain he has never felt so proud of the woman on his arm. It strikes him as odd, perverse almost, that etiquette should dictate they must address one another formally, and yet also require them to have this physical contact. He can feel the warmth of her slender fingers through the soft leather of her glove upon his sleeve. He wishes the inn they are bound for were a mile away, just so he might enjoy the delight of her holding his arm for longer. The sky is heavy with icy rain, and the inclement weather has driven indoors all those who need not be abroad. Those who must brave the cold do so with collars up and heads down, hats firmly pinned or held. Horses trot by with ears turned back against the wind, picking up the pace each time they head in the direction of home, resisting whip and rein should they be asked to travel out again. The many motorcars and cabs that now vie with the broughams, landaus, hansoms, and horse-drawn omnibuses for road space splutter and belch fumes as their engines falter in the low temperatures.

Bram is aware of the thinness of his coat, and the inadequacy of his clothes. Ahead of him he sees Perry striding happily on, his own garments of a far superior cut and cloth. He has not noticed this before, and vaguely wonders how his fellow artist can afford such quality. He realizes he knows little about him beyond that he, too, has come to London, to Mangan, to pursue his love of art and try to develop his talent.

"You walk quickly," Lilith says.

"Oh, forgive me," says Bram. "Am I going too fast for you?"

"On the contrary. It is a relief to find, for once, a man who does not believe women must be led at the pace of a small child. In this weather we should both freeze at such a speed."

"I wouldn't want you to think me too eager for the brandy."

"Oh, it's too late for your character, I'm afraid. I already have you down as a hardened drinker and frequenter of public houses in the mornings."

"And you are a person who would accompany such a fellow."

"I find that I am."

He smiles at her and is so intent on doing so that he almost steps into the path of a hurtling gig.

"Be careful!" Lilith pulls him back to safety. Laughing at him, she says, "It is a good thing you have a companion for your loose living today, else you might not have lived long enough to die a famous artist."

"Then you must always come with me when I visit the many public houses where I am known by name. You owe it to the world of art. How could you live with yourself if I were crushed beneath the wheels of an omnibus because you were not there to save me? Think of the loss to future generations."

She regards him closely for a moment. "Do you always tease your visitors this way?"

"Only the ones I have lured into dissolute habits," he says.

He finds they have come to a stop and stand on the pavement, regarding one another intently, each openly studying the face of the other, neither speaking, as if to do so would shatter the moment.

"Lilith," he forces himself to say at last, "I have been thinking of you constantly. Since the party. Since we spoke . . ."

"Please, don't . . ."

"Bram!" Perry calls from a little farther down the street. "Hurry along there."

They catch up to the others and soon arrive at a weathered door, which is protected from the elements by a dozen layers of thick brown paint, its brass hand plate worn to a thin sliver of metal. The door creaks as Perry pushes it open, and the four of them step inside.

The Soldiers' Arms, in common with many public houses in the city, has been built to accommodate as many drinkers as possible, and what comforts there are exist to encourage the patrons to linger, and to socialize if they will, while not getting in the way of the serious business of imbibing alcoholic beverages. The floor is of broad wooden boards, at least, which is an improvement on some of the compacted earth and flagstones favored in other establishments. A scattering of fresh sawdust upon the floorboards suggests some small effort has been made toward cleanliness, though it will soon be crushed beneath so many wet and dirty boots as to render it ineffectual. Against the far wall there is a high bar, polished by the sleeves of the faithful over years. Gleaming pewter tankards, stout china pots, and chunky glasses are lined up on the shelves behind it. There are casks of ale, flagons of cider, and bottles of harsh red wine on display. On an upper shelf sit gin, rum, brandy, and whiskey. There are twists of tobacco for sale, as well as a humble but serviceable snuff. It is a quiet hour, so that the space is not uncomfortably crowded, and the voices of those present create a low mumbling, rather than the raucous shouts and laughter that might be heard in the evenings.

Bram leads his guests over to the wide fireplace and sees them seated on the shabby but inviting settle, with its treacly black wood and faded tapestry cushions. He goes to the bar with Perry and whispers urgently in his ear.

"Have you any money on you?"

"My dear fellow," Perry looks stricken, "I assumed you were in funds."

"Why would you think that? I haven't sold a painting since I arrived and I've used up nearly all the money I brought with me. I gave Jane two pounds for housekeeping only yesterday." Bram narrows his eyes at Perry's expensive coat. "Have you no savings at all? Nothing, perhaps, sent from home?"

"My parents, alas, do not approve of my chosen path in life. They will not support me in it. I make what I can from selling my sketches, but lately I have been so busy helping Mangan I've produced precious little work of my own. And now he is ill, well, it is difficult to paint, sculpt, or even draw when the house is in such uproar."

Bram cannot argue with this. And he knows only too well how hard it is to scrape a living together. He digs deep in his pockets. Perry does the same. Their search yields the royal sum of three shillings and sixpence.

"Well," Bram does a quick calculation, "we can afford one brandy for each of us here, and a small bottle to take home to Mangan."

"One drink only?" Perry sighs. "What a pity not to be able to spend longer in such delightful company," he adds, looking wistfully in the direction of Charlotte.

"Can't be helped," says Bram, ordering the drinks from the aproned barman. "We'll just have to make the best of it."

They rejoin their companions, who have undone their coats but, sensibly, given the patchy heat supplied by the fire, elected to keep them on. Perry sits as close to Charlotte as good manners will allow and engages her in a discussion about the dancer, Isadora Duncan, who has recently taken Paris society by storm. Bram takes the low wooden chair opposite Lilith, setting the drinks down on the small table between them. He uses the opportunity to study her fine profile as she turns to watch the leaping flames of the burning coals in the hearth.

"How I long to paint you." The words are out of his mouth before he has had time to consider the wisdom of speaking them aloud. The statement sounds far more personal, more revealing of himself than it should be, somehow. Lilith looks at him thoughtfully.

"How would you depict me?" she asks. "As Mr. Mangan has chosen to portray Charlotte—a Grecian goddess, perhaps?"

"Good Lord, no!" The gulp of brandy is already dissolving his reserve.

"Oh? Don't you like the way he is sculpting her?"

"I'm sure he will produce a perfectly stunning piece of work, in his singular way, of how he sees her. But such a pose, such a style, well . . ."

"It is not *your* style."

He shakes its head. "Nor would it suit you."

"Oh? Please tell me, what do you consider would suit me? How is it that you see me?"

He hesitates, uncertain still as to how much he should speak what is in his heart. How much of himself, and of his regard for her, he should reveal. But then the images he carries in his mind of how he would paint her, of how he imagines he could immortalize her, these images are so vivid he cannot resist attempting to share them with her.

"I would have you sit in a darkened room, the light source only from one place. Strong, but partial, so that it would fall across your face were it turned to the side . . ." He shakes his head and snatches off his hat, frustrated at his efforts to be clear, to make her see what he sees. His hair falls into his eyes and he pushes it back with a paint-stained hand. "The contrast should be heightened. A limited palette—browns, blacks, creams only. That way your eyes, well, they would shine with their own luminosity. As they do in life." He becomes more animated, gesticulating with his hands as he speaks. "Your hair loose, of course, dark against your skin . . . not a nude, nothing like that, but bare shoulders, certainly. Pale. Very pale. Again the contrast, do you see? Do you see, Lilith?" He pauses, and then asks again, more quietly, reaching across the table to take her hands in his. "Do you see?" The sensation of her warm gloved fingers in his palms is easily as intoxicating to him as the brandy. He wants to keep this fragile connection. Slowly he lifts her hands and presses them to his lips, turning them over to kiss the soft, white-blue flesh of the underside of her wrists, the slender gap that he can just glimpse between the end of her leather gloves and the fur cuffs of her coat. She gives no answer to his question, but puts her head a little on one side as she watches him, and does not resist when he continues to clasp her hands in his own.

Perry is recounting an anecdote about Mangan letting a model get frostbite because she was made to sit for so long unclothed in his unheated studio. Charlotte laughs a little too brightly, and then calls for more brandy. Bram cannot bear the thought of their time together coming to an end so soon, so he simply lets Perry pour them each another measure from the pathetically small bottle that was intended for Mangan. He looks up at her and finds her staring back at him. He wishes more than anything that they could be alone together, for he knows she will not speak to him in the way she began to in the garden the other night so long as there are other people to hear what she has to say.

Whether or not she is aware of the extent of his inner turmoil he cannot tell, but he is certain she senses something of it. At last she casts her eyes down and, slowly, reluctantly, he likes to believe, withdraws her hands, setting them demurely in her lap. Charlotte and Perry are laughing loudly at a shared joke.

Lilith stands and begins to button her coat. "I am sorry to break up the party," she says with somewhat forced cheerfulness, "but I really think Charlotte and I should be going." She glances around the room which is now filling with more boisterous drinkers.

Bram leaps to his feet, his chair scraping the floorboards as he does so.

"Of course," he says. "We shall find you a cab."

Charlotte and Perry both protest, but follow nonetheless as Lilith takes Bram's arm once more. Outside the weather has worsened, so that the icy blast that blows down Cleveland Street seems to carry in it splinters of ice. They cast about for a hansom or a motor cab, but all that pass are already occupied. Perry and Charlotte, fueled by the coarse brandy, wave and whistle madly in the hope of summoning some sort of transport. Bram stands at the curb with Lilith. Neither of them speaks, and there is a palpable tension between them now. The bleak, gray light of the winter afternoon perfectly matches Bram's mood, for he can see no possible way of improving his standing in Lilith's eyes. She is the daughter of a duke, fabulously wealthy, and beautiful, and could have the pick of all the eligible men in the country. He is the son of a modestly successful steel magnate, with less than a shilling of his own, and a chosen career that might see them both starve.

"Hey!" yells Perry. "We've found one!" He signals wildly to indicate the carriage pulling to a halt a little farther up the street.

"Come along, Lily!" Charlotte calls as she runs after it.

Lilith turns to Bram to say good-bye and, to the astonishment of both of them, he swiftly takes her in his arms, pulls her to him, and kisses her hard, full on the lips. She pulls away, but he holds her tight, so that her face remains only inches from his own. As the wind buffets them and tugs at their clothes, and passersby exclaim or laugh, and Charlotte squeals in amazement, and a motorist blasts his horn, and a nag whinnies, and the shouts of a chestnut seller sing out above it all, Bram falls deep into Lilith's fathomless gaze and hears himself murmur her name, over and over, like a prayer. A prayer that she will not disappear out of his life. A prayer that she will return his passion. A prayer that she knows. That she understands. That she, too, wants what he wants.

"Don't go," he says at last.

"I must," she whispers, her own voice unsteady. "I must."

Bram kisses her again, more tenderly this time, but still with unmistakable fervor. When he finally lets her go, she turns without a word and runs to the waiting cab. He watches Perry shut the door and the driver urge the bony horse into a trot as the carriage bears Lilith away. Away down the street. Away from that incomparable moment. Away from him. But as he watches a smile plays across his face and glee wells up inside him, for Bram knows, he is certain beyond the trace of a doubt, that while he held her, while he kissed her sweet mouth, she kissed him back.

12.

If to be in love is to lose one's self then I am as in love as it is possible to be, for I am utterly lost! My head is filled with thoughts of him, of the man who has so unexpectedly yet so completely claimed my heart. When I close my eyes I see him. When I dream it is of him. When I try to read a novel the words shift upon the page until they spell out his name. I am like a giddy girl, unable to be still or serious for a minute, flitting from one imagining to the next, all of him. Of us. Could there ever, truly, be an "us"? The thought is thrilling, and yet it casts me down also. For in what world do I see a future for us together? Am I to move into the Mangan household, become bohemian, live in chilly, hungry freedom, and break my mother's heart forever? Is Bram to join me as my husband in some corner of Fitzroy Square, without purpose or title or means, humiliated by living off my inheritance, and ill at ease among the society into which he would inevitably be thrust? Both alternatives are inconceivable. I should be despairing, and yet I find that I am not. The delicious, the intoxicating state of being in love is too glorious to be squashed by such prosaic obstacles. That I can have been so quickly transported to this disturbing condition still amazes me. I have tried, these past few days, to pinpoint the moment when it happened. The instant when my view of the world shifted. Charlotte believes it occurred when Bram kissed me. She spoke of nothing else all the way home in the cab that day, and of course there has been no hiding my feelings from her. I may be expert at keeping secrets as a witch, but this is different. This business of love is new to me, and though Charlotte herself claims neither experience nor expertise, it is good to share it. I am glad she was there to see what happened. Indeed, if I did not have her to share my feelings with I believe I should go mad.

But I think she is wrong about my moment of transformation. By the time Bram held me to him and showed me what was in his heart, mine was already lost to him. Only I had not acknowledged the fact, even to myself. I had not dared do so.

And yet, above all this joy, the Dark Spirit is never far from my thoughts. As always, personal desires must defer to coven matters. Aside from the visitations, there is something else that twists my mind into knots of doubt and confusion. Who was it who challenged me at the inauguration? And why? I believe the two things must surely be connected. To have two threats against the coven at the same time cannot be coincidence. I had thought the challenge to be of lesser importance than perhaps it truly is. Taken with the actions of the Dark Spirit I have to look at it anew, have to question the motives behind it.

It is my search for answers to these questions that finds me heading for the shabby house in Bloomsbury while the rest of the world slumbers. I have slipped away alone, unseen. I need a confidante. Someone who might help me make sense of what has happened. Someone I trust utterly.

The carriage arrives at my destination. I alight onto the pavement and the driver, whose discretion is beyond question, flicks the reins quietly, moving away to wait in the shadows. It would not do for curious eyes, however unlikely, to notice the Montgomery carriage parked outside the house of a disreputable bohemian artist in the small hours of the night. I do not knock, but open the door which has been left unlocked so that I may make my entry as quickly and quietly as possible. I have visited the house on a number of occasions, always in darkness, and so have become adept at navigating the flotsam and jetsam of the hallway as we thread through the gloom to the studio at the rear of the building. Mangan is waiting for me.

"Ah!" He takes an unlit pipe from his mouth and holds out his hand in greeting. "The splendid, shining Morningstar. Welcome! Welcome." He grasps my hand in his and does not so much shake as squeeze it warmly. During our meetings I feel I have come to know the outlandish sculptor quite well, and I am aware of how much he has to dampen his natural ebullience and indeed volume if he is not to wake the whole household. He bids me be seated, clearing a space on a dusty chaise. The only light in the room comes from two short candles, and the gray wash of the city night with its blurring streetlamps diffused through the glass roof and frontage. It is not so much illumination as a subtle lessening of the blackness.

"Thank you for agreeing to see me," I tell him, but he dismisses my gratitude with a wave of his pipe.

"My dear, beautiful girl, have not I always insisted you are welcome here whenever you need me? That has been the case since your father appointed me one of your tutors all those long, sunlit summers ago. Now that you are elevated to Head Witch you are, of course, doubly entitled to any help you feel I can give you. I am your friend and your servant."

Not for the first time I have reason to be thankful for my father's foresight. When he chose Mangan as one of my instructors there were those in the coven who voiced their doubts. I recall Lord Grimes protesting that such a man was unsuitable to give any sort of guidance to a young woman. Mangan is known for his wild ways, for his unorthodox living, for his flamboyant nature. Just as he is an outsider in society, so he is seen as a maverick in the coven, often kicking against our customs and traditions, urging us to reform, to move with the ever-changing times. And yet, he is perhaps one of those among us who truly lives his beliefs. He treats all men as equals, and all women, too. He is not hidebound by etiquette, and this gives him a certain freedom. Did Father consider I would need him to balance my rich diet of tradition and heritage? I wonder.

"I do need your help," I tell him. "At the inauguration . . . poor Violet." At last I can hold back my tears no longer. I have kept my grief and sorrow hidden from everyone, but now I can do so no more. I pluck a handkerchief from my purse and sob into it, unable to speak.

Mangan is more at ease with displays of emotion than my father would have been. He leans close and pats my hand.

"Terrible," he agrees gently, "quite terrible. But you must not blame yourself."

"How can I not?"

"I don't say you must not for your own sake. You must not because as Head Witch you cannot afford yourself the luxury of wallowing in guilt and regret."

I am taken aback by the harshness of this comment. He sees my reaction and attempts to soften his words.

"My dear girl, you have taken a huge step for one so young. This . . . honor, this great task, has been given to you without your asking for it. But it is your due. It is both your burden and your blessing. I know you will serve the coven well. And if there is anything I can do to help . . . Anything! Ask, and if it is within my gift, it is yours."

I compose myself, putting my handkerchief away.

"I need to know who it was who challenged my right to be Head Witch."

"Ah, naturally, that would be a sensible concern. Alas, I do not know who it was."

"Have you no idea at all? You have spent so many years in the coven, seen so many new members inducted, acted as tutor to many . . . was not the voice, however distorted, just the tiniest bit familiar? Or the speaker's stance, perhaps? Or his manner in any way?"

"I fear such a man—for we know that much at least—such a man would make certain his disguise was not so easily seen through. In that, he was successful."

"But I felt certain you would be able to tell me something. The spirits, they have been speaking to me. Two of them specifically named you as the person I should turn to. They directed me to come to your house. They were insistent."

"It may be they sought to send you where they knew you would be sure of support and reassurance. I fear that is all I can give to you on this matter, Daughter of the Night." He sits beside me now, taking both my hands in his. "Don't be afraid. There will always be someone foolish enough to want to test the new order; such an action does not necessarily mean the challenger would be a suitable candidate himself, hmm? And in any case, you saw him off! And in fine style, too."

My shoulders sag. I had, I realize now, placed no small amount of hope on the notion that Mangan might know something. "There is more," I tell him. "What prompted me to come to you is something . . . something difficult for me to express clearly. I am certain this . . . occurrence is connected to the challenge. I don't know why, not clearly. I just feel that the two things, both so dark, so threatening, they must be connected. I hoped that if you could shed light upon the identity of the challenger you might also be able to give me guidance as to what to do . . ."

"Shh, my dear girl, you are making little sense. Take a breath. Calm yourself. Whatever it is you are trying to tell me about has clearly upset you a great deal. Take your time. I am listening."

I do as he bids me and then begin again in a more measured and sensible fashion, choosing my words for clarity, making myself say aloud what I have scarcely dared face up to alone.

"I have been visited by a Dark Spirit. More than once. He comes to me unsummoned, uncalled, he . . . he has threatened me. He has threatened the coven."

Mangan, briefly, is at a loss for words. His face shows how seriously he takes this news. At last he says, "Dear Morningstar, I don't wonder that you are distressed. You have every right to be, both for yourself and for the coven.

"As a matter of fact," he says, "it is fortunate you wanted to see me, for there was a matter I wished to talk to you about." He hesitates, choosing his words with care. "Shortly before he died I visited your father and found him uncharacteristically agitated."

"Oh?"

"Yes, he was more restless than I had ever seen him. I questioned him as to what it was that was troubling him. At first he was reluctant to speak of it, and then, once he decided to confide in me, he became quite vociferous. Quite determined that I should hear what he had to say."

"Go on."

"It seems that certain of the spirits with whom he had, over the years, if not regular then at least frequent contact, well, they had been contacting him to warn of a threat."

"A threat to my father or to the coven?"

"Indeed, one must necessarily involve the other, but he gave me to understand the danger posed was to the coven and to all Lazarus witches. They stressed that it was an old adversary who was preparing to move against us."

"The Sentinels?" Even saying their name aloud makes me shiver.

Mangan nods. "Your father believed so."

"He did not speak to me of this."

"As I say, it was but a few days before he died." Mangan shrugs. "Perhaps your father was waiting until he was certain, until he had something more specific to tell you. And then the chance did not occur."

"I can see how that might have happened, but why, then, has he not mentioned it since? We have met in the catacombs. We have spoken at some length . . ."

Mangan pats my hand. "I am a father, too. Would I fill my child's mind with such worries so close to the inauguration? I think not. He can't have known about the challenge, or he would have been compelled to warn you. It may be he considered you had sufficient to occupy your thoughts and your nerves. He may be waiting for the moment to raise the matter." He hesitates and then adds, "I confess, I myself was looking for the right time to talk to you of this. You are young, so newly come to a position of such responsibility, and still grieving for your father. Perhaps I should have spoken sooner . . . Now, of course, we have reason to think that whatever plan there is against us is set in motion."

"You think the challenger was a Sentinel! One of our coven members?" I cannot keep the shock out of my voice.

"It would seem something of a coincidence otherwise, don't you think?"

For a while I say nothing. I need to take in all that he has said. If the challenge was part of something more, something bigger, then I begin to doubt that I have successfully risen to it after all. I was clumsy, my magic as yet not confidently used. Things could so easily have ended badly. Will my challenger report that I am but a novice, and that the Lazarus Coven is in the hands of an unskilled girl?

I search Mangan's face for answers. "Have you ever witnessed a demon summoning before?" I ask him.

"Once, many years ago. Not at an inauguration, though. It was a small coven meeting, convened expressly for the purpose. These skills have to be practiced from time to time, otherwise the knowledge of them would fade from memory and die out."

"And was it . . . was it successful? Was a demon raised, and was it controlled and returned as it should have been?" The vivid memory of the demon hauling me on Maygor's Thread toward the pit, of Violet's shrieks of pain, of the moment her life ended, all assail me as I think of them now.

Mangan gently lets go of my hands.

"These things, as you have seen all too clearly, are very dangerous. The summoning is the least of it." He pauses and stares at the floor for a long moment, and then goes on, "Eight witches entered the chamber that night. Only seven left it."

We sit in silence as we contemplate the full meaning of his words.

"So you see," he says at last, "what you achieved was no small feat. You have justly earned the respect of all those present. And, no doubt, given your detractor pause. Ha! Shouldn't wonder if the fellow wasn't scared half out of his wits himself!"

He cannot contain a short burst of laughter. The sound is so loud in the stillness of the room I worry someone will hear. We listen for a few seconds, but can detect no footfalls or creaking stairs. We are both startled, therefore, when Perry appears in the doorway. Even in the dimness I can see that he is still groggy with sleep and his brocade robe has been hastily thrown on over his nightshirt.

Mangan springs to his feet.

"Ah, Perry. Did we disturb you with our chatter?"

"I . . . forgive me, Mangan, I did not realize you were . . . entertaining." He turns as if to leave, but Mangan hurries after him, taking his arm and steering him back into the room. Now that we are discovered, it is important the confused man be with us long enough for a spell of forgetting to be worked upon him.

"Come along in. Look—Lilith has come to see us."

I nod my greeting to the dazed interloper. It feels strange to be called only by my first name, with no title or formalities. I know Perry will recall none of it in the morning, for Mangan will work a swift spell of forgetting to erase this meeting from his mind. Indeed, he even takes advantage of the young man's presence, sending him into the kitchen to make tea.

We are left alone again. For a while we return to the subject of a possible threat to the coven. He agrees with me that we should convene a meeting of the senior witches as soon as possible, and organize a calling to consult the spirits further. It is now that I think to speak to him of the spirit who was present at the ceremony, but before I can do so Perry has reappeared with the tea and we allow our talk to turn to more personal matters, awaiting the right moment for Mangan to send him to his room and relieve his memory of my ever having been here.

"How is Jane?" I ask. "And the children?"

"All in rude health, as ever."

"And your work goes well?"

"It is both my pleasure and my torment, as it will always be."

I glance at Perry and whisper, "We should have been more careful. We might have woken others in the house."

"I doubt it." Mangan smiles. "The children would sleep on though the last trump sounded, and Jane is a true mother. Nothing stirs her save the smallest whimper of one of her offspring, at which she is up and out of the bed before her eyes have fully opened. Gudrun will not wake before noon, whatever the provocation. And our new artist has his billet beneath the rafters, and no sounds can reach him there."

I experience a frisson of delight at the mention of Bram, and for a moment am distracted by the thought of him sleeping upstairs.

I watch Mangan steer Perry from the room, pausing as he does so to blow me a kiss from the doorway. I compel myself to hold the thought he has given me. As Lilith, I may grieve for Violet. As Morningstar, I must not allow sorrow to weaken me. I must turn my thoughts to the notion that the Sentinels are moving against us, that they may be using a Dark Spirit to weaken me, and that one of them has wormed his way into the very heart of our coven.

At home the next day I cannot settle to anything and am aware of my sharpness with Mama. I must call a meeting of senior witches to discuss what is happening. It is only right that they are informed, and, in truth, I cannot do without their help. I send word that I will await them in the Great Chamber at midnight.

It seems strange to be standing alone in this sacred space now, but I felt in need of a short time of solitude before my fellow witches arrive. How peaceful it is in here tonight, the air not yet disturbed by either the physical presence of the living or the spectral presence of the dead. How different from the last time I was here. If I allow myself to think of that terrible creature I can see him clearly in front of me even now. I wanted to call Violet, to try to speak to her, but I was counseled against it. Lord Grimes was as gentle as he could be when he pointed out that, as she was taken down to the Darkness, she will not be easily called. Such a connection must only be attempted with support, if at all. Oh, poor dear Violet! But I cannot let the memory of what happened change the way I feel about this chamber. This is my domain. Mine. Mine to keep and guard, mine to use. Tonight it will be the meeting place for five senior witches including myself. I have requested them by name, the most trusted and experienced members of the coven. I need their wisdom. I need their help.

I thought carefully about whom I should ask to this meeting. Lord Grimes and Druscilla are old friends and obvious choices, of course. I decided against asking Mangan to attend. He has told me all he knows on the subject of the potential threat to the coven, and his presence can sometimes be a little disruptive. I know I can talk to him whenever I need to. Instead I have called Victoria Faircroft, who is nearly as old as Druscilla, but a very different type of witch. She is positively evangelical about magic and communing with spirits and has struggled all her life with the secrecy that surrounds the Lazarus Coven. I have chosen her precisely because she will take a different view from Druscilla on almost every point. Such a breadth of opinion will, I hope, be useful. The last of our number will be Lord Harcourt, the earl of Winchester. I may not like the man, but he had my father's respect, and his loyalty to the coven is unswerving. And besides, I will soon be his daughter-in-law. I must learn to see him as an ally.

There are seven torches burning in their sconces around the curved walls of the chamber. They cast a welcome warmth, and their jumping flames a lively movement to relieve the solemnity of the place. It is here where I received most of my instruction, here where I practiced my craft. Sometimes more successfully than others.

I am brought back to the present by sounds of approaching footsteps. The double doors are pushed open and the four senior witches stand on the threshold. It takes a moment for me to realize they are waiting for my invitation to enter.

"You are all most welcome," I say. "Please, join me."

Before the doors can be closed Iago scampers through them and comes to wind himself around my ankles. His purr reverberates about the chamber.

"Ahh, how perfectly charming!" cries Victoria Faircroft. "It is so rare to see a witch with her familiar these days, and I do so enjoy the quainter traditions being kept alive."

Druscilla gives a snort. "Really, Victoria, you ought not to go bandying about words like 'familiar.' That sort of talk used to get people hanged, you know," she says, sitting lightly if somewhat stiffly on the front bench. She holds her slight frame erect and contained as ever, and is dressed neatly in black.

Victoria is a blur of floating layers and pastel shades. She wears a gown that looks as if it might have come from a dressing-up box, and has added to it some sort of woolen sleeveless tunic and a trailing scarf. She wears no hat, and her hair is secured not by pins or combs but plaited and twisted upon her head and tied there with strips of silk. She favors long strings of beads, and leans her ample figure on a silver-topped cane as she embraces me with her free arm. The years have not been as kind to her as they have to Druscilla, and arthritis bends and swells her joints painfully. We exchange affectionate pecks, and I am all but overwhelmed by her perfume. At present she is awash with the scent of rose petals, but it is her habit to change flowers every twenty minutes or so.

She ignores Druscilla's remark and stoops to make a fuss of Iago. "Such a dear little thing," she coos. "I myself kept a snow leopard for many years. Excellent company, highly intelligent, you know." She winces as she attempts to straighten up once more.

Lord Grimes steps forward and offers her his arm, helping her to her seat.

The earl of Winchester does not concern himself with anyone but me. He takes my hand and raises it to his lips.

"Morningstar," he says, "you are as beautiful as ever. I trust you are entirely recovered from the . . . *difficult* events at the inauguration?"

"Entirely," I tell him. "It was good of you to come. Good of all of you."

Druscilla states plainly, "You are our Head Witch now, my dear. You will not be refused by any of us. Ever."

Victoria puffs slightly as she struggles to make herself comfortable on the bench. I wonder that over the years no one has seen fit to provide chairs with arms and backs for the older coven members. "It is rather nice to be thought of as some use," she says. "Heaven knows, at our age we are considered something of an embarrassment in the Outerworld. Like guests who simply refuse to leave the party and go home."

"Speak for yourself," Druscilla tells her.

Lord Grimes does his best to keep the peace. "We are fortunate indeed that not all the young consider us nothing more than an encumbrance. Morningstar, once again, permit me to offer my condolences at the regrettable loss of your maid. Please know that if there is anything we can do to help you in your new role, any assistance we can offer, you have only to ask."

The four turn their faces to me expectantly, for once quiet. I am keenly aware that they are all so very much more skilled and experienced, both as witches and necromancers, than I. I try not to let my lack of self-confidence show, particularly in front of Louis's father.

"I have asked you here today because I have become aware of a threat to the Lazarus Coven."

Druscilla shrugs. "There have always been those who are jealous of what we have, and who would try to take it from us."

Lord Grimes nods. "We are ever on our guard."

Victoria gives a light laugh. "Scarcely a year goes by that some coven or other does not declare themselves the *true* followers of Lazarus. Or else they have been inflamed by politics and wish to put an end to a coven composed in the main of aristocrats, such as ours."

"I understand that," I tell them, "but this is something . . . different. Something more specific, somehow, more . . . imminent." I hesitate, and then continue, "I mean to say, the threat is new, but the adversary is not."

A different quality of silence falls upon the assembled company. At last it is Lord Harcourt who asks the question they all have in their minds.

"Are you referring to the Sentinels?"

I nod.

"As you say," he goes on, "they are old foes. It is hardly news that they wish us harm."

"Huh!" Druscilla glares at him. "*Harm* does not say it. They wish us dead. All of us. Finished. Exterminated like so many rats. They would erase all of our work, our teachings, our rituals, everything."

Lord Grimes puts a hand on her arm. "They consider that we took the Great Secret from them."

"And so we did!" she agrees. "We had to. They were not and are not fit to own such power."

Victoria hurries to agree. "Their work was without restraint. Their use of the Elixir reckless and ruthless. They used it not to gain knowledge or to preserve wisdom, not for the greater good, indeed, but to simply make themselves more powerful. And the power of a risen necromancer is quite terrifying."

"This was their goal," Druscilla adds. "To raise the dead of their group, so that these revenants could wield their dark magic for the furtherance of the Sentinels. Had they sufficient numbers of such sorcerers, none could have stood against them."

Lord Grimes shakes his head at the wickedness they have all heard fabled stories of. "It is said some necromancers were put to death—willingly or otherwise, history cannot reliably relate—in order that the senior Sentinels could practice their skills in Infernal Necromancy . . ."

"And to further swell their numbers," says Druscilla. "The Lazarus witches of centuries ago were compelled to act. They could not allow such abuse of the Elixir, such wanton, amoral employment of the Great Secret, to continue."

Soon the three are chattering with some vehemence about the vileness of the Sentinels and their forebears. It is Lord Harcourt who eventually raises a hand for quiet.

"Tell us, Morningstar, why is it that you think they are more dangerous now?"

"My father spoke to Mangan before he died." I ignore the tutting and huffing the artist's name elicits. "Father was very near the end, and he took him into his confidence. He told him he believed that the Sentinels are planning to move against us. They are plotting something, and intend putting it into action soon. The challenger was the first proof of that."

Lord Grimes shakes his head in disbelief. "You are telling us that there is a Sentinel in our coven?"

"I believe so, yes. The challenge was just the beginning."

"But," Victoria looks shaken, "that is impossible. How would he have been inducted? We would surely have sensed there was something wrong. We would have spotted him."

"I believe he is skilled at disguise and at blocking his witch's persona. If he does not want to be detected as a Sentinel, or indeed as a witch at all, he is adept at the deception."

"I will draw up a list of new members at once," Lord Grimes decides. "It would be as well to scrutinize it."

Druscilla leans forward. "Morningstar, if what you say is true, then the first thing you have to understand is that the Sentinels are not witches." There is a murmur of assent from the others. "They are necromancers, some of them, yes, but not witches. Never witches. They are sorcerers." She hisses the word, as if it burns her mouth to utter it. "Their magic is ancient, more ancient even than our own, and fearsomely powerful. But it has its roots in evil. There are more sorcerers condemned to the Darkness than any other humans, and many of them are Sentinels."

"We must alert the rest of the coven to the danger," Victoria insists.

Lord Grimes questions the wisdom of this. "But surely we must take care not to show our hand. Might it not be better to allow the spy to think he remains undiscovered?"

"And so he does!" Victoria points out. "No, our fellow witches have a right to know that we are under threat. Who knows where and when the Sentinels may strike if they are prepared to take such risks as worming their way into our very midst? Think of poor Oswald Tressick."

"But Oswald fell ill at the opera," says Lord Grimes.

"And what caused him to fall ill? I wonder. He was a man of healthy appetites and vigor. Never had a day's sickness in his life."

"You suspect a Sentinel's hand? In a public place?"

Druscilla nods her agreement. "Victoria may be right. In the light of what we now know . . ."

For a long moment nobody speaks. I know I must go on.

"There is something else. I have been visited by an unwelcome spirit. A blackness accompanies him. I believe him to be a Dark Spirit."

Druscilla frowns. She understands the term I have used to mean a spirit from the Darkness, and she is unable to mask her alarm. "He has visited you uncalled?"

"He has. On several occasions. He was here . . . during the inauguration. In fact, his presence affected my ability to control the demon."

Lord Grimes shakes his head. "I knew there was something . . ."

"You heard him, too?" The idea somehow makes me feel less alone, less singled out.

"Not heard, no, but I observed your behavior."

Druscilla nods. "Yes, there was something. I, too, detected a presence."

A thought occurs to me. "Could it be that the two things are connected? The presence of a Sentinel and the Dark Spirit?"

Victoria fans herself with her scarf. "It would indeed be something of a coincidence otherwise. The Sentinels were known for favoring the use of such dangerous beings in their necromancy. A risky practice at best."

I try to order my thoughts. "You mean, the Sentinel summoned the Dark Spirit to the chamber? Was he also responsible for having him hound me?"

"It is possible," Druscilla agrees. "You must be on your guard,

Morningstar. Such a combination of foes presents a very real danger."

Victoria seems to shrink in her seat, looking suddenly every one of her many years. "This is too awful. A new Head Witch, the country in turmoil, war on the horizon—the spirits have been insisting as much for months—the Sentinels infiltrating the sanctity of our coven, of an inauguration! And now a Dark Spirit emerging from the Darkness. It is too much, all at once."

Lord Harcourt gets up and comes to stand beside me.

"It is not more than we can face if we face it together," he says, holding my gaze with his own as he speaks. "Your father had faith in you, Morningstar, and so do we all, but know this. You have our support. Whatever the price, whatever happens, I promise you we will stand by you."

It seems even Louis's father is prepared to offer me his sincere protection, to put his personal feelings aside for the good of the coven. The others nod and echo his words and I feel, just for a moment, a little of the fear I have been carrying these past days, I feel it lessen, feel it lift ever so slightly from my shoulders.

13.

Unlike the Lazarus Coven, the Sentinels do not have a central place of worship and gathering. They select venues for their meetings which are as varied and disparate as the membership itself. There is no rule of inheritance that decrees who should belong, so that each member must be proposed by an existing Sentinel and voted in by the Ruling Elect. This consists of seven men of long-standing allegiance to the group. There is not, never has been, nor ever will be, a female Sentinel. The greatest quality a member can possess is power, and it was long ago decided that while many women are in possession of admirable qualities, when pitted against men, their inherent weakness tells. And weakness will not be tolerated. In fact, new members are rare. Efforts are made to ensure that numbers do not decline, but none presently in charge consider there is an advantage to being greatly numerous, so the need for admitting someone new to this most secret of societies seldom arises.

As Stricklend passes through the great doors of St. Paul's Cathedral and finds the interior temperature scarcely higher than the bitter November night outside, he knows some will question the wisdom of this particular venue choice. Admittedly, there will be few visitors wishing to gain entry, so there will be fewer questions asked about why the whispering gallery and all points above it should be "temporarily shut for maintenance." This aside, other members of the group might consider there are places which would afford more comfort. But then, this meeting has been convened at the behest of Stricklend himself for an issue that is both serious and urgent. Personal comfort was not a matter to which he gave any consideration whatsoever.

His footsteps echo in the cavernous empty space and then soften to the slap of Italian leather on stone as he climbs the stairs at the base of the cathedral's dome. Behind him the verger secures the twisted gold-and-red rope across the entrance. He is aware of two figures ahead of him. One has Maurice Loxton's bulk and is making the ascent slowly and with not a little wheezing. Loxton, a stockbroker with a reputation for ruthlessness and a bank balance to prove it, has been a senior Sentinel for almost as many years as Stricklend himself. Almost. It still causes a certain friction between the two that Stricklend's opinion always carried the greater weight. And now that Stricklend's superiority is unquestioned and unassailable, his fellow Sentinel's jealousy has hardened into a leaden loathing. Loxton's loyalty to the group and to the cause is beyond question. He is sharply clever, a likable enough quality to Stricklend's mind. Even so, there is a self-serving independence about him that niggles at the permanent private secretary. Of course, all men who worship power are themselves likely to be powerful and egotistical. But such self-interest must be checked by a greater love of the cause. If it is not, well, that way lies megalomania. Stricklend has seen it before. More than one great man, during his own time as an Elect, has let his belief in himself override the greater cause. And all have paid the ultimate price for their pride. Loxton needs watching, and Stricklend is the man to do it.

Stricklend slows his pace. Even though the Sentinels will be the only people permitted entry to the area, the practice of secrecy must be maintained. There are two hundred and fifty-nine steps to the gallery, so that the chill of the night has been driven from his bones by the warmth of exertion by the time he reaches the gallery. He walks briskly around the circular walkway, glancing down over the balustrade at the giddying drop to the marble floor below. He affects interest in an inscription on the wall and pauses to read it. Two more figures slip past him. He checks his watch. The appointed hour has arrived. He moves a little closer to the smooth stone of the wall and turns to stand facing outward and upward, as if contemplating the splendid architecture of the dome above or perhaps, inspired by his surroundings, offering up an exultant prayer. But the god Nicholas Stricklend serves cannot cross the portals of the cathedral.

A voice, thin and breathy, travels the circumference of the circle. The words hiss slightly as they loop the gallery, but are nonetheless clear. This is not the first time Stricklend has chosen the Whispering Gallery as the venue for a meeting. The trick of construction and acoustics means that a person standing here may speak his thoughts softly, and they will be heard on the far side, and indeed all around the narrow walkway. Stricklend himself is unimpressed by such parlor games. A point in favor concerning the location, however, is that the lack of comfort considerably curtails verbosity and keeps the meetings short.

"Let all present declare themselves in turn," the speaker instructs.

To Stricklend's immediate left the sequence is started with the first response of "I serve," then from the next point on, until it comes full circle and he, in turn, declares his presence, anonymously, but with the statement "I serve," as is required of them. Tradition also dictates that the Sentinel who called the meeting be the first to speak.

"I have summoned you here in order to further the most important aim, the singularly most pressing need for all Sentinels," he tells them.

"As always, we are happy to answer the call," comes the somewhat sycophantic response from the far side of the gallery. There are similar murmurs of assent and agreement.

"The time has come for action," Stricklend says.

"It might help," says Loxton with ill-concealed rancor, "if you were to tell us precisely what it is you are so concerned about. Now that you have us all assembled, and duty bound to hear you out, spare us all the rheumatism that will set in from these damp stones if we linger too long in this faintly ridiculous building."

"*You*, sir, know full well why I have convened this meeting!" Stricklend's voice is gaining strength and volume and already beginning to give the lie to the name Whispering Gallery. From somewhere farther around the wall he is shushed but pays no heed. "As all here will recall, it was your idea to have the heir to the Lazarus leadership challenged at the inauguration. A plan which succeeded only in consolidating the girl's position." There are murmurings of assent. "Time is passing and we are no further forward. We must act."

"And what would you have us do?" asks another member of the elite from the shadows.

"I suggest there are but three options left to us in order to obtain the Elixir."

At this there is a collective gasp. To name the prize, to speak of it at all, let alone in a public place, feels shocking even to the most seasoned member of the group.

"The first of these is to use the spy that has become an insider of the Lazarus Coven. The challenge at the inauguration was not as successful as we might have hoped, but it was not the fault of the challenger that the outcome was not in our favor," Stricklend points out. "The man is a loyal and experienced Sentinel, and he is now a trusted member of the Lazarus Coven. Our first option, then, is to have him seduce Lilith Montgomery, become her lover, win her over completely, so that he is able to obtain the Elixir from her."

The other Sentinels mutter among themselves regarding the merits of the proposal.

"But," says one, "we do not know that the girl is . . . well, kindly disposed to our man. She might refuse his advances."

"She might," Stricklend concedes.

"And," another points out, "seduction is hardly an activity one can set one's watch to. The process might take weeks. Months even."

"Quite so," Stricklend allows, "which brings me to the second option. We abduct the Head Witch and . . . persuade her to part with the recipe for the Elixir. She alone of the coven members knows both the spell and the formula in their entirety."

"You amaze me." Loxton is beginning to lose patience. "You have so far suggested love or kidnapping as ways to overcome the obstacle before us. In both cases our success would depend on the foolishness, on the weakness of character, perhaps, of Lilith Montgomery. This is the witch who summoned a demon and controlled it sufficiently to send it back to the Darkness at her bidding. This is the witch who is known to be as serious-minded and clever as she is well connected. This is the witch who is, after all, Robert Montgomery's daughter, schooled by him over many years. Do you truly believe she will fall for charm like some naïve debutante? Or that she would be so stupid as to leave the house without guardians?"

"The third route calls for more drastic, more violent action." Stricklend goes on as if Loxton has not spoken. "Which is why I put it to you as a last resort. We must dispose of all the senior witches of the coven, save for the girl. Then, when she stands alone, when she has no real support, we take what we want from her. We may even be able to take the coven, too."

A laugh from the shadows is followed by an incredulous question. "You mean us to become followers of Lazarus?"

"I do not. I mean us to conquer them, and to assimilate the followers, to absorb them into our own group. The Lazarus

Coven would cease to exist and the Sentinels would become the keepers of the Elixir. We would, at last, fulfill our destiny."

At this the other members fall silent. Stricklend knows some will find that the idea has appeal. But it is ambitious. And such ambition, at such a time, might cause them to overreach themselves. Might cause them to fail.

"We must decide," Stricklend tells them. "We cannot let the matter rest any longer. The time is, after so many years of waiting, perfect for us to make our move. The country is in a state of flux with war imminent. The Lazarus Coven have a new and unproven young Head Witch. We have at last succeeded in having our spy infiltrate their number. There will never be a better moment. We must not leave this place until we are agreed upon our course of action, and until we have decided how best it should be executed."

While the Sentinels stand in silent thought, far below them in the choir stalls young men raise their angelic voices upward, ever upward, so that sublime music drifts aloft to soothe the furrowed brows of those in the Whispering Gallery.

Throughout this time of turmoil and disturbance there is one aspect of my life that brings me such joy, it is as if I am two different people at once. Indeed, that is precisely what I am. I am Morningstar, who must put the coven before all else, and I am Lilith, a girl in love. What conflicting emotions stir me! I do my best to give the impression that nothing unusual disturbs my equilibrium, but in this I am not always successful. Charlotte, certainly, has noticed the difference in me, but then she is, of course, in my confidence where my affection for Bram is concerned. I have had to acknowledge to myself that my feelings for Louis cannot compare with what I now feel for Bram. The thought of causing him pain is dreadful, but I know I cannot continue with our engagement. I cannot marry him. To do so would be dishonest, however much it may be what he and Mama want for me. Now that I know what true love feels like, how one can be transformed by it . . . I cannot turn away from it. I know I will have to face Louis, to find the right moment to talk to him. It is something I dread doing, and I admit I am relieved he has gone to his country estate in Hampshire for the shooting, so that I have at least a little time to consider how I will try to explain to him . . . how I will break his heart.

In the meantime, I try to see Bram as often as I can. Ours is not an easy romance to conduct. I cannot introduce him to Mama, who would put a stop to our seeing each other at once. And the grounds she would use to do so would rankle and irk and cause me to inwardly rage, and yet I would know them to be valid. This means we are compelled to meet in secret or, at least, with utmost discretion. In this, Charlotte has proved a great ally, due, I think, as much to her love of the idea of love, as to her affection for me. She provides the necessary alibi, so that I might leave the house unquestioned, and otherwise unaccompanied. Bram has finished his portrait of her, so that when she sits for Mangan—who has yet, helpfully, a fair amount of work to do on his sculpture—he and I are free to spend our time together. And what freedoms exist in that house! We take ourselves up to his garret rooms, unchaperoned, where we can be reasonably sure of uninterrupted privacy. If Mama knew . . . well, she must not know.

The motor cab speeds through the icy streets of Bloomsbury. Christmas shoppers are abroad, and the atmosphere is already festive. Charlotte is full of her plans for the next few weeks, but I find it hard to be attentive. There are things I do not wish to think about, and Christmas is one of them. How will I ever be able to engineer further meetings with Bram if Charlotte is engaged on a ceaseless round of parties and functions? This will be such a difficult Christmas for Mama as it is, I cannot give her something else to fret about. And Freddie grows ever more restless at Radnor Hall, threatening almost daily to return to London. Bram has not spoken of his own plans, but it would be perfectly reasonable of him to go home to Yorkshire. I cannot bear the thought of being parted from him so soon.

"Oh! Do look, Lily, the Mangan children have decorated the house." Charlotte tugs at my sleeve.

Indeed they have. Not satisfied with a simple holly wreath on the front door, most of the lower half of the narrow town house has been festooned with greenery, either fir boughs or holly or mistletoe. The effect is quite mad, but at the same time enchanting. Two of the younger children, tightly wrapped against the cold, are still adding to the decorations, tying string through painted wooden shapes and distributing them here and there as Jane and Perry hold them so that they might reach. They see us and wave. I consider it nothing less than marvelous, the way in which the household has quietly accepted the closeness between Bram and me. I have received not so much as a disapproving glance or any of the more robust responses I might have expected from the great sculptor himself.

Once inside, Charlotte makes her way to the studio. Gudrun saunters out from the drawing room and calls up the stairs to Bram.

"Artist! You have a visitor." She steps closer to me, and for the first time I feel her scrutinizing me, as she leans against the newel post, cigarette in hand, head cocked as she considers me thoughtfully through curls of smoke. "You are a very beautiful woman," she decides, "and our Artist is a very beautiful man."

I am trying to form a suitable response to such an odd statement when she goes on.

"Do you think this is enough, Beauty? Do you think this will overcome all?" she asks, her German accent seeming stronger today than at other times.

"I don't know about that," I tell her. "I think what's beneath the surface is more important."

"Oh? And would he love you if you were plain? Or you him?" She flicks ash carelessly onto the floor. "And what is it that you think lies underneath that matters so much? He is an artist, after all. He cares very much for beauty. They all do."

You won't tell him your secret!

The unexpected voice of a spirit shocks me into open-mouthed silence. He is so adept at catching me off guard. I steady myself. I have decided I will not talk with him anymore. I have asked Druscilla to help me, and we have planned a summoning. I admit I am nervous about it, this spirit has such attendant bitterness and hatred, such as I have never known before. But Druscilla is the most skilled necromancer I know. I am reassured that she will be with me. We will face him together, for face him we must. It is imperative we discover his links to the challenger and to the Sentinels.

You will never be able to tell him what you are!

The voice sounds so vehement, so angry.

Go away! This is none of your business.

Anything you do is my business, Daughter of the Night.

I have not summoned you. This is not the time . . .

Do not forget who you are, Morningstar. You cannot escape your destiny, any more than I escaped mine. To be free of your burden you must rid yourself of it. It was passed down to you, a poisoned chalice because it is not truly yours. You must give it up. You must.

Gudrun is frowning at me, clearly surprised I have no argument to give to what she has said, little knowing that I have another clamoring for my attention. Bram's hurrying footsteps on the stairs save me from having to respond.

"There you are, Artist. Better not keep Beauty waiting," she says, pausing to dust off his lapel lazily before disappearing back into the drawing room.

Bram gives a shrug, then a smile, then snatches up my hand and kisses it quickly. We can hear approaching children and the dog, and before they can reach us he leads me swiftly away, up the stairs to his rooms. Even in my good new coat and fur hat I can feel the temperature drop as we enter the attic space. The fact is, there is very little warmth on the ground floor, and none at all in the bedrooms, and what heat might remain to drift upward simply continues its journey through the frozen slates or holes in the roof. As Bram bustles about boiling a kettle for tea I can see his breath forming small clouds in front of him. He glances at me, clearly unsurprised to see I have not removed my coat.

"I'm sorry," he says. "It is horridly cold up here."

"The tea will warm us."

"If I can ever get this blasted gas to light, the matches are so damp . . . there. Shouldn't take too long." He leaves the kettle and hurries back to wrap me in his strong arms. "It is ridiculous that I subject you to this," he murmurs into my hair.

"There is no place on earth I would rather be."

"There is nothing in the least bit romantic about pneumonia," he warns, "which is what we shall both soon have if we are obliged to hide ourselves away in the roof like, oh, I don't know, a pair of mice."

"Bats," I tell him. "I would rather we were bats." I smile up into his lovely face. "The cold doesn't matter. Nothing matters." For a long moment we say nothing but gaze at each other, reveling in the embrace. He kisses the very tip of my nose.

"I'll bet you couldn't even feel that, your poor dear nose is so frozen."

"Better kiss me again, then."

He does, but not my nose. This time he puts his lips to mine and I melt into the blissful closeness of a long, luxurious kiss. The heavenly moment is pierced by the shrill cry of the kettle. Bram lets me go, grinning. He pushes his unruly hair out of his eyes and claps his hands together, rubbing them in a businesslike fashion.

"Tea," he says, hurrying back to his task. He fills the pot and puts a little milk and sugar in the cups. He is careful to shut the sugar tin and milk away in the shabby metal cupboard where he stores his comestibles. He gives the tea in the pot a stir before pouring it with a flourish from some height.

"Do you know, until I met you I had never seen a man make tea."

"I'm happy to hear I have added so significantly to your life experiences."

"Particularly with the tea making."

"Particularly."

He brings the steaming cups and sets them down on the low table in front of the single armchair. When I hesitate he plonks himself down in it, taking hold of my hand as he does so and pulling me onto his lap.

"Thing with only having one decent chair," he tells me, "is that you have to decide: share or take turns. Sharing is warmer."

"I like sharing."

"Excellent. Then we are in agreement."

"As in so many things."

"Only now you will have to pass the tea over."

I do so carefully and we sit with our hands wrapped around the saucerless cups, sipping at the scalding drink.

"It's too cold to go out today," he says.

I laugh a little. "It might be warmer than in here."

"Snow is threatened."

"We could go to the Soldiers' Arms and sit by the fire." The little public house has become one of our favorite haunts. No one who knows me would ever go to such a place, and the walk there is short, so we are not at any great risk of being seen. But there is the matter of money. Bram was paid well for Charlotte's portrait, and is hopeful for further commissions on the back of it, but none have yet been forthcoming, and we are both aware that the money will not keep him for long, especially if we spend it on brandy. I have insisted on paying my share, but he simply will not let me pay when he cannot.

"Not today," he says. "Today I'd like to do something different."

"Oh?"

He looks unsure of himself, but continues.

"I want to paint you, Lilith. Please say you'll let me."

"Only if you'll allow me to buy the picture from you when it is finished."

"Don't be absurd. How could I let you pay for it?"

"Then I won't sit. It is my only condition."

"Really? Your only condition?"

"Absolutely. A fair price, the minute it is completed."

"I won't want to part with it."

"You can keep it here, show it to Mangan, if you're pleased with it. Perhaps it will gain you some commissions." I do not mention that I can hardly take it home to hang above the stairs at Fitzroy Square. How would I ever explain its existence to Mama?

He thinks about this for a while and then smiles broadly. "Very well, I accept your condition."

I hop to my feet, excited at the prospect of being his model now. "Where shall I sit? I trust you don't expect me to remove my clothes. I would freeze to death before the paint was dry."

"Only your hat," he says, leading me over to where he has the easel set up. I see now that there is a canvas in place and a chair positioned just so on the other side of it. Had he really been so sure I would agree to sit? He already knows me better than I know myself.

You know that he does not, Lilith. He cannot!

The voice is so unexpected that this time it makes me jump.

"Lilith, what is it?"

"Oh, nothing. I . . . thought I saw a mouse. Over there," I tell him, sitting on the worn wooden chair and allowing him to turn my face fractionally to one side.

"There," he says, "that is perfect. There is not much light this time of year, but what there is now falls directly onto one side of your exquisite face, my love. Your hair, though." He frowns. "It should be loose. Do you mind?"

"Not at all," I say, reaching up to take it down from the high bun into which it is coiled.

"Please . . . let me." One by one, with great tenderness, he removes the hairpins. Slowly. Carefully. Allowing each lock of hair to fall naturally onto my shoulders. Such an intimate action, such gentleness, should be blissful, but I am still tense, alert, waiting for the Dark Spirit to speak again, so that the moment is quite spoiled.

When he has finished his task Bram stands back to look at me. "Now," he asks, "are you comfortable? Can you hold this pose, do you think?"

"Quite comfortable," I assure him, though I find I am stupidly anxious. The unwanted spirit is still with me. I can sense him watching. Listening. Ready to remind me of the fact that Bram does not know, cannot know, that the woman he adores, the woman he has lost his heart to, the woman who now sits before him, holds such strange and powerful secrets. I do my best not to let my anxiety show, but Bram is not so easily fooled. He is, it seems, attuned to my own moods and cannot help but see that something is troubling me deeply.

"Darling, please tell me what it is."

"I . . . cannot."

He shakes his head slowly. "Don't you recall what I told you? Nothing you can tell me about yourself would alter my feelings for you. You must surely believe that now. Do you doubt me, is that it?"

"No. No, it's not that."

"Is it . . ." he hesitates, and then goes on, "is it something to do with your fiancé? Breaking off the engagement will not be easy, I know . . ."

"It's not about Louis."

"Then *what*?" He takes my hands in his and feels them tremble. "How can I help you if you will not talk to me?"

Perhaps you should tell him. Tell him what you are and see how he regards you then. It will be interesting to watch his promises of love turn to an expression of disgust.

I leap from my chair, pushing past Bram, my hands over my ears.

"Stop it! Stop it! Stop it! Why can't you leave me alone?"

Bram grabs me and pulls me to him. He is searching my face for answers and knows that my cries are not directed at him. "Who is it, Lilith? Who is making you so very afraid? Tell me."

"I can't! You wouldn't understand."

"I could try."

"It's impossible. *We* are impossible. I shouldn't be here. I shouldn't be seeing you." I try to pull away from him, but this time he will not let me go. I can hear his voice, soothing yet urgent. I can hear the Dark Spirit, goading and laughing at me. I can hear other spirits now, disturbed by the activity of such a powerful soul from the Darkness. I can hear my loyal captains offering their help. I am deafened. I am drowning in all their voices, all their words. I feel as if my mind will burn up from it all. I let out a shriek, and as I do so I unintentionally loose a shock of magic, fiery and dangerous, without direction, that lights up the entire attic space. The heat of it sends Bram hurtling backward, crashing against the far wall. The easel and chair are overturned, the teapot and cups dashed against the floor and smashed, the armchair upended, the bed turned, the mirror burst in smithereens from its frame. The blinding light lasts a second, no more, but when it passes and cools, there is an aroma of singeing hair and wood and dust. I stand very still, my fists clenched, my hair flowing outward, billowing, undulating, as if moved by a celestial breeze.

Slowly, cautiously, Bram gets to his feet. He looks a little bruised, and shocked, but otherwise unharmed. He takes in the devastation of the room and then returns his bewildered gaze to me.

The Dark Spirit has, mercifully, been silenced by my outburst.

I take a long, deep breath and look at the man I love, levelly, calmly. I want to hold close in my memory that dear, loving face in case, after I have spoken, he never turns it upon me again.

"You know me as Lady Lilith Montgomery, daughter of the sixth duke of Radnor. And so I am. But my father also happened to be Head Witch of the Lazarus Coven. A position that, when he died, passed on to me. My chosen name is Morningstar, and I lead a coven dedicated to the art of necromancy, sworn to commune with the dead in the Land of Night for the good of all, and to protect the Great Secret. In short, my darling, darling Bram, you have fallen in love with a witch."

Bram pulls the rough blanket a little tighter around Lilith's shoulders. In his narrow bed they lie together, fully clothed beneath the covers, holding one another in an embrace that he wishes would never end. In those first moments after Lilith told him, after she uttered in all seriousness—and he knew it *was* serious— the word "witch" he had felt as if he were falling. As if nothing he thought he knew would ever be true again. As if he could not, now, be certain of anything. The ground under him might not be real. Indeed, at that moment it had seemed to dissolve beneath his feet and no longer to be able to bear his weight. He knew one thing—Lilith was not lying. Nor did he believe her to be mad. Which meant that what she said was the truth. She was a witch. A witch, she had gone on to explain, who talked to the dead and who was capable of magic. This last was not, in fact, a surprise to him.

I sensed something. I always knew there was something about her. Something . . . otherworldly. She glows with it.

Even so, it is a giant step to take, from suspecting something strange to accepting that the woman he adores casts spells and summons spirits. He considered the possibility that it is he who is mad, but Lilith has done her best, in the hour since her revelation, to reassure him that this is not the case. He kisses the top of her head, breathing in the sweet scent of her hair. He can feel her tender heart beating against his own chest, even through their many layers of warm clothing.

"You are very quiet," she says softly. "I am afraid of what you might be thinking. Of what you might be thinking of me."

"I am thinking that I am the luckiest man alive to be holding you in my arms."

She wriggles free a little and looks up at him, risking a small smile. "Aren't you afraid I might turn you into a frog?" she asks.

Bram shrugs. "I quite like frogs."

Lilith's smile broadens. "I'm not sure I'd want to kiss you if you were all green and warty."

"Better kiss me now, then, while I'm still relatively human."

And she does. A long, slow, sweet kiss that stirs him, making him wish the room were not so very cold, and their clothes not so very thick and plentiful. When she speaks again she lowers her gaze, uncertainty in her voice.

"I . . . I thought you might be repulsed. Revolted. By what I do. By what I am. Or afraid, perhaps."

He shakes his head. "I love you, Lilith. I love *you*, in all your wonderful strangeness." He hesitates before going on, then says, "But *you* were afraid, I think. Earlier. Something terrified you. Won't you tell me what it was?"

"Not today. Not yet. I don't think I can tell you any more right now. Do you mind awfully if we don't talk about it for a little while? Could we just . . . be together? Like this?"

When he nods she snuggles back into him and he holds her tight. He knows that by confiding in him she has allowed him to come closer to her than anyone. He knows that she will tell him all there is to tell, in her own time.

I can wait, my love. Now I know that you trust me, and that you will not run away from me again, I can wait.

14.

The night after my revelation to Bram I sit in the blackness of the unlit Great Chamber, Druscilla at my side. I am glad to be pressing ahead with the summoning. The Dark Spirit has become increasingly frightening and persistent. He seems to know precisely when his words will have the most impact on me, when I am least able to address him. Indeed, I feel that it was because of how unsettled, how badgered, how hounded I felt that I confessed my truth to Bram. Oh, and it is wonderful that the secret no longer binds my heart! I feel able to love him now without the fetter of duplicity. Though, I admit, my relief at having told him is clouded somewhat by the knowledge of what I have done. Have I put the coven in danger? I do not believe so. Have I broken my vows as a Lazarus witch? Yes. I cannot pretend otherwise. To speak of the coven and our work to someone of the Outerworld is strictly forbidden. I do not suppose I am the first to have done so, but am I the first Head Witch? Do I even deserve to be called such, when I cannot follow our creed? I don't know what will happen in the future, but I do know now is not the time to show weakness. The coven must unite against the Sentinels. This is not the moment to reveal any chinks in our armor. For this reason I have decided not to tell Druscilla about my confiding in Bram. Not yet. Tonight we have another matter that demands our full attention.

"I think it advisable," Druscilla is saying, "given the hostility you have spoken of when this spirit is present, that we try only to summon him in voice."

"I agree. His visual presence would be distracting and would somehow make him more threatening."

"Make no mistake, a Dark Spirit can still be extremely dangerous, even when he is here in his most ethereal form."

"I understand."

Druscilla pauses. In the darkness I can sense that she is looking at me as only she can.

"Are you frightened, child?" she asks.

I have to fight to keep the tremor out of my voice. "Nervous, perhaps. Anxious to deal with this . . . situation."

"You are right to acknowledge the seriousness of being haunted by someone from the Darkness. Particularly now, with the Sentinels threatening our coven. And if it is true that they are somehow using this spirit . . . well, that is a grave situation. Imagine how difficult it would be to maintain any secret, let alone the Great Secret, for any length of time, if they have managed to find a Dark Spirit to infiltrate our thoughts. But fear not, we are well prepared. All will be well."

We ready ourselves by reciting the Lazarus creed and a prayer to Hekate for protection. Then we sit in silence. In the treacly blackness I can hear my own blood pulsing through my veins, my heart thudding a little faster than it should, the air dragging in and out of my lungs. I empty my mind, letting down my guard, an open invitation for the Dark Spirit to visit. Druscilla, meanwhile, is silently summoning him as best she can without knowing his identity. She suspects he is a witch or sorcerer of some kind, and I have told her I think him very ancient, but it is not much to go on. Without more specific information it will be very easy for him to resist the summoning, however skillfully done.

We need not have worried. He does not wait to be summoned, but springs into my mind the instant my barriers are lowered.

I knew you would come to me, little sister, I knew you would seek me out.

Druscilla hears my gasp.

"Is he with you, Lilith?"

"He is."

You had no need to bring the crone. If you wish to talk to me you have only to let me into your feverish little mind.

"I do wish to talk to you tonight. Now, here, at the moment and place of my choosing, not whenever it suits you in my private life." I speak aloud so that Druscilla will be privy to at least half the conversation. It is quite likely she will also be able to pick up the spirit's voice, she is so attuned to the Land of Night. It depends how strongly he resists her.

I believe you are enjoying your status as Head Witch. I believe it is making you arrogant, little witch. You imagine your precious coven to be so powerful. You have no idea what true power is.

"Are you a witch, Spirit?"

Witch! How I hate that word. I have no need of your petty spells and conjuring. I am a sorcerer. When I trod the earth I was the greatest sorcerer the world had ever known. I was lauded and respected. There has not been my equal since.

"When was that? When did you walk in the Land of Day?"

Centuries ago, when your witchery was young.

"I don't understand," I tell him cautiously. "If you were so powerful, so revered, how is it that now you are content to serve such a dishonorable group as the Sentinels? Why would you ally yourself to their cause?"

I choose the masters I consider most advantageous to myself.

Druscilla puts her hand on my arm. "Ask him who is the Sentinel who has infiltrated our coven," she whispers. But the spirit has heard and needs no asking.

The old woman is a fool to think I can be so easily swayed! My purpose is not to bargain, not to help the Lazarus witches. I come to state my demands, clear and simple. She is like all Lazarus witches; she sets herself above those who wielded true power with their magic! Such arrogance. There was no greater sorcerer, than I . . . Men, witches, sages of the ancients, all trembled in my presence! All deferred to me! Had I not been betrayed I would be ruling them still!

I am trying to take in all I am being told when beside me Druscilla utters a sharp cry of pain.

"Druscilla?"

She cries out again. It is the most pitiful, heartbreaking sound, and I know she must be suffering greatly to let herself cry so.

"Druscilla, what is it? What is happening?

I hear the Dark Spirit start to laugh. It is a rasping, dry, unholy noise.

Druscilla gasps, "Oh! Lilith, you must send him away!" Her voice is distorted with effort and pain. "Quickly. He is too strong . . . he will stop my heart . . ."

Without hesitating to question or to speak to the spirit further I begin chanting the words of banishment. Over and over, with as much passion as I am able, I speak the antique phrases that will send the spirit back to the Darkness. Still I hear his laughter. Druscilla clutches at me, and I pull her to me, holding her close, willing her frail body to stay strong, to withstand the evil that is inflicting such suffering upon it. She has ceased crying out but is breathing very quickly now, and I fear I will be too late.

Do you think you can protect them all, Lazarus witch? I will turn on all those you love, do you hear me? If you refuse to do my bidding, I will seek out the one who is dearest to you, for I know where your heart lies, and I will crush him, like a beetle beneath a giant's heel.

"Be gone, Dark Spirit! Leave us! I am not afraid of you. I will not heed your threats, and I will not have you hurt this gentle soul. If you wish to fight, then you must do so with me, not this frail old lady." I wait, muttering beneath my breath a prayer for

Hekate to come to our aid. Then, in an instant, the presence vanishes. The quality of the air in the chamber changes. The Dark Spirit has gone.

"Druscilla?" I clap my hands. "Light! Light now!" The torches in the wall sconces burst into flame. Druscilla is slumped against me, her face pale and pinched, her skin clammy, but she holds my gaze and squeezes my hand.

"Fear not, Morningstar. I am . . . I am unharmed."

"Oh, Druscilla, I am so sorry. I should never have agreed to let you help me."

"Nonsense. What am I for . . . if not to help my coven leader? Here, help me sit up a little. That's better." She takes a moment to regain her breath and her composure. "Thank you, Lilith. Your swift action—your very able action—it saved me."

"Why would he cause you such terrible pain? I don't understand."

"I'm afraid I do, because I know now whose presence we have just withstood."

"You know who the Dark Spirit is?"

She nods slowly. "His name is Edmund Willoughby. Your Dark Spirit was not just some lowly sorcerer dabbling in spiritualism, Lilith. He was what he says, the most powerful sorcerer of his day. Of any day."

"The name is familiar."

"You were always an attentive student. You will have heard him mentioned during your instruction."

"He said there has been none like him. No one since. Is that true?"

"It would be hard to either argue with him, or to disprove the claim, because Infernal Necromancy is no longer practiced."

"He raised the dead from their graves?"

"All necromancers of his time would have attempted to do so.

Not all were successful. He was. Though he did not have the Elixir, he does not know the Great Secret—the magic he used, the rites and spells, all were of a very different nature to ours. But he was powerful, and because of that he made powerful enemies. His story is a warning to anyone who underestimates the lust for power the Lazarus Elixir can inspire. Whatever his high position, Willoughby was not satisfied. He became greedy. He knew there was a strength of magic that could surpass his own, and he believed it was within his grasp."

"The power of the risen necromancer . . ."

". . . is surpassed only by the power of a risen witch." Druscilla nods, finishing the quotation from our Book of Divine Wisdom. "It has always been known that a necromancer who is successfully risen would wield phenomenal power. History tells us that Willoughby instructed his assistant to aid him in the process. He was to administer the Elixir. But Willoughby had jealous enemies. They bribed the assistant, and he did not perform the rites. He failed to raise his master, and Willoughby was left to roam the Darkness. Until now."

"Now he has found a way back. Through the Sentinels. He spoke of me doing his bidding. The Sentinels' bidding, do you think? He expects me to give them the Elixir?"

Druscilla's face is serious. "Tread carefully, Morningstar. He is a fearsome adversary. Whatever he wants, he will not care who suffers in order for him to obtain it. Be aware, child. Do not ever let your guard down again."

As she speaks I hear again the words the wicked spirit hissed at me as he tortured poor Druscilla so—*the one who is dearest to you.* Bram! He means to get at me by hurting my darling Bram. When I think of the suffering he has just inflicted on Druscilla, an experienced witch, my blood chills. I cannot leave Bram defenseless against such a creature. I cannot.

Bram holds his hands over the small, enameled, paraffin heater he has just had delivered to his room. It is modest, and old, and not sufficiently large to properly heat his drafty attic studio, but it gives a blissful point of heat. Now he will be able to thaw his frozen paints and restore life to his numb fingers when he is trying to work. At first such a purchase had seemed rash, given his worryingly meager finances, but he has convinced himself it is a necessity.

At least poor Lilith will no longer shiver as she sits for me to paint.

He turns to regard the unfinished portrait on the easel. The lamplight offers only tantalizing glimpses of the face he has come to know so well. The face he adores. He longs to continue with the portrait, but to do so in such feeble light would be a mistake. He steps closer to the canvas and reaches out to touch her cheek, and as he does so he senses he is no longer alone in the room. Wheeling around, he is astonished to see Lilith herself, real flesh-and-blood Lilith, standing in the doorway.

"Bram, forgive me, I did not mean to startle you."

He hurries to her. "You need never apologize for visiting me, any time of day or night. But how do you come to be here?" he asks, leading her by the hand to stand by the heater. "It must be two in the morning . . . I did not hear you arrive, no voices downstairs . . . how did you . . . ?"

"Mangan let me in," she explains. "He was still in his studio and heard my knocking. It seems we are all nocturnal creatures; you were not asleep."

"I find it harder and harder to still my mind sufficiently to sleep," he tells her, running a hand through his unruly hair.

"Oh?" She seems concerned. "What is troubling you?"

He laughs at this, sliding an arm around her waist and pulling her to him. "*You*, Lilith Montgomery. *You* are what is troubling me. Either I am utterly taken up by trying to paint you, or by berating myself for not succeeding in painting you, or for not succeeding in painting anything at all because all I can think of is you!"

She appears relieved at his answer. "Ah. So it is my fault." She smiles briefly, but is quickly serious again. "Bram . . . I need to talk to you. It is . . . it is about what I started to tell you the other day. It is important. Very important."

Still holding her in his arms he resists kissing her, sensing that this is not the moment. "I cannot imagine you would have gone to the trouble of sneaking out to see me at night if it were not for a very good reason. Here, let me take your coat. Look, I have joined the modern age and installed heating!" He gestures at the potbellied stove, but Lilith does not remove her hat or undo the buttons of her winter coat.

"I need to take you somewhere. To show you something. I can't explain until we get there. Will you come with me? Please?"

"Of course." He nods his agreement, snatching up his own outdoor garments, before taking her hand in his. Quickly and quietly they descend the stairs and go out into the dark street, where Lilith has a cab waiting. They sit together in silence as they speed along the empty roads. London slumbers through the cold winter's night. The gaslights give off scant illumination through the freezing fog that billows about them. The density of the air muffles even the clanging of the horse's iron shoes as it trots on, heading north out of Bloomsbury. Bram has not the slightest idea where Lilith is taking him. Nor can he summon comforting words for her, because he cannot begin to guess what it is that has brought her to him in the dead of night, alone. He squeezes her hand tightly and lifts it to his lips, but even then she does not speak, only responds by leaning closer into him, and continuing to gaze out of the window of the cab into the milky miasma.

At last the cabdriver reins in the carriage horse and opens the door for them. Lilith pays him but instructs him to wait, and then leads the way through the tall iron gates that stand at the entrance to the cemetery. The fog has thickened, and the number of streetlamps lessened, so that the interior of the graveyard is rendered a place belonging to some other, liminal kingdom. Tombstones and funereal statuary loom into view as Bram and Lilith pass them. Droplets of the water-laden night air have frozen onto the needles, twigs, and branches of the many yew trees, so that they appear to have grown gray and whiskery with age. Flowers placed at headstones have likewise acquired a patina of ice that will have chilled the life from them by morning. The distortion of all sounds pulls out of shape even the screech of an unseen owl that protests at the unfamiliar presence of people at such an hour. Bram detects movement off to his left and fights revulsion at two squabbling rats which have dug a tunnel beneath the broken lid of a neglected mausoleum. It is only when Lilith bids him stand beside a grave on the far side of an immense cedar tree that Bram recognizes the place as the very spot where he first laid eyes on Lilith.

How transformed the cemetery is. From the sun-filled garden of remembrance I recall it was on the day of her father's funeral, to this . . . this unearthly realm of the dead.

Lilith turns to him now.

"I told you, darling Bram, that I am a witch who speaks to spirits."

"Is this where you come to do so?"

"No. Ordinarily, no." She pauses, choosing her words with great care, then continues. "Do you remember, the other night, I was . . . I was afraid? You saw that I was."

"I cannot forget it. You seemed terrified."

"I had been visited by a spirit. Not one I had called or summoned. One that sought me out."

"Does that happen often, to . . . people such as you?"

She shakes her head. "Mercifully, almost never. The spirits answer our call. They are not welcome to assail our thoughts whenever they choose. Most would not think of doing so. But this spirit . . . he comes at the behest of someone else."

"Someone else? Someone living, do you mean?"

"Yes."

"A witch?"

"No. That is, not exactly. Oh, I am sorry." She shakes her head in frustration. "I am explaining this terribly badly. There is so much you do not know. There is no good place to start, no easy way to tell you what I must. And I would not have dreamed of speaking of so many aspects of my life as a witch, or of necromancy, or any of this, but . . ."

"But?"

She raises her eyes to meet his and he is shocked to see they are filled with tears.

"Bram, you are in danger. I have put you in such dreadful danger."

"You have? I don't believe it."

"It is because of me . . . because of the Dark Spirit who haunts me. He wants something from me. Something I can never give to him. He wants it for the masters who have summoned him and who are using him to weaken me. And he . . . he knows how I care for you. He has found my weakness. He means to threaten you, at the very least . . ." Her voice falters and she leaves the thought incomplete, looking away. "I should never have let you get close to me. It is because of me that this awful creature now aims to turn his vile strength on you! I should not have allowed myself to care for you, nor you to care for me. I will only bring you pain and confusion and . . ."

Bram takes hold of her shoulders and speaks calmly and firmly, even though he feels unnerved by the atmosphere of the churchyard and by what Lilith is telling him.

"Now you listen to me," he says. "I don't care who threatens me, be he man or ghost or . . . anything, or anyone. I will not be driven away from you by threats. I will not leave you to face this . . . monster on your own. Lilith, look at me."

She looks, blinking away tears, and sees the warmth in his eyes. The longing. The passion.

"I love you, Lilith. Just let this fiend try and come between us. Just let him try!"

She straightens her shoulders and sets her jaw. "You're right. I'm being ridiculously emotional. I brought you here to try to explain how I am going to keep you safe, and instead I end up sobbing like some silly schoolgirl. Don't worry. I shan't cry again."

"I'm very glad to hear it. Your tears would freeze to your beautiful face in this fearsome weather." He indicates the inscription on the headstone in front of them. "This is your father's grave. Why did you choose to bring me here?"

Lilith says simply, "Because I want you to meet him."

She takes a step forward. Holding her arms wide, she closes her eyes, and Bram sees her lips move as if she is praying or reciting some well-practiced words. The hairs on his neck stand as a shiver descends his spine.

Is such a thing truly possible? Am I to see someone brought back from the dead to talk to us?

He watches in silence, unable to hear what she is saying, but all too conscious of the shift in the atmosphere around them. The night-dwelling animals and birds cease their fidgeting and fall quiet. Even the fog itself appears to stop its lurching movements. The temperature drops suddenly, several degrees. He begins to tremble and has to make a conscious effort not to allow his teeth to start chattering.

Lilith lets her arms fall by her sides and opens her eyes. She stands still as the stone angel beneath the cedar tree, the eerie half-light robbing her face of all color, save for the sharp green of her irises.

She looks more exquisite, more splendid, yet more fragile and ethereal, than I have ever seen her.

For a long moment nothing happens, and then, slowly at first, but with increasing speed, the fog begins to shift in unnatural patterns. As Bram watches, the misty air appears to pulsate, taking on this form and that shape, until at last a figure steps from it. A tall, lean man, with angular features, whose stern face is softened by the expression he wears as he greets his daughter.

"Lilith!" His voice is clear but breathy. He bows low, formally, adding, "Or rather, Morningstar."

"Papa!" Lilith cannot hide her happiness at seeing him, though Bram can see she is doing her utmost to remain in control of her feelings. He knows little enough about what her coven requires of her or how such things work, but he knows her sufficiently well to feel her reticence, her hesitation. She gives him the feeling that she is doing something of which her father will not approve.

"Father, thank you for answering my call."

"I would never refuse a Lazarus Head Witch. Nor would I refuse my daughter."

"It is as your daughter that I come here today," she says. And Bram sees in her expression the truth of this. It has clearly cost her to seek her father's help. Knowing her as he now does, he can only imagine how hard it must be for her to admit she is in a situation she considers beyond her.

How dearly she must have wanted to prove herself. To him. To me? To herself, certainly.

"I have not come alone," Lilith explains. She beckons to Bram and he steps forward.

Could a man ever have imagined such a strange introduction to the father of the woman he loves?

At once, the late duke's demeanor alters dramatically.

"A non-witch! You have brought a non-witch to witness a calling? You clearly summoned me to reveal myself, knowing that I would be seen! What madness is this? To go against the coven creed . . . !"

"Forgive me, I know . . ."

"Then you also know you have broken your vows. Not only as a witch but as *Head* Witch! How can I have failed so completely in preparing you for your inheritance?"

"Father, this is Bram Cardale. He is the man I love."

"Love!" The duke is so enraged his spirit grows and shifts, losing definition one moment, forming a darker figure the next, pacing this way and that in agitation. "I do not wish to hear of some girlish infatuation! How could you, daughter? How could you throw up all that I have taught you, all that you must know to be right, for some romantic nonsense . . . ?"

"You don't understand, Father."

"Don't I? Do you seriously imagine there was never a moment when I did not yearn to share with my own wife the truth about myself? About our *children*?"

"This is different."

"No. No, this is you being foolish. You have thrown away all that you were destined to be for some notion of love. And what of Louis?"

"I . . . I cannot marry Louis." Before her father can respond to this, Lilith presses on. "Father, I know I have disappointed you, but I came here for your help. I am being haunted by a Dark Spirit. He has threatened Bram. Because of me, Bram is in great danger."

"What better illustration of the hopelessness of your . . . *connection* with a non-witch could there be? Tell me? How can he protect himself? How can you protect him? Do you expect me to do it? You overestimate the ability a spirit has to intervene in matters taking place in the Land of Day."

"But you could warn us, you could watch over him . . ."

"If you are truly being pursued by a spirit from the Darkness there is little I can do."

"There is more . . . the Dark Spirit does not come to me of his own accord. He acts for another."

On hearing this, the duke is silent for a moment. He appears calmer. Calmer and yet more concerned.

"The Sentinels," he says levelly.

"You spoke of your fears before you died, Father. You were right. They are moving against the coven, determined to claim the Elixir as their own."

The duke regards Bram coldly. "Well, Lilith, it seems you have provided them with a very useful means of getting it."

"I will never give it to them! I would never reveal the Great Secret, not to anyone, least of all a Sentinel."

"Would you not? No matter whom they threatened? Would you sacrifice your precious lover, Lilith, and remain true to the coven? Your conduct so far would suggest otherwise."

"Must it be a choice, Father? Must I be made to give up one to serve the other? Is there no other way?"

The duke looks at his daughter's anguished face and then looks away again.

"You are not the first to be faced with such a decision. If the coven is, as you say, under threat from the Sentinels, your first, your *only* concern must be the protection of the Lazarus Elixir. You know that. Personal happiness is a luxury, and you would have it only at the expense of the coven. That cannot happen." For the first time he addresses Bram. "Young man, if you love my daughter, you will let her go. You cannot help her. The Dark Spirit will not harm you if you are no longer involved with Lilith. Take yourself away from her, away from London. If you have no future contact with her, you will be safe. And she will be free to do her duty."

Having spoken his mind, he turns his back on Bram, preparing to remonstrate further with his daughter.

But Bram has heard enough.

"No, sir, I will not."

"What's that you say?" The duke of Radnor is not accustomed to being defied, either in life or in death.

Bram can feel ice forming on his hair and is conscious of his shabby clothes and unkempt appearance. He is conscious that his accent gives away his heritage, that his clothes mark him out as a man of small means, that he is not, in so many ways, a person the duke would have ever considered suitable for his daughter. Such opinions, however, no longer matter to Bram.

"I will not abandon Lilith. She is everything to me. I love her . . ."

"There is more to love than pretty words and kisses!"

"Indeed there is. There is loyalty. You may choose to refuse her request for help; that might be your understanding of love. I will stand by her, whatever the dangers. Oh, I don't pretend to know about your coven, or your creed, or even what is happening right this minute. A man could lose his mind were he to think of it too hard and too long. But just because I cannot make sense of it does not mean I am not fit to help Lilith. We will stand together and I will do whatever it takes to keep her safe and to enable her to fulfill her duty. Because it matters to her. I will not be dismissed like some servant found wanting. I will not be scared off. I am a part of your daughter's life now, sir, whether it suits you or not." He steps close to Lilith and takes her hand in his.

"Please, Papa . . ." she whispers.

The duke shakes his head. "It seems to me you have already made your choice, daughter," he says. And in an instant, he is gone, and Bram and Lilith stand alone at the graveside once more.

15.

The feast of Yulemass is quickly upon us. The chambers beneath Number One Fitzroy Square are abuzz with activity and expectation. As witches gather to celebrate, we assemble in the antechamber. The celebration of Yulemass traditionally begins with a sociable mingling. Some of the minor witches have set out the refreshments which are customarily simple: cheeses, rustic bread, spicy pickles, and fruit. There is also sufficient red wine intended to relax, but not to inebriate. Tonight is the Eve of Midwinter, an occasion where the coven meets to reinforce the bonds of brother- and sisterhood, and later to call a spirit as a group and to question the soul that presents itself on all manner of subjects. This is the year's longest night, when the hours of darkness are greater than those of daylight, and those who have crossed the Rubicon are most active and eager to make contact. All coven members who are able attend, without masks, to celebrate the continuation of the Lazarus Coven, the successful protection of the Great Secret, and the privilege and wonder of being able to commune with the dead. It is a joyous event, albeit one that has, in the past, resulted in momentous portents. For the midwinter Yulemass is very much under the control of the spirits, not of the necromancers, and in this it is a singular and important event in the witches' calendar. Mindful of this Druscilla and I have gone to some trouble to build up a layer of protective magic around the

Great Chamber. We do not want the Dark Spirit of Edmund Willoughby joining us tonight, under any circumstances.

After I took Bram to the cemetery, after Father refused to help us, Bram and I sat up in his rooms until dawn. His unswerving support, the calm way in which he accepted my father's appearance at the graveside, the way he stood up to my father, all have endeared him to me even further. For hour upon hour he asked me questions and I did my best to answer them. Poor darling, his head must have been filled with so many disturbing and incredible things by the time the morning light alerted us to the beginning of a new day. But, in order to keep him safe, he must know. He must come to understand as much as possible about the coven. About what it is we do. About what I am. My heart still constricts when I recall Father's disappointment in me, his anger at what I have done. All my life I have sought to please him, and now I have broken his heart. I must prove to him that Bram is worthy of my trust. And the first part of that proof will be my ability to face the Dark Spirit. I will keep Bram safe. I will protect the Elixir from the Sentinels, and whomever they send. Perhaps then my father will forgive me.

Iago and I arrived early for the gathering. This is a rare time when I am not expected to wear my Robe of Office, or even my witch's cloak, but may dress how I please. I have chosen one of my new black gowns, the dressiest of those bought at Mrs. Morell's shop. It is made of the softest velvet, cut to fall in gathered sweeps to my ankles, and to move sinuously against my body as I walk. The darkness and heaviness of the fabric are relieved by sections of lace capping the short sleeves at my shoulders, with more lace from the low-cut bustline up to a high collar. It is the most glamorous garment I have worn in months, and I admit to feeling special in it. I felt such sadness at not having Violet with me as I dressed for the evening. She always enjoyed Yulemass, and we shared so many of them together. I have tried to call her, to summon her spirit, but without success. Druscilla attempted to help me, but we can detect no trace of her. She is hidden from us, I know it, deliberately kept from us. And there is nothing I can do. I tried to think what she would have liked me to wear, and chose a long, slender twist of gold. It is a necklace my father gave me, a piece of witch's jewelry, quite outlandish and heavy, and really unsuitable for wearing anywhere other than at a coven meeting. The sleek golden rope loops three times around my neck, falling in long loose loops past my waist, with its intricate links causing it to both shimmer and shift as I move. I selected black lace gloves which stop just above the elbow, so that the only flesh visible—aside from that glimpsed through the pattern of the lace—is a short stretch of my upper arms. I had Alice do my hair for me. I had given her to believe that I was going out to a small private party. The lie served while she worked, but I cast a gentle spell of forgetting as she left my bedroom. She is a pleasant enough girl, and an able maid, but I cannot trust her not to talk below stairs, and my dressing in such a way while in mourning would make tongues wag. She piled my hair high upon my head, sleek and sophisticated, securing it with a gold dragonfly tiara. When I looked at my reflection in the mirror I felt, for the first time, that I truly am the Head Witch of this coven.

"Morningstar, my dear." The slightly wheezing voice of Lord Grimes, Master of the Chalice and most loyal of Father's friends, makes me turn. We embrace warmly. I am aware my position would be far more tenuous had I not the unquestioning support of such witches.

"Master of the Chalice, welcome. It is good to see you."

"You look divine, child. Your father would be so proud. Might he appear to us tonight, do you suppose?" he asks, taking the goblet of wine one of the minor witches is offering him with a nod of thanks.

I am careful not to let my sorrow show, for I know very well my father will not appear to us. "Tonight it is not we who will decide who comes," I remind him.

"Of course, you are right, and oh, isn't that the beauty of Yulemass? I do so enjoy the element of surprise. Over the years there have been some wonderful communications, you know? Truly astonishing. My goodness," he says, sipping his wine, "this is splendid. I'm not sure Lord Robert would have selected such quality."

"Of course he would. He always wanted the best for his fellow witches."

"Naturally, but . . . hmm"—he drinks some more—"I think I would have been more selfish and kept such a vintage for myself. Ah, the earl of Winchester approaches. He will no doubt be anxious to offer you his support, as Head Witch and as someone soon to be a member of his family, eh?"

I wince at the reminder that I have not yet had the courage to face Louis and break off our engagement. It has suited my cowardice that he has chosen to stay in the country for now. He writes to me often, and tells me how he misses me. My letters to him are somewhat stiff and say nothing of any importance. He must surely detect the lack of warmth in my words.

The earl stands before us now, every bit as handsome as his son, perhaps lacking the viscount's youthful vigor, but easily making up for it with the gravitas and charisma of maturity. He bows low.

"Morningstar—how brightly you shine this evening."

"Welcome to Yulemass."

He drops his voice. "Druscilla tells me you and she have taken measures to ensure there will not be any . . . unwelcome visitors tonight."

"Indeed."

"I am eager to learn what else you have done in regard to the matter of the Dark Spirit."

"Else?"

"As Head Witch you cannot be content to simply ward off a being who is in the employ of the Sentinels. Have you formulated a plan? I confess, I had expected to hear from you sooner. Another meeting of the senior witches needs to be called . . ."

"Rest assured, nothing is more pressing in my mind than the Sentinels. However, I do not believe this is the occasion to discuss the matter."

"But the matter is gravely serious . . ."

"And it is precisely for that reason that I will not talk of it further during Yulemass festivities. Believe me, Lord Harcourt, nothing occupies my mind more, and I will not trivialize the business of the Sentinels' threat by conversing about it in whispers and snatches."

Without giving him the opportunity to press me further I slip away into the crowd.

Already the claret is starting to work its own unique magic and the antechamber is filled with the buzz of relaxed banter and chat. Druscilla and I share a brief embrace, and I am thankful for her strong presence and her continued guidance regarding the Dark Spirit. Victoria Faircroft is dressed even more flamboyantly than usual and is flirting with Lord Grimes. Many present have known each other much of their lives. Meaningful friendships, true bonds, and alliances have been formed over the years. We are a strong coven, and I am, at this moment, so proud to be even a small part of it, let alone its Head Witch.

At last it is time to move into the Great Chamber. As always I experience a powerful combination of excitement and affection as I enter our sacred space. The chamber is bedecked with silvery birch and glossy holly twisted into wreaths and swags. There are three times as many candles in the sconces and stands, so that light dances across the painted floor and flashes off the jewels worn by the gathered witches. Everyone finds a place to sit on the benches around the circle. The senior witches take their places on seats placed in front of the high altar, facing the sacred space. As Head Witch my position is on the middle chair in this row. I feel a nervous tension grip me as the torches are dimmed in their sconces, so that a low, flickering light fills the room. We all stand to recite the Lazarus creed and to say our necromancers' prayer. Repeating the ancient words together, hearing their singular rhythm throb through the chamber like its very heart is both stirring and comforting. However archaic our rituals, however morbid our practices, however close to the darkness we venture in our journeys to the Land of Night, this is a part of me. This is familiar, and real, and powerful, all at once. This is what I was, after all, born to do. The central focus of Yulemass is the joint communing with a spirit, called forth specifically to tell us what he or she sees for the future of our coven. The Master of the Chalice is charged with this summoning, rather than myself. This leaves the Head Witch freer to question whoever appears before us than if I were engaged in the calling.

A respectful silence falls as the sacred words are spoken.

The air thickens slightly, as if some mysterious new ingredient has been added to it. There is a curious taste in my mouth, too. This is not uncommon. Sometimes the flavor can be quite revolting, which is off-putting, but on this occasion I detect sugar. No, something sweeter, if that is possible. Honey, I believe. Next, faintly at first, comes the sound of singing. It is a high, pure voice, and as it grows stronger a figure takes shape within the circle. The blurred outline of a girl slowly grows stronger and clearer, until we can all see her standing before us. She could have been no more than sixteen when she died, and is dressed in a pretty lace cotton dress of palest blue. It can be hard to determine the time from which the spirit comes, but by the style of her clothes and the way her hair is curled, I estimate she trod the earth some two hundred years ago.

"Welcome, little sister," I say, standing to greet her, giving her what I hope she can see is a warm smile. She looks quite sad. And why would she not? What must have happened for her to die so young? I want to ask her, and to comfort her, but this is not the way things are done. We are taught to keep our feelings in check when conversing with the deceased. We must not make the contact personal. This is not only to maintain a professional detachment, it is for the protection of the spirit, as well as for our own protection. A close personal connection could prove dangerous. There are well-documented incidents of what can happen when a necromancer crosses that particular line. All young witches who practice necromancy are told these stories as cautionary tales. My father recounted the time, when he was himself a minor witch, learning his craft, and he had been present at a calling. The coven had convened to consult on the matter of succession, as the recently departed Head Witch had left no heir. The aim had been to call a reliably wise and insightful spirit, one who had helped them before, and to, in effect, give this guide the casting vote in the selection of a new leader. No one could have foreseen what would happen that night. It transpired that one of the senior witches, a woman with a dramatic nature, had grown close to another spirit guide. To say that they were lovers would be incorrect, as, of course, the visiting deceased had no physical form through which to express affection or desire, though he may well have felt both. But there had indeed developed a relationship that was intense and exclusive. And, it turned out, lethal. The lovelorn spirit had appeared in the circle during the meeting, highly emotional, and bewailing the fact that the witch had begun to spurn him and had, he knew, taken an earth-treading lover. He was enraged and distraught, and, not unnaturally, the witch in question sought to calm him. In doing so, she stepped into the circle. In an instant the spirit changed from pathetic to demonic. The truth was then revealed. He had gone into the darkness and gained powerful black magic to enable him to exact his revenge. Before anyone could prevent it, he grabbed the witch and took her down with him into the darkness. She was never seen again. The coven members made strenuous and sustained attempts to find her, to call her or her demon lover back, but she never answered.

The girl now standing in the circle has clearly never stepped into the darkness, even though she has dwelled in the Land of Night for two centuries. She looks about her with curiosity and a little awe, but is not frightened. I notice she is holding some flowers in her hand. Small blue ones with yellow centers that I believe to be forget-me-nots.

"You are welcome, my dear," I tell her. "Thank you for answering the call. We are the Lazarus Coven, and we seek only to ask your guidance. Please know that you are safe here, and that we will do nothing to put you in harm's way, nor to prevent you from returning to your rightful home when the time comes. What is your name?"

The girl looks at me for a moment with wide blue eyes and then starts to slowly walk around the circle, looking out at the faces that peer back at her. "Amelia," she says in a childish voice, before returning to singing the little song she had begun earlier. She certainly seems at ease in the chamber, and, although surprised, is not perplexed about being called. It never fails to astonish me how young some spirit guides are. Children sometimes answer our calling. The gift of foresight which the dead receive when they arrive in the Land of Night does not discriminate between infants and adults. All are given the ability to look into the future of those still left in the Land of Day. What differs is the individual's skill in clearly explaining what they see. Added to which, being human, however altered, spirits can be, on occasion, capricious, or even spiteful. It is their knowledge, after all, their gift. Not all of them want to share it. Some even allow themselves to be called with the express purpose of wielding their power, enjoying a position of influence and respect which they may never have had while living.

It is the job of the necromancer to elicit the truth from a visiting soul. It is not always easy.

"That's a pretty name," I say. "And those are very pretty flowers."

She nods, looking at the blooms in her hands and stroking the petals thoughtfully. "I picked them myself," she tells us. "From Grandmama's garden. Such a sunny day. I miss the sun so."

She seems so fragile, so delicate. I must treat her carefully.

"We have come together to celebrate Yulemass."

"I do not care for midwinter. Nothing grows in the garden at midwinter."

I want to ask her if she has a garden of sorts in her home on the other side of the Rubicon, but I know I must not. We are not allowed to question spirits about the Land of Night. If they choose to tell us, all well and good, but our purpose is not to delve into the mysteries of that existence. We are concerned with helping and protecting the living.

"Amelia, we feel we are in a time of great change. Will you help us? Will you tell us what challenges lie ahead, so that we can be better prepared to face them?"

"Everything is changing," she says, still pacing slowly around and around in the circle, still playing with her flowers. "Everything."

A senior member of the coven raises his hand for permission to ask a question and I nod my consent.

"Child, some here believe war is coming. That it cannot be stopped. Do you see it? Will there be war?" he asks. The quality of the silence in the chamber changes perceptibly. Many feel they know the answer to this grave question. None of us truly wants to hear it.

"Oh yes," Amelia tells us. "There is going to be a war. A very big war. Lots and lots of people will die."

"How many?" Another of the senior witches cannot contain himself and asks the impossible question without seeking permission. I frown at him. This is too specific. He sees my expression and tries to make it easier for the girl to respond. "Hundreds, d'you think? Thousands?"

Amelia shakes her head sadly. "Oh no," she says. "Millions will die." Before we have a chance to react to such a statement she goes on. "So many young men. Boys, really. Poor, poor boys, lying and dying in the mud. No good air to breathe their last breath with. Sinking in the stinking mud." The terrible words sound somehow so much more dreadful spoken in her soft, singsong little voice. Suddenly she looks up at one of the minor witches and points a thin, white finger at him. "Your son will die!" she declares. There is a collective gasp of horror at this and the witch clutches at his heart. Amelia wheels about now, pointing here, there, everywhere, singling out witch after witch after witch. "And yours! And yours! And your son, too. And yours, and yours . . . !" On and on she goes, causing shock and despair throughout the chamber.

I try to follow her gaze, to see exactly whom she has picked out. She moves at such speed and finds so many to tell it is hard to discern them all, though each who has been selected knows it. And, as he is seated next to me, I know I am not mistaken when she singles out Lord Harcourt.

"And your beautiful boy, too. He will be among the first to die."

Louis! I turn back to the earl. To hear of the impending death of a loved one is surely the greatest terror of all who speak to spirits. The man is impressively still and silent, bearing whatever pain and terror he feels without the least outward sign of it, as he has been brought up to do.

"Amelia!" I call to her, gently but firmly. I must stop this dreadful roll call of doom and gain something from her that might be of use. She stops and turns to look at me, cocking her head. "I know this must be hard for you," I say, "but we are grateful, truly we are, for your insight. Nothing is foretold that cannot be changed if we are prepared to try." I have to believe this. All necromancers must, else what is the point of our art? Would there really be anything to be gained simply by being informed of the imminence of death?

"You cannot stop the war. It is coming, whether you will it or no."

"That may be, but we can lessen the horrors it will bring. We can shorten the duration by our actions, perhaps. We can advise the men in power so that the worst, the terrible outcome you describe, might be averted. Can you help us, Amelia? Can you tell us who we should speak with?" I know that if she has, as she claims, foreseen such details as the deaths of the families of some present here, she must also be able to see who controls the armies, who makes the decisions, who should be pleaded or bargained with. Who must be stopped, whatever it takes.

Amelia thinks for a moment. "I might know," she says. "But why should I tell? What will you give me if I tell? Will you let me feel the sun on my face again?"

"I'm sorry, my dear." The Master of the Chalice steps in gently. "It is not in our gift to do such a thing."

She looks at him sulkily. "But I want so to sit in the garden once more."

"You are welcome to visit my garden," I tell her.

"But only like this." She stamps her foot. "Like a ghost. I want to feel warm again. To smell the flowers."

"Amelia . . ." I try to comfort her, I want to. For her own sake, as well as ours. But she is upset now, and does not want to listen.

"Then I shan't!" she says crossly. "I shan't help you." She scowls at me now. "Especially you! You are the one they want. You could save those boys. You know you could."

"Amelia, I could not . . ."

"Yes you could, if you wanted to. And they will make you do it. They will take you away and make you do it!" she shouts.

There is consternation in the chamber now. None of us can know exactly what she means, but it is clear her vision involves me and my abilities as a necromancer.

"Who will take her?" the Master of the Chalice demands of the girl. "Who is it who threatens our Head Witch?"

"I'm not going to tell you. I don't want to. I . . ." She stops suddenly and glances anxiously about her, over her shoulder, searching above her head and then behind her. All at once she has become terribly frightened.

"What is it, child?" the Master of the Chalice asks her. "Do not be afraid."

"I can hear them!" she cries. "Oh! Can't you hear them?" She begins to run now, and even tries to jump out of the circle. When she finds she is unable to do so tears of terror stream down her pale cheeks. "Oh no!" she cries.

Now I hear them, too. We all do. Bees. In seconds, dozens of them have come up from below and joined the girl in the circle. She flaps her arms and hands, batting them away with her flowers, screaming. The smell of honey grows stronger. Now I understand. Now I see the curious mark on her top lip, which I had taken for a mole or birthmark but which must have been the bee sting that killed her. And here we have brought her into a confined space and now it is filled with the greatest fear she has ever known.

"Send her back!" I hiss at the Master of the Chalice.

The earl of Winchester objects. "No! We must hear more."

"She must go back."

The earl is on his feet now. "We need to know more. She has given us nothing!"

"She is terrified," I tell him. "She is suffering. She will tell us nothing further now."

Amelia is on the floor of the circle, desperately trying to cover her head and her face, to protect herself from the bees.

"I don't understand," says the Master of the Chalice. "How did the bees come through? We did not call them."

"Send her back now!" I shout at him.

He nods and quickly chants the necessary words. He does so with skill and speed, but even so it seems an age before Amelia begins to fade before our eyes, the sound of her cries growing ever more faint, until all that remains is the echo of the buzzing bees as they, too, vanish.

The chamber is in commotion. Those who were spoken to are in shock and others seek to console them. Some start talking animatedly of what action should be taken, and how soon we might call another spirit who could help us. They are all so shaken by what has happened that few among them seem to hear what I can hear. A low, distant voice. A whisper almost. Or rather, a strong voice, but far away, slowly growing stronger, coming nearer. Now I can see, in the center of the sacred circle, a shimmering shape, the beginnings of a figure, starting to take form. How can this be? We have neither called nor summoned anyone further. The crossing is strongly protected by our own magic, so that the uninvited shall not enter the Land of Day.

And yet the bees came. The bees got through. Someone, or something, enabled them to do so. Someone, or something, who knew what they meant to Amelia. Who knew what they would do. But why? Why torment the girl? Why, if not to prevent her from helping us?

Which can only mean that malevolent forces are at work here.

Self-serving, dangerous, wicked forces. The protective magic Druscilla and I worked so hard to place about the chamber was not sufficient. And now a powerful force is materializing as I watch, and I know that I am once again in the presence of the wicked spirit of Edmund Willoughby. Only this time he is not content to pursue me only in voice. This time, he plans to show himself. The figure is not yet sufficiently formed to have human features, but it is without doubt a tall, thickset man. And I can hear the words he speaks more clearly. Or rather, the word. One word, over and over and over.

Lilith! Lilith! Lilith!

I step as close to the edge of the circle as I can without touching it and raise my hand. Some of the senior witches are aware of the spirit's presence, but without pausing to confer with anyone else, without arming myself with the grimoire or Maygor's Silver Thread or anything that might protect me, I send a spell of banishment as boldly as I am able.

"You may not enter here!" I tell the fearsome spirit that chants my own name. "You are not welcome. You are not wanted. You were not called. You were not summoned. Return from whence you came!"

The voice twists into a loud hiss. The figure dissolves and is gone. The circle is empty once more. I find I am holding my breath. I release it, and gulp steadying air. As I turn away from the circle I find the earl of Winchester watching me, his face dark, his eyes full of tears.

16.

Bram realizes his defenses against the winter weather are inadequate when he finds a small drift of snow on the floor in his room.
The wind has dislodged the newspaper and clothing scraps he used
to stop up the holes in the roof, and thin, dry flakes have been
falling all night. He climbs out of bed, stumbling about in the
half light of the December dawn. He has taken to sleeping in his
clothes, with a woolen hat jammed onto his head, and two pairs
of socks to prevent his toes being numb by morning. Even so, he
quickly shrugs on his coat. Rubbing his hands together, he casts
about for matches and then stoops to strike one and set it to the
wick of the paraffin stove. He has scant fuel left, and is eking it
out as best he can. The money from Charlotte's portrait will not
last long, though at least he has an appointment at the end of the
week with another prospective client. A Mrs. Wilding has twin
daughters who wish to be painted together as a birthday present
for their father. They have agreed on a price for the work, and he
is to paint them at their home.

At least I shall be warm there, he thinks, *even if it means I must
trudge across London four times a week until the portrait is finished.*

He reaches out and touches the canvas. The paint is still sticky.
A freezing space with air damp from the stove is a poor environ-
ment in which to attempt to work with oils. The moisture in the
air means the painting takes forever to properly dry, so that he has
to wait many hours, sometimes days between sessions. The low

temperatures mean the paint all but freezes in the tubes and is difficult to mix, but at least his new stove has gone some way to remedying this. He has chosen to depict Lilith using a limited palette of muted browns and blues. The effect is dramatic, if slightly somber. And somehow mysterious.

The thought of not seeing her, of there coming a time when she might disappear out of his life completely, causes him real physical pain.

Footsteps on the stairs shake him from his thoughts. There is a knock at the door and, without waiting for a reply, Gudrun lets herself in. She has two cups coffee on a small tray and a cigarette between her teeth. Bram takes one of the drinks from her, wrapping his fingers around it gratefully, sniffing brandy in the steam.

"I heard you stamping about up here," she tells him. "It is as if I am living beneath an elephant."

"Did I wake you? I'm sorry."

She shakes her head. "Who could truly dare sleep in this cold? We might never wake up." She saunters over to the easel. "Ah, your little *liebling*. Very good, Artist. Really, it is very good. You have found your muse at last."

"Oh, I think she will only let me paint her once."

"Pity. She stirs something in you." She gives him a blatantly vulgar glance which, much to his annoyance, causes Bram to blush. "So, you have not yet taken her into your narrow little bed."

"I don't see that is any of your business."

"Don't be such a prude. In this house everything is everybody's business."

"Perhaps I prefer to keep some things private."

"Why?" She shakes her head, genuinely baffled by this. "Do you think your sex life is so very different from anyone else's? What do you think Mangan is doing to me when you hear him roaring in the night, hmm? What is he doing with Jane, on the days when she can be bothered to care? How do you think the house came to be full of children?" She folds her arms, still smoking, sighing at him. "You English make too much fuss about sex, anyway. How long are you going to go on torturing yourself with Beauty? What are you waiting for? She's never going to marry you."

Bram frowns now and looks away from her, contemplating his feet.

"You surely do not think this?" Gudrun laughs flatly. "My God, Artist, you do! You think Lady Lilith, daughter of a duke, who has ridiculous amounts of money and could marry a prince if she wanted to . . . you think she is going to marry you?" She laughs again. "Has she even broken off her engagement to that handsome viscount of hers? I have not read of it in the paper."

"If you've just come up here to mock us, mock me, you can take your nasty coffee and leave."

"Oh, I have hurt your feelings. Forgive me, Artist. I grow cynical. Why shouldn't she marry you? Why not marry for love? There is plenty of space in here, after all. Jane can help look after your beautiful artist babies. And Mangan won't mind, though of course he will expect you to share her with him. Do you think Beauty would like that? Some highborn ladies find the wild man exciting. Perhaps yours is no different."

Bram has never in his life wanted to hit a woman, but he knows he is as close to doing so now as he will ever come.

"Get out," he says.

Gurdun shrugs, drops her cigarette butt to the floor, and grinds it out with her heel.

"I'll go," she says. "I'll leave you to your dream of love in a perfect world." She pauses as she passes him. "Just don't leave it too long to enjoy her, Artist, or you may miss your chance. Because one day she won't come knocking on your door anymore, and it will be because she has married some dusty, dry aristocrat with a big house and a grand title. Still, there is always, as you

English with your relentless optimism will say, the lining of silver in the cloud." She smiles at him from the doorway. "An artist always does his best work when his heart is broken. You will see."

🕷

We passed a dreary Christmas at Fitzroy Square. Father's absence was all the more painful for the memories of happy times gone by. Against all odds I persuaded Freddie to stay at Radnor Hall, so it was just Mama and I who sat down to a Christmas day meal for which neither of us had any appetite. For the sake of the servants, we observed the traditions the house ordinarily followed for the festive season, though of course these were muted by our status of mourning. Mama was reluctant to take part in anything, but I convinced her that the staff should not be done down. Duty, as always for someone of my parents' generation, is the clarion call to arms. Christmas Eve saw her giving out small gifts beneath the exquisitely bedecked tree in the hall. Together we attended a service at St. Bartholomew's on the Strand at midnight. She was even persuaded to come to the door to listen to carol singers on one occasion. She and I knew, however, that such involvement did not necessarily reflect her own inner spirits, and we were both relieved when the festivities came to an end, the decorations were put away, and life in the house was allowed to return to its quiet winter rhythm once again.

Aside from fretting about Father and how he now thinks of me, and watching my mother struggle with the endlessness of her grief, the most difficult thing for me to bear has been separation from Bram. We have scarcely been able to meet at all these long, dark months. Mangan finished his sculpture of Charlotte in time for it to be presented to the Pilkington-Adamses by Christmas, so there has been no excuse for me to accompany her to the house in Bloomsbury. She has been stalwart in providing an alibi for us when she can, but since her mother decided to take the family to their Scottish estate for the New Year and has seen fit to keep her there, we are without our best ally. We write notes and letters, but must be careful that even these are not seen by Mama, who would set about asking all manner of questions. She would not approve of Bram. Indeed, I can think of no way of presenting him in a light that would make her look at him favorably. Any thought of the future casts me down, and my cowardly tactic for enduring this is simply not to think of it.

As if there were not obstacles enough in the path of our seeing each other, the events of Yulemass have complicated things still further. An emergency meeting was held, with only the senior witches present. It was decided that I should not be left at any time unguarded. I railed against such a decision, reasoning that I have my own guardian spirits who accompany me whenever I am out of the house. It is well known among coven members that I have an able and trustworthy escort in my Cavalier captains. But there is fear among my fellow witches now. The threat to me is unavoidably a threat to the security and perhaps even the continuation of the coven itself. Those who were singled out by Amelia for the dreadful prophecy of loss she brought with her are understandably anxious that we strengthen our position. Further spirits have already been called or summoned in an effort to gain more detailed information of what lies ahead, and of what might be done to change things. Sadly, we have found little comfort, for the consensus seems to be that war is inevitable. Amelia was, alas, right about this.

In addition, we have taken to holding regular meetings of the whole coven, in order to maintain and strengthen the bonds between witches, to cast and enforce spells of protection and incantations designed to alert us to danger. We have set up groups within the coven, working in rotation, undertaking frequent callings and summonings of spirits that may give assistance or comfort in these difficult times. Some are able to pass on specific, if fragmentary information about the forces that oppose us, whether Sentinels or foreign militia. Others suggest courses of action that might prove sensible, or warnings if certain members or their family are in particular peril. It seems our work as necromancers will become ever more important, both in the coming war abroad and our own, closer to our coven home.

The earl of Winchester has insisted one of his own guardian spirits, a fearsome Goth, accompany me when I am out after dark. This has horribly curtailed my movements. While I might persuade the spirit to wait outside Mangan's house, he still reports back to his master regarding my whereabouts. And the earl has taken it into his head that the closer Louis is to me, the safer he becomes. Indeed he has clearly been pressuring him to redouble his efforts to press me for a date to marry, and has insisted he return to London. Last time he called at the house I felt terrible, seeing how worried he is and knowing I can only add to his difficulties now. He looked so very frightened, and yet did his best to sound cheerful and brave, that my heart went out to him.

When I am trying to be sensible I wonder, could the earl be right, perhaps? Might it be that if Louis and I were to form such an alliance, a pairing of witches and a joining of two ancient families of necromancers, might he be saved? If that is the case, it could be seen as my duty to marry him. And how happy it would make Mama. But what of Bram? What of love? There are times when it seems I must consider everyone else before myself, and Bram barely at all. If I were Mama I would know exactly what to do. I would marry Louis.

And now at last winter is fading and we are beginning to emerge from its gloom into spring. Today Freddie is expected home. Part of me longs to have him here, but I am wary. From Withers's reports it seems he has been spending longer and longer time away from the hall. Who knows what he has been doing. I have sent a friendly spirit to watch over him, but it is a difficult task to do well. Freddie might not be a witch, but he is aware of our practices, and clever enough when it suits him. Over the years he has become quite adept at evading anyone Father or I have sent to guard him. After all, who are they guarding him from if not himself, and how can they possibly succeed in that?

The glorious early spring morning is too good to miss, Bram insists, and they cannot possibly pass it indoors. Besides, the portrait is finished. He is secretly delighted with it, and he senses that Lilith is, too. He knows he has captured the essence of her, and the muted hues he chose have worked better than he dared hope.

Winter has now fully relinquished its grip on London, and brave new life can be found forcing its way up from previously frozen flower beds, bare branches, and even between cobbles and paving slabs. Small birds flit to and fro gathering twigs and beakfuls of all manner of snatched materials for their nests. The sun is still low in the sky, and the days not yet lengthened into spring proper, but there is a sense of regeneration, of renewal, of hope. This rebirth of slumbering life has infected Bram with what he knows in his heart to be a misplaced optimism. He has even managed to persuade Lilith that they can venture out in public together for once.

The second he sees her slender figure standing by the entrance to the zoological gardens he knows the darkness of winter, of her time of mourning, of the most acute phase of her grief, all have passed. She is quite changed. Although still dressed in her sumptuous black woolen coat, she has chosen a hat of silver-gray, with matching gloves. He marvels at how such a tiny lifting, a minute step of barely a shade, can bring about such an alteration. Her complexion seems rosier, brighter, more alive.

For a brief moment she does not see him, so that he is free to enjoy watching her. As he does so he notices something curious.

Lilith takes out a handkerchief to dab at her dust-smarted eyes. As she is putting it back into her bag she drops it. It falls to the ground, and she stoops to pick it up, but she does not reach the ground. Instead, the small square of cotton and lace appears to rise up to meet her outstretched hand. Bram marvels at what it must be like to have magic as part of one's everyday life. At one's disposal for things both trivial and important.

And then she looks up and spies Bram, and her green eyes shine, and the smile with which she greets him warms his heart. As soon as she reaches him he snatches up her hand and presses it to his lips. For a moment they stand close, without speaking, desire fizzing between them. At last she pulls away.

"Come along," she says, smiling, "I want to visit the wolves."

They walk on past the aquarium, beyond the new Mappin Terrace with its bears and arctic animals, and to the very edge of the zoological gardens where a wooded area borders Regent's Park. Here a shaggy-pelted wolf pack have been given an unlikely home. Lilith loops her arm through Bram's, and they watch the lupine family stretch and yawn and stir themselves for a new day.

"They don't look at all savage," she says.

"That's because there is a sturdy fence between us and them."

"No, it's because they are never hungry. They don't have to hunt. Everything is given to them."

"I shouldn't imagine they mind. Look at that one, he's positively plump," Bram points to a black wolf lolling beneath a silver birch.

"It isn't right. They should be living wild, not in a park."

But Bram is not listening. He pulls away from her, his eyes wide, his expression stricken, as he feels the weight of a terrible coldness, a dreadful dark energy, enter his body.

"My God!" he cries, struggling for air. It is as if he is being crushed from within, his lungs pressed as though in the grasp of some unseen giant, his heart constricted, unable to beat as it should.

"Oh, Bram! What is it, what's the matter?" She gasps as Bram staggers backward, clutching at his head.

He opens his mouth to speak, to try to tell her of the fierce ringing inside his skull, of his fight to breathe, of the blackness descending upon him, but he can form no words, can make no sound.

I am dying! Dear Lord, my body surely cannot withstand . . .

"Bram! Listen to me. You must listen to me!"

Lilith kneels beside him as he slumps against the railings of the wolf enclosure. Behind the iron bars, the animals are suddenly awake, alert, pacing swiftly this way and that. Bram knows Lilith is talking, telling him something, but he is so very dizzy, in so much pain, it is hard to make out her words.

"It is the Dark Spirit. It is Willoughby. He caught us unawares, here, in daylight . . . I let down my guard. My darling, you must do what I tell you."

"Argh!" Bram screams as a stab of pain pierces his body.

How can this be?

"I can see no one!" he gasps. "I hear no voice."

"But I do. He is mocking me. He is . . . he is showing me what he is capable of. What he can do. What he will do if I refuse to give him what he wants."

"Give him . . . *nothing!*" Bram insists through clenched teeth.

"Stay awake, my darling! He is trying to manipulate your mind. You must not fall unconscious. The stronger you fight him, the better able I will be to send him from you."

Lilith leaps to her feet, oblivious to the anxious stares of passersby. A young man steps forward to offer his help, but she waves him away furiously, standing guard over Bram, trusting nobody. "Leave him be!" she cries. "He is not yours to inhabit. I command you, return to the Darkness where you belong and release this man from your grasp!"

The confused onlookers move back. They think Lilith is talking to them, and her words appear those of a madwoman. Bram knows different. He knows she is trying to control the Dark Spirit. He bends forward, clutching at his chest.

I will not be broken like some toy in this vicious game!

He forces himself upright, clinging to the railings. Behind him the black wolf also stands its ground, head low, hackles raised. He catches its eye as he hauls himself to his feet. Its teeth are bared and it emits a ferocious growl. It is the growl not of a hunter after its prey, but of an animal in terror.

Lilith has set up a chanting. The small collection of people nearby has thinned as men lead their women away from the lunatic and her ailing friend. Someone has summoned a keeper, but he stops short when he sees the wildness in Lilith's eyes as she holds her arms wide, her voice growing ever stronger and louder. Bram is aware that he has no breath left in his body, and if he does not take in air very soon, he will pass out. Try as he might he cannot force his chest to expand, cannot overcome the force that restricts him.

The gentle morning has been transformed into an atmosphere of turmoil, with an unnatural wind stirring up dust and whipping the branches of the nearby hazel bushes and birch trees. Lilith is shouting now, her words whisked away by the swirling gusts that snatch at her clothes. Her hat flies from her head, her hair is tugged from its pins, so that it billows out and tangles about her face. Bram sees she is giving her all, but that it might not be enough. His vision is beginning to blur and dim at the edges, and unconsciousness cannot be more than seconds away.

And then what? Then what?

He staggers along the iron fence, causing the black wolf to spring toward him, barking and snarling. He knows he must do something to stop himself from falling into that darkness. Summoning his last vestige of strength, he pushes his hand through the railings directly in front of the wolf. Instinctively, the animal lunges forward and sinks its teeth into Bram's flesh.

He screams. And that scream forces his reluctant, failing body to take a deep, life-giving gulp of air. Oxygen surges through him. And in that instant, when he is stronger, and Willoughby's hold is weakened, Lilith works her magic, and the spirit is sent spinning away. Far away.

In the time it takes a wood pigeon to alight on a nearby branch and cease its flapping, the normality of the March morning is restored. The wind disappears. Birds take up singing once more. The wolves, puzzled, lope off to find shade. The keeper inquires after Bram's health and, once reassured, returns Lilith's hat to her. Lilith takes it from him and swiftly works a spell of forgetting on the keeper and the startled onlookers. She may well have been recognized, and it would not do for gossip to spread and the incident to be reported in the newspapers. She and Bram hurry down the winding path away from the scene.

Bram pulls a handkerchief from his pocket and wraps it around his bleeding hand. He puts his arm around Lilith's shoulders partly to protect her, and partly because he fears his legs might just give way beneath him without her support. They find a bench at the far side of a picnic area. It is still sufficiently early in the day so that the place is empty, so that they will not be overheard. He sits down heavily, his hair falling in his face, willing his racing heart to steady itself once more. Beside him Lilith tenderly takes his wounded hand and examines the bite.

"It's nothing, really. I'll have Jane find me some iodine when we return to the house. What was that . . . *thing* trying to do?"

"To hurt you. To frighten you. To warn me."

"He certainly succeeded on the first two counts."

"Oh, Bram, forgive me, it's my fault. We are so far from the cemetery, or my home, and in a public place, in daytime . . . I never imagined Willoughby would be so bold, so reckless as to harm you here. I should have realized . . ."

"But, from what I recall, you told me the spirits are stronger at nighttime. That they cannot do a great deal alone, other than haunt and scare people, unless . . ."

"Unless they are being manipulated or assisted by someone in the Land of Day. Which is precisely what must have been taking place. The Sentinel was very close. I could feel him, as soon as he began to work through the Dark Spirit he revealed his presence."

"He was here? In the crowd?"

"Possibly. Or at least, here in the gardens."

"And he is here still?" Bram asks, looking about the flower beds and shrubbery, trying to imagine evil lurking unseen somewhere even now.

"He is not spellcasting or communing with a spirit, so he will be easily able to mask his presence."

"Good Lord, Lilith, he could be anywhere. He could be anyone."

"He could."

They fall silent for a while, before Bram shakes his head. "I need to walk. I can't sit still."

"Do you feel quite well?"

"My heart is leaping, but don't worry. I'm perfectly well."

"Your poor hand," she says, kissing his bandaged fingers gently.

"My left, fortunately, not my painting hand. It will heal soon enough."

Lilith moves forward and slips her arms around his waist, leaning against his warm, strong chest, putting her ear against his heart so that she might listen to its uneven rhythm. It is a gesture of such affection, such intimacy, here in the open, in this public place, that Bram feels tears sting his eyes. He blinks them away and turns to enfold her in his arms.

"Perhaps we should run away to a wild place," he says, contriving a smile. "Somewhere far away where no one knows us. Where we can just be Bram and Lilith, the disheveled painter and his beautiful muse."

"That would be wonderful," she agrees, but in the way a person does when they are entering into a fantasy, a dream, rather than putting a plan into action.

Bram steals a chaste kiss, meaning only to be tender, but she takes his face in her hands and holds him, returning his kiss with a passion that shocks him.

"Come away with me," she says.

"You have a tropical island in mind?"

"No, but I could take you to Radnor Hall."

"What?"

"To our estate in Radnorshire. I'm serious, my darling. Why not? There is nothing wrong with organizing a weekend party."

"Oh? And who else would you invite? I can't wait to hear who you think would find me suitable company. Keep in mind I've never shot anything and I cut a very poor figure on a horse. Nor have I ever attempted to pass myself off as a witch."

She shakes her head, laughing. "No one. That's the beauty of it. I wouldn't invite anyone else. There would just be you and me."

"And a modest crowd of servants."

"We only keep a small staff there while we are up in London, which is most of the time now. Mama prefers it here. I think she mainly tolerated the place for Father, and for us when we were children. She will not go there if she does not have to. Oh, Bram, do let's go! Even for a week. I think we would be safer there."

"Spirits can't travel?"

"They can, but whoever it is who is controlling this one would not know we were going until it is too late. A Sentinel must use a train or car like the rest of us. And if he were to follow us, he would not get within two miles of the house. The estate is large. We would be safer there, at least for a while. We could be just the two of us. Together."

He tries to take in the full implications of what she is telling him. The idea of having her to himself, day and night, is too marvelous to contemplate.

"But, we would have to come home . . . I shouldn't . . . compromise you, Lilith."

"Bram, look at me." She places her hands firmly on his shoulders, and her words are level and serious. "I am a grown woman. I can make up my own mind. I love you. I want to take you to Radnor Hall. After . . . after what has just happened . . . well, I refuse to think beyond that. If you don't want to . . ."

"I do!" He laughs.

"Then it's decided. I'll make the necessary arrangements. We can catch the train to Ludlow."

"And when we are there, will you tell me more? About what it is you do. I know how much it means to you, the coven, I want to understand. Will you tell me?"

"I will. I will tell you so much your head will spin and you will become bored of the very idea of witches and who they are and what they look like and how to spot them." She laughs, and is then quickly serious again. "We cannot risk things going on as they are, Bram. I have to find other ways to protect you. And I have to think about how I am to confront the Sentinels. Time away, with you, is what I need."

"When?" he wants to know, completely caught up in the idea now, pulling her tighter to him. "When is this wonderful, marvelous, incredible thing to happen?"

"Two weeks from now," she says. "After the Anstruthers' ball."

"After the ball," he echoes, smiling, and they stand there,

embracing, listening to the strange cries of creatures from far-away lands who don't belong but who have discovered a way of going on in the curious world in which they find themselves.

Later, alone in his bed that now seems unpleasantly empty without Lilith next to him, Bram chases sleep unsuccessfully. The idea of a week away with her, out of London, spared the interference of her mother or the many friends she has in the city who would, no doubt, be happy to tell Louis of his fiancée's interest in another man. It is beginning to worry Bram that she has not yet broken off the engagement. She has told him she is looking for the right moment, that she wants her brother home, that she has to find a reason and that it should not be Bram, that she wants to find a time that will not upset coven business. These last two bother him most. Surely, if they are to have a future together, she *should* tell Louis that she loves someone else, that she loves Bram. Is she ashamed of him, after all, despite the fact that she repeatedly tells him this is not the case? And what if her loyalty to the coven weakens her resolve to follow her heart? Louis is a witch, too, she has explained. They share, then, a very special bond.

One which I cannot hope to match.

He turns over, pulling the inadequate cover up to his chin. The cold is not helping in his quest for sleep. He decides he must have a hot drink and clambers out of bed, fumbling in the darkness for matches. He lights an oil lamp and then sees the kettle is empty. Cursing silently, he pushes his already socked feet into his shoes and heads for the kitchen. He descends the creaking flights of stairs as quietly as he can, mindful of the fact that it must be well past midnight and Jane would not thank him for waking any of the children. The house is silent and still, but when he reaches the hall he is surprised to hear low voices coming from Mangan's studio. He can make out the gruff tones of the artist himself, but does not recognize the second speaker.

Who would be calling at such a time? There is surely not sufficient light to view any artwork.

Curiosity overcomes him. He sets his lamp down on the bottom stair and walks carefully along the hallway to the doorless gap that leads through to the studio. He does not enter, but waits in the dusty shadows, listening. Peering through the gloom he can make out two figures, both seated by a surprisingly lively fire in the hearth, which gives off the only illumination. In the dancing light Bram sees Mangan, a glass of brandy in his hand, nodding as his visitor speaks. This second figure is short and broad and has a voice with a smile in it.

"My dear Mangan," he says, "I agree with you entirely upon this matter, but I am at a loss to know what else we can do."

"She is a strong-headed girl," Mangan points out. "She will not be easily restricted in her movements. Nor should she be. We must allow her to govern herself, surely."

"Indeed, but, well, she is young. She may not wish to admit to herself how much danger she is in. Morningstar's safety must be our main consideration."

Morningstar? Lilith's coven name! Why would this man know it? Why would he be discussing her position as Head Witch like this? Unless . . . unless he, too, is a witch!

Bram feels his blood pounding against his temples as realization dawns.

Unless both he and Mangan are witches!

The thought is so astonishing that he stumbles, barely managing to prevent himself from falling into the room. He flattens himself back against the wall, hardly daring to breathe. If the two men have heard anything they give no sign of having done so beyond a short pause in their conversation. Bram waits until they are settled to talking again, noting that they have moved away from the subject of Lilith, before tiptoeing back along the hallway, taking up his lamp, and hurrying as silently as he is able back up the staircase, his hands trembling as he grips the banister. Once back in his room he slumps into the armchair, his head in his hands, struggling to make sense of it all.

He acknowledges to himself now how flimsy was his grip on reason and good sense when Lilith confessed to being a witch. It was as if he could accept anything from her, anything about her, because of his love for her, because he knows he would do anything not to lose her love. And talk of Louis and the coven, well, it was just that, to him. Talk. Something strange and fantastic that happened elsewhere, to other people. But now, finding out that Mangan, too, was a part of her coven, the discovery seemed to break whatever hold he had on what is real and what is make-believe.

Mangan! All this time in the same house as him and I never suspected anything, never saw anything different in him beyond artistic eccentricity. And his visitor, who is he? And who else is a witch? Am I surrounded by people who secretly cast spells and summon the dead? Is Jane a witch, too? Is Gudrun? My God, how will I ever know? How will I ever be certain of anything again?

17.

My bedroom resembles a shipwreck, with garments, shoes, stoles, and suchlike strewn over every surface. Iago is thoroughly put out by all the excitement and fuss and is sitting on a green velvet chair in a bad temper, his tail thrashing from side to side. He refuses to be persuaded to change his mood, and is all out of purrs. It would, no doubt, be chaotic enough if it were only I getting ready for the ball, but with Charlotte here, too, excitement and fluster have been raised to levels beyond the endurance of any self-respecting cat.

"Oh, Lilith." Charlotte stands in front of the looking glass turning this way and that to better view the dress she is trying on, "I am not sure this is right. Is it right? Alice, what do you think? Is this the right dress? Oh, my goodness, the first ball in an absolute *age,* and I am incapable of choosing what to wear. Lilith, I blame you entirely. You look so divine in that gown, I shall pale beside you." She slumps down on the bed. "I may as well go in that ghastly creation my mother found for me. It will make no difference. I shall be a wallflower the entire evening."

Laughing, I throw a small cushion at her. "Really, Charlotte, you should know better than to fish for compliments here. Alice is far too busy to waste time flattering you, Iago can only growl at the moment, and I refuse to enter into the delusion that you will look anything other than exquisite, as you always do."

"Oh? And do you suggest I wear Mama's choice of gown?"

I stifle a giggle. "Very well, I admit there are some garments even you would struggle to shine in." I cast about the muddle of silk, velvet, and chiffon. "Here." I select a svelte golden dress with a pearl-encrusted bodice and lengths of sheer satin falling in rippling folds to the floor. "Put this one on. The color will be perfect with your hair. And you can wear your lovely ropes of pearls."

"It is beautiful . . . but a little fussy, perhaps? All those seed pearls . . . No, it won't do. Alice, help me, I shall try the raspberry velvet once more."

Still laughing, I experience a sudden pang of sadness. My enjoyment of the ball, however much it is a welcome diversion, cannot be complete because Bram will not be there. He occupies my thoughts so very much, and I would love to dance with him, to have him hold me, in front of everyone. To have him see me in my finery. But I have not yet spoken to Louis. The fault is mine. I know I am putting off doing so, and it is cowardly of me. If Bram and I are to have a future together I must free myself from my promise to Louis. I must tell him about Bram. And I must do so before rumor and gossip deliver the news for me.

After what happened at the zoo, well, I know the only way to keep Bram safe is to keep him close to me. And to do that, we cannot continue our romance in secret. I must break with Louis. I must face Mama and tell her I intend to marry Bram.

But even then, he will not have the protection that I enjoy, because I must keep him separate from the coven. I have already broken my vows by telling him the truth about myself and by revealing what I have of the Lazarus witches. How would the coven members react were I to tell them that I have taken him into my confidence? They would be shocked. Horrified. Some might consider me to have failed in my role as Head Witch. How could I make them understand? How could I convince them that we are right to trust those who love us, and that those we hold dear are deserving of all the protection we are able to give them? I chose not to keep the fact that I am a witch from the man I love, but I must keep *him* from my family of witches. Must my life always be built upon secrets, secrets, secrets?

For now though, I will turn my thoughts to the ball, for Charlotte's sake, and for Freddie's. He has waited such a long time to emerge from the gloom of mourning. I must not spoil it for him with my own preoccupations. I sit on the stool of my dressing table and browse through my jewelry box. I have promised Mama I will not allow my appearance to be in any way brash, though after so many months of somber dressing, the ivory chiffon I am wearing feels shocking even without jewels. I admit to feeling wonderful in it. The corset Charlotte insisted I buy is barely worthy of the name, it is so light. It cleverly gives me the shape to suit the slim silhouette of my gown without in the least restricting my movement. Such freedom feels a little wicked. The dress itself is from Paris, absolutely the latest thing, Mrs. Morell assured me, designed to make the most of careful draping of the fabric. The waist is high, so that the skirts fall elegantly, the sheer silk underskirts a mere whisper against my body. Charlotte notices what I am doing and tuts loudly.

"Lilith, put those baubles away. There is only one necklace you should wear tonight, and you know it."

"Oh, Charlotte, no, I couldn't possibly . . ."

"But you must!" She steps forward in such agitation that Alice is forced to let go of the corset she had been lacing for her. "This is the first ball since you came out of mourning. It is an important occasion. You have to show that you are back in society for good and proper now."

"But, Charlotte . . . such flamboyance . . ."

"I swear, if you do not wear the Montgomery diamonds I will accompany you as I stand!" She draws herself up proudly. "What do you think Lady Annabel would make of your party including a woman in her underclothes? How would *that* sit with her notion of what is proper?"

I begin to laugh. "Well, they are very expensive, very pretty underclothes . . ."

"I mean it, Lilith. Put those diamonds on this minute."

I feel a small thrill run through me.

Alice is smiling. "Shall I fetch the key, my lady?" she asks.

I nod. "Thank you, Alice."

Charlotte squeals with delight. Alice leaves the room for a few minutes and returns with a key on a ribbon. I take it from her, slide the small oil painting on the wall above the fireplace to one side, and unlock the safe, muttering the required incantation under my breath as I do so. I pause, my eyes closed for several seconds until I hear the lock release. I take out the green leather case and set in on the dressing table, sitting down once more. The three of use stare at the large, gold-embossed box. As I open it, the diamonds catch the light and sparkle and flash almost blue. Charlotte gasps. I hear Alice sigh. I reach in and let my fingers caress the cold, hard stones. As always, they seem to sing with a very special magic of their own. I lift up the cascade of platinum and gems and hold it to my throat. Alice fastens it for me and the necklace rests heavily against my skin, sending tiny shocks and shivers through my body.

Behind me Charlotte claps her hands with delight. "Oh, Lilith! Now I know we are going to have a simply divine evening!"

Only a few weeks ago I could not have imagined being so excited about the ball. After the Yulemass revelations the mood in the coven was dour, and the future seemed bleak. We have consulted further spirit guides, who have given us some reassurance, but the mood among my fellow witches is one of anger and fear, and many have taken practical steps to prevent tragedy if they can. While we may not avert war, we can be better prepared, and those who were singled out have begun putting plans into action to protect their sons. Some have already been shipped off abroad. Others will be given positions that keep them as out of harm's way as is possible. Of course, those "boys" who know of the prophecy as they were present themselves, have, to their credit, refused to be shielded in such ways. They reason that it will be as much their duty to fight as anyone else's and they must take their chances. Louis is one such stalwart youth. He has told me of heated exchanges with the earl, but he has refused to be sent away on some spurious diplomatic mission. He will stay and face what comes. He knows that I admire his courage, and I believe that gives him some comfort. It is largely because of Amelia's revelations that I have failed to find the courage to inflict more suffering on Louis by breaking off our engagement. It feels horribly disloyal, given what lies ahead.

And of course I have Freddie to think of. Louis and he are still friends, and I know he will think I am a fool for turning away from such a match for the love of a penniless artist nobody has ever heard of. Freddie has, as yet, given me reason to hope that he may be lifting himself out of his dark troubles. I have not once, these past weeks, been summoned to Mr. Chow Li's to rescue him, and though he is still frail and given to sleeping through whole days on occasion, he seems a little steadier. A little stronger.

But the greatest cause for my delight is Bram. When I am fearful for him, and for our future together, I hold tight to the thought that we will soon be out of London, in the comparative safety of Radnor Hall. Together at last. Bram has purchased the railway tickets, and we are to meet at St. Pancras station tomorrow, at noon. I have already told my guardians I will not be needing them. No one knows I am going yet, not even Mama, whom I will tell at the very last minute. There is really very little danger of anyone causing me harm so far from London. The Dark Spirit will not have his master to aid him, and I believe my own strength as a witch will keep us safe there.

"Yes!" Charlotte claps her hands together in delight. "Oh yes, Lilith, this is the one. This is perfect, don't you agree?"

She looks glamorous and pretty beyond words in the dark pink velvet, and I tell her so. Iago jumps down from his chair and comes to wind himself around my legs, clearly having decided he will give his affection, albeit grudgingly. I scoop him up in my arms.

"Poor puss, to have to put up with all these women and their silliness."

"Indeed it is not silliness," Charlotte tells me. "This ball marks the end of a very long, dreary winter, and I for one intend to enjoy myself enormously."

When Bram arrives home after a shopping errand for Jane he finds the household abuzz. Through the noise he discerns the fact that an invitation has been received for Mangan to attend the Anstruthers' ball this very evening. Gudrun is to accompany him, and can be seen through the kitchen doorway washing her hair in a bowl, instructing Freedom to heat more water on the stove. The twins are doing their best to dance in the hallway, though they cannot decide who should lead, so keep falling over. Honesty, being the eldest of the girls, is considerably put out at not being allowed to attend and has set up a ceaseless wailing to make her point. Mangan himself can be heard roaring from the bedroom, demanding the whereabouts of his gold cuff links and accusing Jane of having taken them to the pawnshop. George has found the spot in the studio with the best echo so that his bark might be heard above the growing cacophony. Jane spies Bram and distractedly takes the bag of flour and packet of butter from him.

"Bram, dear, don't just stand there. They are sending the carriage in an hour," she explains, taking him by the arm and steering him toward the stairs. "Get yourself dressed, do."

"Me? But surely I haven't been invited?"

"'Mangan and Friends' the invitation read. Gudrun will go, of course, and Perry, and you, dear. Now hurry along. If Mangan's collar studs are not found within the minute I fear blood will be shed."

"But . . . what about you, Jane? Aren't you coming?"

"Good Lord, no. Who would look after the children? Besides, I've nothing to wear, and haven't the time it would require to make myself look sufficiently presentable." She stops bustling, just for a moment, and Bram can see she is thinking about what she has just said.

"I could look after the children," he tells her. "Really, I wouldn't mind."

She smiles at him. "You are a dear, sweet boy, but no, it's better you go. Mangan will want his protégé with him." She stands gazing into the middle distance so that he wonders if she is looking into her past, or trying to see her future. "Run upstairs, now," she says, "I believe Perry has a spare set of evening clothes that might fit you."

He allows himself to be propelled up the staircase, as Jane trots up the rickety wooden treads behind him in answer to Mangan's cries for help. Before she turns on the landing she pauses, still clutching the butter and flour, and says to Bram, "There will always be sacrifices to be made, living with Mangan. I'm happy to make them, as long as I have him, d'you see?"

Her face is such a mixture of pride and sadness that Bram cannot tell which emotion wins out. He finds he is looking at her differently now, searching for something hidden. Something strange.

No, not Jane. Surely not Jane. That Mangan should be a witch is perhaps not such a surprising thing after all. But not Jane.

He heads along the passageway and knocks on Perry's door.

"Bram, my dear fellow, not a minute to spare. Come along in."

"Jane tells me you might be able to help with clothes. I've nothing even close to being suitable."

"Fear not, I am well equipped." He starts pulling garments from his wardrobe. "Jacket and waistcoat should fit all right, and I've plenty of shirt fronts and collars . . . here, ah yes, and here. The trousers might be a tad short, but not ridiculously so. Have you shoes? No? Not to worry. Here we are." He loads him up with an armful of evening wear.

"Do you know them, the Anstruthers?" Bram asks.

"Me? Heavens no. Quite the aristos, madly rich. People get into fights for an invitation to one of their soirées, let alone a ball. Should be a splendid affair. And plenty of prospective clients for both of us, don't you think?"

"I expect Mangan thinks so."

Perry laughs. "Yes, I expect he does. Oh well, we shall know our place then, the penniless artists touting for business. Isn't that so, Gudrun?" he calls out to her as she passes the door.

Gudrun peers into the bedroom. Her hair is wrapped in a towel, turban-style, making her look even more aloof than usual and not a little exotic.

Should I simply ask her? Simply put it to her that I know her secret and see if she, too, confesses to magical talents?

"You are brave tonight, Artist," she tells Bram.

"Oh?"

"You must know your Beauty will be there."

Bram experiences a shiver of excitement as he thinks of meeting Lilith, tonight, unexpectedly, no doubt looking more wonderful than ever. The thought that such an encounter might be difficult for her, for both of them, has already flitted through his mind, but he chooses to dismiss it. He finds he wants to see her, wants to observe her in her world, surrounded by her people, being the Lilith he never sees when she is huddling in her coat in his freezing attic, or hiding on a settle in the Soldiers' Arms.

It will be a test of sorts, a test of their love for each other. He knows that Gudrun considers it will be so, and it irks him that she should find this amusing. He will not let her see that he is in any way apprehensive. Besides, tomorrow he will be on a train, with Lilith, bound for a week of just the two of them, far away from all the endless demands their London lives make upon them.

The venue for the ball is the Anstruthers' fine, redbrick house on the edge of Hampstead Heath. By the time the Mangan entourage arrives there is already a queue of carriages and motor-cars depositing guests on the broad gravel sweep that leads to the grand but understated double front doors. Smartly liveried footmen, drivers, and maids scamper to and fro, offering a hand to assist ladies from their conveyances, taking proffered hats and canes as the gentlemen enter the hallway, and whisking away empty vehicles. Sumptuously dressed women of all ages slip fur stoles gracefully from their backs to expose pale, chilly shoulders, an impressive selection of jewels, and a no-less-amazing variety of necklines. Bram is immediately conscious of the ramshackle nature of the group of which he is a part. Gudrun looks ravishing in an unconventional sort of way, which would suit the occasion and her status as Mangan's mistress and muse perfectly well, but her hair is still wet and she is never without a cheroot in her hand, so that the effect is somewhat spoiled, and she looks to him even a little mad. Mangan gives the accurate impression that he cares nothing for clothes, and has been forced into some semblance of evening attire on the insistence of his wife. If he had come wearing a fez and a paisley silk smoking jacket he would have presented himself as most think of him—an eccentric artist. Had he found a well-fitting and elegantly cut set of tails and trousers he would have appeared successful and debonair. As it is, he sports an ancient jacket that looks what it is: a relic from the past. His shirt collar still lacks the requisite number of studs to keep it in place, so that it is already riding up at the back and sliding around at the front. His trousers are the ones he was, only yesterday, wearing to dress a piece of Portland stone, and his left shoe has a flapping sole. Bram decides he looks as if he gave up dressing halfway through and just came as he was. Which is probably almost exactly what happened. With his wild, bushy hair and abundant beard he looks not so much the artistic genius as the local lunatic. His cause is not helped by Perry, who walks beside him immaculately and expensively turned out. Bram himself was fortunate to fit into his housemate's jacket and trousers well enough at least not to draw attention to himself.

But perhaps there are dozens of people here who know of Mangan's other identity, and will overlook all his peculiarities because they think of him only as a witch. How many? I wonder. How many attending this elegant ball tonight are themselves witches?

Mangan pauses on the threshold. He looks about him and takes in the scene with a sweep of his arm. "We are entering into a bastion of the old order, my friends. Be vigilant. Their world is a seductive one. They will flatter and fawn and pour syrupy words in your ear. There is a danger of losing one's self."

"Or at least," observes Gudrun, "one's self-respect."

"But nice to have some champagne," Perry points out.

"Ah!" Mangan grips Perry's arm. "How many great artists have sold their souls while under the spell of that golden poison, hmm?"

Bram leans closer and speaks softly. "I thought we were here to find new commissions."

Mangan's beetle brows wriggle in distress. "We must prostitute our art or starve, it is true, but, oh, how it pains me to do so! To think that we must display the charms of our talent as if on some street corner to attract the lustful glances of the moneyed classes."

"Surely," Bram says, "that money will buy us the freedom to also do our own work, our best work."

Mangan slaps him on the back with bruising enthusiasm. "Ah-*ha,* the pragmatic optimism of youth. God bless you, young Bram. I for one will take a place in that rosy future you paint for us. Come! Let us enter the fray." He straightens his unstraightenable tie, dusts off his sleeves, sets his shoulders back, and leads them forward.

The Anstruthers' ballroom is grand in every sense of the word. Bram has never seen a room in a private house with such extravagant proportions, such opulent decor, or such glamorous occupants. For a moment he thinks his nerve will fail him, and he glances back at the door to see if a swift and discreet exit is a possibility. But Mangan has already been spotted by an art lover who is intent on engaging the whole of his party in conversation. The orchestra has not yet begun to play, but even so there is a surprising amount of noise. Excited chatter, cheery greetings, the clink of glasses, the stepping or striding of more than two hundred well-shod feet, all combine to form an amorphous hubbub, through which only the odd word can be understood. Bram feels unequal to the task ahead of him. How can he hope to impress people like this? He is a nobody. Mangan likes to refer to him as an "undiscovered talent," but now he feels merely as if he is Bram from Yorkshire, in borrowed clothes, with no money and only two commissions to his name. He has none of Mangan's flamboyance or Gudrun's unshakable self-confidence.

And what will Lilith make of my presence here, in a place I so evidently do not belong?

He worries that his appearance among her splendid and wonderful friends will only serve to highlight the differences between them. The gulf between them. The uncrossable divide that is made up of their positions in society and her membership in the coven.

For I can no more become a duke than I can become a witch. That is the plain truth of it.

And then he sees her. The sight of her takes the breath from his body. He has never seen her properly out of mourning, and has grown accustomed to the somber clothes she was required to wear. He had always considered they suited her. And yet, now, seeing her wrapped in delicate layers of ivory chiffon, with matching silk gloves which stop at her upper arm to reveal a short, tantalizing glimpse of her winter-pale skin, he decides she has never looked more radiant, more beautiful, and if he is honest with himself, more unattainable. About her neck she wears a diamond necklace of breathtaking splendor. It seems to Bram to symbolize the glamor of her world. A world he has no place in.

It is hopeless. I am a dreamer to believe otherwise.

Once again he feels the urge to turn and flee, but it is too late. Charlotte, standing next to Lilith, has spotted Bram and Mangan, and has taken her friend by the hand to hasten across the ballroom floor in their direction. There is no chance of running now. He watches Lilith closely, scrutinizing her expression as she recognizes his face in the crowd. Even so, he cannot read what he sees, cannot be certain if she is pleased or displeased to find him there. He knows her well enough to know she is expert at guarding her true feelings from any onlooker.

"Oh, Mr. Mangan!" Charlotte fizzes with glee. "How wonderful to see you here. All of you. My parents will want to speak to you. They are so very pleased with the sculpture. It is quite the talking point among visitors to our house, you know. And your painting has been attracting interest, Bram. Is that not so, Lilith?"

Bram looks at her, waiting for her answer. Waiting to hear the tone of her voice so that he might discern her mood, her reaction to his being there.

"I was not aware you were acquainted with the Anstruthers," she says.

"I was fortunate enough to be included on Mangan's invitation," he explains, giving a rather uncomfortable bow, feeling faintly ridiculous that he is having to greet so formally someone he has held in his arms and kissed.

Mangan laughs loudly. "Fortune favors the brave!" he declares, stooping to kiss Lilith's hand. "My dear Lady Lilith. You look . . . enchanting," he tells her.

Bram finds himself bridling a little at the joke between them. The shared secret.

Could not Lilith have told me Mangan is a member of her coven? Why did she leave such a thing for me to discover by myself?

Perry bounds into the conversation. "We are on a mission to secure commissions," he says, causing Charlotte to laugh and comment on the rhyme. The two fall to happy chatter, and Bram envies Perry the ease with which he conducts himself. Mangan has been collared by a pair of elderly ladies with fluttering fans, so that Bram and Lilith are left free to speak. Except that he is so tongue-tied he starts to panic that the moment will pass and she will be snapped up by someone else before he can summon some sensible words.

"Is your brother here?" he asks at last, remembering that he was the reason behind Lilith attending the ball.

"He is." She scans the room. "There, just in front of the orchestra."

"He looks very like you. I think I could have picked him out myself."

"We are alike in some ways, yes."

She is being unbearably polite and reserved. Bram is about to abandon caution completely and simply ask her if she minds him being there, and to explain that Mangan insisted he come, and to apologize if this is difficult for her in any way, but also to say that it is wonderful to see her, and that she looks utterly divine. But a tall, blond figure comes to stand close to Lilith. A proximity that suggests a familiarity that rankles Bram. He detects a minute alteration in Lilith's demeanor, which worries him further.

"Oh, Louis, this is Bram Cardale, the artist you have heard me speak of. Mr. Cardale . . . Viscount Louis Harcourt."

She does not say "my fiancé" and yet he is. Still. And a witch besides. I cannot tell which of us is more uncomfortable in this situation, Lilith or I. I must not make matters worse.

Awkwardly, he thrusts out his hand. "I am a pupil of Richard Mangan. The sculptor. You will be familiar with his work, of course."

For one agonizing moment it looks as if the Viscount will not take Bram's hand, but then he does so, shaking it firmly.

"Isn't everyone? Excellent stuff. Not that I'm any judge. Not an artistic bone in my body, have I, Lily? You've always told me so."

Bram has to resist grinding his teeth at the use of Lilith's pet name on this man's lips.

"You must come to the studio one day," he says. "I would be happy to explain the pieces there to you."

"I tried to persuade Lily to take me with her when she accompanied Charlotte for her sittings, but she refused me. Said genius must not be disturbed."

"I said nothing of the sort." Lilith colors a little.

"Well, you wouldn't let me, in any case. I believe you like to keep your little secrets and you didn't want me joining your bohemian arty group."

"Now you're talking nonsense, Louis. Why don't you go and find someone to pester for a dance? The orchestra is about to play."

He clutches dramatically at his heart and reels away. "Ah! You have a cruel streak in you, Lilith Montgomery—to speak to your own fiancé in such a way! But I shall not stay where I am not wanted. When you've finished talking about art and genius remember that I have the first waltz and a polka booked on your dance card." So saying he disappears, grinning, into the crowd.

They watch him go, then Lilith raises her gaze to meet his and gives a faltering smile.

"I am sorry," she says. "That was . . . difficult. I should have . . ."

"Told him? Yes, you should." The words come out sounding far harsher than he intended.

Lilith frowns and briefly closes her eyes. He opens his mouth to take it back, to say he is sorry, but he is drowned out by the opening bars of a Strauss waltz.

He puts his hand on her arm. "Lilith . . . I had to come. Mangan wanted me here. And . . . I wanted to see you so very much. You look exquisite, my love."

She opens her mouth to reply, but Louis reappears, bounding from the milling crowd.

"Our dance, I believe," he says, offering Lilith his arm. She lets him lead her away, glancing back at Bram too briefly for him to be able to read her mood.

The music increases in volume. The hosts take to the floor amid much applause, and somehow, in all the excitement, Lilith melts into the crowd and is gone. When Bram sees her next, Viscount Harcourt is holding her tightly to him as they waltz expertly around the ballroom.

From his vantage point in the gallery overlooking the ballroom, Nicholas Stricklend has a useful view of everyone in whom he has an interest. His position also has the advantage of removing him from the hurly-burly of the revelries in which most of the guests are engaged. He does not enjoy social gatherings of any sort, but particularly dislikes those that involve such large numbers of people, all galloping about, quaffing poor champagne, and attempting to outdo one another in the weight of their jewels, the elaborateness of their gowns, and the volume of their laughter. The resulting fug of human heat turns his stomach. That the Anstruthers' ballroom boasts a minstrel's gallery is a bonus indeed. Better still, they have seen fit not to fill it with minstrels, but to position the orchestra below. With the dancing underway the gallery has all but emptied, which suits Stricklend very well.

He notices the earl of Winchester, who is not dancing, but watching his son with an attention bordering on obsession. As well he might. For his own part, Stricklend is pleased that the Yulemass prophecy has opened up another avenue to obtaining the Elixir—one that need not rely on anything so crude as the abduction and torture of the new Head Witch of the Lazarus Coven.

He can see Lilith Montgomery being whirled about the room to the accompaniment of Strauss's oompah in what he decides is a proprietorial manner by the young Viscount Harcourt. While Stricklend does not choose to partake of friendships of any sort which involve physical contact, he has spent many years observing those who do. And all that he has learned brings him to the conclusion that the viscount is smitten, but the duke's daughter is not. There is a stiffness about her back and shoulders, a tension in the way she carries her head, a lack of softening toward her dance partner that are at odds with the seemingly sincere smile she bestows upon him. The viscount, in contrast, grips her about the waist as if she might try to fly from his arms, and never for one instant takes his disconcertingly penetrating gaze from her face. He does detect, however, a certain affection on Lady Lilith's part, but it appears to be something born of family ties, and of duty, rather than passion. It is however, he is quietly confident, an attachment that will be sufficient for his needs. The girl trusts the young man, that much is clear. Indeed, she apparently trusts most of the assembled company. Or else she merely finds safety in being in a crowd. How could anything untoward, let alone anything threatening, possibly happen to her here, in this dazzling place, surrounded by all these sparkling people? On his arrival Stricklend observed her guardian spirits waiting with laudable patience and loyalty at the entrance to the house. He was not surprised to see the dashing Cavaliers who always accompany her, but the hulking Goth is a new addition to her personal guard, and the second he spotted Stricklend he sent a burst of particularly unpleasant will in his direction as he passed.

As he watches the Lazarus witch dance, he catches something in her movement, a subtle inclining of the head, a sweeping glance in a particular direction, a focus in one part of the room. It does not take him long to find the object of her attention—a tall, good-looking man in ill-fitting clothes. He has the hair and eyes of a poet, but there is a line to his mouth that is full, yet quite severe, quite basic. What can such a girl as Lilith Montgomery, blessed in so many ways, want with a nonentity such as this? And yet, there is a strength about him, an intensity that does draw the eye.

Stricklend searches the throng for another who is necessary to his plans. At last he sees the tall, angular figure of the seventh duke of Radnor, glass of champagne in hand, already a little unsteady on his feet and evidently more interested in drinking than waltzing. Frederick Robert Wellington Montgomery can pass muster at the glance, but will fall woefully short of the mark under closer inspection. His skin has about it the fragility of one whose health is compromised. His jet-black hair is not fashionably floppy, but lackluster and lank. His eyes are at once restless and weary. If Stricklend were given to pity he might feel some for this somewhat pathetic creature, for his lot in life was not of his choosing. But a stronger young man would rise to the challenges of being born into witchery, necromancy, and aristocracy. Freddie Montgomery is weak, and Stricklend can find not the smallest iota of sympathy for one who had so much given him, and fell to weakness. Still, his flaws will prove useful to the Sentinels, and for that the permanent private secretary finds himself grudgingly grateful.

He checks his pocket watch and then turns toward the main entrance to the ballroom. At precisely fifteen minutes past ten, a strikingly glamorous young woman with a winning smile and an appealing swagger to her hips enters the room. She looks up at the gallery and sees him. Stricklend tucks the gold watch back into his waistcoat pocket and gives her a single but definite nod. She returns the gesture, and scours the room, taking out her fan, which she works coquettishly beneath her dark eyes. At length she finds her target and sashays between the guests until she stands directly behind Freddie. Stricklend watches as the woman taps him lightly on the shoulder. The young man turns, sees her, takes in the risqué loveliness of her, and smiles back. Within moments she has him laughing and stroking the back of her hand. Seconds later the pair thread their way, arm in arm, through the throng, and leave the ballroom together.

Satisfied, Stricklend adjusts his jacket minutely and quits the gallery, taking the ornate spiral staircase which descends to the dance floor. The waltz comes to an end, amid much gloved clapping, and is quickly followed by a minuet. Ladies study their dance cards. Men hurry this way and that looking for their partners. As Lilith turns about in search of her brother, as Stricklend knew she would, he moves forward and presents himself with a low bow.

"Lady Lilith, Lord Frederick has asked me to tell you he has had to step out for a moment, and so regrets he will not be able to partner you for the second dance as he promised."

Lilith regards the stranger before her with puzzlement.

"Had to step out? Step out where?"

"Oh, not from the ball entirely. He promised you will see him shortly."

"Oh. I see."

"In his absence, might I perhaps prevail upon you for this dance myself?"

"Forgive me, sir, but do I know you?"

"It is I who am at fault. My name is Nicholas Stricklend, and I have the honor to be permanent private secretary to the minister for foreign affairs. A dull title, I understand, but there it is."

"And how do you come to know my brother?"

Stricklend pauses and does his best to arrange his features into what he hopes is a gentle smile. The lie he is about to present is distasteful to him not because it is a falsehood, but because it paints him as having a weakness, and a weakness of a variety that he finds particularly repugnant.

"Let us say your brother and I, we share a predilection for adventures of a singular and, some might say, moribund nature." He watches her face with interest as she processes this information.

"I have no wish to associate with anyone who leads my brother into the destructive pastimes that are destroying his health and his mind. Will you kindly tell me where he has gone?"

"All in good time. Let us talk while we dance."

"I will not dance with you, sir." Lilith turns on her heel, but Stricklend calls her back, his voice still soft, his demeanor, should anyone observe it, friendly.

"Dance with me, Lady Lilith, or you will never see your brother alive again."

18.

I struggle to take in what I am being told. There is something so very frightening about this stranger, I knew it the moment he spoke my name. I knew it before he uttered those terrifying words. I have no choice but to let him take my hand and lead me onto the dance floor. As we step this way and that, following the music that I scarcely hear, instinctively avoiding other dancing couples as we glide about, we must appear, for all the world, a perfectly respectable and undistinguished pair of dancers. This Stricklend is probably ten years my senior with a strong, fearsome energy about him. A dark, dark energy. I contemplate calling my guardians. I know they would come quickly to my side. But what manner of confrontation do I imagine I could instigate here, in the ballroom, among all these people? No, I must let him speak. He wants something from me, and Freddie is in great danger. I have no alternative but to play his abhorrent game and listen to what he has to say.

"I fear," he begins, "I am not such an able dance partner as Viscount Harcourt. You and he are friends of long standing, I believe, and now engaged to be married."

"What has my relationship with Louis Harcourt to do with Freddie?"

"I am merely curious."

"You have just informed me my brother is in peril, Mr. Stricklend, I have neither time nor interest in your curiosity. Say what it is you have to say."

"As you wish, I will dispense with niceties."

"I fail to see how there can be any in this situation!" I snap, causing Charlotte, who has just danced past me, to turn toward me with a worried frown. I must remain calm. I contrive not to meet her quizzical gaze.

"It really is quite simple, Lady Lilith. I am here to ask you for the Lazarus Elixir, for the spell that it requires, and for a list of its components."

A chill grips me. Such a dread that I am robbed of words for a moment. When finally I rediscover my voice I cannot mask the tension in it.

"Are you quite mad?" I ask. "If you know of the existence of the Elixir, then you must be sufficiently informed about the workings of the Lazarus Coven to know I would never, under any circumstances, relinquish its details. Myself and my fellow witches are sworn to protect the Great Secret, with our lives, if necessary."

"And with the lives of others?"

The terrible man even manages a polite smile as he forms the question which leaves me in no doubt as to what he has planned. The Elixir in return for Freddie. A simple trade. I glance about the room, but there is no sign of my brother. I am not surprised. I am not being challenged by the sort of person who would fail to put into practice the greater part of his threat. I know that. And now, thinking about what my father taught me, thinking about the dangers and threats he warned me of for so many years, I know who it is who stands before me. Ridiculous tears blur my eyes. I will not cry! I will not let this . . . *creature* see that I fear him. That I understand the gravity of the situation. I take a breath and raise my chin, putting a little more energy into the dance. I see his expression alter fractionally, registering surprise at my determination, I think.

"I have never, to my knowledge, stood in the presence of a Sentinel before," I tell him.

"To your knowledge," he repeats. The thin smile has gone now, and I can see from the lines on his face that this sterner, harsher countenance is more natural to him. "We do not announce ourselves," he goes on, failing to resist the temptation to talk about his precious group. "Secrecy is the mainstay of our creed. Secrecy and strength. And we are strong, Lilith Montgomery, make no mistake about that. We mean to have the Elixir, and have it we shall. One way or another. You might consider yourself fortunate that I decided to offer you this chance to avoid any . . . unpleasantness. Leave with me now, take me to your beloved chamber—oh yes, we know all about that, we know all about *you*—take me there, give me what I want, and your pitiful brother will be returned to you unharmed."

"And if I refuse?"

He pauses for just a few seconds before answering, but the melody suggests the piece is about to end, and I sense he does not wish to prolong our discussion beyond this single, hateful *danse macabre*.

"As I said, we will have the Elixir. The time is right for the Sentinels. We will not be denied what is rightfully ours any longer. The only choice you have in the matter is whether you give it to us or you have it taken from you."

The music stops. I let go of his hand and step back. Around us guests clap with delight, and the mood is happy and carefree, and yet in front of me stands a man who threatens to be my nemesis. I swallow the cry in my voice that would burst forth if I let it. The cry for Freddie. The cry for the girl, the sister, the lover, I cannot ever be. The cry for the fact that no one can ever mean more to me than my duty to the coven. The noise level in the room is enough that I can be confident only Stricklend hears my words.

"I am Morningstar, Head Witch of the Lazarus Coven, and I will never reveal the Great Secret, to you or any other Sentinel, no matter the threat, no matter the sacrifice!"

Before he can respond I turn on my heel and march from the ballroom. From the corner of my eye I see Louis watching me go. I hurry on so that he cannot delay me. The one thought on my mind now is to find Freddie.

In the hallway, maids and footmen scurry to assist me, offering to fetch my cape or call a driver, but I tell them I am feeling faint and I need a quiet room to sit in for a few moments. A sprightly maid leads me upstairs and shows me into a small bedroom. I decline her further offers of help with my clothes or fetching water and suchlike and she leaves me. The second I am alone I stand at the window, eyes closed, and call to my guardians. As they rejoin me I bid them show themselves. At such a time I have a very human need to see them, to make them feel as tangible, as substantial as the threat to me, even though they are not.

My brave captains are the first to come. Their fury at my distress is evident, and they are all for taking off after Stricklend and tormenting him, but I don't believe he would feel threatened by them. Sentinels are known to have powerful individual defenses against either spiritual or physical attack. Instead I dispatch them to search the house for Freddie.

The Goth I will send to watch Stricklend closely.

Do you wish me to confront him, mistress? I can enter his thoughts and see what lies there.

I doubt even you could breach whatever shields he has in place. No, better you merely observe him.

He will know he is being watched.

That can't be helped. At least I will know his whereabouts. If he leaves the ball, tell me at once.

The Goth then fades to nothing before my eyes. I struggle to still my racing pulse and focus my fractured mind. Freddie is still close by, I can sense his presence, but it is feeble, like a fluttering moth that could expire at any moment.

"Oh, where are you, Freddie?" I whisper. "Where are you?" With my eyes closed I can watch my Cavaliers as they charge through the house, room after room, floor after floor, until the youngest and swiftest comes upon a body, supine and inert upon a chaise.

Here, mistress! Here!

Where? Oh, yes! I see him.

I run from the room taking care not to be seen by any curious servants. I have to climb two flights of stairs before I find my way to the guest suite on the third floor. In contrast to Mr. Chow Li's, this is a pretty place, a place of good taste and refinement and respectability, but the end result is the same, because what has gone on here is the same. I fall to my knees beside my darling brother. He has removed his jacket, and his shirt sleeves are rolled up. His left arm trails to the ground, and from it a thin line of fresh blood that still drips to the floor.

Carefully I turn him over so that I can see his face.

"Freddie! Oh, my poor, dear Freddie!" His skin is a ghoulish green, his eyelids closed, his mouth open. I place my hand against his brow and let out a small scream. He is cold. Dead. Gone. I am too late. Too late! No!

"No!"

Mistress, should he be shaken? Try to rouse him.

Should we call a spirit physician? Or one who treads the earth still?

No. No, there is nothing to be done. I am too late.

My tears fall unchecked now, splashing onto Freddie's lifeless chest as I lean over him. I have failed him. I have failed Mama. I could not protect him, from himself, or from Stricklend and the

Sentinels, and now he is dead, and Mama's poor battered heart will be broken forever.

"Oh, Freddie." I gaze at his face, stroking his broad smooth brow.

And in that instant, his eyes spring open.

I gasp, wondering if I can have been mistaken, if, after all, he is still alive and there is still hope. But no, I can see there is no life in those beautiful green eyes. They stare back at me, accusing, reproachful. And when he speaks to me his blue lips do not move, for it is his spirit voice I hear.

Lilith, help me!

"Freddie! Oh, I am so sorry. So very, very sorry."

You have to help me.

"It is too late. I can do nothing."

Make me live again. You can, Lilith. I know you can. I'm not ready to die. My life cannot be over, not yet, not like this. It wasn't meant to be this way. Please, I am so scared. Please, help me!

"Freddie, you don't know what you are asking . . ."

Yes I do. I heard you and Papa talking. He told me all about it when I was a boy. At first I didn't believe, and then when I did I was frightened. But I know you can do this, Lilith. You've got to help me. You've got to. Father wouldn't let me die. You mustn't!

I look down at his ghastly, terrified face. How can I leave him like this? How can I let him go into the Land of Night when he is so very frightened? All of a sudden he is just my baby brother and it is up to me to protect him. It is not fair. He has been made to suffer because of my position in the coven—Stricklend has struck at him to try and get what he wanted from me. None of this is Freddie's fault. Well, if he must pay a price for my being the Lazarus Head Witch, then it is only right that he should benefit from who I am, too.

I stand quickly, wiping my tears from my face, and hurry to

open the door. I shout down for some help and a footman arrives breathlessly.

"My brother has been taken ill and I must see he gets home immediately," I tell him. 'Please have my driver bring the carriage round. Is there a door at the rear of the house?"

"Yes, my lady."

"Good, we shall use that. I do not wish to disturb the other guests or cause a fuss. We must do this discreetly, do you understand?"

"Of course, ma'am."

"As soon as you have sent word to the driver, come back here with another footman. My brother is unconscious and will need to be carried."

The journey back to Fitzroy Square is barely three miles but feels interminable. I have the driver run in and fetch Withers. We pretend to take Freddie into a room at the back of the house, saying we do not want Lady Annabel worried, but in fact we slip into the garden, Withers carrying Freddie's limp body in his arms, and hasten down the secret stone stairwell into the catacombs below.

Bram's attic rooms seem bleak and bare after the opulence of the ball. By the time he slumps onto his bed, still wearing Perry's second-best clothes, his head is throbbing from a surfeit of noise and champagne. In the distance, the sonorous bells of Big Ben chime four.

The dark before the dawn, he tells himself.

And yet he has little hope that the new day will bring with it any cheer. He closes his eyes against the gloom of his dreary home and at once Lilith's face swims before him. She has shunned him, he is certain of it. Going to the ball was a mistake. She did not want him there. He did not fit. It was as simple as that. He watched her dance, first with the viscount, and then with a man he did not know. And then she left. Left the ballroom, left the house, left him. Just like that, without a word. What else could he make of it, other than that his presence was not welcome? Perhaps the truth was that she had only ever considered him someone to be kept a secret. Bram noticed that Louis Harcourt also left the ball, not long after Lilith.

The pain in his head will not let him sleep, so he sits up, rubbing his eyes. He strikes a match and puts it to the oil lamp hanging from a hook above him, turning the wick low to save fuel.

She looked so wonderful, so very beautiful. Among all those glamorous people she still stood out, still shone with some special light.

He reaches over to the table and picks up a sketchbook and stick of charcoal. Narrowing his eyes, he recalls the way she wore her hair, and the cut of her gown. He starts to draw, timidly at first, and then with growing confidence. He can see her so clearly, the tilt of her head, the graceful line of her neck, the neatness of her back, the curve of her hip as she danced. He finishes one sketch, tears it from the block, letting it fall to the floor, and starts another. This time he tries to catch the way she holds herself when she stands still, shoulders back, but not stiff, her dark eyes watchful, always watchful. He draws another picture, and another, and another, until his hands and cuffs are black with charcoal smudges. At last he sketches her mouth, only her mouth, full and sensual, lips slightly parted. As the oil in the lamp dwindles and burns out, Bram lets his hand rest on the paper, his eyes closing again, as he drops into a fitful, dream-ridden sleep.

My senses tell me day has broken, though down here in the catacombs there is not so much as a sliver of daylight to indicate that night has fled. I have been so involved in my magic these past hours I have not been aware of the passage of time. I could never have imagined the power that resides within me, had I not taken the decision to save Freddie from the Land of Night, whatever it takes. The first surprise was the clarity of my own resolve. Since the instant I set upon this path, I have not felt a moment's hesitation. Freddie was not meant to die; he is too young to have his life so needlessly snuffed out. It was not his fault he found himself caught up in a conflict between rival magic orders. The quarrel was not his, and he should not pay the price. I am his sister, I love him, and I will do whatever I can to help him. Indeed, it was my failing that I could not keep him safe in the first place.

And then there is Mama to consider. She is so very fragile. I fear losing her only son now would send her into a place of such despair that I might never bring her from it.

But, above all this, I am a necromancer. My whole existence is, and has always been, defined by my ability to commune with the dead, to summon spirits to divine the future and gain insight, to use their magic to strengthen my own spells of protection so that I might do good in the world, protect my family, and continue to keep the Great Secret. Surely, it would be denying what I am *not* to use my gift to help my brother. What would be the point of all those years of study and training, all my father's diligent instruction, all the strength and wisdom of the coven, if I could not use my craft to save someone I love? For centuries, necromancers before me have done just as I am doing now, and many had not the purest motive of all as I do—the motive of love. I can use the Elixir, I can raise Freddie, I can sustain him with spellcraft and regular treating with that precious potion that is at the very center, the heart, of what a Lazarus witch is. There is a price to pay, I understand that. And I will see that nothing is taken that is not paid for. I will not give away the Great Secret, and I will see to it that no one is harmed through my actions. I know I am breaking my coven vows by attempting Infernal Necromancy. Would Father have done as I have done? Would he have sacrificed Freddie? I must follow what I feel to be the right thing. Perhaps, after all, this is a way that my loyalties can be brought together—my loyalty to my family and to the coven. Should not the Lazarus witches be able to withstand such a deed? Will I be cast out for my actions? I cannot know. I only know I cannot abandon my brother.

As soon as Withers had laid Freddie gently on the floor at the center of the sacred circle in the Great Chamber I bid him leave me and see that I was not disturbed by anyone, even a fellow coven member. There was nothing further he could do to assist me. Indeed, this was the first time, in all these years, that he had ever set foot in the rooms beneath the house. I sensed his wonder, his awe, but he was intent on helping me and knew that this was not the time to ask questions. I am blessed to have such a friend. So is Freddie.

Anyone who is involved in the raising of spirits will have to cross the veil that divides the realm of the living from that of the dead. The followers of Lazarus have named these places the Land of Day and the Land of Night, and see them as separated by the Rubicon. We are taught how to venture to the habitat of the dead, but we only do so from a position of safety. We may call a familiar and willing spirit anywhere, though it is customary, and more sensible, to do so either at our home or at a place where those spirits visit to test the boundary themselves, such as graveyards, sacred spaces, and crossroads. What matters is that we make the connection only while we are firmly and securely rooted where we belong. The Head Witch is often seen as a natural conduit for conversations and prognostications with those in the Land of Night, and over time, I know I will spend more and more time in their company. I will have to guard against being drawn to their melancholy but beautiful world too much, for it is not where I belong, not yet. But it is strangely alluring. It is peopled with our loved ones who have gone before us, as well as with spirits of incredible wisdom, so that there is a risk witches begin to detach themselves from their terrestrial life. I saw it with Father. At times he would become withdrawn and fretful. I understand more already, even after a few short months as head of the coven. The home of the spirits is without pain, without base bodily drives and needs. There is such a beauty in its purity, it is truly wonderful. This pull, this constant yearning by the spirits for us, and by our own souls for the peace and bliss of such an existence, will be at its strongest when I embark on the act of Infernal Necromancy, for that is what I must do to save Freddie.

But this seduction is not the greatest danger that I face. That comes from the Darkness. The Darkness is the deepest level of the Land of Night, where demons and creatures of our nightmares dwell. The place emits a powerful and venal energy. Its inhabitants are jealous of those who still tread the earth and delight in causing us suffering. Their chief goal is to capture the unwary and drag them down to their pit. Even experienced necromancers have been lost to the Darkness. I recall only too well how close I came to being taken into the abyss by the demon I summoned at my inauguration. I must be on my guard.

Which is why preparations for the Raising have taken me all this long night. The necessary objects have been assembled. I have spent several hours invoking spirit guardians, calling on witch spirits and departed necromancers to assist us, and offering prayers and entreaties to our Goddess protector, Hekate. Should I prepare inadequately, should something go wrong . . . should I be taken, then Freddie, too, is doomed. Doomed and damned, for the spirit being called for Raising would be in a highly vulnerable state, and without me would fall victim to the nearest avaricious demon or twisted creature.

I am wearing the Robe of the Head Witch, and have Maygor's Silver Thread wound about my arm. Standing before the statue of Hekate I look into the face she presents me, the other two gazing out in opposite directions, watching, ready to warn of danger. She is very beautiful, and tonight her eyes seem gentler, somehow. Does she fear for me? I wonder.

"Stay with me, Queen of Witches," I ask her. "Please, do not let this Daughter of the Night fall into the pit of everlasting darkness. Guide me, so that I can do what it is I have to do."

At last, I am ready. I turn my back on the altar now and step into the circle. I had Withers place Freddie's body along the Rubicon, as he hovers on the threshold of the Land of Night. With his death so recent, calling his spirit back would be a simple matter, particularly as we were so close in life. Summoning the power required to make his body live again and his spirit to inhabit it, so that he is returned as near to his previous state as is possible, that is far more difficult, and success is far from guaranteed. He is still dressed in his evening clothes, and he looks quite peaceful, with his eyes closed and his hands folded across his chest.

I have the witch's trove in the circle with me, and take from it a vial of bone dust, which I sprinkle onto my palms, rubbing them together. The grit is harsh on my skin, but bones provide an important connection between the living and the dead. Next, I take up a lighted candle and walk around Freddie's body, pouring a thin stream of melted wax to form a loop on the floor about him.

From beneath my cape, I extract the golden key which hangs on the slender chain around my neck. Kneeling in front of the trove, I remove a smaller box from inside it. This is made entirely of ebony, black and gleaming, without ornament or carving. I unlock it and reach in for the blue glass vial that sits snugly within. The second my fingers touch it I feel its heat. The warmth travels up my hands, my wrists, my arms, so that by the time I have lifted it from the box my whole body is aglow with the heat it gives off. For a moment I stand transfixed, staring at the innocuous-looking bottle with its cork stopper and wax seal. The

Elixir. I am holding it in my hands. The Great Secret is contained in it, and I am about to set it free. Others are aware that it has been disturbed. Urgent whispering and chattering fills my head, but I ignore it. From somewhere deep below, somewhere in the Darkness, I hear sighing and calling, but I must not be distracted. At the edge of the circle, I place the chalice on the ground before me. With infinite care, I break the seal on the vial and gently ease out the stopper. There is no smell at all, rather a sense of energy being released.

Cautiously, I tip the bottle and pour seven drops of the precious, ruby liquid into the chalice. I replace the cork and set the bottle back in its box, which I lock once more before returning it to the trove. When I take up the chalice I find my hands are shaking as I walk back to the center of the circle, holding the chalice up in front of me.

I am still wearing the diamond necklace. I close my eyes and let my fingers select one small stone. It is no longer cold, but warmed by my own body. Quickly I work the platinum thread counterclockwise until the gemstone unscrews from its setting and drops into my palm. I hold it aloft, my eyes still closed. As I recite the ancient words of the Raising spell I close my hand tight about the diamond. I feel its hard surface resist my grip, the sharp edges digging into the flesh of my palm. And then, slowly, magically, it yields. Yields and crumbles until it is not more than fine sand. I open my eyes now and look down at Freddie. He looks so very far away from me. Fear grips me. What if I fail? What if I make a mistake?

I must not.

Carefully, I let the diamond grains fall from my hand into the chalice. A thin wisp of green smoke rises briefly from the Elixir and then vanishes.

I often call spirits, but this is different. These are not the gentle words I use to speak with my spirit guides or even the incantations for summoning new spirits. My mouth is dry as I call out the words that will summon a dead spirit in its own body.

"Exurgent mortus et ad me veniunt!" My own voice sounds unfamiliar to me, the power of the command lending it weight and nerves adding an edge. There is a pitiful moaning from beneath the sacred circle, but Freddie does not stir, either in spirit or body. I call out again, *"Exurgent mortus et ad me veniunt!"* There is a howling from beyond the Rubicon now, a fearsome, unearthly noise. I must be vigilant. The call is unspecific at this point, as the spell requires, and there are those other than Freddie who might try to answer it. As I form this thought there comes a loud banging, and the ground beneath my feet pulses upward, as if being pummeled by some mighty fist. I press on with the ritual.

Kneeling beside Freddie, holding the chalice in one hand, I rest my other palm over his eyes. "When these eyes open once more, they will see." I touch his brow. "When this mind stirs, it will think." I put my hand on his chest. "When this heart beats again, it will feel." I place my fingers on his cold, blue mouth. "When these lips part again, they will speak." My pulse is racing now, and it is taking a great effort of will to ignore the hideous noises coming up from under the circle, and not to panic at the way the floor is bulging and stretching as it is repeatedly kicked and thumped by something with monstrous strength.

I lean forward and put the edge of the chalice to my dear brother's lips. There is such a small quantity of the Elixir that it seeps into his mouth easily. I place the chalice on the ground and slip my arm beneath his head, raising it up onto my lap. All at once I can feel the same heat that infused me flooding through his body, chasing away the chill of death. Then I see his fingers move. They move! Spirits save us, the wonderful potion is working! He begins to twitch, his arms jerking, his feet kicking out against nothing, his head thrashing from side to side as if he is asleep but in the grip of a terrible dream.

"Wake up, Freddie," I whisper, and then, louder, "wake up, Freddie!"

With one enormous surge of energy he is propelled out of my arms and upright, standing, but not standing, as his feet are not in fact touching the ground. I fall backward and have not time to get up before his eyes spring open and his mouth, too, and he lets out a shriek, the sound of which will stay with me until my last day of treading this earth. He looks filled with panic and fear, arms flailing, hands clawing at the air, gasping for breath. But those eyes *do* see! That heart *is* beating!

He turns and his gaze finds me. He coughs and splutters, trying to speak. I get to my feet and approach him, hand outstretched.

"Freddie, don't be frightened. I am here. I am here."

The color has returned to his flesh, and the strength to his limbs. Within moments he is restored. Completely restored. As the energy in him settles and finds its equilibrium his feet at last connect with the floor, so that he is standing quite naturally. He looks about him, then at his hands, his arms, his body, then at me. And then he smiles, and it is a good, happy, *real* smile.

"Freddie!"

"Lilith . . . I am . . . I am quite well." His voice is hoarse, but otherwise unaffected. "You saved me, darling sister. I knew you could! I knew you would." He takes a step toward me.

And the ground opens up and swallows him.

Suddenly the chamber is filled with screams. I hear Freddie's heartbreaking scream of terror as he is dragged down into the abyss. And I can hear my own roar of rage.

"Freddie, no!" I fling myself to the edge of the yawning chasm that has opened up at the center of the circle. The stench of the pit fills my mouth and stings my throat as I look into the dark hole, searching for any sign of my brother, but it is too gloomy, and there is too much foul-smelling smoke. I detect movement, only, so that I am aware of beings of some sort flinging themselves about below. Some are winged. Others scrabble at the stony sides of the crater. I can still hear Freddie crying out, calling my name. I hold up my arm and flick Maygor's Silver Thread into life, so that I can whip it into the hole. "Freddie, catch the rope! Catch hold of the rope." But it is too dark for him to see it, or for me to direct it toward him. I quickly use a simple enchantment, "Light! Light now!" I command, and a phosphorescent glow illuminates the pit. What it reveals is more terrifying than anything my imagination could have supplied. The hole deepens into a seemingly bottomless shaft of stone, cut through the earth, with rocky ledges here and there, upon which crouch demons and cursed creatures too dreadful to survive in the light of day. Freddie is clutched by one such being, held fast on a ledge. I see that it is intent on taking him down lower, and I know I must act fast. Maygor's Silver Thread will only reach so far. Another demon tries to take Freddie, but the first one will not give up his prize willingly, and so is forced to fend it off with a clawed hand. The light seems to trouble them, so that for a few moments I have the advantage.

"Freddie, there! Grab the rope." He tries and misses, then tries again, and this time he has it! At once the enchanted thread coils itself firmly around his wrist. I close my eyes and offer a prayer to Hekate, begging for some of her great strength. Instantly I feel the power course through me, so that I am able to stand at the crater's edge and haul Freddie up. Hand over hand, I reel the rope in. The demon has had to release Freddie to fight its attacker. I must work quickly. At last Freddie reaches the top and is able to grasp the edge with his hands. But the demon has not abandoned his prey yet. It lurches up through the choking air of the pit and grabs onto Freddie's legs, pulling him down. Freddie yells and claws furiously at the wall of the crater. I redouble my efforts, but their combined weight is too much. I cannot hold on! Maygor's Thread tightens itself protectively around my arm. If I do not pull Freddie up, I will go down with him. This time, there will be no escape. My feet skid across the surface of the sacred circle until I am inches from the hole. Then, just when I am certain all is lost, my three Cavaliers lay their ghostly hands on the rope, lending me their own ancient energy. Slowly, agonizingly slowly, we drag Freddie from the abyss. The second he is safe I leap up and whip the Silver Thread against the floor, shouting the command that will reseal the fissure, sending the demons back into the Darkness where they belong.

I am breathing like a runner, gulping good air at last. My muscles tremble from the exertion. Freddie scrambles up and backs away from me shaking his head, plainly scared beyond reason by what has just happened. By what he saw. By what he now knows to exist.

"Those *things*," he gasps, "those terrible . . . creatures! Was that Hell, Lily? Was it? Was that where I was supposed to go? Where I *am* supposed to go?"

"No, Freddie, no, not there, not you . . ."

"Why not? How can you be certain? Those things . . . they wanted to take me . . . they thought I belonged there. Dear God, Lily, you have made me into a monster, and now the other monsters want me for their own!"

"No, Freddie, listen to me, it isn't like that."

"I have to get away!" He starts to dart about the chamber, and then rushes at the door, heaving at the great beam that bars it.

I hurry after him and put a hand on his shoulder, but he shrugs me off and will not be stopped.

"Get away from me!" he screams. "Leave me alone! I have to get out. Have to get away!"

And before I can stop him he has wrenched the doors open and fled, out of the antechamber and up the stairs. I run after him, and I am amazed at how fast he is, how quickly he bounds up the stairs. By the time I emerge from the summer house I just catch a glimpse of him leaving the garden through the small door past the mews. I know I cannot catch him. I am weakened by my efforts in the chamber. Hekate lent me her strength when I needed it most, but it has ebbed away now, and my own, flimsy body is exhausted from the unnatural demands I have made upon it. Freddie, in contrast, seems supernaturally strong now. I quickly summon my Cavaliers and instruct them to go after him.

Find him, stay with him until I come. Do not leave his side.

Yes, mistress.

I know they will be able to do as I have asked. What I am less certain of is whether or not, when I find him, I will truly be able to help Freddie. I have raised him from the dead, the Elixir has done its work, but he must be tended, he must be looked after. The effects are only temporary and so the Elixir must be taken regularly. If he stays too long without the precious potion his spirit will start to fade, and his body, his poor, dear body, will slowly begin to rot.

19.

When Bram wakes up it is to find Gudrun sitting on the end of his bed, sifting through the many sketches that are strewn about the place.

"So," she says without looking at him, "did you get to dance with your princess last night?"

Bram wearily props himself up on one elbow. His head throbs horribly and his eyes feel puffy and sore. He rubs his temples and yawns, tasting the fur on his tongue.

"What do you want, Gudrun?" His voice is croaky. He stretches his legs uncomfortably, dismayed to see how creased and crumpled Perry's clothes are.

"Poor Artist," says Gudrun, still studying the drawings. She shrugs. "Anyway, now you will see I am right."

"Really? How so?"

"I told you a broken heart makes the best art." She waves a handful of the sketches at him. "These are magnificent."

He looks at them properly now, and even with his slightly blurred vision, he can see that she is right. They are the best he has ever done. He takes one from her gingerly and studies it more closely.

Lilith, how he loves the sound of her name in his head. *My beautiful Lilith.*

He goes to put the painting down on his bedside table and his gaze falls on two railway tickets. He snatches up the clock. It is twenty-five minutes to noon.

The train! My God, the train.

Leaping from the bed he grabs his valise from beneath it and dashes around the room snatching up what he can—a handful of underwear, one, two shirts, trousers, his shaving brush—he stuffs them into the suitcase and slams shut the lid, buckling it quickly.

"My goodness, Artist, you are in such a hurry," says Gudrun, watching him with an irritatingly amused expression.

Bram ignores her. The events of the night before are fading. What matters now is today, meeting Lilith, getting out of London with her. Leaving the room without explanation or good-bye he races down the stairs and out of the house. He is groggy and uncoordinated, but the fresh spring air revives him.

She will be there. I know she will be there. And we will leave this stinking city and go somewhere quiet and peaceful, and I will tell her I love her and she will forgive me for being there last night, and everything will be wonderful.

St. Pancras station is abuzz with travelers, most of whom seem intent on getting in Bram's way. He pushes through the crowds, abandoning manners in a desperate effort to get to platform three. By the time he arrives most passengers have already boarded the waiting train. He scans the faces milling about, searching for Lilith.

Might she have already boarded? No, she wouldn't do that. I have the tickets. She would wait for me.

The platform empties as the last passengers step up into their chosen carriages and the guard walks briskly along slamming doors. Still there is no sign of Lilith. Bram begins to run, pointlessly up and down.

She will come. She must come.

The last door shuts with a loud clunk, the guard raises his flag and blows his whistle. The train gives an answering blast and, with the creaking and clanking of pistons and traction, begins to roll slowly forward. Steam billows back from the funnel as the engine gathers momentum. Bram stands, hopeless and bewildered, staring back along the empty platform until the tail end of the last carriage has chugged past him and disappeared out of view.

The energy born of eagerness and passion drains out of him, so that he sits forlornly on his suitcase, chin in hands. He upset her at the ball, he is certain of it now. He should never have gone. His presence there served only to underline the differences between them.

She has thought better of seeing me. She has seen the hopelessness of it all.

For a moment he is so certain of this he can see no other possible explanation. Travelers walk around him, barely giving him a second glance. Porters wheel luggage past. A small child is dragged by the hand, wailing, his mother's heels clicking on the floor as she marches on. It seems to Bram the world is going on without him, that he is no longer properly a part of it. If, indeed, he has ever been. Then, hidden deep inside himself, he locates a small kernel of hope.

What if she has been unavoidably detained? What if she intended to meet me, wanted to, but was prevented from doing so?

He searches for possible reasons, for plausible explanations for her absence. There must, he has to convince himself, there *must* be some reason other than the unthinkable. Other than that she has thrown him over, and he will never see her again.

Perhaps she is in difficulty of some sort? Could it be she has been visited by the Dark Spirit again? I know how terrible that vile creature's strength is, what pain he can cause. She might need me, even now, and be unable to send word to me.

The ridiculousness of their situation suddenly fires a useful spark of anger in his belly. He stands up. What manner of world are they living in when one human being cannot contact another, contact someone who cares deeply for them, when they are in need? It is preposterous. If she needs him, he will go to her. He will go to her, and who cares what anyone else thinks or says? He springs up with renewed purpose, snatching up his valise, and makes his way hurriedly back through the throng and out of the station. He attempts to hail a cab, but there are none to be had, so instead he sets off at a loping trot for Fitzroy Square. It is not far, but his clothes are unsuitable for such exertion, his collar quickly chafes and his shoes soon start to rub, threatening blisters. He ignores such trifling discomforts and hurries on, so that by the time he reaches the railings of the square's garden he is hot and a little breathless, and damp with perspiration.

The striking house that is Lilith's family home looks so pristine and lovely in the early spring sunshine that Bram hesitates. He is suddenly acutely aware of his own appearance. He is still dressed in borrowed evening clothes, in which he has slept, and has had neither wash nor shave. He attempts to tame his hair with his hand, straightens his jacket. He is on the point of approaching the house when a car rounds the corner of the square at some speed and pulls up outside the front door of Number One. Bram hangs back. He recognizes Louis Harcourt as he leaps from the car and bounds up the steps. His knock on the door is quickly answered, and the viscount goes inside. In less than a minute he reappears, and Lilith is with him. She is dressed in a simple pale gray jacket and skirt with a darker matching hat and gloves. She seems to hesitate before getting into the car, looking up at Louis, her face full of anguish. And as she does so, he takes her in his arms and holds her in a warm, tender embrace. When he at last lets her go Bram clearly sees him wipe a tear from her cheek, before Lilith steps into the waiting car, Louis taking his place beside her, and they speed away.

Bram reels backward as if he has been struck. For a moment

he thinks the Dark Spirit has come to assail him again, but no. He knows that the shock that has forced the breath from his body, the pain that constricts his heart, is the grief of heartbreak.

Gone. She has gone from me!

Suddenly, he sees everything in a different light, the perspective shifted, the truth he was blind to before now revealed. Lilith had not broken off her engagement with the viscount because she still loved him. She had danced with him so closely at the ball, the two of them clearly deeply attached to each other. She had left the ball without a word of explanation to Bram, and then failed to meet him at the station. And now, now he had witnessed their continuing affection.

And it is Harcourt she has chosen to leave with, not me.

He stands for a moment, confusion and hurt muddling his mind, the agony of his loss sweeping over him like a storm-built wave, so that he has to grasp the garden railings to steady himself. Only when he is certain his legs will carry him does he begin his journey back to Bloomsbury.

He arrives home to find the house empty. He wanders through the unusually quiet hallway, the absence of dog and bicycles suggesting Jane has taken the family to the park. Bram drifts into the deserted studio. He is numb now, the sharp pain he experienced earlier replaced by a dullness, an emptiness, a weighty sense of being utterly lost. He pulls his hat from his head and sits heavily on a lump of unworked stone. Somewhere in the garden a blackbird sings with inappropriate brightness. Bram's dry mouth is aggravated by the dust that habitually fills the air in the studio. He coughs, spluttering, the sound echoing off the hard surfaces of the room.

Perry's voice startles him. "You sound like a man in need of a drink," he says, coming from the darkness of the hallway clutching a bottle and glasses. He pulls up a wooden stool and sits opposite Bram. "If you don't mind my saying so," he prattles on as he pours generous measures for both of them, "you look fright-ful. Here, this should pep you up."

On any other day, Bram might have questioned the need for brandy, have questioned Perry's readiness to produce it, have questioned there being any in the house. On any other day, he might have paused and thought at least of eating something, or of drinking water to steady his already twisted stomach. But not today. Today all he wants is something to ease his suffering. Something to blur the image he cannot shake from his head of Lilith being held close by Louis. Of Lilith going. He drains his glass and then holds it out to be refilled. Wordlessly, he downs the second measure.

"I say." Perry laughs lightly. "Steady on."

"Another," Bram insists.

Perry watches him a moment longer and then asks, "Want to talk about it, old chap?"

Bram shrugs and shakes his head. "No. Yes. No! What is there to say?"

"Clearly something is amiss."

"She's gone, Perry. She's made her decision, chosen the way her life is going to be, and it does not include me."

"Ah."

"Yes, *ah*." He leans forward, elbows on knees, turning his drink around in his hands, staring at the silky liquid inside as if it might reveal some sort of answers, some sort of explanation, some sort of action he might take.

"I assume we are talking of the delectable Lilith?" Perry asks.

"I was a fool ever to think she would consider me. Seriously consider me."

"I thought she was rather keen—"

"She's chosen Louis," he cuts in.

"I see. Pressure from her family, perhaps? Someone considered more . . . suitable?"

"You don't know the half of it," Bram tells him.

Perry seems about to respond to this but says nothing, topping up their glasses instead.

Bram shakes his head. "You know, I don't believe it is that . . . family pressure. She was prepared for disapproval from her mother, yes, and telling her fiancé . . . breaking off their engagement . . . of course it would be difficult. But, when we were together . . . being with her meant everything to me."

"You love her."

"Ha!" He gives a mirthless bark of a laugh. "That is such a small word for what I felt. What I *feel*. The truth is . . . enormous! The way she affects me, the way she consumes me so completely . . . To be with her, to love her, I have lost myself to her utterly, do you understand what I'm saying? Can you? Can anyone? Do I?" He runs a hand through his tangled hair.

"You don't think you were mistaken?"

"No."

"Or perhaps that you might . . . win her back?"

"We are not in a situation to play games," he says, glancing at Perry. "There are . . . complicated things about our being together. If she has decided she cannot be with me, then . . . I will not change her mind."

"So, what will you do?"

"I don't know. I don't know! How can I know?" He stands up, draws back his hand, and hurls the glass against the wall. The resulting smash falls horribly short of the noise he was hoping for. It goes no way to expressing the mixture of rage and sadness that are now, fueled by the brandy, surging through him. "I must get away," he says at last. "I cannot stay here. Cannot be in London, where she is, and be without her. I cannot."

※

As the motor car speeds through the sunlit streets I glance at Louis. His profile, against the strong light, is visible only in silhouette, but even so I can detect the grim set of his mouth. He answered my cry for help and came at once, as of course he must, but he is deeply shocked by what I have done and unable to successfully mask that shock.

"How could you do it, Lilith?" His voice is scarcely more than a whisper. "How could you bring yourself to do it?"

I know that he is not simply asking me how I found it within myself to undertake such a difficult piece of magic. He is questioning my loyalty to the coven. My integrity. As well he might. I have justified my actions to myself, but I will not as easily convince others that I did what I *had* to do.

The driver turns down Tottenham Court Road, slowing the speed of the vehicle so that we might better scour the pavements and the roads and the alleyways we pass in the hope of spying Freddie. My guardians were caught out by his incredible turn of speed. They reported back to me that, despite their best efforts and the considerable advantages they have moving about in spirit form, they were unable to keep up with him. I have even consulted the earl's Goth, who has confirmed fleeting glimpses of him in various places but has been unable to pinpoint his whereabouts.

With each passing minute I begin to doubt the wisdom of what I have done. I do not doubt my motives: I wanted only to help my dear brother. And when I first saw the work of the Elixir! I was in a state of awe; how could anyone fail to be? To see the Great Secret brought into being before my eyes—the giving back of life to one who has had it taken—nothing could have prepared me for it. The reanimated Freddie who stood before me in the Great Chamber was not some ghoulish revenant, but Freddie restored. Living again. Moving, breathing, feeling, thinking, speaking as freely and with as much force as he had done before his heart had been stilled by the wretched poppy. Indeed, if what my captains recount of him since is accurate, his physical capabilities seem greatly improved. Magnified considerably, in fact.

What concerns me, what troubles me so greatly now, is the possible state of his mind. He seemed to tolerate the strangeness of finding himself . . . awake again, but oh, how terrible it must have been, to be dragged down into that pit, to see what he saw, to smell the fires of the Darkness, to be mauled and held, and very nearly stolen away, by those fiendish creatures! Freddie has never had the steadiest of characters, how will he withstand such an experience? By the time I had brought him back out of the chasm he was forever changed. He looked so terribly afraid, as if he would never know peace again. And I am responsible for that.

"We must find him, Louis." I cannot stop myself stating the obvious. I know it is pointless to say this, childish even, but I need my friend's support now so very much. I expect him to reach over and take my hand. To comfort and reassure me. But he does not. I have stepped too far away from him. I have done something too dreadful.

Without looking at me he says, "Of course we must. Can you imagine the scandal if he is discovered, raving and shouting at any who will listen? What a tale the newspapers would make of that!"

"No one will believe him. They will think him ill."

"They will think him mad. As he most probably is."

I flinch at the harsh truth of this but can think of nothing to say to it.

Louis goes on. "Besides, it is not just your family reputation you have to concern yourself with, you realize that, surely? The coven members will soon know what has happened, that is obvious, but the minute word of this gets out *others* will know."

I stare down at my gloved hands. He is right. This is where the real catastrophe could lie. I have been so overwhelmed by my personal tragedy, by the prospect of losing Freddie, that I have closed my mind to the greater stakes being played for. For we are no more than pieces in a terrible game, I see that now. A game of Nicholas Stricklend's making. He must have known I would never simply give him the Elixir. He must also have known that I would, if it came to it, use it to save my brother. The Sentinels were the group of sorcerers my father feared most. Every Lazarus witch is taught to be on their guard against those who would take the Great Secret from us, and the Sentinels were always the lurking terror in the dark, the inhabitants of our nightmares, the greatest threat to the coven. If they find Freddie before I do, I will have to go to them, too. For if Freddie does not receive the Elixir . . . it is too horrible to contemplate. I would be in no position to bargain with them then. How could I let Freddie meet such a horrifying end? My loyalty to the coven would be broken forever. I would be an outcast. And the Sentinels would have what they wanted, to use for whatever nefarious deeds they have in mind, without a care for the weak whom they have all been taught to despise.

A dreadful thought flashes through my mind. If Freddie is taken, then the route to the Great Secret lies with me. The Lazarus Coven cannot allow me to give it away, whatever my reason. The surest way to stop that happening would be to stop me. I study Louis once more. No wonder he will not look at me. If we do not find Freddie, will it be he who sees to it that I no longer threaten the coven? Has he been chosen to make certain I am silenced forever? Could he do it? His father could. No doubt, it was his father who made sure he came to me. Oh, Louis, what have I done to you, to all of us?

"There must be someone he would go to," Louis says. "Some friend . . ."

I shake my head. "Freddie had only fair-weather friends. There is no one he could turn to now. Nowhere for him to run . . ." I stop suddenly. "Of course! Mr. Chow Li. He would go there."

"Where? Who are you talking about?"

"It doesn't matter. Just tell the driver to take us to Bluegate Fields."

Louis does not question the unlikely location but taps his cane on the glass in front of us and instructs the driver as I have asked. We swerve violently to make a sharp left turn, and I notice a motor cab behind us doing the same thing. I watch for a moment and am certain it is following us.

Three men, my lady.

My Cavaliers have seen it, too.

Who are they?

We cannot say. But they are dangerous men. And they are armed, mistress.

Stricklend has sent them, I am certain of it. He means us to lead him to Freddie.

I lean forward and call to the driver. "Please, you must go faster. Turn here, yes, this little street. It will lead us where we want to go." From the corner of my eye I notice Louis regarding me with astonishment, no doubt puzzled by my acquaintance with the route to such a place. The car turns again, just as quickly, throwing me against Louis. He steadies me, but does not use the moment, as he surely would have only yesterday, to hold me close or kiss my hand. Through the rear window I see we still have not rid ourselves of our unwanted escort. I am anxious that we do not play into the Sentinels' hands, but we have no choice. We must find Freddie.

I continue to give directions as we leave the district of Westminster and travel east through Holborn and toward the docklands. Passing the Fenwick clock tower I notice it is nearly one o'clock. An hour after I should have met Bram at St. Pancras station. How long did he wait for me? What must he think of me now? After all the tumultuous events of the night, it is the thought of how badly I have treated Bram that brings unwelcome tears to my eyes. Will he forgive me? Could I ever make him understand? I cannot see how.

We leave the more prosperous areas, and soon Louis's fine automobile stands out as something ostentatiously expensive against the drab backdrop of the grimy terraces and warehouses. The sun shines here just as brightly as it does in Fitzrovia and Bloomsbury, but that light is sucked into the dullness of the dark brick and stone of these mean, dirty streets. The colors are dulled with grit and poverty. The clothes people wear seem a uniform of drudgery and utility, save for the occasional scarlet ribbon or gaudy petticoat on show from women of a certain type still plying their trade on street corners.

"Are you sure your brother would come here?"

I nod sadly. "It is the only place he could come. Tell the driver to stop. We shouldn't take your motorcar farther, and anyway, the lanes will soon be too narrow and rough for it."

As we climb out of the comfortable cocoon of the vehicle I see that we have at last evaded our pursuers, at least for now. I urge Louis to hurry, and we scurry down a side alley toward the Thames. My guardian spirits stay close, swords drawn. Though unseen, their presence will deter opportunist rogues, who will sense danger, even if they do not know why. More importantly, the Cavaliers will ward off any spirits Stricklend may see fit to send after us. I cannot rule out such a tactic. I am sure he is capable of it.

"Lilith, are you certain you know where you are taking us?" Louis is becoming increasingly unnerved by the curious stares and unwanted attention we are garnering. In our fine clothes we are unhelpfully noticeable. I do not answer, but press on quickly, not wanting to speak any more than is absolutely necessary. If our appearance draws interest, our voices would do so also.

We are rounding the corner into the street which contains Mr. Chow Li's house when I see Freddie.

"There he is!" I cry out, unwisely, forgetting in the excitement of finding him that we do not wish to alert our followers as to where we are. "Freddie!" I call to him. "Please, wait!"

But the second he sees us he turns and runs. My heart constricts at the thought that I now inspire such fear in him. We scramble after him, tripping over the pieces of a broken cart and slipping through all manner of rubbish and detritus. Freddie is incredibly quick, but his progress is slowed by the obstacles, both inert and human, that are in his path.

I call again, but he is not listening. We chase him down through the storehouses and inns, past a tannery and a glove factory. Small children scatter as Freddie tears through them, and then they re-group to taunt us as we hurry after him. We are getting closer and closer to the river, so that soon I can see it as well as smell its dank, sour odor. Freddie's flight takes him along its banks toward Tower Bridge, which is the only crossing here for some distance if he is not to find a rowing boat or a ferry. As he reaches the bridge, Louis shouts out.

"Montgomery! Have a care, man—you are being hunted!" he yells, pointing wildly to the three figures who are closing fast on Freddie from a side street.

"Oh, Louis, they will reach him before we do!"

Frustration at my own lack of speed drives me on, but I cannot keep pace with the men. By the time I set foot on the great stone bridge Freddie has reached the first of the two towers which house the lifting mechanism that raises it for taller ships. He hesitates, and in that instant his would-be abductors move into place so that they surround him. He backs up against the railings of the bridge, desperately looking this way and that, searching for a means of escape. Louis catches up and shouts at the men to leave him alone, tackling the nearest one. I stop and steady myself. I am no use to my brother running like a flimsy girl. I must use what strength I have more effectively. I take a deep breath and bring all my thoughts, all the power of my mind to one point, so that I see only the tall, bony figure who is now striding toward Freddie. With a prayer to Hekate for strength I send a swift spell of movement that snatches up a small stone on the road and hurls it through the air. My first attempt falls wide, but my second finds its mark, and the man shrieks, clutching at his head, and is sent reeling backward. Louis has struck a fierce blow to the first man's jaw, and he lies on the road clutching his face, spitting out teeth. My poor brother is transfixed against the railings of the bridge, seemingly incapable of either fleeing or defending himself. The third man lunges at him, at precisely the moment Louis reaches him. There is a brutal fight. I hear Freddie cry out, and catch the glint of sunlight on a blade. Louis screams, and the three are tangled together in a desperate struggle. What happens next occurs with the speed of a lightning flash, and yet the movements of all those involved are somehow leaden, heavy, slowed to an unnatural rate, so that I see every tiny detail, which will remain forever seared into my mind. The assailant raises his knife toward Freddie. Louis attempts to grab his wrist. Whether or not this affects the action of the henchman I cannot tell, but the result is catastrophic. The shard of steel slices across Freddie's throat, opening the flesh. All three men are put off balance by the violence of the movement and tip, as one, over the top of the railings. To the shocked cries of onlookers, they tumble from the bridge, down, down, down, narrowly missing a laden coal barge, so that they enter the metallic-gray water of the Thames locked in a deadly embrace.

20.

It occurs to me it is unlikely this shabby building that has leaned against St. Mary's Convent in Holborn for so many years has ever before attracted such interest. A queue three people thick and easily threescore long winds back from the front steps down the drizzle-rinsed street. Those standing in line might have been chosen for the uniform drabness of their clothes. Watching them now through the grubby window of the makeshift kitchen it is as though I am witnessing all the color in the world dissolving in the rain, to be replaced with the browns and grays of misery and struggle. And surely there can be no better picture of both. Women, old people, and children, compelled to stand for hours waiting for the charity of the convent to provide them with the only hot meal they will see today. And while their bodies are starved of food, their hearts ache for absent loved ones, longing for the day they will return, dreading the knock on the door that brings a telegram to mark the end of hope.

"Lilith, dear, have you finished those pots? Sister Agnes is about to open the doors," Sister Bernadette tells me as she passes, puffing slightly under the weight of the basket of bread she is carrying.

"Goodness," I say, wiping my hands on my apron and hastening after her, "where did all those wonderful loaves come from?" Shortages have affected all manner of food, but none more so than wheat, now that the U-boat campaign has a stranglehold on the supply ships from America. The sight of a whole baker's tray of fresh, white bread is rare indeed.

"Diverted from their journey to the Ritz." Sister Bernadette grins.

"You must have friends in high places indeed."

She laughs at this. "Surely the very highest of all!"

In the room that now stands in for a canteen, all is ready. Three enormous containers of steaming broth stand on sturdy tables, two nuns or volunteers behind each.

"Ladles at the ready, Sisters," Bernadette instructs, glancing at the clock on the wall. One o'clock precisely. It amazes me every day that this small miracle of punctuality is brought about. We are woefully understaffed, and the queues grow longer with each passing meal. So many hungry people. So many weeks, months, years of gritted teeth and hardened hearts.

Sister Agnes unbolts the front doors and those at the head of the line step forward. Each brings with them a receptacle of varying degrees of size and suitability. In the twelve months I have been helping out at the soup kitchen I have seen everything from tin mugs to chamber pots and even a horse's nose bag presented to be filled with the lifesaving meal. Today there is a buzz among those waiting at the sight of the bread. I take up my position at the end of the last table and break chunks from the loaves to press into eager hands. Some of the children are pitifully thin. It pulls at my heart to see them so.

I have tried to explain to Mama that we cannot sit by and wait for the war to end; that there are those so much less fortunate than us who need our help. But she does not understand. The world she knew is vanishing, and nothing makes sense to her any longer. She has retreated inside her own version of how life is or how it was. If losing Papa tested her, losing Freddie broke her, as I had feared it would. Even now, years after that terrible afternoon on Tower Bridge, I can see him falling, see the blade drawn across the whiteness of his throat. Hear the splash as he entered the water. I will always believe it was my fault that he died the way he did. I should have protected him from the Sentinels. I should have saved him. I failed him, and now he is dead and gone and he has taken the better part of Mama with him.

I can only thank the spirits that Louis survived. He told me later that he had summoned his magic as best he could but that the speed with which everything happened prevented him from saving himself unaided. He recounted how the three of them plunged deep into the Thames, unable to disentangle themselves from one another. Stricklend's thug broke his neck as they hit the water. Louis said he felt my spirit guardians helping him, pulling him upward. It was his father's summoned Goth who dragged Freddie from the depths and propelled him to the embankment. But my poor dear brother was beyond help. Death had him in its clutches once more and would not have its fingers pried loose a second time.

The coven was in turmoil, of course. For a while it looked as if I would be cast out. But with war upon us, with the Sentinels' threat now an open one, with a figurehead who has declared himself, it was decided that to lose a Head Witch, to have to find another, would be too damaging to the coven. I am still goaded and harassed by the Dark Spirit. It is as if the Sentinels, having failed in their attempt to gain the Elixir by controlling me through my love for my brother, are awaiting their moment, biding their time. And while they wait, they send their spirit servant to haunt me, to wear me down, no doubt, in the hope that by giving me no peace I will be less able to withstand their next attack, whenever it comes.

"Are you going to give us some of that, love?" An elderly man stands in front of me, his bowl of soup raised expectantly.

"I'm sorry, yes." I give him as big a piece as I dare. Too generous a helping would have Sister Agnes remonstrating with me in an instant. I realize I had drifted off into my own thoughts and shake my head as if to banish them. No good can come of dwelling on what cannot be changed. There are others who need me now.

It takes two hours to feed everyone who has come seeking food. By the end of the queue we are scraping the great tin cauldrons and the bread has gone entirely. A further hour is required to wash up and clean away so that the kitchen will be ready for use in the morning. Glancing at the clock I see it is already nearly four. I have promised Mama I would take tea with her, and I must not be late. Small moments of normality seem to help her. I quicken the speed of my washing and wiping until Sister Bernadette, sensing my hurry, bids me go home, assuring me they can manage and will anyway do better without me charging about the place like a clockwork mouse.

I whip off my apron and call my farewells over my shoulder as I go. Outside I break into a trot. I have grown accustomed to looking a sight and no longer pay attention to the looks of surprise my disheveled state sometimes attracts. It is hard to be concerned about such trivia as untidy hair or an unflattering garment. It is little enough that I do in this terrible time. Vanity has no place here.

I arrive at Fitzroy Square flushed and perspiring. My dress is one I chose for the freedom of movement it allows me and for the durability of the fabric. I hope that I might sneak upstairs and quickly change and redo my hair, but my mother's voice reaches me in the hallway.

"Lilith? Lilith, is that you?"

"Yes, Mama. I'm just going up to change."

"I have been waiting. Withers has brought the tea up. Come along. You know I hate to drink it when it has become stewed."

With a sigh I brush down my skirts and attempt a cheerful expression before heading into the drawing room.

As always my mother's frailty distresses me. She has become so insubstantial, so delicate. She sits by the fire in a winged chair that dwarfs her.

"There you are. Oh, Lilith, darling, you surely haven't been out of the house looking like that?" Her hand flies to her mouth and her shock is genuine.

"I've been helping out at St. Mary's, Mama. You remember?"

"Of course I do. I have not entirely lost my wits, whatever you may think."

"I think no such thing."

"Don't you? You regard me as if I were an imbecile at times. And yet I am not the one who goes about looking as if I have fallen from a carriage into a puddle."

"There is no point in dressing up, Mama."

"I am not suggesting 'dressing up,' as you call it. I am merely observing that if anyone appears to have lost their sense of what is reasonable it is not me. Really, Lilith, when everyone else is making such an effort. Look at all those brave young men going off to war. Do you see them looking a fright?"

"No, Mama."

"No, of course you don't. They wouldn't dream of turning out shabbily. It would be letting the side down."

I have to bite my lip to prevent myself from saying something I know I will later regret.

I continue to plead a headache so that I am able to avoid having to dine anywhere with Louis or indeed with Mama. Mrs. Jessop has a light supper sent up to my room on a tray, but in truth I have little appetite. The sight of the poacher's pie, pickles, and crusty rolls all lovingly and lavishly prepared by Cook earlier in the day starts up the gripe of guilt in my stomach. How is it that I have so much when others must go to their beds hungry? And is Mama right, after all? Am I a hypocrite? It has taken a war to wake me from my privileged slumbers. And yet my engagement to Louis continues. I never told him of my feelings for Bram. I should have, perhaps. Should have offered him the chance to turn me away, knowing that I had been in love with someone else. I fully intended doing so. But then, after Freddie, well, it seemed to matter less, where my affections lay. Bram had gone, and I had let him go. There was a moment when I thought I would find him, find him and tell him what had happened. Attempt to explain the inexplicable. Ask him to forgive me for letting him down. Make him see that I loved him still. Love him still. But the events of that terrible day served to remind me of how difficult it would be to make my life with a non-witch. Of how much danger—*constant* danger—Bram would be in if he were to be with me. How could I hope to protect him? How could I ever convince myself I could keep him safe when I had so utterly failed Freddie?

And Louis had nearly died trying to save my brother. Trying to undo the harm I had caused. And Mama, poor Mama. She has so little left to light her dark existence now. The prospect of my marriage to Louis is some small crumb of comfort that it is within my power to give her. And yet I put off and put off and put off the wedding. So long as this dreadful war lasts no one is able to press me on the matter of a date. To celebrate a marriage with all the fanfare and expense such a union would demand—it would be in poor taste, unseemly, simply wrong, when so many are suffering. As long as the war continues I can avoid becoming Louis's wife.

I finish brushing the tangles from my hair, and Iago springs onto my bed beside me, his legs moving a little stiffly now, and a few gray hairs around his eyes giving away his age. I lie back on top of the covers, too restless for sleep, yet weary. I cannot recall the last night I slept well. I know only it was some time before the Anstruthers' ball. Before Stricklend murdered my brother. Now the small, quiet hours are filled with the threat of nightmares and remembering. Nightmares about Freddie, about what I did to him, and how I failed him. And remembering the one other living person in this world who has ever made my heart dance. Bram. I know him to be living, even though I have not seen him or heard from him since the ball, because I frequently call upon one of the more reliable spirits who can assure me that he still treads the earth. It gives me such comfort to know he is safe. Comfort and hope, though I do not deserve such a gift. Would he ever forgive me for treating him so badly? I failed to meet him at the station that day as I had promised, and I sent no word of explanation. Mangan told me he had left London, returned to Yorkshire. I started so many letters to him but never posted one. He has never written to me, but then, why should he? I later discovered that he enlisted soon after war broke out.

My spirits tell me they do not see him in Darkness, so I know he still lives. At present, they do not hear heavy guns near him, so I am certain he is not in France now, and I thank the heavens for this. I pray daily that he be spared. Even if he is lost to me, I dearly want him to be safe. To be happy. I hope that he is able to know true happiness again one day. I fear I never may.

Iago sets up a rumbling purr and curls up next to my feet. I lean forward and stroke him gently.

"You may be ready for sleep, my little friend. I am not." I pull on my robe and step into my brocade slippers. The rain has ceased gurgling through the gutter outside my window, but it will be a damp and cool October night outside. I pull my green cloak about my shoulders and make my way down the wooden stairs and out into the garden. The trees have already shed most of their leaves, and their branches drip water onto the sodden lawns and paths. It is really too wet to sit anywhere, so I settle to pacing around the garden, slowly shutting out the nighttime noises of the city that drift over the walls. The streetlamps are no longer lit at night, and their glow has been replaced by the sweeping searchlights that scour the skies for the deadly zeppelins that come to drop their bombs on us. But tonight all is quiet. Quiet, that is, save for the urgent whispering of the spirits who have been waiting for me to come to them.

Where have you been, Morningstar?

Lilith! Lilith!

We thought you had forgotten us, Daughter of the Night.

I am here. I will always be here.

So many dead! So many terrible things.

The way I commune with the spirits has undergone such a change since war began to tear countries and families asunder. Now, all I have to do is to still my thoughts, to open my mind and my heart, to allow them to come, and the voices start up their clamor for my attention. Some are old friends, and all I recognize. There is the kindly grandmother who frets over suffering and is horribly dismayed by the war. She frequently tells me of young men, so very young, who have passed to the Land of Night, cut down before they had a chance to live their lives. She often weeps, setting up a chorus of wailing among the more sensitive spirits. Since the Yulemass calling, Amelia has come to speak with me from time to time. I am pleased to hear from her, but her sadness endures, and I wish there was more I could do to help her. I never hear from Father, which is a constant source of sadness for me. Sadness and guilt, for I know why he will not come. At times, I find communicating with the spirits brings me more pain than comfort, but I am a necromancer. I am here to allow those spirits to have their voice. It may be that their divinations can be of help or give solace to those of us still treading the earth. Or it may simply be that I am a cypher for the anguish of those who have crossed the Rubicon. Either way, I cannot turn my back on them.

I pause under the denuded walnut tree, leaning against its ancient trunk, the smooth bark cool against my back even through the thickness of my cloak.

Morningstar, you are welcome.

Good evening, Grandmother, who have you brought with you this peaceful night?

Oh, there is no peace to be had in these terrible times! The living have lost their wits and the dead cannot rest.

We must all do what we can to help one another.

Use the Elixir!

Who said that?

I am astonished to see a shadowy shape form on the grass in front of me. The earlier clouds have drifted away and a fair moon allows me to see that the figure is that of a young man. It is most unusual for a spirit to actually show themselves outside of the chamber, and without being formally called or summoned. I feel a chill enter my body as I realize he is wearing the uniform of a British soldier from the present. As he takes a step closer I gasp, for the slanting moonbeams fall upon his youthful face to reveal he is missing an eye and half his jaw has been blasted away. The wound is horribly fresh. Wet mud glistens upon congealing blood. I fight to keep my reaction hidden.

What is your name, soldier?

Alfie. Alfie James.

I am truly sorry to see you so terribly hurt, Alfie.

Mortar landed in our dugout. Everyone died. Every one of us broken and ruined.

You asked about the Elixir . . .

There's so much talk of it . . . down there. Among the dead.

What . . . what do the spirits say about it?

Some say as you should use it. You could, if you wanted to, couldn't you? Use it to bring us back. To give us another chance.

Yes, Morningstar! You can help us.

The cries and entreaties multiply until I cannot think for the cacophony. I throw my hands over my ears instinctively, even though I know I do not need them to hear the sounds the deceased make.

Stop! Please stop. You do not understand. The Elixir cannot be used in such a way . . .

Why not?

Are you afraid?

Is it because of what happened to your brother?

Freddie! Is Freddie among you?

He won't come. He doesn't want to talk to you.

But you will help us, won't you? Please? Please, Daughter of the Night.

I can't! It . . . wouldn't work. You don't understand. It wouldn't be right.

Is it right that I died at seventeen?

Oh, Alfie, I am so sorry.

You used it to try and save your own brother. Who's to say you shouldn't use it for us, too?

They fall to shouting and arguing until I am forced to flee. I run back down the gravel path, across the lawn, and into the house, not stopping until I am in my room. Iago is startled awake by my sudden entrance and sits up, green eyes glaring at me. I stand panting, struggling to steady my breath and my racing heart, waiting, listening, fearing the hordes of spirits might follow me, might assail me with their cries anywhere now. For what is to stop them? They all know of the Elixir. Is that my fault, because I used it? Perhaps those Lazarus witches who sought to have me thrown out of the coven, or at least stripped of my position as Head Witch, perhaps they were right. I have unleashed a hunger for new life among the spirits. The Land of the Dead cannot sleep now. The war is swelling their numbers, the dark power of violence stirs them, and I have shown them that there is a way they can tread the earth once more.

They are no longer content to stay where they are. If they have become sufficiently bold to address me uncalled, to argue so vehemently, to question my actions and demand things of me, what will they do next? Will they assail the thoughts of those who are not necromancers or witches? Will they set about haunting? Will they never be at peace? It seems that by using the Elixir on Freddie I have opened their minds to the possibility of resurrection, of letting them cross back to the Land of Day!

What have I done? What have I done?

The steelworks at night is a throbbing cauldron of industry. The mezzanine office is set in a separate building from the furnaces, yet Bram is still conscious of their intense heat. It is as if a barely tamed dragon were kept across the yard. But it is here, in the high-ceilinged factory which used to make nothing more threatening than cutlery, that the real danger is to be found. At the start of the war Cardale's Steel, like all other factories in the area, was commandeered to produce munitions for the war. Now, at the benches below the glass-walled office, women work with careful efficiency assembling the bombs and bullets that will, God willing, one day bring the fighting to an end.

Are we engaged in a futile mission? he wonders. *We produce the means of killing in order to put a stop to the killing. It is as if the war has rendered all good sense beyond us.*

His time spent in the trenches of France has left his spirit sapped and his faith in those in control of the armies shattered. He saw nothing there in that struggle, in that slaughter, to convince him that more of the same will bring peace. Now, home on a rare few weeks of leave, awaiting news of his next posting, he has welcomed the activity of helping his father at the steel yard.

Anything rather than remain idle. For without purpose to occupy myself, to occupy my thoughts . . .

It had been easier, he found, to bear the suffocating pain of losing Lilith while he was away. Away from anything that might remind him of her or of what might have been. But now, back in England, watching the brave young women at their hazardous work, he cannot help but think of Lilith. And thinking of her, conjuring her face in his mind's eye, still causes his heart to constrict. Still causes his breath to catch. He has become aware, over the years, that he cherishes this pain now. It is as if the heartache is all he has left of her, and he is unwilling to let it go.

He regards the scene below him with an artist's eye and contemplates picking up his sketchbook. After leaving London he had not the heart to paint, but in France he found fresh inspiration. He chose not to depict the carnage and horror but focused instead on the courage of the young men he served with, attempting to capture them in his battered notebook. In the determined concentration of the female workforce now employed at Cardale's, he sees an equal bravery.

Bram notices one of the women pause in her task. She looks up, not at him but toward the high windows that give only a view of the clouds. He sees her cock her head, listening. He, too, listens. At first he can hear nothing above the hammering and clanking on the factory floor, but then, faintly yet clearly, he makes out an altogether more chilling noise. His eyes meet the girl's at the moment they both recognize the throaty whir of the zeppelin. The women exchange glances. One reaches over to pat the trembling hand of another. Not one of them starts for the door. In the distance bombs can be heard bursting upon houses and factories with fatal inaccuracy. Should one find its target here the resulting explosion would wipe the buildings and all inside them from the earth, leaving no trace. Every worker knows it, but still they stay. Still they press on with their given part of the war. The air-raid siren has not sounded, suggesting the threat is still some way off. Bram has witnessed the calm courage of these women before and knows they will not desert their posts unless absolutely necessary.

From the far bench come the first faltering notes of a popular song. Other voices join in, and soon the singing fills the space, the defensive town guns lending a muffled percussion to the stalwart choir. At length the artillery falls silent. The threat has passed them over. This time.

Bram's father arrives and hurries up the metal staircase to the office. He opens his mouth to speak, no doubt to urge his son home, but changes his mind.

He knows me better now. He has learned more about me in my absence than ever he did while I was home.

Cardale senior holds out a telegram.

"This came for you, lad" is all he says.

Bram takes it from him and finds he has no reaction left to give when he reads that his next posting is to be in Africa.

21.

Despite the stove burning and the soup bubbling in its giant pots, the kitchen at St. Mary's is bitterly cold today. A cruel easterly wind has got up, strengthening over the past day or so, and it seems to force its way into this building through every gap it can find. Even as I hurry to help Sister Agnes set up the table, the exertion does not properly warm me. What must it be like for those with insufficient money to properly heat their homes? For myself, I know that part of the chill that troubles me resides inside, and comes from the dread I feel at the way in which the spirits suffer. They call to me so very often now, farther and farther from the usual places in which we used to commune. And they are so terribly distressed, I find it almost impossible to comfort them. There is to be a coven meeting soon, and I am undecided as to how to talk to the other senior witches about this. I would dearly welcome their help. Lord Grimes has been Master of the Chalice for many years, and he must surely have experienced something similar in other times of conflict. But I am concerned that my own actions have had more of an impact than I dare to believe. Perhaps the behavior of those in the Land of Night is indeed unprecedented. Perhaps it is my fault, and will be seen as such. Dare I raise the matter at the coven meeting? What would Druscilla say? She has already expressed her disappointment at my actions. Victoria, I think, understood. Others kept their views to themselves. To admit my fears that what I did has somehow caused lasting ill effects in the Land of Night . . . I cannot imagine how such an idea would be received. Nor if there is anything any of us can do about it.

"We are ready!" calls out Sister Bernadette, clapping her hands to alert everyone to the fact that the doors are about to be opened.

I take up my position behind one of the stew pots. The queue is longer than ever, and those in it have been made more desperate and more miserable by the cold. It is heartbreaking to see small children, some of them barefoot, sent out on their own to stand in line for hours to receive a meager bowl of soup. I am struck by the abundant red hair of one of the older boys, and it is only in my staring at him instead of concentrating on my ladle that I realize I know him.

"Freedom?" I ask quietly. "Freedom, can it be you?"

The boy frowns at me. I sense he recognizes me but that he is reluctant to acknowledge me. And who could blame him? Surely to be found in such a place, bowl raised for charity, is better done anonymously. Yet I must talk with him.

"Do you remember me? I came to your father's house with Charlotte. It was some years ago, you were not such a grown-up young man then, of course. And . . . I came to visit Bram. Do you recall?"

At the mention of Bram's name I fancy the boy brightens a little, but it is a fleeting alteration in his expression.

"Hurry up!" comes the cry from farther down the line.

I quickly spoon food into Freedom's dish, and notice that the twins are with him, too. They are boisterous as ever, as only small children can continue to be, whatever their circumstances. It disturbs me to realize, though, that they still seem small, as if they have not grown at a normal rate. How much must their diet have suffered to have this effect? The queue shuffles forward and the boys begin to move on. I have heard of Mangan's stance as a conscientious objector, and I know that his refusing conscription will ultimately land him in prison. I am assailed by a combination of guilt and longing when I think of that chaotic house in Bloomsbury. I have not returned there since losing Freddie, and Mangan's attendance at coven meetings has become less and less frequent. He has all but withdrawn from society, his pacifist beliefs and his German mistress rendering him an outcast. He knows me well enough to understand my reluctance to visit. Even so, I fear I have been a poor friend, and the sight of the children here, reduced to queuing in the soup kitchen, makes me ashamed of myself. I will call on Mangan and see if there is anything I can do to help.

I fully intended to make my visit directly after my shift at St. Mary's, but my plans are changed by the arrival of a note, delivered by Lord Grimes's second footman. It is short, missing some of the Master of the Chalice's customary warmth and its tone is urgent.

Morningstar, you are needed. Please come directly. Let us meet at the north gate.

I cannot conceive of a reason Lord Grimes would ask me to meet him in secret, away from his home, unless it is on pressing coven business. Business that he does not wish to address in his home, or, it appears, with other witches present. I know at once that the north gate refers to a specific entry to the cemetery where my father's empty grave lies.

By the time I have divested myself of my apron, donned my coat, and made my apologies for leaving early, darkness has already fallen. London is currently a place full of sorrows, and seems even more so at night with most streetlamps left unlit in an attempt to thwart the hateful zeppelins. Happily, I am comfortable in the dark and am able to employ the heightened senses of a witch to safely navigate my way through Holborn, threading nimbly between the people who find themselves compelled to be abroad, walking briskly east, beyond Fitzroy Square, skirting Regent's

Park, and on toward the graveyard. As I draw nearer to our rendezvous point, I begin to wonder if Lord Grimes has noticed the restlessness of the spirits and wishes to talk to me about it. Or could it be that he has news regarding the Sentinels? He is not a man given to panic, and I can be sure he would not have arranged such a meeting if he were not greatly concerned about something.

I am but a few paces from the tall iron gates when I sense that I am being followed. No, not followed, *pursued*. I cast about me, but there is no one else to be seen in the street. No one, that is, living. What I see looming out of the night shadows renders me unable to move. The darkness itself seems to take shape and to form into a towering figure, more than eight feet tall, its features human but blurred, its presence one of pure menace. The realization that the power of the Dark Spirit has enabled it to manifest itself in such a fearsome form astonishes me. It is as if Willoughby has been feeding upon evil energy in the years since he last stood before me. Now he is more terrifying, more powerful, and more determined upon his intended victim. And that victim is me.

The apparition bounds toward me, covering the ground with awesome speed. I have mere seconds to galvanize myself from my stupor. I fling myself through the gate and stumble onto the dusty ground of the churchyard, just as Willoughby swoops. The swiftness of my movement has saved me from his grasp. I am aware of gasps and moans all around me: a chattering of spirits disturbed from their slumbers. Spirits that are, nowadays, so easily brought forth, as if they no longer sleep deeply, but rather are waiting.

While I have evaded the phantom form of the Dark Spirit, I am not beyond the reach of his magic. Magic that has increased and intensified since our last encounter. There swirls about him a foul-smelling mist that reaches for me, filling my nose and mouth with its unearthly poison. I clamber to my feet and force myself to stand firm. Beneath the dim glow of a lone streetlamp I see a carriage drawn to a halt and two men emerge. It is clear that, with the aid of Willoughby, they mean to snatch me away, and no doubt deliver me to the waiting Sentinels, most likely Stricklend himself.

I think not.

"You underestimate me, Dark Spirit. You and your master," I tell him. Willoughby turns, drawing himself up, his very presence sufficiently forbidding to make the men from the carriage pause in their step. That they don't flee in terror tells me they must at the very least be minor Sentinels themselves. I quickly cast a spell of disturbance, slamming shut the heavy gates that stood ajar between me and my earthbound assailants. If they have any spellcraft themselves they do not have time to use it. I begin an incantation to return a spirit to the Darkness, which is sufficient to cause Willoughby to have to muster his own power to resist me. At the same time I send a spell of small fire at the carriage. The canvas roof of the little vehicle is aflame in seconds. The horse whinnies in alarm, and the driver struggles to control it. The men are forced to return to beat at the fire which has taken hold. The terrified horse gives in to his natural instinct and bolts, sending one man sprawling onto the pavement, the other clinging to the carriage as it speeds away. A shout goes up and a policeman's whistle sounds. From farther up the street come running footsteps. I open the gates with another spell and hurry through them, relying on the fact that Willoughby will not want to confront me when I am among people. I feel his dark magic fading as I hurry to join the small crowd who have gathered to assist the panic-stricken horse. Only when I am certain the Dark Spirit has gone do I turn for home, cursing my own stupidity at being drawn into such a trap, wondering if Lord Grimes's footman who delivered the fake note to me is the only one of his servants to be in the employ of the Sentinels.

Stricklend is unaccustomed to being kept waiting, but if he is forced to linger somewhere, the earl of Winchester's drawing room is a pleasant enough place to do so. The family home of the Harcourts is a solid affair, its rooms stout and broad, its frontage foreboding, its decor utilitarian. That this is a man's house is glaringly evident. No woman has softened the edges of the grand wooden furniture with cushions or curlicues, or framed the tall windows with swags or bows. The earl has been a widower for many years, and until his son succeeds in marrying Lady Lilith, there is unlikely to be a female incumbent at Clifton Villas. As Stricklend drifts around the room casting his eye over a fine Louis XIV escritoire, he ponders the extra value the earl must place upon his only offspring, given that he has no wife to distract him and no other heir.

"Ah, Stricklend, forgive me." The earl strides through the door bringing with him his own enduring energy. "I was detained on business of the House. You know how insistent junior members can be that their cause is of the utmost urgency."

"Lord Harcourt." Stricklend offers a stiff bow. "Indeed, even in the Lords I fear there is no escape from the idealistic young."

The earl stands facing him, holding his gaze, deliberately challenging. "And were we not just such hopeful youths ourselves once?" he asks.

"A very long time ago, perhaps. Happily, the years have cured me."

Lord Harcourt gestures toward a high-backed Knole sofa and takes a seat in the one opposite. He knows the game well. Outside of Parliament, the two men are in opposition in all things. The Lazarus Coven and the Sentinels are sworn enemies. This is the man who has threatened his son. And yet they will observe the rules of engagement. They will be polite. They will conduct themselves with dignity. Nonetheless, the earl has no desire to drag out the meeting any longer than is necessary.

"I assume you are here to measure progress in my son's efforts to win over Lilith Montgomery. I can inform you he dined with her not three nights ago."

"I am aware that he did." Stricklend pauses to allow this minor triumph of information to rankle, then adds, "However, there is a world of difference between sitting at table with a dozen others and enjoying a more intimate liaison. No wedding date has been announced, I take it?"

"It has not," the earl concedes. "But—"

Stricklend holds up his hand. "Please, do not insult my intelligence by telling me that their friendship continues to deepen. The plain fact is that, for all his charms, your son has failed to win Robert Montgomery's daughter's hand in marriage. They are *affianced,* it is true, but their engagement is a long one, and those who know about such things tell me a wedding is, frankly, unlikely. No, I am sorry to say, waiting for the viscount to secure what we want is no longer an option."

The earl blanches but makes an impressive attempt to cover his anguish.

"Then . . . what do you propose to do? I have tried my utmost to get what you asked for. My son has been sincere in his attempts to ally himself to Lilith. You must surely see that we are not to blame if the plan has not brought about the desired result?"

"My dear Harcourt, it is not a question of apportioning blame. Where would be the benefit of recrimination and reproach? No. I am not here to admonish you for your failure. I come, as a representative of the Sentinels, simply to offer you a choice."

"A choice?"

"Quite so. Time is a harsh master, you will allow, which means we have not the luxury of more gentle options than these: Either you yourself obtain the Elixir for us, complete with the necessary spell to accompany it, which will, naturally, include the divulgence of the Great Secret, or we will remove from you the burden of fatherhood."

"You will kill Louis!"

"Would that there were another way. Our original ploy of using the seventh duke to manipulate his sister ended badly for all concerned. Your son has not succeeded in the more . . . romantic option. We believe that, given your position in the coven and your closeness to the Montgomery family, you are best placed to get the Elixir yourself. Particularly given suitable motivation."

"But the Elixir is kept in the catacombs of Fitzroy Square . . ."

"Which you could no doubt gain access to."

"Well, even if I could, I am not in possession of the Great Secret. That knowledge is handed down from one Head Witch to the next. Only Lilith knows the truth of it."

"Then when you obtain the vials I suggest you also obtain this *truth* from your precious Morningstar. Or bring the girl herself and let us do it. We have no particular preference."

"She will not tell me." The earl shakes his head firmly. "I promise you, she will not divulge that Secret to anyone."

"Really? We shall see. If you are not capable of getting the information from her, then bring the store of the Elixir, and bring your haughty Head Witch. When we have both, we will do the rest."

22.

As I sit in my room composing a letter to Mama I struggle to find suitable subjects about which to write. After the events of recent times, and the failed abduction attempt, I determined it was no longer safe to have her here in London. With some difficulty, I convinced her that the increase in the number of zeppelin raids was reason enough to send her out to Radnor Hall. The bombing alarmed her so, I knew she would be eager to escape it, and yet she does not like our country house. I believe she feels closer to Father here. Closer to Freddie. I was forced to spin another lie concerning Withers's health, telling her that he was unwell and badly needed the restorative peace and air of the countryside. At last she agreed to go. In my letter, I reassure her that the house continues to run smoothly despite her absence—although of course she is keenly missed—and that the servants are coping without Withers. I tell her what is blooming in the garden, which is very little just now, with spring reluctant to appear, as if such a cheerful season should be skipped as a matter of propriety amidst all the gloom of wartime London. I cannot mention anything that touches on the suffering people are experiencing here. To speak of the difficulties faced by Mangan's family would only distress her. I dare not mention Freddie. I know she likes to talk of him, but to engage in the fantasy that he is still alive is surely to compound the problem. I can only hope she will adjust given time. And of course I cannot write to her of what is

325

on my mind. How many times, I wonder, did Father long to unburden himself to the woman he loved most in the world, but was unable to do so because she knew nothing of him being a witch? I do not think I have ever felt so very alone. But who can I turn to in the coven? And Bram. If he were here would I tell Bram everything? Could I? Could I ever make a non-witch understand?

I try to put my mind to finishing the letter, but all of a sudden I am assailed by a feeling of such dread and fear that I drop my pen and clutch at my heart. My chest is so tight I can hardly breathe, and I know without a speck of doubt that Bram is in terrible danger. In front of me the splotch of ink from my dropped fountain pen spreads thickly across the white sheet of paper, as blood might spread across pale flesh.

"Bram!" I cannot help calling his name aloud in a breathless whisper of despair. "Oh, Bram!"

I must discover what is happening to him. I am so disturbed, so frightened, that it is hard for me to still my feverish mind sufficiently to call a spirit. I know many are close. I call to an old friend, a spirit who has helped me locate Bram more than once before.

I am here, Daughter of the Night.

Tell me please . . . is he hurt? What do you see? What can you hear?

I see him very still. His eyes are closed.

Does he breathe? Does he live?

Yes, he breathes. He lives.

I find I have been holding my own breath and now I gulp air once more. He is alive! Wounded, it appears, but alive. Perhaps that wound will be enough to bring him home. Oh, the thought of it moves me so! How have I endured all this dark, empty time without him? I know he loves me, or at least, he did love me. Will he still feel the same way after I let him down so badly?

After I abandoned him? Will he still want me? Is there a chance, after all, that we can be together? If a witch and a non-witch together is folly, then we will only be one small jot of madness in all the murder and muddle that this war has brought. Surely love is what matters? Love *is* what matters.

Fine sentiments, sister.

I know at once who is there.

Iago lets out a hiss of terror and arches his back, ears flat, teeth bared. He continues to growl, staring into the corner of the room. I jump to my feet. I am already shaken by what has happened to Bram, so that it takes me a moment to compose myself sufficiently to face Willoughby's spirit. As I do so, to my amazement, he begins to take shape in front of me.

"How dare you!" I speak to him aloud, feeling that it somehow puts distance between us and helps me believe that he is not present in my mind. If he wishes to appear, then I will talk to him as if he still treads the earth. "You are not invited and not wanted," I remind him. "Your masters have failed in their attempts to take what is not theirs, what will never be theirs. Your persistence is as pointless as it is unwelcome."

Do you think they will give up so easily, after centuries of waiting for the right moment? If they draw back it is only to regroup. To choose a moment that suits them best before redoubling their efforts. You cannot fight them off forever, Morningstar.

The shadows in the corner of the room appear to grow denser and take human form. Iago continues to growl. I stand my ground as the figure emerges, tall, strong, with a face that could be described as handsome were it not for the harshness of his eyes and the evil that surrounds him like a cloak of bitterness.

"Freddie is gone and Bram is beyond your reach. The Lazarus Coven has never been better prepared and better protected. You must realize that the Sentinels will never succeed. Go back to the Darkness where you belong."

And whom might I find there—your brother, perhaps? Your little maid? You should never have made her a witch, you know. She wasn't strong enough. Nor were you strong enough to save her. How many more loved ones will you sacrifice to your cause, Daughter of the Night? How many?

And he is gone. Disappeared in the beat of a bat's wing. As if he had never been. But he was here. And the words he spoke tear at my soul. I place my hand over my heart and wait until it steadies before quickly putting on my green cloak. I must go to the chamber. I must summon spirits in the safety of the sacred circle and ask for their advice. It is clear I must act, but I cannot do so alone. I need the guidance of far older souls than my own.

As I cross the garden I become aware of further whisperings of the spirits. They are ever present now, and I fear what might happen if the Sentinels were ever to regain the Elixir and the Great Secret. So many souls, lost and wandering, hankering after a physical form again. How readily they might try to cross the Rubicon if Stricklend were to practice his dark magic again. What is more, they are also affected by the collective fear that washes through the city when the zeppelins come, bringing with them their lethal cargo. By the time Iago and I have descended the twisting stone stairs, however, I realize that there is something else. Something more. I have been here during other air raids, but I have never heard so many voices, so noisily raised. It is as if Land of Night spirits are all trying to make themselves heard, each and every one of them. Louis was right, they are no longer content to remain where they belong, many of them. And it is my fault. They saw what I did for Freddie. They think I could bring them all back to tread the earth.

But I cannot!

I will go into the Great Chamber and will do my best to settle these poor spirits and to ask guidance from those who know more about these things than I ever shall.

I push open the ornate double doors, separating the wings of the giant dragonfly that decorates them, and step into the room that is so sacred to our coven. The shock of finding that the space is not empty makes me gasp. A figure, a man, stands in front of the altar, his hands upon the witches' trove, which is open, its lid flung back on its hinges. Although I might reasonably have expected to find a spirit taking form here, this is not one of the deceased. This is a living person. A person who is known to me. I gather my wits quickly. Iago stops at the sight of the intruder. I clear my throat and make my voice as steady as I am able.

"Lord Harcourt. What brings you to the chamber at this hour, uninvited?" I ask.

"Lilith." He smiles at me, seemingly untroubled at being found trespassing. "The friendship between our families is many generations old. Would you refuse me entry to your home?"

"Refuse, no. If I were asked. But you chose to come here in secret. That is . . . curious." My gaze has lighted on his left hand and I see to my horror that he holds the casket containing the Elixir. Now all is clear! Stricklend has sent him. He must have known the earl would be familiar with the catacombs. How long, I wonder, has it taken him to devise a method of getting in unseen? Of gaining entry without alerting any of my guardians from the Land of Night or Day?

I silently call my Cavaliers, but they do not come. Or rather, they cannot. I sense their struggle and know that they are being held. This has been a carefully considered course of action. The earl has seen to it that my spirit guardians are kept from me. What else has he planned? Trying hard not to let my fear show, I step forward. The torches around the room burst into life as I bid them do so, but I leave some unlit, the better to conceal from the earl my trembling hands.

"My father always said you were a useful ally but that you would make a dangerous enemy. I see that he was right in this."

"As in so many things."

"You have the Elixir. I assume you intend taking it to Strick-lend." Lord Harcourt's facade of calm slips for just a second. Just long enough for me to see that I have disconcerted him. I press home my meager advantage. "I must say, I am surprised and disappointed. I had thought better of you. I know you and Father did not always see eye to eye, but you had his respect. And mine. Until now." I begin to walk around the perimeter of the Sacred Circle. Slowly. Carefully. Iago follows, his lithe little body tense, his tail whipping from side to side.

Outside, bombs continue to fall. Even down here the walls shake as nearby buildings are burst apart. "I could never have imagined," I go on, "that you, a senior witch of the Lazarus Coven, would betray us, would break your vows, would hand over the Elixir to such a vile and dangerous creature. For what, Lord Harcourt? What has he promised you? What did he have to offer you that persuaded you to trade your own soul?"

The earl's face darkens. "Do not presume to judge me, Lilith Montgomery."

"I do presume! Any Lazarus witch would judge you likewise. You are a traitor!"

"You are not so blameless, Morningstar! You were ready to break your vows to save your worthless wretch of a brother!"

"I broke no vows to save my brother! As Head Witch I alone am permitted to use the Elixir. I did so out of love. And I paid a high price for what I did. You would give away our most treasured possession, sell it to a man who would use it for spirits alone know what dreadful purposes."

"Who is to say they are dreadful? Why should we be the ones who decide who should use the greatest of all the necromancer's tools? Why not him?"

"You make a poor argument to justify your actions, my lord."

"But you have no answer for it! Why is our refusal to use the

Elixir the right and only way? You yourself saw that it might not be. You yourself, Lady Lilith. Are you so different?"

"From that monster? The man who had Freddie killed? I most certainly am! And what is more, I did not divulge the Great Secret. That remains safe with me, and was safe even as I used Infernal Necromancy to raise my brother from the Land of Night." I stop, for we have both come to the silent question that now drowns out all other sounds. "Tell me, Lord Harcourt, how do you intend obtaining the Great Secret from me? I see you are alone. Do you plan to torture me, perhaps? Do you think my father did not teach me how to use travel with the spirits to avoid the torment of pain? Do you think to frighten me like a young girl, spooked by stories of horror? There is no one dear to me you can threaten here now. My mother is far away and well protected. Freddie is gone. Even . . ."

"Even . . . ?"

I know in this instant that he has been informed of my feelings for Bram, and find myself in the unlikely position of being thankful that Bram is at this moment somewhere on the other side of the world, and being tended by doctors and no doubt guarded by fellow soldiers.

"There is no one else I care for. Save Louis, of course, but you would hardly threaten your own son." Something in his expression, some minute alteration in his stance, a fleeting fear in his eyes, gives him away. Now I understand. He is not doing this for the promise of riches or glory. He is doing this for Louis. He is acting out of love, just as I did for Freddie.

He sees that I understand, and I fancy it weakens rather than strengthens his resolve. I take a step toward him. He instinctively steps back, holding the casket away from me.

"Don't do this," I beg him. "Louis would not want you to. Please, do not do this."

"You could simply have married him." The earl shakes his head, blinking away tears. "He loves you. You know that. You've admitted as much. If you'd ceased prevaricating and married him, the two of you would have become close. He could have persuaded you to share the Great Secret with him willingly, I'm sure of it."

"No."

"Yes! That way, none of this would have been necessary."

Another bomb falls, very close this time, causing plaster to fall from the north wall and the chalice on the altar to teeter. Iago flattens himself against the cold stone floor.

"I will never let you have the Great Secret for Stricklend. He is a wicked man. He would use it badly. Cruelly. Dreadfully. Without restraint. Without care. Without morality. Such a person must not ever be given such terrible power, surely you see that?"

The earl stands straight now and his eyes harden once more. "I knew you would not tell me what I need to know. I have known you all your life, Lilith. I knew that without the leverage of a loved one I would not be able to pry the secret from you. But Stricklend is different. Stricklend is a Sentinel. He has his own skills. His own strong magic. He will get what he wants from you. Of that there can be no doubt."

Before I have a chance to ask him how he intends to get me to wherever it is the Sentinels are waiting for me, I hear footsteps on the stairs and two burly men burst into the room. I summon a spell of disturbance, flinging one of the benches across their path. One of the henchmen trips over it, the other continues toward me. I raise my hand and use a spell of small fire to set flames dancing along his sleeve. Alarmed, he stops to beat at them. I seize my moment and run at Lord Harcourt to try to wrest the casket containing the vial of Elixir from him.

He tightens his grasp. "Do not make this any more unpleasant than it need be, Lilith. I must have it."

"No!" I try to summon my guardians, to call upon Hekate to lend me her strength, but there is powerful magic here, far more powerful than anything Louis's father could manage alone. A cold sweat dampens my neck as I become aware of a familiar, loathsome presence. Willoughby! The Sentinel has his pet spirit here, in the chamber, acting as a conduit for his own magic. No wonder my friendly spirits are blocked and my own magic diminished. My suspicions are confirmed when I see a ragged shadow emerge from beneath the altar. Iago leaps to stand in front of me, hissing fiercely at the shape that moves closer and closer. The poor cat is too terrified to run, and too loyal to leave me. In a second he has been hurled across the floor of the chamber.

"Leave him alone!" I cry, just as Lord Harcourt's men lay their hands upon me. "You are making a terrible mistake. You must not help Stricklend. You must not!" I am hauled backward. The earl follows me, still clutching the casket.

"Louis will never forgive you for this," I tell him. "Never."

"Louis need never know what has taken place. Stricklend will send you to join your beloved father, you might even thank him for that. And when you are gone, as you have no natural successor, I shall make sure that I become the next Head Witch of the Lazarus Coven, and one day Louis will take my place." For the briefest of moments I see some remorse in his expression. He seeks to rid himself of it by another attempt to justify his actions. "Remember, Lilith. I do not choose between a modest life for my son or a distinguished one; I choose this life for him or none at all."

It is as his men drag me through the doorway and out of the chamber that I hear the bomb fall. The bomb that will hit us. The others hear it, too. For several terrible seconds we stand rendered incapable of movement, listening to doom speeding its way down through the night sky, ripping the blackness apart as it plummets toward us. And then everything happens as if in one fluid, almost balletic movement. One of the men lets go of my arms and turns to run. The other almost instinctively, I think, grips me tighter. But he only does so for a fraction of a second, for it is then that the roof explodes above us. There are screams. There is no time to run. I could try to find protection beneath the altar, but I know that only something much stronger will save me now. I close my eyes and call upon Hekate one final time, while bricks and stone and timbers and choking dust rain down upon us, as the largest bomb ever dropped on London finds its mark on Number One Fitzroy Square.

23.
1919

I hardly recognize the reflection that peers back at me from the full-length mirror in my new bedroom. The severity of my recently bobbed hair is lessened somewhat by the pearl-encrusted headdress that will hold my veil in place. I have quickly grown to like the sleek lines of my short hairstyle, and it is a relief not to have to spend hours taming and dressing long tresses every day. Mama, with a new forthrightness that has come to her with age, has declared it hideous. Louis likes it, which matters, I suppose. I am still sufficiently old fashioned to believe a bride should at least attempt to present herself in a manner which pleases her husband-to-be.

Turning slowly before the looking glass I take in the cut and detail of my wedding dress. I could not have done without Charlotte's help these past few months, and she outdid herself in finding me such an excellent designer. One who, spirits be thanked, listened to my requirements and produced something that does not make me feel ridiculous. The lines are modern, slender, skimming my narrow curves, emphasizing my naturally angular silhouette. The fabric, in contrast, is Chinese silk and antique lace, beaded with pearls. The combination is very pleasing. When the day comes, I will, I hope, make Mama proud and Louis happy.

"Thank you, Mrs. Morell, I'll take it off now. No further fittings will be necessary."

"You are satisfied with the finished dress, my lady?"

"I'm delighted with it. You have all worked so hard and done an excellent job. Thank you."

I hold out my arms so that she can undo the tiny covered buttons at the cuffs.

"You look exquisite, my lady," says Mrs. Morell. "I will see to it that the veil is sent over to you the moment it arrives from Paris," she assures me, clapping her hands together in a gesture of delight that also prompts her assistant into action, so that I am soon out of the gown and back in my own more mundane clothes.

When I am alone again I take Iago in my arms and the two of us step out of the wide glass doors onto the balcony to enjoy the view of the Thames at night. This outlook, directly opposite the Houses of Parliament and with vistas both up- and downriver, was the reason that I chose this penthouse apartment. After the house at Fitzroy Square was destroyed I knew I did not want anything so grand, or so big. Mama is, against all expectations, happily settled in Radnor Hall and has no wish to return to living in London. Times have changed. It is no longer practicable or desirable to employ a large retinue of servants. And besides, there is only me. It is surely a foolish indulgence in this modern age to keep a dozen maids and footmen and suchlike all dancing attendance upon one person. And when Louis and I are married, well, Clifton Villas will be our town residence. I cannot say I relish the prospect. It is a gloomy house, with little charm, and a great many rooms without sense or purpose. Perhaps, given time, I can persuade Louis that my lovely apartment would suit our needs better. It certainly suits mine.

By the end of the war this poor city was badly battle-scarred. The bombing raids had not been many, but they had left their mark. Added to which, the sheer lack of everything, including manpower, meant that buildings went untended for years; parks were either allowed to run wild or were plowed up to grow food;

monuments and landmarks stood neglected; lead was stripped from roofs, and railings from the front of houses to further the war effort. The process of regeneration has been a slow and painful one. This building, completed only months ago, and erected to stand with its toes almost in the Thames, presents its broad, fiercely modern frontage toward the Victorian gothic of Parliament across the water. I like this juxtaposition. As a Lazarus witch, I am at once a part of something ancient almost beyond memory, but I am also of the generation that must, perhaps more than any before us, look forward and construct a new, bold future, putting the pain of the recent past behind us.

Iago wriggles in my arms and I set him down on the balcony. He springs up onto the little iron table and sets about washing his paws. He is quite aged now, but his fur is still black as midnight, and he is still as lithe and light on his feet as ever. He has had no trouble adjusting to his new surroundings and seems to enjoy our high vantage point as much as I do. I doubt he appreciates the finer points of the design of the building, however. I think the place quite wonderful. After my childhood spent surrounded by the dark clutter favored by followers of Victorian fashion, and then Mama's giddying swirls of Art Nouveau at Fitzroy Square, I was at once drawn to the fresh, clean lines and elegant simplicity of Waterloo Court. The apartments are spread over seven bone-white floors, all with balconies overlooking the river, with woodwork, windows, and smooth railings picked out in pale mint green. Some people have expressed their horror at the bold shapes and unfamiliar proportions that this new style dictates, but I find them perfectly fitting for the age we are now in. Frivolity and frippery would be out of place. The era of excess has gone. How much more dignified, more honest, somehow, this modern fashion is.

Of course I would rather Fitzroy Square had been spared. It was our family home, and I had been happy there. Its being bombed was yet another cause for heartbreak for Mama, and I forbid her from visiting the ruins. Not only was the house damaged beyond saving, but lives were lost that terrible night. Many of the servants were still downstairs in the kitchens or had moved to the shelter in the basement area to the front of the house. Some, though, had already gone up to their attic bedrooms and were killed the instant the bomb fell. We lost Cook and Sarah, the scullery maid. And our housekeeper, dear Mrs. Jessop, whose absence Mama feels dreadfully.

Iago and I were lucky to escape with our lives. Most of the catacombs caved in under the weight of the collapsing house and the force of the bomb blast. If ever I needed proof of the protection magic can give, it was there when I found myself standing unscathed among the rubble. All around me was devastation. What had been a fine house was reduced to so much debris, broken windows, shattered bricks, even the twisted wreckage of Mama's beloved iron staircase, like the spine of some great slaughtered creature. Through it all came a pitiful mewing. Iago emerged, ironically saved by the wicked blow Willoughby had dealt, as it had left him lying winded beneath the lintel of the double doors to the chamber. And there was the casket containing the precious vial of Elixir, risen to the surface through the random force of the blast, a precious piece of flotsam amid a sea of chaos. Everything else the coven possessed by way of sacred items for worship and necromancy was lost. The Great Chamber is sealed forever, and in it lay Maygor's Silver Thread, the witches' trove, and the chalice. I thank the spirits the priceless drops of the Elixir were spared. The casket holding the single existing vial is now safely hidden in a place I am confident it can remain undisturbed, the Montgomery diamonds nestling snugly with it.

It has been hard to witness Louis's grief at losing his father. He loved him, naturally, and I have agonized over whether or not to tell him the real reason for the earl being in the catacombs that night. To burden our friendship, to start our married life together with the weight of such a secret is not easy. But I have decided there is no benefit to him knowing that his father was about to betray the coven. Or that he was prepared to sacrifice me in doing so. The man is dead. He can do no more harm. And how much harder it would be for Louis to accept his death if he knew that his actions were all for him. It would take from him the memory of the father he adored, and saddle him with guilt for his death. No, it is better he never knows. I will simply have to bear this hurtful knowledge alone, for his sake.

As darkness falls, London begins to sparkle with lights. It is a cloudless, late spring night, and the stars are too beautiful to miss. I step back into my bedroom and walk through to the hallway where I take the lift installed specifically to access my roof garden. The mechanism whirs softly as I am borne up through the ceiling, and out onto my very own high plateau. The space is comfortably large enough for reclining chairs, tables, and a small swimming pool, but it is not for these that I have made the ascent today. At the far end of the garden, with its low rendered wall, white-painted, and a door displaying a detailed replica of the dragonfly that once adorned the doors of the Great Chamber, sits the glass-domed construction which speeds my heart a little each time I enter it. Once I realized that the catacombs were lost forever, I knew I needed somewhere I could connect with the Land of Night. If this could not, for practical reasons, be underground, then where better than high up in the darkness of the nocturnal sky, as close to the starry heavens as it is possible to be? The engineers who constructed Waterloo Court rose to the challenge of my request for an observatory splendidly, and I shall be forever grateful for the fine results of their labors.

Inside, although there are in fact walls surrounding the space, they are barely noticeable, for they are less than a yard high, the rest of the construction being entirely of glass. And what glass it is! The specially made panes, some flat, others curved, are slotted into a spider's web of slim iron, giving a startling view of the skies above, as well as the city stretched out below. I love to come here on stormy nights, when the wind and rain assail my transparent shelter, but I am kept dry and snug, able to experience all the wildness of the elements without so much as getting wet. And on clear nights, such as this one, I feel as if I have been raised up to dwell in the heavens and browse among the crystal stars. There is a telescope in the north of the room, mounted on gleaming brass fittings, so that I may study the celestial bodies more closely. It is a diverting pastime, perhaps the one guilty luxury I permit myself in these troubled times.

When the coven lost its home, it fell to me to provide, or at least to find, a new one. There were many ideas put forward by senior witches, all of a uniformly gothic and gloomy nature. But I felt the need for change. For a sacred space that would signify our commitment to the future, as well as the past. Who is to say that we must dig downward to reach the spirits? It is only tradition that has dictated this. We are not in the business of plucking the dead from their graves; we do not require them to physically clamber to the surface, so why must we burrow underground like moles? Spirits exist on a plane all of their own. It is the night that gives us best access to them, not the subterranean dark. There was much dissent among the coven at my idea. I expected it. But I held to my view. I even said that I would be happy for the senior witches to have an alternative venue for their meetings, so long as they realized that I, as Head Witch, would maintain the sacred space where I chose to. They were, after all, free to stay away from meetings held here if they wished. After a deal of argument it was agreed that the observatory would be the new home for the Lazarus Coven, so long as it proved successful. I had cushioned seating installed around the inside of the low wall, and the floor is painted exactly as the one in the Great Chamber had been. If spirits were reluctant to come to it, the matter would be reviewed. In fact, the spirits have shown themselves happy to come here when called or summoned, and to feel very at home in the airy, ethereal space.

There was another reason for my wish to free our rituals and meetings from such a place as a catacomb. I still wake gasping and panic-stricken some nights when the sight of what I saw in the Darkness when Freddie was nearly taken into its depths fills my nightmares. To think that I might have lost him to such a place. To such . . . beings. The Darkness holds all that is bad in this world once it no longer treads the earth. I will do all I can to stay away from it and not to put my fellow witches near such danger ever again.

A bell in a small alcove by the door rings gently, alerting me to a visitor. I pick up the telephone on the wall next to it.

"Who is it, Terence? Oh, please send her up to the observatory. And would you be so kind as to bring a tray of gin and tonic, too?"

One further advantage of the observatory over the catacombs is that it can be used for entertaining my friends. I could hardly have invited them into the Great Chamber, even if its existence had not been a secret.

Charlotte arrives in her customary flurry of excitement, with Terence, my rather aged butler, trailing in her wake bearing the tray of drinks. I know him to be uneasy with heights, so that he has to steel himself to walk about on the roof garden. He is certainly no Withers, but he is quiet and diligent, and since he'd been wounded in the war and lost an eye, I know he would have struggled to find a position elsewhere. He lives with other servants in the building in the staff rooms in the basement, which suits us both. There is a restaurant on the ground floor from which food

can be sent up, as well as my own small kitchen where Terence
assembles breakfasts and suppers. Mama cannot fathom how I
manage to live like this, but I find it blissfully uncomplicated and
far more private than life at Fitzroy Square ever was.

"Lilith, darling!" Charlotte kisses me quickly and then flops
onto a chaise longue, tugging off her gloves and removing her
hat. "Goodness, coming up here is like visiting some rare bird
up in its aerie."

"I think that would make me an eagle."

"Really? Oh no, that won't do. Much too predatory."

"An owl, perhaps? I am something of a night bird."

Terence hands us both tall glasses of gin and tonic with generous slices of lime and lashings of ice. He picks up Charlotte's discarded accessories and leaves us, walking a little unsteadily back
to the lift door on the far side of the garden.

"No, owl won't do," Charlotte goes on. "They are too plump,
somehow. I have it! You are a phoenix! You have risen from the
ashes of Fitzroy Square and flown up to this lofty perch in all your
glorious colors!"

I laugh at her. "Charlotte, what nonsense you spout. I am the
least colorful person I know."

"Oh well, have it your own way." She sips at her drink. "I must
say, that new man of yours might be unsteady on his pins, but
he's a whiz with the gin bottle."

"He's settling in."

"How you manage without a lady's maid I simply cannot imagine. Lord knows it's an utter nightmare trying to find servants
these days. Any worth having are all snapped up. Perfectly good
maids have got all sorts of modern ideas into their heads since
the war and now don't want to be in service. I mean to say, how
is one supposed to function? Mummy says if things continue the
same way we shall be forced to give up Glengarrick."

"Oh, surely not. The estate's been in your family for generations. Can't you just, well, manage with fewer footmen?"

Charlotte looks at me as if I have taken leave of my senses. "Lilith, darling, these are my parents we are discussing. They have no notion of 'managing' when it comes to servants. They think the setup you have here quite extraordinary. No, it will be down to me to save them, I fear. I shall simply have to marry well, marry quickly, and marry money."

"Well, that sounds straightforward. Have you a lucky groom in mind?" I ask, sitting on the chair next to her.

"Don't tease me. All very well for you to be smug. You know you've bagged one of the few decent bachelors going. How is darling Louis?" Charlotte settles deeper into the chaise and savors more gin.

"He's very well, thank you."

"Counting the days to the wedding, no doubt. Should be quite an occasion. Though so sad he won't have his dear father there." She pauses for form's sake before adding, "Still, nice to be marrying an earl instead of a viscount, one would imagine."

I know I should disapprove of so many things about Charlotte, but she has been a stalwart friend to me through difficult times, and she does make me smile.

"I'm sure the perfect knight, armor gleaming, will come galloping up to your door any day now, begging for your hand," I tell her.

"Huh! I've had precisely two proposals of marriage since the beastly war ended. One was from a friend of Father's who is more than twice my age, and the other from Sticky Stackpole. I mean, *really*. Someone has to tell him that cultivating an abundant mustache will not disguise the fact that he has a weak chin and an even weaker mind."

"But he is ridiculously rich."

"There is no such thing, Lilith. Which you should very well know. Once you and Louis unite the Montgomery and Harcourt fortunes you will be quite the wealthiest couple in London, I shouldn't wonder." She is thoughtful for a moment and studies me closely. "You are looking a little thin. Are you eating properly?"

"Now you sound like Mama."

"You won't do that gorgeous gown justice if you're all thin and scrawny."

"I'll bear that in mind."

"Most likely wedding day nerves getting to you."

"It's weeks away yet."

"But it will be a splendid event. Any girl would be a bit jittery, I'd have thought. So long as that's all it is?"

"What do you mean?"

She sits up and puts her hand on mine. "You are happy about marrying Louis, aren't you? Oh, I know I joke about marrying for money and all that, but you understand what I truly believe, Lily. One should marry for the right reason. You do love him, don't you?"

"Of course I do," I reply with practiced ease, though I no longer know whom I am trying to convince more, Charlotte or myself.

"It's just that, well, he has wanted to marry you for so very long, and you always said no before."

"Things change, Charlotte. People change."

"I suppose so. Only . . ."

"Charlotte, if you have something to say don't you think you ought to come out and say it?"

She sits up, setting her glass down on the pale ash table. She takes both my hands in hers and squeezes them tightly.

"You simply do not look like a love-struck bride to me."

"Oh, Charlotte, really, we are not silly girls . . ."

"No, listen, it's just that I know how you look when you are in love, Lily, because I have seen it once before, and this is not the same." She smiles at me and adds, "I have never seen anyone as *infuriatingly* beautiful as you were when you were with Bram!"

I keep my voice level but avoid meeting her eye.

"That was a long time ago, Charlotte. Everything is different now."

"Is it? Are you telling me if he were to walk through that door now I wouldn't see that same transformation in you? Because to be perfectly frank, darling, I believe you are still every bit as much in love with him as ever you were, and what you feel for Louis is not the same, is it?"

"Perhaps not," I say, "but who is to say it is not more . . . sensible?"

Charlotte lets go of my hands and waves hers in a gesture of despair. "Lily, *please*! We are talking about being in love—I don't see in the slightest what *sensible* has got to do with anything."

I say nothing, for what can I say? I cannot tell Charlotte that, before that fateful zeppelin raid, I had myself decided I would find Bram again and tell him how I felt, because I believed love matters above all else. I cannot tell her how what happened changed things yet again. That how Lord Harcourt acted, what he was prepared to do, and what I must do to fulfill my obligations as Head Witch of the Lazarus Coven, all these things made me realize that no one but another witch could understand me. That it would be unfair, in fact, to love and be loved by a non-witch, for they could never understand the danger that surrounds me. The constant vigilance I must maintain because of what I am. Louis understands. Louis accepts all of these things, because we share that common path. Marrying Bram, even if I could find him, even if he would forgive me, even if he still wanted me, would be wrong. It would be unfair, unkind. It is better I do not see him again. Yes, marrying Louis is the right thing to do, however unromantic Charlotte thinks me. It is the sensible thing to do.

24.

From the window of the bedroom that currently serves as his studio, Bram has a good view of the finer houses in Skimmerton. His mother offered little resistance to the idea of his using the room. She was so pleased to have him home again she would, he thinks now, have agreed to his commandeering the drawing room if he had only asked for it. His father had not been so accommodating.

"Thought you'd done with all that," he'd said, seeing Bram wincing as he attempted to raise a paintbrush to easel height. "Would have thought you could put that arm to better use, now that the hospital has seen fit to send you back to us."

The rifle bullet that found Bram's shoulder had seen him spend the final months of the war in a ward full of similarly wounded soldiers. He counted himself fortunate. His injury had healed, leaving only a scar and some residual weakness and occasional pain. After the months he had endured in Africa, fighting disease and hunger as much as the enemy, watching his brothers in arms fall victim to the deadly Blackwater fever or malaria day after day, trudging through the swamps along the Rufiji River or baking beneath the equatorial sun alongside the Ugandan railway, he knew he had been lucky to come home at all.

"I've said I'll come in to the steelworks with you, Father. I can enjoy my painting in my spare time."

His father's answer had been a disapproving grunt, but Bram

has stuck to his word. For months he has traveled across town to the steel yard and spent his days in the office, carrying out his father's instructions, familiarizing himself with the running of the works. And as soon as he is free he hurries home to his paints and his canvases and picks up wherever he left off, with whichever painting currently holds him spellbound. He has never felt so inspired, so in the grip of some artistic fever of creativity. It is as if, after touching the edge of oblivion, after the smell of death filled his nostrils and almost claimed him, he is reinvigorated with the desire, the *need*, to put what he has seen, what he has felt, what he has known, onto paper. To strive to capture the presence of those who were lost. To depict what they went through, and to show the strange land where they fought, suffered, and, some of them, died. He has been entirely taken up with his mission this past year and a half. And now it is done.

He turns back from the window and considers what he has achieved. The paintings stand leaning against every wall, stacked against one another, carefully wrapped and bound and ready for their journey down to London. So many images. So many faces.

But have I succeeded? Will others see what it is I have struggled to show? Or will they simply find figures? Compositions. Clever slants of light or depths of shadow, but nothing more. Nothing more.

Moving to the bedside table he picks up the letter he received from Jane the previous week. Reading her words he can hear her warm but harassed voice in his ear.

". . . so you simply must stay with us when you come up for your exhibition. Mangan will be so very pleased to see you. He has not yet recovered his health entirely. The months he spent in that dreadful place weakened his lungs forever, I fear. Thank heavens darling Lilith was able to come to our rescue and secure him a place working on a farm in Somerset. You know, he took to the work! Can you imagine?"

Indeed, Bram can imagine. He can just see Mangan coming

to grips with plowing fields or milking cows and then setting about telling everyone else how it should be done. The image makes him smile, but he knows the reason he reads and rereads Jane's letter is for the pleasure of reading of Lilith. To hear news of her is to feel a tiny bit closer to her once more. He resolved, while lying wounded in the hospital in Nairobi, that if he made it home he would seek out Lilith. Go to her and tell her how he felt. Make her see that the gap between them was bridgeable, and that there was no one else he could ever envisage being with. He would convince her that somehow they would find their place in the world, together. The war has changed things. What stood in their way a few years earlier surely did not, could not, matter so much now. He would find her. He would speak with her. He would make her see.

But men make plans and the gods laugh. Perhaps it was the fever I suffered after I was wounded that gave me such a ridiculous view of how things might be.

He forces himself to read on, make himself face the bleak reality that the second page of Jane's letter contains.

". . . Charlotte is quite the darling of high society now and is in the newspaper on the arm of some duke or other nearly every day, it seems. Or course, Lilith was so very busy with her war work, doing so marvelously in the soup kitchens at St. Mary's Convent. And now she is to be married. I think you met her husband-to-be, the Earl of Winchester? He was still a viscount back then, of course, but his father was killed quite recently, in an air raid. How people have suffered! Mangan seems to recall Lilith's fiancé being at that rather grand ball you went to some years back, do you remember? You and Perry looked terribly dashing, and poor dear Mangan was barely let through the door, he looked such a fright! We saw the notice in the *Times*. So I suppose she will cease being Lady Lilith Montgomery and become Lady Lilith Harcourt instead. Oh, say you will stay with us at least until the week after your show finishes, so that Mangan may have plenty of time with you, do . . ."

Lady Lilith Harcourt. Louis. Of course. She was always going to marry Louis. She was always going to marry an earl. She was always going to marry a witch. Why wouldn't she marry an earl?

Bram folds the letter and puts it in his jacket pocket. He is not quite ready to dispose of it yet. He will go to London. He will stay in the familiar muddle of the house in Bloomsbury and enjoy letting Jane fuss over him, and see the children, and spend time with Mangan. He will hold his exhibition, show his work to the world, and brace himself for its reaction. But he will not look for Lilith. He will not hold her hand and tell her what is in his heart. He will not.

He busies himself checking the packaging on his paintings, and marking them off against the list he has made, with the layout of the hang attached. As he does so, his eye is caught by a slim, unwrapped canvas standing in the corner of the room behind some works that are unfinished. He knows what it is. He knows what he will see if he chooses to look at it. Who he will see.

Cross with himself now, he strides over to the corner and drags the canvas from its hiding place. Without pausing, he takes the painting and carries it to the empty easel, where he sets it up and stands back, mouth grim, determined to face his fears. Lilith's enigmatic face gazes back at him. The artist in him is struck at once by the quality of the work. It is one of his best, and he knows it. The man in him is struck by the beauty of the subject.

Dear God, Lilith. What spell have you cast over me?

In his heart he knows that he did not imagine her love for him. That it is more than likely duty and loyalty and fear that have made her abandon him and turn away from the possibility of a life together. And he believes, if he allows himself to do so, that were he to go to her, to take her hands in his, to meet her soulful gaze, and to tell her he still loves her, he still wants her, he would see in those glorious, wild green eyes that she still loves him, too. There and then, he resolves to try one more time. To risk the pain of possible rejection. To risk humiliation. To risk falling again into that kind of madness into which he descended those lonely years ago when she spurned him.

We could be together. We could find a way. If she still loves me. For after all, surely there is no greater magic than love.

🕷

It is a warm April night and the window is open. Sitting on the cream sofa in my bedroom, my eyes closed, I can hear the chimes of Big Ben announcing the hour. Nine o'clock. Louis will be here any minute to take me to Charlotte's fancy-dress party at the club she has booked for the purpose in Kensington. I would rather not go. Not only because of my natural dislike of such large, rowdy gatherings but because there are so many spirits whispering in my ear tonight. Some of them seem so lost. Others have pressing matters they wish to discuss with me. How can I leave them to go off and indulge in hours of frivolous society? Why do I allow myself to be persuaded to attend such things? I know the answer is Louis. He loves me to go, so that he may show me off, as if I were some sort of rare wild animal he has managed to trap. And, of course, there are Charlotte's feelings to consider this time. This party is one of her fund-raising events. We have all bought our "tickets" to attend, and the money will go to one or another of the several good causes of which she now finds herself patron. She would be hurt if I did not attend.

There is a knock on my door and I bid Terence enter.

"Lord Harcourt is here, my lady."

I take a slow breath and then release it, mentally sending the spirits on their way. I do not want any of them thinking they might accompany me to the party.

"Thank you, Terence. Would you help me with this, please?"

He hurries forward and takes my ceremonial cape from me. With some difficulty, for I am taller than he is, he succeeds in draping it around my shoulders and helping me to fasten the ornate clasp at the front. It is a rare treat for me to be able to go out in public dressed as a witch. The fashion for fancy-dress parties has allowed me this small pleasure. Beneath my cloak I am wearing a favorite velvet gown. There is a medieval look to it, with long sleeves looped over a finger on each hand, and a low-slung gold-stitched belt sitting on my hips. Earlier I rinsed my hair in lemon juice so that it shines as it swings, the blunt cut stopping level with my jaw. I have kohled my eyes, and chosen my favorite dragonfly tiara, so that I do indeed resemble an exotic witch from an ancient land.

Downstairs, when Louis sees me he smiles broadly.

"What a wonderful costume, Lily. It suits you terribly well. Why is that, I wonder?" He kisses my hand and leans forward to touch my cheek. He is dressed as a vampire count, though he has decided against donning fangs. He still manages to look danger-ous somehow and, disconcertingly, more like his father.

"Louis. I hope you aren't planning on biting unwary maidens tonight."

"Even Charlotte's parties don't get quite that wild."

"Don't be so certain."

Louis's chauffeur has the motorcar outside and we are sped the short distance through the nighttime streets. People are out enjoy-ing the pleasant evening. Couples stroll arm-in-arm along the river. A few horse-drawn cabs still ply their trade, retaining some-thing of a romantic appeal in these fast-moving modern times. Within minutes we are at the party venue and are escorted inside by a doorman liveried as some sort of Arabian pirate.

Louis whispers to me as similarly attired maids take our coats. "Oh dear, was there some theme or other we were supposed to know about, d'you think?"

I shake my head. "No, don't worry. I've already spotted two Marie Antoinettes and a Robin Hood."

The party is an uneasy marriage of old and new trends. The club itself has been recently refurbished and is a wonderful example of Art Deco, from its newly built facade, through the arrangement of the interior, to the smallest detail of the decor. The reception area has as its central focus a wonderful mural of angular shapes arranged in a starburst. Colors are clear, lines are crisp, with the thinnest strips and lines of gilt highlighting the geometric designs and shapes.

Charlotte's choice of fancy dress, however, hopes to appeal to the partygoers' fondness for the elaborate prewar balls we used to attend. There was always fierce competition in some quarters to win the prize for the best costume. Rivalries ran for several seasons, with outfits becoming ever more elaborate and outlandish.

"Lilith, darling!" Charlotte, exquisitely turned out as Titania, complete with gossamer wings, floats over to us and embraces me in a flurry of chiffon and seed pearls. "You look simply divine, as always. Oh, Louis, it is beastly of you to look so heart-stopping when you are firmly engaged to the most beautiful woman in the room. What *are* the rest of us supposed to do?"

She leads us into the throng, through the foyer, and into the main room that is not quite a ballroom, more a modern dance hall, with a bar to one side. There is a small stage, where an energetic jazz band is playing loudly. Waiters in vaguely Middle Eastern costume of several centuries ago weave through the merrymakers, silver trays of mysterious cocktails and glasses of champagne held perilously high. Already I wish I were back in the calm of my own apartment. I do not feel like dancing or engaging in the idle chatter I am required to find interesting.

Louis senses my resistance and sends to me a little spell to evoke the smell of roses. As he had anticipated, it makes me smile.

"That's better. Can't have you glum so close to our wedding

day. People will think you've gone off the idea of marrying me," he says, pulling me through the melee. "Come on, let's dance."

"But, Louis, I don't know this new one. I've no idea . . ."

"Nor have I. Let's make it up as we go along, shall we?"

He holds me tightly, picking up the upbeat tempo, expertly guiding me through the other dancers as we invent something between a foxtrot and an as yet undiscovered sequence of steps. I can tell he is enjoying himself, and I don't wish to spoil his evening. All around us the young and the not so young are dancing, laughing, and drinking with something akin to desperation. It is as if their very lives depend on their having a good time. As if the only way they can banish all the pain, all the loss, all the sadness of the war, is to fill each moment with wild enjoyment. But that very desperation is itself a kind of loss, as if they have misplaced the spontaneous, sincere happiness of old and replaced it with something contrived. Something that is only on the surface. Something pitiful.

We pass the next two hours dancing, drinking, and exchanging words we can barely hear above the din of the party with a curious assortment of historical and legendary figures. The evening becomes ever more surreal, as a gigantic rabbit attempts the Charleston with Queen Elizabeth I, and at one point three Julius Caesars are spotted playing a game of poker on the bar. I find myself withdrawing, overcome by a melancholy brought on by the sight of such determination to have fun. And part of the frenzy, it seems to me, is to distract us from noticing what is surely the most poignant difference between this party and a similar event that might have been held six years ago: the room contains easily three times as many women as men. And among those men who have survived to be here, plenty carry visible wounds bequeathed to them by a dying bomb or a bullet. One can only guess at how many endure scars of the invisible kind.

"So, Beauty, I see the war has not changed you."

The voice is instantly recognizable. I turn to see Gudrun behind me, sitting elegantly atop a bar stool, smoking a cigarette through a long black holder. She has had her glorious red hair cut and firmly set into ripples that gleam beneath the party lights. She is dressed in a glamorous satin dress without the slightest attempt at a costume. She looks a little thinner than when last I saw her. A little older, yes, but something else. There is a wariness about her now. A watchfulness. I cannot claim to be surprised. To be a German living in London through the war must have been a horrid experience.

"Hello, Gudrun. It is good to see you again. Is Mangan with you?" I peer past her.

"At such a charade? Huh! He would sooner eat his own foot. No, Mangan dislikes such gaiety these days. He is not in the best of health now, thanks to the wonderful British penal system. He prefers quieter occasions." She draws deeply on her pungent cigarette and then exhales slowly, blowing smoke through her nose, letting the plumes drift away and watching them as they go, before she speaks again. "Besides, Mangan does not receive the number of invitations he used to."

"Surely he was on Charlotte's guest list."

"Oh, yes. But he would never pay for a ticket. Neither would nor could, in fact. No, I am only here because my patron brought me. See, over there." She points to a rotund man whose age and girth are making it difficult for him to stand the pace of the revelry. "He is a buffoon, but a loyal one. The only man left in London prepared to buy my work. He thinks one day Germans will be back in fashion." She laughs at this, a dry, mirthless sound.

"But you still live with Mangan's family, back in Bloomsbury?" I ask, though in truth I know. I have seen Mangan several times since the end of the war. It is true, he has suffered some lasting damage to his health, but his time in the countryside has restored him a little. He is trying to work again, I know, but people have long memories. He and Gudrun are no longer fashionable, he for his stand against the war, she simply for being German.

"Where else would I go? Mangan is trying to sculpt again. The work is really too heavy for him now. I have told him he should work in something lighter, something smaller, but, ach, you know Mangan. When did he ever listen to reason? Perry is busy doing whatever it is Perry does. Jane feeds people. The children make noise. All as if the war never was."

"Except that it was."

"Yes. It was." She tips her head back and downs her champagne, and then waves the empty glass at a distant waiter to summon more. "I hear you are getting married, Beauty."

"Yes. Next month."

"Poor Artist, have you forgotten him completely?"

"Of course not."

"So, in this case, you will be coming to his exhibition next week."

"Bram has an exhibition here? In London?" I cannot keep the breathlessness out of my voice. Bram. Here. And painting again!

"At the Dauntless Gallery in Cork Street. I'm surprised he has not sent you an invitation to the private view. But, of course he won't mind if you just turn up anyway. Perhaps you could bring your fiancé."

I am too distracted to rise to Gudrun's provocation. Bram. Here. In London. Most likely staying at Mangan's house. I experience a piercing stab of jealousy at the thought of him spending time with Gudrun but not with me. But then, that is utterly ridiculous. I was the one who did not go to the station as I had promised him I would do, five years and a lifetime ago. I was the one who fell silent, who turned away. Why should he contact me ever again? Why would he think to come and see me or to send me an invitation to his show? Why would he? And even if he did, I could not accept. I am engaged to Louis. My life is moving on, and it would be wrong to pretend otherwise, to him or to myself. It is true times have changed. Perhaps there are not the same barriers between us that there once were. But some remain. I am still a witch. Bram is not. No, I cannot see him or go to see his paintings, much as I admit I long to do so. In a few weeks' time I will be Lady Lilith Harcourt, Countess of Winchester, and there is an end to it.

25.

When Bram enters the house in Bloomsbury he sees so few changes that he is taken back to the very first time he came to Mangan's home. The dog has gone, and the children are each a little taller. Jane has gray hair now, and Perry has lost the bloom of youth, but otherwise, much is as it was. The hallway is still full of coats and boots and clutter. Doors are missing from doorways. Electricity has been installed but is not used. The hole in the wall from the house into the studio space remains. The air of pandemonium under light restraint continues.

"Children, run along, do." Jane shoos three small boys ahead of her down the hallway. "Bram has had a long journey and the last thing he needs is all your noise. Come along, dear, Mangan is so looking forward to seeing you again. Freedom, go and put the kettle on, will you? Such a helpful boy. Couldn't have managed without him when Mangan was away." She pauses and lowers her voice. "You will find my darling husband a little . . . older," she warns him. "He is not as robust as once he was. Still," she adds, brightening again, "having you here will be just the tonic he requires. I'm certain of it."

Bram braces himself for an elderly Mangan in a bath chair, so he is astonished to find the great man halfway up a ladder, paintbrush in hand, putting the finishing touches to a startling mural that covers one entire wall of the studio.

"Mangan, my dear, Bram is here," Jane calls up to him.

"What's that? Bram from Yorkshire? Well, don't just stand there gawping, my young friend, make yourself useful. Pass me up another pot of paint, would you? Over there. The pea-green. That's the one. Want to get this tree finished before Jane starts clucking like a mother hen and insists I put my feet up. Woman thinks I'm an invalid."

"I think no such thing, I simply believe a little rest and some soup from time to time might just stop you wearing yourself to a frazzle. Talk him down from there, Bram, dear, *do,*" she says, leaving them with an exasperated flap of her hands.

"Woman would have me spoon-fed if I let her."

"She's only trying to look after you."

"I am perfectly sound in wind and limb, as you can see," says Mangan, letting go of the ladder to brandish his paintbrush expansively. He teeters horribly, and for a moment Bram thinks he will fall, but he grasps the wooden tread above him once more and continues applying paint, seemingly unperturbed.

"That's quite some mural," says Bram, taking in the image of a sweep of English countryside, complete with farm, barns, stream, and hedgerows. Many artists might have rendered such a scene cloyingly sentimental, but in Mangan's hands it is depicted as something vibrant, bold, and bursting with life.

"This place saved my life, Bram, I don't mind telling you. I was rescued from that Stygian hellhole of a jail and transported to this other world. I have never lived in the countryside, but, my word, there is so much we can learn about ourselves. When we are returned to nature, working the land with our hands, these hands, look at the calluses, honestly earned, through toil and effort, in all weathers, at one with the elements. I was . . . invigorated. Whatever Jane likes to tell people, I feel reborn, full of energy, and ready to work again!"

"Paintings this time, then? And on such a scale."

"Oh, no, this is for me. An *aide-mémoire* of my time spent tilling the soil. Not that I need one, no, no, but I confess, I miss the open landscape. I wanted to have it here with me still." He starts to descend the ladder. "No, I shall return to my sculptures, my true calling." He reaches the ground and stands in front of Bram. "Not that there is a demand for works in stone just now, but I daresay there will be again, when the world has recovered its senses and is in its right mind once more."

"And you really think it will? Recover its senses, I mean?"

Mangan narrows his eyes at Bram for a moment. "What? Where is that glorious youthful optimism I remember you for?"

"I may have left a little of it in Africa."

"Ah. Yes. Bad business that. Still." He drops his brush into an open tin of paint nearby, paying no heed to the fresh splash of green that joins others already decorating his worn trousers. He clasps Bram to him in a manly embrace. "Good to have you back with us, Bram from Yorkshire. Splendid. Yes, splendid indeed."

Bram experiences a flash of memory of the time he overheard Mangan talking to a fellow coven member. The images in his mind are shadowy, but the recollection is bright and sharp, of the night he learned that Lilith is not the only person close to him who is a witch.

This man counts me as his friend. There exists between us a mutual trust. And yet he keeps a secret so large I wonder there is space enough for it even in this rambling house.

"Why so serious, young man?" Mangan frowns at him. "You have the world at your feet, or will presently. This is no time for the maudlin reflection I judge you are now engaged in." He narrows his eyes and then goes on. "Or could it be a troubled heart that is giving you such a dyspeptic appearance all of a sudden?"

Bram shrugs. "You know Lilith is soon to be married?"

"I know Jane has been fussing about having nothing suitable to wear for some months now. I know all over London the great and the ennobled are dusting off their finery, and licking their lips, no doubt, at the opportunity to display their wealth and good taste, or the lack of it, at what I am told will be the wedding of the year."

"I'm sure it would be an occasion of unrivaled glamor," Bram says.

"Would?" Mangan raises his eyebrows. "Is there any doubt that the marriage will go ahead?"

"I . . . hope so."

"Ah-*ha*. So that's how it is. Well, well. You've set yourself a challenge there, my friend."

"Do you think me unworthy?"

"Indeed I do not."

"Do you think me unwise?"

"Ha! When has wisdom had any say in affairs of the heart?"

"We are from different worlds, Lilith and I."

"Nonsense, you both lived in London."

"She is the daughter of a duke. My father is a man who made his own money."

"The war changed everything, haven't you heard? These things matter so much less now than they used to."

"She is very rich. My father so disapproves of my painting he will likely leave me a pauper."

"Then she'll have money enough for both of you."

There is a beat. Bram holds his nerve.

I must speak. I must.

"She is a witch, and I am not," he says.

Mangan gasps loudly, then recovers himself. He stares hard at Bram and sees there is no point in denial. It is a moment before he asks quietly, "And does such a fact frighten you, Bram from Yorkshire?"

"It does not. No more than *your* being a witch frightens me."

Mangan's mouth opens and then closes again before a grin

spreads slowly around his face, lifting his features, and erasing some of the hardship of recent years.

"My word, young man. You are every bit as remarkable as I knew you were. Knew from the very first moment we met, I did. That you were special. That you were destined for something . . . extraordinary."

"I'll second that!" Perry's voice from the doorway startles them both. They turn to see him entering the studio carrying a tray of tea. Bram wonders how much of their conversation he has heard.

"Tea!" Mangan is horrified. "The man journeys from the north of our country, via Africa, if you please, he comes to see us, the returning hero and feted artist, and you offer him tea? Fetch a bottle of something, Peregrine, for pity's sake. What will he think of us?"

"I will think that tea is perfectly acceptable, and that in any case there won't be a thimbleful of brandy left in the house, as a bottle opened here is a bottle emptied, I seem to remember," Bram tells him.

Mangan stares at him open-mouthed and then erupts into loud laughter, slapping him on the back, causing Bram to wince since his shoulder is still tender enough to suffer under such enthusiastic treatment.

"Your memory is both unforgiving and accurate, my young friend. Come, find a perch, tell me of these paintings of yours the whole town is talking about."

And so the three of them sit and talk of art and inspiration and the challenge of marrying the two successfully. Bram can see that Mangan has indeed aged; that his skin has sagged a little beneath his cheekbones; that his wild hair has thinned some; that the blue of his eyes has faded a tone. But the man's inner strength, his drive and his passion, still remain. The more they talk, the more animated he becomes. Perry fulfills his usual role of supporting his mentor. Bram wonders that he is content to be always the pupil and to never, apparently, push forward his own work.

He loves Mangan, that much is clear. Perhaps it is enough, to be a part of someone else's genius instead of striving to reveal one's own. I'm not sure it would be for me. Not now I have rediscovered the joy of painting.

Mangan turns the conversation to Bram's exhibition. "And now you are to have your own show, and already the art world is abuzz with excitement at this new talent. Hah! As if we did not know what you were capable of. I wish you every success, young Bram," he says, raising his chipped teacup in a toast. "It is hard-won and well-deserved. Enjoy your opening night."

"But you will be there to celebrate with me, naturally."

"Ah, it is good of you to think to include me in your moment of triumph, but I fear my presence there would be . . . unhelpful."

"What?"

Perry leans forward. "You see, people are still a little sensitive about the war and about what others did or did not do . . ."

"But surely Mangan contributed in his own way. The farm laborers were essential."

Mangan sighs. "Alas, there are not many that will view my actions in such a kindly light."

Perry, for once, allows his feelings of irritation and frustration to show. "It really is too bad. Even people who have for so many years adored Mangan's work, people who know him to be a man of integrity, they have turned against him."

"It is true. Not only because of my opposition to the war, but, well, I fear having Gudrun here placed me beyond some sort of pale."

Bram shakes his head. "It seems to me we fought a war so that people could be free to follow their own consciences. Are some still to be hounded because of where they were born or what they believe in?"

"The war may be over," Mangan says, "but we live in an uneasy peace."

Perry nods. "There is a danger that if Mangan were to attend the private viewing of your exhibition, if people were to see you allying yourself to him, well . . ."

Mangan finishes the statement for him. "You would be tainted by association. Your career might very well be over before it has begun."

"But that is appalling."

Mangan shrugs ruefully. "It is the world in which we find ourselves."

"Well, it is not the world I slogged through swamp and jungle to protect," he says, slamming his cup down on the tray with such anger the handle snaps from it. He jumps to his feet. "I would very much like it if you, sir, and your entire household, would do me the honor of attending the first night of my exhibition as my guests."

Mangan grins up at him. "Do you insist, Bram from Yorkshire?"

"I absolutely insist," he says. "And the devil take anyone who doesn't like it!"

Less than a week after their conversation, the day of the private view is relentlessly warm. By the time Bram has overseen the hanging of the final painting and all is arranged to his satisfaction, he can feel his shirt clinging to his back beneath his jacket. He glances at his pocket watch. There is not time enough to go back to Bloomsbury and change.

They will have to take me as they find me. After all, it is my pictures they are coming to see, not myself.

He tries to imagine Mangan caring, or even noticing, that he is in a disheveled state, and the thought makes him smile. The gallery owner and his assistant bustle about instructing the caterers where to set up the drinks. Bram takes the opportunity to pace the three rooms that display the accumulated work of nearly four years. The collection has come about entirely from the sketches and notes he made while in Africa. A half-dozen damp, dirty, battered sketchbooks, carried with him over hundreds of miles, through relentless rain and enervating sun, smudged with charcoal and smeared with fat from campfire meals, these were the seeds that grew into over fifty paintings.

The pictures look so orderly and finely framed here in the smart gallery, beautifully lit, and carefully positioned to show each to best effect, Bram scarcely recognizes them as being the same works that filled the spare bedroom in his parents' house. There they were left on easels, works in progress for weeks or months at a time. Or stored in random batches in corners, to be later plucked out and reworked again or, in some cases, wiped completely from the canvas, so that he would pick up the original sketch, travel back with his mind's eye to that place, that time, that face, that light, and begin again. But now there are no more chances to polish and to hone. What hangs on the walls in this gallery, on this day, must serve to represent all that he felt those long, hard months. All that he discovered, partly about Africa but mostly about his fellow man.

In the third room, at the very end on the far wall, is the painting that can still move him to tears if he lets it. He steps closer, steeling himself against emotion. The gentle face of the army chaplain gazes back at him. He is shown in a close-cropped portrait, three-quarters profile, the low light of the equatorial sunset warming the dusty tones of his face and hair, his pipe held lightly in his smile. Bram starts to feel rage replace the tenderness the picture evokes.

What a waste. What a dreadful waste.

"Ah, Mr. Cardale, there you are!" The gallery owner—an

elderly academic who left Oxford to immerse himself in the world of art—ushers Bram back toward the reception area. "Can't have you hiding away in here when the first guests are due to arrive any minute. Dear, dear. This is your moment, Mr. Cardale, this is the day when you are discovered, and your praises sung. And sung they will be, I assure you." He pauses in his bolstering up of Bram's confidence to take in the portraits and landscapes that surround him. "My, my, but aren't they something terribly special? I can't tell you how proud I am to have your work here. Can't tell you . . . Are you happy with the hang, Mr. Cardale, is it to your liking?"

"It is all so much better than I could ever have expected, Dr. Travis. I can't thank you enough. I only hope the public, and the critics, are as kindly disposed toward my offerings as you are."

"Oh, the public have more sense than one might suppose. They will surely see the talent on display here today. As for the critics, well, try not to mind them. Their livelihood depends upon their saying something no one else has thought of, and it makes most of them rather bad tempered."

Bram has not felt so nervous since the moment he disembarked onto the harbor at Mombasa. His stomach churns, and the bullet wound in his shoulder sets up its familiar ache. He finds he is afraid, not so much of failing as an artist, of remaining penniless and obscure, but of failing the subjects of his paintings. He has kept them to himself all these years, until he finally found the courage to venture out with them. Now he is fearful, so that he regrets exposing them to what might be hostile viewers. And then there is Lilith to think about. Having finally summoned the courage to send her an invitation he has suffered agonies ever since.

Will she come? She did not send word, did not respond to my invitation. And if she does not come, will it be because she no longer cares for me or because she cares too much? Too much for a woman about to be married to someone else. And if she does come, how will she judge my work? How will she judge me? Have I a chance of winning her back? The smallest chance?

At last people begin to arrive. Some are keen followers of art. Some are there to be seen to be there. Others might hope there is money to be made from this new artist. Others still had nothing better to occupy them this Friday evening. Soon the gallery is so crowded Bram wonders anyone can actually see the paintings at all. The wine is disappearing fast, and as it does so the noise rises. And it is a cheerful noise, full of praise and compliments. The mood of excitement and approval is unmistakable. Dr. Travis is beaming. He grabs Bram's arm as he rushes past.

"You are a success, Mr. Cardale, as I knew you would be. Yes, a very great success!"

Bram feels almost as pleased for the gallery owner as he does for himself.

There is a commotion at the front door which can only herald the arrival of Mangan and his party. The artist's resonant voice carries even to the inner room, as he enthusiastically praises the paintings on show.

"Genius!" he declares to anyone within range. "A natural talent. A painter for our times, of our time. The perfect chronicler of these cruel years. Such pathos! Such insight!"

Bram tries to make his way through the crowd. He sees Perry, who waves to him. Gudrun is there, looking fabulous and drawing glances both admiring and quizzical. Jane leads in the string of children, all scrubbed up and shiny faced, eyes bright, and clearly thrilled at being included in something so grown-up and important. For a while it seems the gathering is happy to listen to Mangan's opinions, as he is only voicing what many of them are thinking. But then someone recognizes him, and someone else recalls the stance he took over the war, and another someone lets it be known that his mistress is German. And the mood changes.

The alteration is as swift and as marked as the cessation of a storm at sea. There is a sudden quiet and an uneasy calm. Bram sees panic on Dr. Travis's face, who has taken in the situation and must surely see his hopes and aspirations fading in front of his eyes.

"Mr. Cardale," he hisses into Bram's ear. "You must ask your friend to leave at once!"

"I will not."

"I beseech you! He will ruin us all."

Bram pushes through the now-subdued guests and at last reaches Mangan.

"Ah! The artist himself. Congratulations, my friend," he cries, pumping Bram's hand. "A triumph. Triumph."

Bram speaks into the tense silence that follows, still holding Mangan's hand, addressing the gathering as he speaks. "Any small triumph that I might lay claim to, if triumph it can be called, would never have come to be had it not been for the guidance of this man," he says. "When I knew nobody, indeed, knew nothing, this great artist took me in. He showed me what could be achieved. He taught me to have the courage to be honest in my work, to tell the truth. I would not be a man of courage if I were to turn my back on him now. This man, and his family," he pointedly takes in Gudrun with a sweep of his arm, "they have made me what I am. They are my friends."

There is a silence where all the air seems to have been sucked from the room. A moment of tension filled with unspoken accusations and questions and private fears. And into it comes the sound of one person clapping, softly, with gloved hands, but firmly enough to be heard. Everyone turns toward that small sound of solidarity, and there at the back of the room stands Lilith.

"Bravo!" she declares. "Bravo!"

And the room erupts into enthusiastic agreement.

It is some time before Bram can reach Lilith. She stands, waiting calmly, watching him being congratulated and adored by the crowd who have decided, as if they were one, that he is to be admired. He is a true artist. He is a success. He is a man whom people will want to know, will claim to know, and whose art they will buy, and as such, anyone he considers a friend is deemed acceptable.

Bram's heart is dancing by the time he is close enough to Lilith to breathe her in. For a moment he cannot speak, cannot find the words that he has formed in his mind so many times, in so many places, for so long. Now, in her presence once again, his yearning for her is too great. He cannot articulate it, but neither can he speak to her of anything else. Not now. Not this time. He starts to panic that she will think him displeased that she has come, will misinterpret his silence as hostility and slip away from him again.

"Don't go," he says at last.

She smiles at this. Just smiles.

"I didn't think you'd come."

"I found I couldn't not. In the end." She glances at the nearest painting. It is of a campfire next the Rufiji at night, with faces aglow from the low flames. "They are wonderful. Quite wonderful," she says.

"The faces or the paintings?"

"Both."

They fall silent again, but she has turned her gaze back upon him and holds him in it. Lilith's eyes are wet with tears she does her best to blink away. Bram becomes aware that people are moving toward them.

This moment will pass and I will lose her again!

Recklessly, he says, "I hear you are to be married."

She shakes her head slowly, the tears now falling despite her efforts. "No, I am not," she tells him. "Not anymore. Not now."

He snatches her hand and presses it to his lips, tasting the saltiness of her dripped tears on the fine, white leather.

When Fordingbridge announces a caller, Stricklend reacts with mild irritation. He was about to leave his office, and was looking forward with some relish to an evening in his rooms at the top of Admiralty Arch, taking in the sunset over the palace while enjoying a well-earned glass of single malt whiskey. He has had a testing day, compelled to sit through dreary meetings concerning the reorganization of civil service departments, a business that has been grinding on ever since the end of the war well over a year ago now. If any real progress has been made it is hard to see where, and Stricklend feels as if the matter is simply an exercise in giving people who no longer have a purpose in Whitehall something to do.

"Who is it, Fordingbridge?" he asks, with little interest in the answer.

"The gentleman has given his name as Peregrine Smith, sir. He assures me that he is known to you and that you will want to receive him." The factotum, already in his habitual bent pose, flinches at the expression on his master's face. "Forgive me, sir, perhaps I was wrong to bother you with a caller at such a late hour. I shall inform the gentleman that it is not convenient . . ."

"No. Send him in." Stricklend is too thrown to toy with Fordingbridge. "Send him in at once and see that we are not disturbed."

"Yes, Mr. Stricklend, sir."

"Not disturbed under any circumstances! Do you understand?"

"Completely, master, yes, sir. Right away, sir," he says, backing hastily out of the door.

Stricklend regains his poise and stands behind his desk. When his visitor enters the room he allows no sign of his inner turmoil to remain visible.

"Good evening, Stricklend. Your man looks quite terrified.

What do you do to him to keep him in such a constant state of terror, I wonder?" Perry drops his hat and cane on the Chesterfield with a nonchalance that causes Stricklend to grind his teeth.

"What madness is this?" he demands. "Why have you come here, unexpected and without disguise, in working hours for all to see? Have you taken leave of your senses?"

"I have not. Do calm down, dear fellow. There really is no call for such alarm. What does it matter if someone sees me? Nobody here knows who I am, and besides, this place is full of people far more interested in themselves than anyone else." He flops down on the sofa and gestures toward the firmly closed door. "Any chance your little man will bring us a glass of something? I feel in need."

Stricklend ignores his request and sits down, resting his arms on the desk in front of him to help steady his nerves. He is unaccustomed to being spoken to in such a way. He is astute enough to know that his subordinate would not be taking such liberties if he was not in an unusual position of strength.

"Why don't you come to the point and tell me what has brought you so rashly to my door?"

"No drink then? Oh, very well. Now, don't look so glum, you will want to hear what I have to say." He pauses for effect, clearly enjoying stringing Stricklend along. "You are a lucky man, Stricklend. You have sailed close to the wind these past few years. Others in your position, well, they might not have survived. Difficult times, indeed. But," he grins, "all your troubles are at an end. For I bring you the means to acquire, at last, that which you have been chasing after for so long."

"Really? Tell me more."

"You could look a little more pleased."

"Don't play games with me, Smith. I have no time for such nonsense."

"You do surprise me. I have always thought of you as the consummate games player. As you wish." He sits forward on the leather sofa, his excitement clear now. "Last night I attended the opening of an exhibition of paintings by a new artist by the name of Bram Cardale. Ring any distant bells?"

"The artist who lived for a time in the house you inhabit, with Richard Mangan. He was, for a short while, I recollect, romantically linked, shall we say, to Lilith Montgomery."

"The very same."

"I understood he left London some time before the war and the two were no longer in contact."

"Your information is correct, but no longer current. I saw dear Bram with the Lazarus witch at the gallery, and it was plain for all to see that they are in love. So much so that they were unable to hide the fact, despite her being engaged to Louis Harcourt. I anticipate news of her breaking off that connection imminently."

"And you think we can use this . . . Cardale, this painter, we can use him to persuade the Montgomery girl to finally give us what we want? She loved her brother, but a similar ploy was unsuccessful, you will recall."

"Oh, we all recall that, my dear Stricklend. But then, you see, we had it the wrong way around. We did away with the duke in order to bring the girl to heel. I propose we turn the tables."

Stricklend feels the first tingle of real excitement as he realizes his spy might just have hit upon possibly the only way Lilith Montgomery would reveal the Great Secret. She would not tell it to him, not even for love, after what happened with Freddie. But she might just reveal it to her lover, given the right set of circumstances. All Stricklend has to do is bring those circumstances about, and he knows he will savor every minute of doing so.

26.

The rose garden in Regent's Park looks particularly beautiful in the early summer sunshine. It is really too soon for the roses to be at their best, but there are buds aplenty, and sufficient blooms for the warm air to be filled with their sweet scent. Louis and I sit, not quite touching, on a green iron bench among the flower beds. Children have been brought out to play, and dash along the paths in their pretty spring clothes. A family of doves is busy nesting in the dovecote, cooing softly, flying hither and thither collecting moss to line their nests.

There is a tangible sadness emanating from Louis. I have given him back the engagement ring and he turns it over and over in his hand. The solitaire diamond flares in the sunshine. When at last he speaks his voice is low and has lost its usual brightness.

"Why did you choose to break my heart in such a delightful place, Lily? I have always been fond of the rose gardens, and now you have ruined them for me forever."

I can think of nothing to say in reply. A small boy runs past, chasing a squirrel which is adept at keeping tantalizingly out of his reach. He is wearing a dark blue sailor suit and has an unruly muddle of curly blond hair which bounces as he runs. A girl in a crisp white pinafore and sunny yellow dress hurries after him, calling his name. I wonder if Louis is thinking of the children we will never have together.

"I cannot go ahead with the wedding, Louis. I care about you too much to marry you when . . . It wouldn't be right."

"We could have been happy, I know it. I love you terribly, you believe that, don't you? And we understand each other, you and I. We have grown up together. Our families are close. We move in the same circles. Dash it all, Lilith, we are both witches."

"Louis . . ."

"It has to be said. You don't seem to want to face facts. And the biggest, plainest fact of all is that you are Head Witch of the Lazarus Coven, Lilith Montgomery. It is who . . . it is *what* you are." He hesitates before going on, struggling to compose himself, wrestling with his own emotions so as not to let his hurt and anger make him speak harshly. "*I* know what that means. I understand. I can support you." When I say nothing he goes on. "Does he even know? Have you told him?"

I hesitate and then nod.

"Good Lord, Lilith! How much have you told him?"

"As yet, not a great deal."

"Then you have had these feelings for some time indeed. When?" he asks suddenly. "When did you tell him?"

"Before the war. Before . . . before what happened with Freddie. After that I came to think that it was impossible. That it would be wrong to allow a non-witch into my life in such a way."

He runs his hand through his hair and for a moment I think he will actually begin to weep. "All this time . . . You sent him away, but you never stopped loving him, did you?"

I shake my head slowly. I close my eyes to shut out the pain I have inflicted.

"Lily, for pity's sake, have a care. There are very few non-witches who know of the existence of the Lazarus Coven. You don't know this . . . artist well at all. You said yourself you haven't had any contact with him for years. You haven't met his family . . ."

"I know how I feel about him."

"And those feelings may very well be affecting your view of what is sensible and what is not."

"I'm sorry if you don't like the idea of my telling him about the coven."

"This has nothing to do with what I do or do not like!" he snaps, perhaps more firmly than he had intended. He takes a breath, then says again, "Nothing at all. I only urge caution."

We fall to silence once more, and it is a quiet filled with regret and sadness. A young couple stroll by, arm in arm, with eyes only for each other. Somewhere nearby a dog barks.

A wood pigeon in the tree behind us starts to sing.

Louis says flatly, "You must love him very much."

I cannot look at him or I shall cry.

"I am sorry, Louis. Truly, I am."

"So am I, Lily," he says, turning to gaze out over the roses. "So am I."

Bram is early for his rendezvous with Lilith. He knew he would be, as he set off from Mangan's house, but he is so eager to see her, so happy at the thought of being with her, he is almost light-headed with it. He could not stand a minute more pacing his old attic room, and so walked briskly through the streets to Fitzroy Square. Lilith had warned him that although the house had been cleared, the site had not yet been built upon and that it was a disturbing scene. Still he is not prepared for the impact the place has on him. The garden square remains undamaged, as does the run of houses on two sides of the square. The remainder of the houses are gone. Some, like Number One, were obliterated when the bomb fell. Others were so destabilized by the blast and the ensuing fires that they had to be taken down. Most of the rubble has been removed, but the street resembles nothing so much as an enormous open wound. The crater has been filled in, leaving only an impression of it, an indentation. Bram stands with his toes at the edge of it, wondering that anyone could have survived such devastation. Lilith told him she was in the chamber, far beneath the house, but he has since learned that few who were there that day lived through the bombing. He feels a coldness wash over him at the thought of Lilith lying crushed and trapped far below the surface, with him thousands of miles away. How terrible it would have been for her to die like that. For him to lose her like that.

"Hard to imagine there was ever a house here."

The sound of Lilith's voice startles him. He turns to find her standing behind him. She is dressed in a simple dark green dress with slender shoulder straps, a low waist, and a hemline that stops well above her slim ankles. It is made of chiffon over a silk under-dress, so that it shimmers and floats as she moves. Two delicately stitched dragonflies are embroidered onto the neckline. She wears short pale-mint gloves, and a particularly fetching cloche hat of a brighter green, with her shiny, blunt-cut hair just visible underneath it. She could be any smartly dressed, fashionable young woman, but she is not.

She is Lilith. My Lilith.

"You look wonderful," he tells her. "Completely wonderful. But a little sad. It must be difficult for you, coming back here."

"It is. Although it reminds me how lucky I am to be alive. Others in the house were not so fortunate."

"It is difficult to believe anyone could have emerged from such wreckage."

"I was deep underground."

"In the special chamber, is that what you called it?"

"The Great Chamber." Lilith steps close to him and slips her hand through his arm. "Come along," she says, "it wouldn't do for us to be late."

She leads him back to the motor cab she has waiting and they leave the wreckage of the square behind them. It is a glorious day, the sky bridesmaid's blue, the parks in bloom and the trees in full leaf. Along their route this prettiness is interrupted now and again by gaps where a house has been obliterated, the space in the street jarring like the shocking glimpse of a missing tooth. As they travel through Holborn, Lilith points to an unremarkable church.

"St. Mary's," she tells him.

"The convent where you helped out?"

"Yes. The nuns are marvelous. I admire them enormously, Bram." She squeezes his hand so that he studies her face for the meaning behind her words. "If I were ever in need of a safe place, the convent is where I should go. I would trust them with the most precious of things. Always," she says. "You will remember that, won't you?"

He nods, smiling. Uncertain why she is telling him this, but recognizing that it is important to her. "I'll remember," he says.

They journey on down to the Thames and along the embankment for a mile or so before turning along a row of graceful Victorian town houses in Chelsea. The cab driver pulls up outside a tall, redbrick building, and a footman hurries out of the house to open the cab door for Lilith. Bram joins her on the pavement and feels a nervousness take hold of him.

"It will be all right," Lilith assures him. "They won't bite."

"Is reading minds another of your hidden talents, then?"

Lilith smiles. "I rather think it was your face I read."

"I had hoped I appeared calm and confident."

"I'm sure you do, to other people."

Together they enter the London residence of Lord Grimes. They are taken directly through the restrained yet expensive decor of the hall and out via French windows to the long walled garden at the back of the house. Outside, all is genteel elegance and enjoyment, and reminds Bram of the way things were done before the war. Liveried servants move swiftly and silently among the guests, silver platters held high, wordlessly distributing ice-cold champagne cocktails and delicate canapés. There is a gentle murmur of polite conversation. When Lilith had asked Bram to attend the garden party with her, she had told him that all those attending—aside from Bram himself—would be members of the Lazarus Coven. The many hours she had spent attempting to explain to him what that meant, what her life as a witch was like, had left him in no doubt that these were not ordinary people. His own experiences of Lilith's magic, and his suffering at the fearsome power of the Dark Spirit, have shown him vivid glimpses of the other world that they inhabit. Even so, standing among the pretty flower beds and lawns, sipping his cool drink from a fine crystal glass, watching the smartly turned-out men and exquisitely dressed women chatting happily, it is hard to accept that he is, in fact, surrounded by witches.

And the woman I love is one of them. The thought is no longer new to him, yet each time he considers it he finds it freshly amazing.

Lilith gently steers him into the midst of her fellows. She is at once greeted warmly by their host. She kisses his cheek.

"Lord Grimes, allow me to introduce you to my friend, Bram Cardale."

"Ah, the artist!" He offers Bram a firm handshake. "Delighted you could come to my little gathering. Lilith speaks so very highly of you, I am exceptionally pleased to meet you at last."

"It was kind of you to invite me, Lord Grimes. You have a very beautiful garden."

"Oh, nothing to do with me, I assure you. My gardener won't let me so much as prune a rose, so alas I can take no credit."

"Lilith, darling!" A bent and arthritic woman swathed in layers of diaphanous pink fabric, her hair rigidly waved, descends upon them, arms outstretched. Behind her a straight-backed elderly woman turns a piercing gaze onto the newcomer.

Lilith whispers in Bram's ear. "Brace yourself, my love." She turns to smile at the pair and then says, clearly and firmly, raising her voice just a notch so that all may hear, "Victoria, Druscilla, may I present Mr. Bram Cardale. Bram, you are now in the company of two of the most gifted witches you will ever meet."

Idle chatter is abruptly replaced by stunned silence.

Bram and Lilith rehearsed this moment, and she had been at pains to have him understand the impact it would have. Certainly he is acutely conscious of the sudden alteration in the mood of the party. That a non-witch be invited to a social event of coven members is unusual but not without precedent. That the Head Witch should choose that occasion to break the vow of secrecy, to boldly expose her fellow witches, to show that she has spoken of the coven to one from the Outerworld, is shocking in the extreme.

"What is this?" Victoria is already trembling with outrage.

Lord Grimes hurries to Lilith's side. "Morningstar . . ." he begins, and then realizes his own slip and corrects himself, ". . . Lilith. Have a care."

She smiles at him and then addresses the guests. "Now that I have your attention, I would like all of you to meet Bram Cardale, the man I intend marrying. He is a non-witch, but he will be my partner through life, and I will not lie to him. I will not keep the greater half of myself a secret from him."

"*Faith in silence!*" shouts one elderly male witch from the far side of the lawn. "That is our creed."

Victoria is shaking her head solemnly. "I believe our Head Witch has lost her mind along with her heart."

Others begin to voice their disapproval. Bram takes Lilith's hand in his.

How much must this be costing her? To incur the displeasure of the whole coven. To hear them question her suitability for her position of leader. She is risking so much for me.

"Times have changed," Lilith says. "If the Lazarus Coven is to survive, we must change with it. Perhaps we have kept ourselves apart from the Outerworld for too long."

"But still"—Victoria is unconvinced—"to break your vows, Morningstar. And to thrust this . . . *person* upon us without consultation . . . it is not in keeping with our laws. We do not use secrecy to set ourselves above others but to protect the coven and the Great Secret."

"And how can my husband-to-be help protect me if he does not know the truth? Already he has been subjected to the power of the Dark Spirit of Edmund Willoughby."

Another witch speaks her mind. "You should have considered that before choosing a non-witch as your partner. It is you who have put him in harm's way. And now you weaken the strength of the coven by your actions."

Others voice their agreement, so that soon many are calling out their fears, criticizing Lilith, demanding that some sort of action be taken.

Quietly, Druscilla holds up her hand for silence. The senior witch commands great respect, so that despite passions running high, everyone is soon quiet once more.

Druscilla steps closer to Bram. She raises her walking stick and prods him with it, as if testing to see if he is real. She prods him harder, and he realizes she is in fact testing his temper.

"What manner of man are you, Bram Cardale?" she asks.

"Perhaps you should better ask that question of somebody other than me."

"Morningstar loves you." Druscilla shrugs. "It seems to me we should trust her judgment."

Victoria waves her arms in a gesture of exasperation. "The girl is in love, Druscilla. Her judgment is skewed by a handsome face and no doubt honeyed words."

"You are speaking of our Head Witch!" Druscilla snaps, frowning fiercely at Victoria, before turning her glare on the rest of the company. "You would all do well to remember that. Morningstar is our rightful leader, the appointed head of our coven. She asks that we accept this man into our community."

"A non-witch!" Victoria repeats.

"At present," Druscilla concedes. "And perhaps he will remain so. Or perhaps not."

Lilith moves to stand beside her mentor. "Druscilla, what are you thinking?"

"Many members of this coven were not born witches, though they apparently choose to forget that fact now. They were proposed by Lazarus witches, put forward, accepted, and inducted."

"But never like this," Victoria points out. "Our existence was never divulged to anyone without our consent. Morningstar has broken with tradition . . ."

"And so she might. It is her right to govern us *her* way. She trusts this man. And I confess"—she turns back to Bram and he experiences the powerful sensation that she is able to see into his very soul—"I find there is . . . something about him. Some raw material, some . . . spark. Well, young man. Would you be willing to be tested? To be scrutinized and challenged and, should you be deemed suitable, to be instructed in the ways of Lazarus?"

Bram gives a polite bow. "I am willing to do whatever is necessary for the woman I love, Druscilla. I promise."

Lord Grimes hurries forward, breathlessly attempting to save his party and restore a happier mood. "A toast, ladies and gentlemen. Charge your glasses. There we are, that's it." He holds his own champagne flute high. "To Bram Cardale," he calls out, "welcome!" And behind him a shaken band of witches echoes the toast, "Welcome!"

❋

I have never watched a man sleep before. Bram looks even more beautiful than when he is awake. With the tension gone out of his face, he looks younger, less troubled. His hair is madly long now. I cannot imagine him with it shorn for the army. What a time he endured in Africa. He has spoken of it only a little, but enough that I can see how it hurts him to remember. One day he will tell me everything. As I have told him. I had not dared consider, *really* consider, how he might react to learning the whole truth about me, and to the idea of him eventually joining our coven and becoming a witch himself. If I had, my nerve would have deserted me, I am certain of it. For some time I had not even dared voice the notion to myself. But then, when I let the thought take hold, it seemed so right. He is so attuned to the world around him, so sensitive to the nature of the people he meets. Perhaps it is the artist in him that makes him—what was it Druscilla said?—"raw material" that might be nurtured into a witch one day. Or perhaps that extra something, that thing that sets him apart and can make for a lonely life, perhaps that is the magic that makes him able to produce art that moves people. How are we to tell which comes first, and which inspires the other? Either way, I am so happy to think he will come to enjoy the wonder of belonging to the coven, and the marvels of knowing and using magic. He will be receptive to the spirits—he has already demonstrated that. And I know he will, in time and with careful instruction, become a fine necromancer.

And now here he lies in my bed, naked and warm. When we left the garden party I knew that this is where I would bring him. I wanted him to know me completely. I needed to know *myself* completely. We did not speak, all the way here in the cab. By the time we arrived it was dark. I had Terence bring us some champagne and smoked salmon and then dismissed him for the night so that Bram and I could be properly alone. We sipped our drinks and ate our food at the small table in my bedroom in near silence. We both knew what we wanted, what was going to happen. The anticipation was delicious! Every inch of my body tingled at the thought of him touching me. By the time he stood up, stepped round the table to me, and pulled me to my feet, I ached with desire for him. I had never allowed myself to be so free.

And yet I was reminded, even then, of my other allegiances. The spirits were drawn to my heightened state and started whispering in my ear. I was furious. How dare they! Am I never to be allowed any privacy? I sent them away, refusing to listen or to speak with them. I warned them that if they did not respect my right to a private life as a woman, they would lose my friendship and service as a witch forever. Either they believed me, or they felt suitably uncomfortable at invading my personal life, I cannot know which. In any case, they departed, so that I could give myself to Bram, body, heart, and soul.

As if sensing he is being watched, Bram stirs. He stretches his strong arms, and his eyelids flutter open. He offers me a slow smile.

"Don't you know it is considered the height of rudeness to stare?" he asks.

"I seem to remember coming under your scrutiny for hours at a time, day after day. For weeks, in fact."

"That was different. You were posing for an artist, not sleeping while somebody gazed at you."

"Somebody?"

He laughs quietly, slipping his arm around my waist to pull me to him. The sensation of his skin against my own again is every bit as thrilling as the first time I experienced it.

"A very lovely body," he murmurs into my hair.

At once I feel a longing for him coursing through me. He is so strong, and yet touches me with such tenderness. He smells of life and vigor and desire and my thoughts start to spin away as he kisses my throat, my shoulder, my breast.

When at last we lie wrapped in each other's arms again, letting the breeze from the open balcony doors cool our damp skin, I know that I was right, this time, to follow my heart. Father always taught me to trust to my mind, to judgment born of thought, of reason, of knowledge. He would allow the use of a witch's instinct, yes, but a woman's yearning? The compulsion to love? To adore and be adored? Never. And yet it is right for me to be guided by this. For now I have an ally in life. Someone who cares about me above everything and accepts me for what I am, even if that is beyond his true understanding. Whatever lies ahead, I will not face it alone. Gradually I will help him to see that what it is I do is not so frightening, not so disturbing. He will be my safe haven. When I am adrift in the stormy seas of magic and the spirit world, it will be Bram who calls me home.

Moonlight falls through the open curtains. Slipping from under the tangled sheet I pull my cream silk night-robe around me, tying it at the waist.

"Come along." I reach out my hand and Bram takes it. "It is a beautiful night, let's not miss it." He follows wordlessly until I become suddenly shy at his nakedness. "Perhaps you had better put your trousers on first," I say, feeling I should look away but not wanting to. My own lustfulness makes me blush.

"Why? Can we be overlooked up there in your aerie?"

"That's just what Charlotte called it."

He smiles. "Well, if there's any danger of her showing up I'd better do as you say."

I find watching him slip into his narrow-fitting trousers almost as erotic as watching him slip out of them. He leaves his broad, smooth chest bare. My own desire both shocks and thrills me. I walk briskly to the lift, letting Bram jog to catch up. He slides shut the iron door of the cage and we ascend to the roof.

It is indeed the most glorious night. The stars are outshone by the lustrous pearly moon that glows directly above us. Below, the city slumbers, with only night workers and a few revelers moving about, subdued in the lamp light. Humans are not by nature nocturnal, but witches often are, and of course necromancers do their best work drawing on the energy of the night. Will I ever be able to make Bram see the beauty of it all? To welcome midnight as joyously as others welcome dawn? I think I will. I think he will suit the strange new life that awaits him.

We have not been seated on the smooth walnut bench more than ten minutes when I am startled by the sound of the lift being called back down.

"Who can be using it?" I cannot keep the anxiety from my voice.

"Perhaps Terence needs to speak with you."

"He would call up on the telephone. He is far too discreet to intrude."

We both stand and watch the lift return. The ornate ironwork of the cage obscures the figure within, until the doors open, and onto the rooftop steps Nicholas Stricklend. I instinctively stand in front of Bram, but he moves forward and places a protective arm about me. Terence arrives breathlessly at the top of the spiral staircase that services the other side of the roof garden.

"I am so sorry, Lady Lilith. He would not be stopped."

"Don't worry, Terence. It's not your fault."

The butler hesitates, sensing something is amiss. He retreats to the top of the stairway but lingers there.

Bram addresses our unwelcome visitor. "Who are you? And what do you mean by forcing your way up here uninvited?"

"My name, as your hostess very well knows, is Nicholas Stricklend."

"Stricklend!"

"Ah. I see Lady Lilith has told you all about me. How illuminating. She must trust you completely, Mr. Cardale. It is Mr. Cardale, is it not? Or have I been embarrassingly misinformed?"

Anger surges through me. I know what he is about. I know why this fiend has come here.

One of my Cavaliers chatters urgently in my ear.

We tried to stop him, mistress, but he used his demon spirits to bar our way.

I force myself to sound strong. "How dare you come into my home! I will never give you what you want, surely you realize that."

Stricklend sighs. "I am aware it will be difficult for you, Morningstar. May I call you that? I feel we can converse more honestly as witches, don't you?"

"You have no right to call yourself witch, *sorcerer*. And I have no wish to converse with you at all. Leave my home at once!"

"Alas, I cannot." He begins to move toward us. Bram tightens his grip on me. I hold my ground. "The Sentinels have waited long centuries to regain what was taken from us. What is rightfully ours. The decision was made that we would wait no longer. The time has come to restore the Elixir to its rightful masters. And that time has come because of me."

"Many Sentinels have existed before you, Stricklend," I tell him, "and I have no doubt many of them thought themselves up to the task you have set yourself. There are accounts of attempts to uncover the Great Secret. Every Lazarus witch learns of them during their instruction. None of these misguided efforts to steal the Elixir from us was successful. They all failed. As will you!"

"I will not leave without what I have come for, make no mistake about that."

Beside me Bram shakes his head. "You are quite mad."

"Really?" Stricklend is unimpressed. "If you consider me so, then I can only wonder what you think of the accomplished necromancer you now have in your embrace. She raised her own brother from his coffin, did she tell you that? I must say I admire your broad-mindedness, Mr. Cardale. Perhaps it is your . . . artistic nature that allows you to view your beloved's darker habits so charitably."

I am about to reply and I can feel Bram clench his fist, but before either of us can respond we are thrown to the ground. The force of Stricklend's spell is astonishing, and it catches us both off guard. I am still fighting for breath as I stagger to my feet. What I see next freezes me to the spot with fear. Stricklend has used his strong magic to fling Bram up into the air and now has him suspended, helpless, twenty feet above the roof garden. In an instant he has conveyed him farther away from me, so that now he is beyond the balcony wall. If he were to drop now, if Stricklend were to let him drop, he would plummet ten floors to the street behind the apartment building.

"Bram, keep still!" I shout at him. He listens to me and ceases his futile, dangerous struggling.

"It is a simple trade," Stricklend says, "you give me what I want, and I will give you back your lover. If not . . ." To underline his point he lets Bram drop suddenly six feet before stopping him again.

Behind me Terence shouts and rushes toward Stricklend. I try to warn him, to stop him, but in an instant the Sentinel has sent a spell at the poor, frail man, so that he crumples to the ground and lies silent. I feel my stomach turn over. My Cavaliers offer their assistance.

We will help you, mistress! We can assail your enemy, catch him unawares, beat him back.

No! If you interrupt his concentration you may cause the spell to be broken and Bram will fall. The risk is too great.

"I grow tired of waiting for your answer, Morningstar. Are you content to watch another loved one die?"

A calmness descends upon me as I realize what it is I must do. I experience no fear, no panic, only a firm certainty. There is no other path.

I look at Bram. He has mastered his own fear and his face is resolute. I know he is thinking of me, of how to make this easier for me.

"Don't do it, Lilith," he calls to me. "Don't give him what he wants. You can't. You must not."

I instruct my guardians clearly, so there can be no doubt.

Use all your strength. Save Bram. Let nothing prevent you. Nothing. Only save him.

But mistress . . .

Do as I tell you!

Stricklend sees what is happening and begins working another spell. It could be one to stop my captains helping or it could be one to send Bram plummeting to his death. I cannot know. In the moment his attention is drawn away from me, I summon all my strength. My witch's strength. Silently, I call on Hekate to come to my aid, to give me even a fraction of her power. The power to stop a beating heart or to force breath from a body. I call on any listening spirits to contribute their energy to what I must unleash upon Stricklend. I wait as long as I dare, trusting that if Bram falls, *when* Bram falls, he will be caught by my spirit allies and brought to safety.

Stricklend curses. The spell he is using to suspend Bram is affected. I hear a shout and see Bram tumbling, not quite falling, but turning, over and over. Stricklend's magic is precise and expertly controlled, but it is hampered by his having to defend himself from my own spells. I know I have only a fraction of the time I really need to work a spell of disturbance, a fierce and painful one, against Stricklend. I recite the ancient phrases at great speed, tripping over the unfamiliar sounds in my haste. He becomes aware of what I am doing and his face darkens further.

"You insult me, witch! Do you think I am afraid of you? You have no notion of the magic of which I am capable. The Sentinels once possessed what you and your Lazarus brothers and sisters so arrogantly consider to be yours. We have worked, for generations, toward reclaiming the Elixir, to having it restored to us. And over those long years we have honed our skills, developed our talents, passing down this knowledge and ability, working and practicing our art, utterly intent on our prize. The Sentinels have never had such a leader as the one who stands before you now, Morning-star. I am the apotheosis of that ambition. All those centuries of magic are distilled through me. I can crush the life from any being who treads this earth—man, woman, witch, or sorcerer. And I will crush you. All of you."

So saying he utters harsh, guttural words, enforcing his magic, so that I see magic fizzing and crackling in the air around him. The Cavaliers are whirling around Bram in an effort to protect him, but Stricklend is too powerful, and I know that if he releases the spell he is building to, they will not be able to defend Bram against it.

It is a simple matter to step in front of my adversary, to put myself directly between him and Bram, to stand in the path of the evil magic that was meant for the man I love. As I do so I hurl my own half-formed spell at Stricklend with all the fury I can command. As my own magic finds its target I see Strick-lend drop to his knees with a cry of pain. But not before he has sent forth his own vicious spell. At least, as I fall to the ground, I have the satisfaction of knowing that not only is Bram protected but that the wicked Sentinel is, for now, disarmed. The charge of blackness that he has released finds its target not in Bram but in me. It is not the piercing stab of a dagger, as I might have expected, but the blow of a hammer, as if a giant has wielded the thing, and my flimsy body has taken the full brunt of the strike.

I can hear someone calling my name. It is Bram, his voice full of anguish. My vision blurs and shapes swim before my eyes. I know I should breathe. I try to, but little air will enter my body. I feel I am filled instead with some solid, suffocating substance that repels life. I am aware of figures moving. Stricklend turns and flees, clutching at his side where the arrowhead of my spell found its mark. And suddenly Bram is here, cradling me in his arms.

"Lilith! Oh my God, my darling Lily."

"You are safe, my love."

"It was me he meant to hurt! What has he done to you?" He holds me close, kissing my face, saying my name over and over.

Oh! My body is failing. Soon I, too, will be nothing but spirit. I must pass on the Great Secret. Dare I risk doing it after I have crossed the Rubicon? What if I am prevented from returning somehow? Can Stricklend's hatred reach me even in the Land of Night? I cannot take the chance. I will tell Bram. I can trust him. I have to trust him.

"Lilith," Bram calls to me again. "Let me send for a doctor."

"No doctor. You must listen to me . . ."

"There must be something I can do."

"Bram, please. I am dying . . ."

"No!"

"I am not afraid. No necromancer fears death. I will cross the Rubicon to the Land of Night and join my Gentle Spirits there."

"No." He is weeping now, and it breaks my heart to see him so lost, so afraid. "Please, my love, don't go. Don't leave me."

I reach up and touch his face. "I am sorry. My only regret is that I must leave you. My poor love. Forgive me, my darling, but there is one more thing I would ask of you . . ."

"Yes. Anything. Anything."

"The Great Secret. It cannot die with me. I will entrust it to you."

"But . . . I am no witch."

"You must pass it on. Tell Louis. He will guard it with his life, I know he will."

Bram is shaking his head, not wanting to face what is happening.

"You have to be strong, Bram, my darling. Please, do this for me." I gasp as my body screams out for the air it is being denied. Stricklend's spell is slowly crushing the life from me.

Bram steadies his voice and strokes my cheek. "All right. Lie still, my love. Tell me what it is that you have given your life for. I promise I will tell no one but Louis."

I nod. I want to be gentle, to explain, to make him understand, to hear him forgive me for abandoning him, but I have so little strength left. So little time.

"The Great Secret reveals the final ingredient needed to assemble the Lazarus Elixir. Without it, the potion is powerless, it cannot work." My heart is thudding, laboring, stuttering now, with irregular, unnatural beats. I must press on. "Three drops of blood from a baby. Newborn. It must be collected before the infant is an hour on this earth. A silver pin, pricked into the heel, and the precious drops collected."

"From a newborn?"

Suddenly, through the haze of my fading senses, I am aware of a thickening of the air behind Bram. A movement of some force, some malevolent force. Too late I realize we have been overheard. Willoughby! Willoughby's Dark Spirit was here all along, waiting, listening. Stricklend knew I would be forced to pass on the Great Secret. I was the intended victim all along. He knew that only at the point of my death would I divulge what he wanted to know! The shadowy shape shifts and is gone again. Gone to its master!

"Oh Bram, we have been tricked! I have been so stupid! The Dark Spirit was here." I try to sit up, shaking my head. I have not enough breath to explain. "He will take what he has learned to Stricklend. If that monster knows . . . don't you see? No baby, no mother, would ever be safe again."

"Hush now, Lilith, do not distress yourself further, please, my darling."

"You have to stop him. Promise me, you and Louis. And Druscilla. Ask for her help. Promise me!"

"I promise. Oh, God, Lilith!" Bram's eyes fill with tears again as my body is wracked with a painful spasm.

"One more thing, Bram, it is vital . . . listen . . ."

"Yes, my love, I am listening. What is it?"

"At the convent. Ask for the casket . . . Sister Bernadette. And Bram, you must remember, a *girl* baby." I can feel myself fading. My limbs are weightless. There is no longer any pain, merely a sensation of floating, of drifting upward. I can hear the spirits calling to me . . . "The precious drops of blood must be . . . taken from a *girl* baby to raise a woman. From a . . . *boy* baby to raise . . . a . . ." As I form the words they sound to me as if they come from some far distant place, rather than from my own mouth. And at last I am free of my body. Free of my earthly ties. And the blessed blackness of the night envelops me, swaddles me, embraces me, until at last I am absorbed into the dark where no stars shine, no light glows, save for that of the phantasmagoria that rises to welcome me to my new home.

27.

"No!" Bram's cry of pain cuts through the cool night air. He clutches Lilith to him and rocks her in his arms, his tears falling unchecked now. He knows she is dead. Knows she has gone to another place. A place she has known of and understood all her life, but not a place he can fathom or ever conceive of going to. "Don't," he begs her. "Don't leave me, my love." He pulls back to look at her exquisite face and kiss her cold lips. She looks so pale, her skin is almost transparent, as if her body might fade away, too. "You are too young, too precious," he tells her, shaking his head, refusing to accept what has happened. "And I love you too much." He buries his face in her hair, breathing in her scent, the thought of releasing her unbearable.

And then it comes to him. The realization of what he must do strikes him with such clarity he cannot question it. Quickly, he picks Lilith up. He sees Terence's lifeless body and knows he is beyond help. He carries Lilith to the observatory. Inside, the air is almost as cool as outside, but he is aware of a strange disturbance in the atmosphere, and he knows that he is not alone. He is able to detect the presence of many spirits. "Guard your mistress," he tells them as he lays her down on the cushioned chaise. He kisses her one more time and then hurries away, back down the stairs. In the bedroom he pulls on his jacket and boots, before racing down to the foyer of the apartment block, where he hands the concierge a five-pound note.

"Send for Lord Harcourt, the earl of Winchester," he tells him. "Say that Lady Lilith has urgent need of him. He must come at once. When he does, admit him, and send him up to the observatory where he must wait for me. Be sure and tell him: he must wait for me. Lady Lilith is unwell, do you understand?"

Satisfied that the man will carry out his instructions, Bram rushes out into the night. The hour is late, but he succeeds in finding a motor cab.

"St. Mary's Convent, quick as you can," he tells the driver. He knows what he must have, if Louis is to save Lilith, and he is certain he knows where Lilith would keep it.

A place of safety, she told me. A place of trust.

When the cab arrives at the church he makes sure the driver will wait for him and then hurries inside. The vestry door, like that at the front of the church, is unlocked, so that he is able to run across the courtyard to the entrance to the convent itself. He hammers on the iron-studded wooden door and calls loudly. With surprising speed, the nuns arrive. Bram tells them who he is and asks for the only name he recalls Lilith mentioning. When Sister Bernadette steps forward he speaks directly to her.

"Lilith left something in your safekeeping," he tells her, barely able to sound rational but knowing it is imperative he do so. "I must have it. I must take it to her now. Her life depends upon it," he explains. "Sister Bernadette, there is not time for me to explain. I believe you know why Lilith trusted you with what was terribly precious to her, terribly important. She chose to tell me of this place, of what she had done, to tell me about you. She would not have done so had she not wanted me to act on that knowledge if the need arose. Please, without the contents of that box, she is lost to us forever." He is suddenly aware of how mad he must look, making demands in the middle of the night, his hair wild, his bare skin showing through his unbuttoned jacket.

Sister Bernadette considers his request carefully, while the other nuns make their disapproval known.

"Coming here at such an hour, in such a state!" Sister Agnes is furious.

"We should call the police," says another nun.

"That will not be necessary," Sister Bernadette assures them. "Sister Margaret, fetch the box belonging to Lady Lilith."

Sister Agnes objects. "She left it in our care—we ought not to give it up to some drunkard who brings us from our beds!"

"Quickly, Sister Margaret, if you please." Sister Bernadette is adamant and will not hear any further argument on the matter. "I believe it is what Lady Lilith would want," she says calmly. When the box arrives, she hands it to Bram. "Do your best for our dear friend," she tells him.

"Thank you, Sister." Clutching the box and its priceless contents to him, he runs back to the waiting motor cab. Although the driver is swift and the streets empty, the journey back to Waterloo Place seems desperately slow. Bram feels that all he tries to do moves at a hopelessly leaden pace and that his efforts will be in vain. He reaches Lilith's apartment just as the concierge is letting Louis in. He too has dressed hastily, though he still manages to appear cool in his expensive wool trousers, waistcoat, and white shirt.

"Cardale, what the devil is all this about? I've been told Lilith is unwell? Has a doctor been called?"

"She is in the observatory, we must hurry," he tells him, wrenching open the door of the main lift and beckoning him in. "Come on, man, there is no time to lose." As the elevator whirs its way upward Bram tries to explain what has happened, though he finds it hard to believe his own words as he hears them spoken aloud. He reminds himself that none of it will seem so fantastical to Louis, for Louis is, after all, a witch, like Lilith. When they get to the door of the observatory, he pauses. "I must warn you, Harcourt, it is . . . shocking . . . to see her like this."

Louis nods curtly, and the two go inside.

Lilith is just as Bram left her, lying on the chaise longue, looking heartbreakingly serene and beautiful. Bram hears Louis gasp at the sight of her, his hand flying to his mouth. Bram stands beside him. "She . . . she told me the Great Secret," he says.

"*You?*" Louis is incredulous. "But . . ."

"There was no one else. She knew she was dying. She was frantic at the thought she would take the knowledge with her to her grave."

"She could have told me afterward, though I can't expect *you* to understand that. She could have come to me as a spirit and told me."

"For pity's sake, I don't know why she told me. Perhaps she was afraid she wouldn't be able to come back . . . that you wouldn't be able to reach her. I don't know, I don't know! All I do know is that she trusted me to tell you, and I will, but you must promise me one thing first."

"How can you stand there and strike bargains? How can you think about making gains for yourself when Lilith lies here . . ." He cannot bring himself to name her state.

"I want nothing for myself," Bram says. "I want you to use the Elixir. Use it on Lilith."

"What!?"

"You can save her. You are a senior witch. You know the spells, she told me all the senior witches learn them. I have the Elixir." He thrusts the box into Louis's hands.

"But such a thing is forbidden. And anyway, to attempt such a thing alone would be folly of the highest order."

"For pity's sake, Harcourt, think of Lilith."

"You don't understand. I've never . . . what you ask is beyond anything I have ever done. It is far from simple, and success is far from certain."

"There is not time to perfect the skill. It is now Lilith needs you." Seeing that Louis is unconvinced he goes on. "She is so young. She is such a good person. She cared more about me, and more about protecting the Great Secret, than about anything else. She was prepared to give her life for it. But she doesn't have to, don't you see? We can save her. She told me what it meant to be a necromancer. I can't pretend I understood everything she said, it's so much to take in, so much to comprehend . . . but I believed every word of what she said."

Louis looks down at Lilith. He briskly wipes a tear from his eye.

Bram tries to find the right words. "If it goes wrong, you can say I made you do it. That I wouldn't pass on the Great Secret to you unless you tried."

Louis's face hardens. "If it goes wrong, we will damn her to the Darkness—did she tell you that? Did she talk of the hell that waits for spirits who are lost? Have you any true conception of what risk we are taking here, not just for Lilith but for ourselves, too?" He stands, shaking his head, still clutching the box that holds the Elixir and the Montgomery diamonds, staring at it.

Bram sighs. He closes his eyes for a moment, and then puts his hand on Louis's arm and says, "I won't make you do it. I can't. To use what I know, to withhold it from you . . . that would be wrong. It would not be what Lilith would want. I will tell you the Great Secret, whatever you decide to do. But I believe saving her would be right." He reaches down and touches Lilith's sleek, shiny hair. Looking back up at Louis, he says quietly, "Bring her back to us. If you love her, please, bring her back to us."

Stricklend finds himself in an unaccustomed state of agitation and is amused to realize that the experience is not unpleasant. He has been waiting for this moment for so long, has planned for it, worked for it, killed for it, and now the hour has come: he is to have the complete Elixir in his hand and use it to bring a dead man back to life. The anticipation is exquisite torture. He allows himself to pace the narrow path between the headstones and funereal statuary. The cemetery is still and quiet, with not a breath of wind to stir the trees or whistle around the tombstones. He takes out his gold pocket watch. Its face is clearly readable in the light of the full moon. Two o'clock. Perry has been gone over an hour, and must surely return soon. There are not many hours of darkness left, nighttime being unhelpfully short these late spring months. He requires the cover of the night not only to shield his activities from curious eyes but also to strengthen his magic. As a Sentinel, he has long practiced spellcraft of many sorts, but never before has he attempted Infernal Necromancy. He knows that such rituals as are needed work best before sunrise. With the Elixir in his possession, the Coven of Lazarus all but vanquished, there is one step left to be taken. Proof of the efficacy of the potion. A successful application of the Elixir before he announces to the group that he has it, and none will be able to question his authority as the most able, the most powerful necromancer the modern age has ever seen.

Stricklend cannot help congratulating himself on a plan, thus far, excellently executed. The Dark Spirit was able to eavesdrop on Lilith's final words as she divulged the Great Secret to Bram. As Stricklend had known she would. To have what he has striven to obtain all these long years is thrilling enough; to know that the Head Witch of the Lazarus Coven is dead is an extra delight. Willoughby assured him that he listened to Lilith Montgomery's final utterances and watched her die before making haste to join Stricklend at the duke's grave and give him the vital information. Perry had all too readily agreed to go in search of the blood of a newborn. Stricklend had instructed him to go to the nearest hospital, posing as a medical student, armed with enough money to bribe all but the most pious of midwives.

Hearing brisk footsteps, Stricklend turns and sees Perry striding through the yew trees. He has to stop himself sprinting forward to demand the final Elixir ingredient from him. At last the younger man reaches the duke of Radnor's graveside. He holds out a small bottle with a cork stopper.

"Here." He speaks urgently, with a tremor in his voice, whether from excitement or fear Stricklend cannot know. "I have it. I have it."

He takes the bottle from him and holds it up, letting the moon's beams gleam through the dark red liquid it contains. "We must hurry. There is not much time," he says. The grave has become a makeshift altar. Stricklend already has all the other ingredients for the Elixir assembled, right down to the diamond dust. He has long had in his possession the incantations, but now that the final essential part of the Elixir is his, nothing can stop him.

Stricklend has had a quantity of the incomplete concoction kept in readiness for this very moment. All it requires is the addition of the blood of the newborn, and the ritual can begin. With great care, he adds the required amount of the still-warm ruby liquid to the black, pre-prepared potion. At once, his heightened senses detect a stirring of spirits about him. As if they know something momentous has begun. He turns to face Perry.

"Are you still willing?" he asks.

Perry nods. "I am."

"Your loyalty, your bravery, your sacrifice, will be rewarded."

"My reward will be my immortality. I will be the first revenant raised by the Sentinels in centuries. Many will come after me, but I will be the one to take the first step and herald a new era where the Sentinels have dominion over death." With an edgy eagerness he moves to the grave. The ceremonial objects have been arranged in such a way as to allow space for him to lie among them. He quickly settles himself on the cold, hard stone that covers the grave.

Stricklend moves closer. He swiftly conjures a Sleeping Spell, so that Perry is asleep in a matter of seconds. Then, more slowly, with more deliberation and care, he casts a Stopping Spell. He has chosen a kind, painless one, but one that he has used before and knows to be effective and reliable. Perry's slumbering form seems to tense slightly, and then his hands jerk once, twice, three times. There follows silence. Stricklend feels for a pulse at the young man's throat. Finding none, he is satisfied that Peregrine Smith is indeed dead.

The quiet is broken by an eerie wind that appears from nowhere. It makes a mournful sound but does not cause the leaves or branches of the nearby trees to move. It brings with it a coldness that settles upon Stricklend. He remains unperturbed. He knows enough to expect a disturbance among the deceased. His studies have taught him to proceed with caution, for in raising one dead soul, others may attempt to free themselves from the constraints of death. Some will be human, some will not.

He picks up the vial of bone dust and sprinkles its contents over the altar, rubbing the last grains between his palms. He lays his hands upon Perry's cooling body and begins to recite the words he has carried in his head for years in anticipation of this night. He continues with the chants and prayers, all the while aware of the growing restlessness among the residents of the cemetery. He can hear their calls and cries now, as plainly as if they were standing next to him. As he proceeds, he catches fleeting glimpses of ephemeral figures as they flit about the graveyard.

Stricklend raises his arms and lifts his voice to the night sky. *"Exurgent mortui et ad me veniunt!"* He calls back Perry's spirit, knowing as he does so that others will answer the call. He repeats the summons two, three times more. Next he places his hand over Perry's eyes.

"When these eyes open again, they will see."

He touches his brow.

"When this mind stirs once more, it will think."

He touches his mouth.

"When these lips part, they will speak."

He puts his hand on his chest.

"When this heart beats again, it will feel."

Stricklend picks up the Elixir and pours a tiny amount into the ceremonial chalice, which he raises high, saying a short prayer sacred to the Sentinels. He takes from his waistcoat pocket a tiny, perfect diamond. Closing his palm around it he utters the words that will reduce it to a fine powder, so that he is then able to add it to the Elixir. He stoops over Perry and slips his hand beneath the dead man's neck, so that he can tilt his head forward. He places the edge of the chalice to his lips, letting three drops of the nec-romantic liquid drip into his slightly open mouth. Setting down the chalice, he leans over and takes Perry in his arms, lifting him up as if he weighed no more than a child.

"Wake up, now, boy," he tells him, with more fondness than he has ever spoken to anyone in his life. "Wake up, and be born again!"

For a long moment there is a supernatural stillness, as a calm before a storm. Stricklend feels the body in his arms grow sud-denly heavier. So heavy that he is forced to set him down on the gravestone once more. As he watches, Perry starts to twitch and to tremble. His eyes spring open. He tries to speak. At first he can make no sound, then, spluttering a little, he finds his voice.

"Yes! I am returned . . . I . . ." He turns over and pushes him-self up so that he is kneeling. His movements are unsteady and erratic, but he quickly begins to regain his strength. He stretches out his arms, examining his hands, looking at his skin, touching his face, taking deep, deep breaths. He looks up at Stricklend. "It works!" he cries, beginning to laugh loudly. "It works, Stricklend, it truly works. Look at me! Look!"

And Stricklend does look, and what he sees when he looks almost stops his own heart.

For though the flush of youthful life did indeed return to Perry's face in the first moments of his reanimation, now he is undergoing a further change. A terrible, terrible change. As Stricklend watches, the young man's skin starts to pock and wither with terrifying rapidity, so that soon his whole face is covered in scarred, shriveled skin, as if he were not simply aging but decaying, rotting, at a greatly accelerated rate.

Stricklend's expression alerts Perry to his own hideousness. His hands fly to his face a second time, and then he, too, screams as he sees the condition of his putrefying hands.

"No! What is happening? Something has gone wrong! Stricklend, make it stop! Make it stop!"

But Stricklend cannot make it stop. The spell has been cast, the magic evoked, the Elixir given. There is no turning back now, no preventing the process running its course. It is clear, as Perry begins to writhe upon the ground as his internal organs also start upon the path of horribly rapid decomposition, that something has indeed gone wrong. While the Elixir and the spell were powerful enough to call up life once more, there is only flawed magic to sustain that life. And what magic there is now churns and flails within Perry, fighting to maintain its hold, unable to stabilize, to regulate either itself or the transformation it has brought about.

If Stricklend thought to attempt anything to help Perry, he is prevented from doing so by a cacophonous rumbling that heralds the opening up of a fissure between himself and the pulsating young man in front of him. The unrestrained power of the corrupted spell has reached the creatures of the Darkness and affected their release. As Perry at last falls still, nothing more than an empty corpse once more, the raw hole in the ground next to him belches forth foul-smelling smoke, and the roars of beings who were never intended to tread the earth. A clawlike hand reaches up from the depths and takes hold of Perry's ankle. In one unnaturally quick movement it pulls his body into the pit. Stricklend starts to walk backward, slowly, keeping his eyes on the entrance to the abyss. He sees a demon, crouched low, scramble up the far side of the crater and bound away among the tombstones. Another, slightly larger, with a bulbous head and small, piggy eyes, hauls itself up onto the grass. It cocks its head on one side as if considering Stricklend very carefully.

"What a foul little beast you are," he tells it. "So very unattractive and so very unwelcome." He speaks to gain precious time, all the while casting a Suffering Spell in the demon's direction. When it strikes home the creature squeals, thrashing wildly at its invisible assailant. Stricklend seizes the advantage and begins to use the incantations he has learned from his study of the necromancer's art. Incantations against just such an event. Spells and chants which, he sincerely hopes, will send the escaping monsters back where they belong, and seal the wound in the earth that is allowing them out. All around him spirits whisper or cry out. He observes several specters wandering among the graves. The power of the Lazarus Coven is only now revealed to him, and he finds himself in awe of it. It takes all his concentration, all his considerable skill, to slowly drive back the emerging demons. As he battles on, he begins to feel his own strength waning.

"Willoughby!" He summons the spirit. "Help me. You are a creature of the Darkness, help me send these wretches back where they belong, unless you want to dwell there for all eternity. Fulfill your pledge and serve the Sentinels as you swore to do."

Beside him a looming figure strides forward into the fray.

I open my eyes.

At first I cannot be sure where I am or whether it is night or day. My vision is blurred, the focus skewed, so that for a short while I lie still, waiting for things to become clearer. I have the curious sensation that I am dreaming, and yet at the same time I am quite certain that I am not. I am aware of voices, but they seem distant. Slowly I come to realize that some are the familiar, insistent whisperings of the spirits. Others are spoken by people who still tread the earth. I know those voices so well. Why does it take me so long to recognize them?

"Lilith? Lilith, can you hear me?"

Yes, yes. Oh! I make no sound. I want to speak, but my voice is still sleeping.

"Lily, my love . . ."

Bram?

"Bram?" At last I can form his name properly. "My eyes . . . where are we?"

"Shh, lie still. All will be well. We are in the observatory. It is still night. The stars are shining just for you, do you see?"

I rub my eyes and blink away the strange heaviness in them. And, gradually, I can make out the cloudless indigo of the sky and its celestial diamonds. I blink some more and my sight is properly restored. It is a relief to see Bram's dear face gazing down at me. But he looks so terribly anxious.

"Have I been . . . unwell?" I ask, and then I see that Louis stands behind him. "Oh, Louis. Why do you both look so concerned?"

"Do you not remember, Lily?" he asks me. "Do you not recall what happened?"

I shake my head and become conscious of the fact that my limbs feel restless. Restless and weightless. Now that the heaviness of my sleepy state has melted away, it has been replaced by a wonderful feeling of well-being. I sit up, the movement momentarily causing a little dizziness.

"Do you feel . . . quite well?" Bram asks me.

"I should feel a great deal better if you would both stop looking at me as if I were an invalid."

Bram moves away a little. Louis asks again, "Do you recall nothing?"

And then, in that moment, in one mind-shaking instant, I do remember. I remember everything. I remember Bram being suspended over the edge of the building. I remember Stricklend. I remember the Dark Spirit. I remember being wounded.

I remember dying.

I remember dying!

Suddenly I cannot breathe. The shock of the recollection has knocked the air from my lungs. I leap to my feet, gasping. Bram tries to hold me. I know he means to help, but I cannot bear him to touch me now, not now. I fight for breath and gulp it down. My sudden movement has brought on a lurching dizziness, so that I have to clutch the back of the chaise to steady myself. I am aware of the loudness of my own heartbeats as they thud in my ear. I can feel the blood whooshing through my veins. I would almost swear I can feel my body regenerating, replenishing, rebuilding itself, stronger and better than it has ever been. I have the impression I have woken from a month of sleep, and feel utterly rested. All my senses are heightened. I can hear small, nighttime birds far below in the trees of the embankment singing sweetly. I can smell the coffee being brewed in the kitchen of the little bakery two streets away. And I can feel magic. My own magic. Oh, how it fills my body! My whole being fizzes and crackles with it. As the giddiness and panic pass I take a few tentative steps. Around me I can feel my guardian spirits. And I can see them! Not just as I ordinarily can whenever I have called or summoned them, but all those dear to me, here, beside me, as real and bright and full of life as the days when they trod the earth.

Welcome, mistress!

My handsome Cavaliers! My brave soldiers.

Will you walk in the gardens with me, Lilith? Will you pick flowers with me?

Amelia. Dear little Amelia.

So many spirit friends.

"Lilith." Bram's voice snags my attention and the spirits recede. "Do you understand what has happened to you?"

Thinking back, stamping down the panic that revisits me when I allow the thought to form in my mind, I know I must make myself face the truth of what has happened.

"I am alive because I have taken the Elixir. You, Louis, you must have worked the spell. And you, Bram, my darling, you must have brought him here."

Louis shakes his head in wonder. "Oh, Lilith, I have never in my life been so terrified of doing anything."

I manage a small smile. "It appears you are a fair necromancer, Lord Harcourt."

"Do you feel well?" Bram asks.

"I feel *magnificent!*" I assure him. And the three of us laugh at the lunacy of it all. I hold Bram's gaze then. Can he truly love me now? What am I, after all, if not a living corpse? I would be revolted, repulsed, repelled by my own body, if I were not experiencing such glorious strength, such invigorating, blissful magic. But Bram cannot know how I feel. To him I might have become some terrible ghoulish creature. I hold out my hand to him, wrist uppermost. "I am truly alive, my love. Touch me. I am warm. My heart beats. My blood flows. Feel my pulse. Won't you take my hand?" For a moment I am afraid he will recoil from me now, that he will not be able to love the unearthly revenant being I am become. But he smiles, his beautiful face relaxing.

"If you want me to hold your hand, you'll have to come down first."

"Come down?"

"Look at your feet."

I look and find that I am floating, drifting some distance above the floor. Giggling, I force my feet to find their way back to the ground. I reach out for Bram, happy for him to hold me now. When he touches my skin, he flinches as the heat of the magic within me stings his own flesh. Disconcerted, he tries again, cautiously. I do my best to control this new, elemental force that I have been reborn with. This time I am aware of a tingling sensation in my palm and fingers as he takes my hand.

Relieved, Bram smiles. "I shall have to be careful," he says.

"I . . . think I have much to learn about my new . . . status. I'm sorry if I hurt you."

"It was nothing. It doesn't matter. I thought I had lost you forever," he murmurs into my hair, his eyes still wet with tears. "I could not bear to live on without you. I begged Louis to do it. I fetched the Elixir and the necklace from the convent, I told him the Great Secret, and I pleaded with him to bring you back."

"Louis, you took such a dangerous step. Oh!" I see through the window Terence's body, a small dark shape on the roof terrace. I hurry outside to him, but I know already that his spirit has gone. I kneel beside him and hold his cold hand.

"Stricklend," Bram says. "Terence tried to help you. Stricklend didn't hesitate for a second. Murdering an old man meant nothing to him."

I cannot help but feel responsible. "I should have protected him," I say.

"You cannot help everyone, Lily," Louis tells me.

"Stricklend will crush anyone to get what he wants," I say. "Terence is not his first victim, and he certainly will not be his last." A terrible thought comes to me. "Louis, when you used the Elixir to raise me, was Willoughby here?"

"Willoughby? Edmund Willoughby, d'you mean?"

"There is not time to explain. Did you feel the presence of a Dark Spirit?"

He shakes his head. "No. There was a great deal of activity. I . . . I expected that, I suppose. You know I've never practiced Infernal Necromancy before, Lily. There was a lot going on, a commotion, spirits stirring . . ."

"But not a *Dark* Spirit, Louis. You would know the difference."

"No. No, I'm certain of it. No Dark Spirit."

I find I am able to breathe again properly, but my relief is short-lived when Bram says, "But, Lilith, Willoughby was here. After Stricklend left, you said you saw him, that he overheard . . . Don't you remember?"

"Oh, yes! How could I have been so foolish? It is coming to me now. Bram, Stricklend never intended to kill you. He knew I wouldn't reveal the Great Secret to him. He knew I would only tell it if I knew I was dying, to pass it on. Ordinarily, that would have been to the heir to my title, or at the very least to a senior witch. But there was none. Only you, my darling. Stricklend knew I would tell you, and he left Willoughby here to eavesdrop."

"Lilith, you could not have known." Bram does his best to comfort me. "It isn't your fault . . ."

"It is my responsibility. The Great Secret is in the hands of the most wicked of men, a man who will use it for his own gain, his own power, not caring how many people he harms. Stricklend has what he needs to wreak havoc, and I gave it to him." I shake my head slowly. "Which means, I must be the one to take it from him again."

"Lily . . . ?" Louis shakes his head.

"What do you mean?" Bram is anxious. "What do you plan to do?"

I hold up my hand and close my eyes. I call to my spirit guardians.

Where has he gone, my captains? Where is Stricklend now?

Two of us stayed with you, mistress. The third followed the sorcerer. He tells us the villain is in a graveyard. He stands close by a giant cedar tree.

"My father's grave," I tell Bram and Louis. "He has gone to Papa's grave."

Bram is puzzled. "Why? Why would he go there? Why now?"

Louis knows. "What better place is there than a cemetery if one wishes to raise the dead?"

"I must stop him." I stride toward the stairs. "He must not be allowed to use the Elixir!"

"Lily, you can't go alone," says Louis.

"He's right. We will come with you."

"No! It's too dangerous."

Louis overtakes me on the staircase calling back over his shoulder, "We can take my motorcar. I am a witch, Lily, do you really think I would allow you to do this unsupported? I can be of use."

I hesitate and put my hand on Bram's arm. "He's right, Bram. He is a witch—I may have need of his skills. And he will have some protection of his own. But you, my darling, I cannot let you come with us. You would be so vulnerable . . ."

"I've let that bastard kill you once, Lilith, I'm not going to let it happen a second time. Stricklend may ooze all the vile magic he wants, but he's still flesh and blood, isn't he? Fortunately the army taught me how to shoot straight. Harcourt, have you a gun?"

"I keep my shotguns in the country, but I do have one rifle and a pistol in my house here in London."

"Then we will fetch them on our way. Come on."

He takes my hand and we run down the stairs. Louis has brought no driver but gets behind the wheel himself, and soon the engine of the motorcar is running. It is pointless my resisting the plan, as I can see the men have made up their minds to help me. If Bram is to stand beside me, I must at least allow him to arm himself. In truth, I know I may very well have need of their help. I have scarcely had time to adjust to my new . . . condition. Druscilla told me there is no magic more powerful than that of a risen witch, but how do I know what I am capable of? How long might it take me to master my new gifts or talents? One way or another, Stricklend must be stopped.

28.

We tear along the embankment of the Thames and then head north, halting as briefly as possible at Clifton Villas to collect the weapons. As Louis drives on I watch Bram load bullets into the guns and test the sights of the rifle, and I marvel at how our lives have shaped us and brought us together for this moment. I am acutely aware that I am altered in so many ways. While my mind struggles to come to terms with the truth of what I now am, my body seems quicker to make the necessary adjustments. My senses continue to heighten, so that I am all but overwhelmed by the myriad sounds I can hear, the smells I can detect—not least the sourness of the nighttime river—as well as minuscule reactions to the air upon my skin, or Bram's touch as he holds my hand. And my other sense, my witch's sensitivity to magic, has increased to become the greater part of me. Magic sings through my veins and electrifies my fingertips. Will I be able to govern it? To wield it as I need to? This night we will all three of us be tested to the very limits of our various abilities.

Within minutes we arrive at the cemetery. We leave the car outside the high iron gates. Bram carries the rifle, Louis the pistol. The instant I set foot within the boundary of the graveyard I am assailed by disturbed and agitated spirits. They clamor and call out, some angry, some frightened, all stirred by the activities that have taken place here. I notice spectral shapes flitting between the headstones, and clearly spy at least two demons.

"We are too late!" I tell the others. "Stricklend has opened a way into the Darkness."

"And a way out," says Louis, pointing to a low, growling creature behind a mausoleum.

Bram raises his rifle.

"No!" I tell him. "Let it be. I will try to send it back, to send them all back. But first we must find Stricklend and Willoughby."

"It's so dark," says Bram. "And this place is vast. They could be anywhere. We should split up and search."

"There is no need." I lead the way as I speak. "I know precisely where he will be." Without hesitation I head for my father's grave. That is where my Cavalier saw him. That is where he will remain until his task is complete. Or until I stop him. I must not be distracted by the foul beasts and tortured souls who dash hither and thither. The closer we get to the fissure in the Rubicon, the nearer to the source of the bitter magic that is being so ruthlessly used, the louder the spirits cry out to me, begging me to help them, to rescue them from the Darkness, to send them to the Land of Night, or even to make them live again and tread the earth once more in the Land of Day.

They know. They all of them know what I am become.

At last we reach the mighty cedar tree. Beneath it I see a swirling mass of spirit forms and phantoms and shape-shifting sorcerers attempting to escape their purgatory. In the midst of it all stands Stricklend, and at his side, as perfectly human to look at as if he had not lived several hundred years ago, Edmund Willoughby. This Dark Spirit is working hard to hold back the hordes that would escape and to rid his master of the troublesome demons. Stricklend whirls about as I approach, and it is satisfying to see the surprise on his face at finding me here.

"You!" he hisses. "Even now, you seek to thwart my plans. Even though you are . . ."

"Dead? Oh, come now, you surely did not believe I would be so easily disposed of."

Bram and Louis stand on either side of me. Stricklend sneers at their guns.

"I see you have your own little army, Morningstar. How quaint. Clearly you feel the lack of your own corporeal presence, now that you are required to walk only in spirit."

"You are quite wrong about that," I tell him, letting my magic lift me up, slowly raising me to stand several feet off the dusty graveyard floor. My hair ruffles as I rise, and my night-robe flutters at the gentle movement. I use a spell of disturbance to snap a slim branch from the tree, grasp it in my hands, and crush it into woodchips, which I let go so that they blow away on the unearthly wind around us. "You see, I *do* have a body. One that is working really rather well just now."

Stricklend gapes. "You . . . you are *risen?*"

"I am."

"But how? I don't understand. I used the Elixir myself. I worked the spell, the incantations. I followed the ritual to the letter. Every utterance, every ingredient . . ."

"Including that of the Great Secret that you had your pet sorcerer's spirit snatch from my dying words!"

"It didn't work!" Stricklend insists. "The magic was flawed. It went wrong."

I look about but can see no corpse. "What hapless follower was prepared to die for you?" I ask him, shaking my head. "You are not fit to use the Lazarus Elixir, Sentinel. You and your kind never were. You never will be." And in that second I send a spell of disturbance stronger than any I have attempted before. Stricklend is thrown backward, sent crashing against a tombstone, where he staggers, gasping for breath. "You are not fit to use any magic, for you wield it without mercy, without morality, without care for anyone or anything!" I am shouting now, and the power of my own voice amazes me. I keep a finger pointed at the dazed sorcerer, forcing him down to the floor. "I will send you to the Darkness to dwell with all the nefarious, cruel, murderous members of your society who have gone before you!"

A shrieking to my left causes me to hesitate. A female wraith, long dead and clearly insane, is rushing at Louis. I see him work a spell of disturbance to halt her, so that she thrashes wildly against her invisible bonds. While Louis is occupied with her, two demons lumber toward us. Whether they are acting on the directions of Stricklend and Willoughby I have not time to tell, but soon they are upon us. I drop to the ground and spellcast to force one back, but the other reaches Bram before he can raise his rifle to his shoulder. The fiend snatches the gun from him and hurls it away into the shadows of the yew trees, before leaping upon Bram. A shot rings out and the thing falls still and silent. Louis stands, visibly shaken, his handgun smoking. During the commotion Stricklend has cast a spell of his own upon Louis. He cries out, clutching at his heart, and I know at once that he is suffering the same dreadful pain that the Sentinel inflicted on me.

Louis drops his gun and falls to the ground. I call to my Cavaliers to protect him, as I ready myself to send another spell in Stricklend's direction. But Willoughby is too quick for me. He belches forth a foul-smelling cloud that envelops me, filling my nostrils, making me splutter and cough, causing my eyes to stream. I hear yet another demon roaring and Stricklend barking orders at Willoughby. The poisonous mist threatens to choke me. Through it I can make out Bram snatching up the dropped pistol and firing at the Sentinel, who curses as he dives behind a headstone. In an instant he has flung further magic at Bram, who cries out but does not relinquish his gun.

I can feel myself growing heavy, my movements slowed and weakened by Willoughby's venomous miasma. It is difficult to think sufficiently clearly to spellcast. I can hear poor Louis gasping and I know that Stricklend will soon crush the life from him. Bram is doing his best to fight off demons and the blows of the Sentinel's smaller spells. I must act.

Mistress, let us help you!

No, my captains, help Bram. He cannot save Louis alone. Help them.

Stricklend laughs. "Your followers are no use to you now, Morningstar. Did you truly believe they could stand against a Dark Spirit, and against me? They are nothing but a drain on your own . . . *disappointing* talents. I have to say, I would have expected more from a risen witch." He sneers. He increases Louis's suffering and bids Willoughby drag Bram to him. My poor darling fires the handgun again and again, but his aim is skewed by Willoughby's magic, and not a single bullet finds its mark, either in the demons or in Stricklend. Soon Louis lies terrifyingly quiet, and Stricklend stands behind Bram, an arm tight around his throat, while the Dark Spirit renders his captive too weak to fight his way free.

"Face your failure, Morningstar. You have lost the Elixir. You have lost your precious lover. He must have seen you risen. He knows how it was done. When I have finished here—when *you* are finished—I think I will avail myself of his strong body and his unique knowledge. I believe he will provide me with the perfect volunteer for my next attempt to use the Lazarus Elixir. What do you think, Morningstar? Do you think I will succeed this time, hmm? Will he be raised like you, or will he suffer the same ghastly fate as my first revenant? Perhaps I will keep you with us long enough for you to witness his rebirth or to witness the flesh rotting from his bones before he is condemned to the pit."

I sense a shift in my own psyche. An alteration in my very self. The rage and frustration at what Stricklend is doing; the heartbreak at seeing my loved ones suffer so; the fury at what is being done with Lazarus magic—all combine to fire the transformation that had not yet fully taken place. I am revenant. I have been called back, taken from death, retrieved from the Land of Night to tread the earth again, and only now, now that the spark has been ignited, only now does the magnitude of what that truly means reveal itself. Deep inside me something stirs. Something ancient that has been awakened. It is the magic of hundreds of witches past, the enchantments of centuries. It is the wisdom of the sages who have studied arcane and long-forgotten arts. It is the strength of the skilled necromancer. It is the power of a risen witch. It is awe-inspiring and terrifying. And it is *mine*.

I fling my arms wide and Willoughby's toxic fog vanishes from me at once. My hair begins to fly wildly, and my night-robe billows about me as if stirred by a swirling vortex. There is the sound of wind rushing through the branches of the great cedar and the somber yews. My feet leave the ground and I travel upward until I am standing a yard or more clear of the dry grass of the graveyard. I can feel magic coursing through my veins. My breath is loud as a sighing giant. My heart is the drumbeat of distant thunder, audible to all. My skin glows, luminous in the caliginous night. My eyes flash bright as emeralds caught in supernatural light.

Demons and ghouls stop their slavering and growling and cower before me, whimpering. With startling ease I push them back to the fissure, back, sliding across the gravelly ground, send them skidding and tumbling over the edge, returning them to the Darkness.

Willoughby will not be so swiftly dealt with. The Dark Spirit bounds across the space between us, hurling his fetid spectral form at me, aiming to stifle my own magic with his vile presence. Before he can reach me I open my mouth and let forth a single, pure note of noise. A similar sound, some years ago, rendered Bram's studio wrecked and singed, but that occasion cannot begin to compare with this. This sound, this solid, white-hot noise, stops

Willoughby in his tracks, blasting his own protective magic from him. Headstones nearby are toppled. A stone angel explodes into smithereens. Stricklend, still clutching Bram, is thrown off his feet, the pair landing heavily upon my father's grave. Tongues of fire catch the dry grass and the branches of the cedar tree, so that soon the entire graveyard around us crackles and spits as it burns. The Dark Spirit is unnerved and disoriented and I seize my moment.

"You do not belong here!" I tell it. "Your time was long ago, and you used your magic badly. You will not return to cause more suffering. I will not allow it! Go back into the Darkness, where your wickedness can do no more harm." So saying I sing out again, at the same time flinging at him a spell of destruction that has come unbidden, unknown, into my mind, the words foreign and guttural and torn from the archaic memories that are now mine. Willoughby roars and writhes, but he is no match for me. Not now. Not ever again. As he plunges into the pit his furious bellowing can be heard growing fainter and fainter the deeper he falls.

Slowly, I turn my gaze upon Stricklend. At last, I see fear on the face of the Sentinel.

"You are right to be afraid," I tell him. "You have abused the Great Secret; you have shown yourself to be unworthy of using the Lazarus Elixir. You have already done such harm. You have hurt those I love for the last time, Sentinel."

"No, wait. Listen to me." He crawls backward, struggling to maintain his spell over Louis and another to weaken Bram, who still fights against his stranglehold. "*Think,* Morningstar. Think what we could achieve together, you and I! A risen witch and a Sentinel . . . we would wield untold power. There is nothing we could not do. Nowhere we could not rule."

"I have not come here to listen to you, Stricklend," I state calmly. "I have come to finish you."

I will the flames on the burning tree to grow hotter, fiercer, wilder. Suddenly the heavy bough above us cracks and falls, blocking Stricklend's retreat. He casts around for another escape, but to his right is the rupture into the abyss, and in front of him I stand. He tightens his grip on Bram, whose strength is slowly returning the more alarmed and agitated Stricklend becomes. Louis is silent now, and I pray to the spirits I will not be too late to save him.

"Let Bram go, Sentinel," I command, but he shakes his head. I narrow my eyes. "I said, let him *go*!" My words are accompanied by more leaping flames that catch Stricklend's sleeves. He is forced to relinquish his hold on his prisoner. Bram slumps forward, clambering to his knees, gasping for breath, as the Sentinel beats furiously at his clothes to put out the fire. I begin to force him back toward the brink of the pit. He snatches at the gravestone, and then at Bram, grabbing hold of his ankle. Bram is still too groggy to fend him off, so that he too begins to shift toward the hole. For a dreadful moment I recall Violet at my inauguration and how I lost her.

"I will take him with me, witch!" There is a hysterical edge to Stricklend's voice now. "I will drag him down into the Darkness with me!"

I pause, halting the magic that is moving the men across the graveyard floor. Turning, I see a strong ivy that twines its long way up one of the tallest yew trees. I open my palm toward it and bid it come into my hand. As I watch, the glossy green vine uncurls itself from the trunk of the tree and travels toward me. It snakes its way around my arm and into my hand. I close my fingers about it and draw a deep, refreshing breath. As I breathe I close my eyes and picture the leaves of the ivy shimmering and shivering as they change from green to black to silver. Only when I know the magic has taken hold do I open my eyes. The plant is transformed, so that now I have my own, pulsating, enchanted Silver Thread.

I raise my arm, drawing it slowly back to its full extent. Then I flick my wrist and fling my arm forward with all the strength I can muster, and the Silver Thread flies out, with a fearsome, singing whip-crack. It finds its mark. Stricklend yells. As the thread returns to coil around my arm I see blood bursting from a deep line across the Sentinel's face. Again I draw back my arm, and again the shining ivy whips forward, this time curling around Stricklend's throat. With a swift yank, I haul him sideways. His cry is throttled as he at last lets go of Bram, scrabbling at the thread, unable to pry it off. In desperation he throws a spell of his own, causing a piece of burning branch to fly at me. It strikes me upon the shoulder, the heat melting my night-robe, searing it into my skin. I cry out, but I do not flinch or falter. Not for one second do I take my eyes off my foe.

"Your time is at an end, Sentinel. You will not tread this earth again, in body or in spirit. I curse you and condemn you to the Darkness for all time!"

He opens his mouth to scream, but there is not time enough for him to do so before the Silver Thread tightens as I pull it, unraveling from his neck, sending him spinning over the edge of the crater, and finally, into the pit. I whip back the thread and stride forward, all the while chanting the words that I know will close the rupture and seal Stricklend's fate.

At last I come to stand upon the very ground that was only moments ago rent open and spewing such evil. There is a rumbling, as if the earth itself is reluctant to accept all the wickedness it must hold within it. I fight to steady my own galloping heart and ragged breathing. Slowly, the cemetery begins to quiet. The flames I created shrink and disappear. The air settles to its more normal, nighttime stillness.

Bram staggers to his feet and hurries to me.

"Lilith! My God, Lilith . . ." He wraps his arms around me,

holding me close, even though I still fizz with magic, and must feel strange and more than a little frightening in his embrace.

"Bram! You are safe."

"Your shoulder—you're hurt." He tenderly looks at the burn that has seared my skin.

"It is nothing, merely a memento. Oh, but Louis . . . !"

We run to where he lies. Bram helps me turn him over. His face is so very pale.

"He is breathing!" Bram tells me.

I place my hand on his brow, letting whatever magic I might possess, magic that I as yet do not even begin to comprehend, magic that might counter Stricklend's spell, letting it help him if it can.

"Wake up, Louis," I say softly, then again. "Wake up."

He gasps, a shuddering breath, and then his eyes open. I let out a cry of relief.

Louis takes a moment to come to his senses, and when he speaks, his voice is cracked and hoarse. "Good grief, Lily." He surveys the devastation around us. "Remind me not to make an enemy of you."

I smile at him. "You could never do that, dear Louis."

I become aware of shifting shapes behind me. The others sense them, too, and appear alarmed.

"All is well," I promise them. "We are among friends."

Slowly, cautiously, the spirits begin to reveal themselves. My faithful Cavaliers. Amelia. Many spirits known to me, and others new, but all come willingly, happily, in friendship. I stand up to greet them properly, and am astonished when they kneel in front of me. They whisper their thoughts and praise.

We are here to serve you, mistress.

Spirits bless you!

Welcome, Queen of the Night.

Bram helps Louis to his feet and they stand beside me.

"Well," says Louis, who can hear every word, "it seems you have been elevated."

I find myself, ridiculously, blushing. "I do not deserve such a title. I have not earned it."

"What title?" Bram wants to know.

Louis explains, grinning, "Our little Lily is a risen witch now, Cardale. No longer Daughter of the Night, she is Queen of the Night."

Queen of the Night, Queen of the Night!

The spirits echo my new name over and over.

Bram smiles at me. "It suits you. I have never seen anyone look more regal than you do at this moment."

I meet his gaze.

"Can you love me still?" I ask him. "Can you wish to be a part of . . . of all that you have seen? You know what I am become. You have witnessed the danger that surrounds me. I was so afraid for you . . . Are you certain you still want to be with me? I mean . . ."

"Hush." He puts a finger to my lips. "Where else would I be?"

High up in the branches of the cedar, a blackbird begins its tuneful song, starting up the chorus to herald the morning, as a thin, silvery light begins to lift the night from the city.

I take Bram's hand in mine.

"Well then, my love, a new day is dawning," I tell him. "Shall we face it together?"

Acknowledgments

The Midnight Witch presented all manner of interesting challenges for me. I wished to immerse myself in a time and place that is extremely well documented, so that my first task was to present it anew. I also wanted to create a complex tale, with story layers that reflected the strata of the era, and that would at the same time reveal a hidden seam of magic and witchcraft. If I have succeeded in my aims, it will be due in no small part to the guidance and hard work of my editorial team, Peter Wolverton and Anne Brewer. I am hugely grateful.

Thanks also, as ever, to my long-suffering and supportive family, and particularly on this occasion to my mum—beta reader and cheerleader combined.

TURN THE PAGE FOR
AN EXCERPT FROM

The SILVER WITCH

by *Paula Brackston*

Available in April from
Thomas Dunne Books/St. Martin's Press

★

PROLOGUE

It is as if she has always known that one day it would come to this. One day she would have to face it. Her darkest fear has been there to test her from a distance all her life. Years of imagining, thinking, wondering what it would be like to be swallowed up by the waves, or swept away by a fast-flowing river, or held beneath the sunny surface of a sparkling swimming pool, all have led to this place, this moment.

Gingerly, she moves toward the edge of the boathouse jetty. Her fingers are already losing their color in the damp chill. She crouches then sits, lowering her feet into the water. The intense cold is a shock. Her breathing accelerates as she twists around and lowers herself over the edge and in. The ancient, neglected wood is slimy with algae and her fingers start to slip. She gasps, clawing at the wet wood, but cannot get a firm grip. With a feeble splash she slides into the water, bursting into tears of relief and terror as her feet find the silty lake bed. The water level is just above her waist. Raising her arms, elbows bent, she edges toward the entrance, inching her way along the uneven surface. The sloping uneven surface. By the time she reaches the gable end of the boathouse the water is up to her armpits. She knows she is in danger of hyperventilating. Of being sick. Of fainting.

No, no, no! Mustn't trip, mustn't stumble. Small steps. Come on, feet, pretend we're running. Running in slow motion. Fleet feet. Strong steps. One foot in front of the other.

She pushes through the reeds, causing small waves to bounce back at her from the timber walls. She raises her chin as the water sloshes against her face. With every step she fights rising panic. Panic that threatens to send her falling into the water. Panic that might be the finish of her.

She reaches the low boards that block the exit. The moment has come. Now she must dive beneath the water, push through into the unknown, fight the tangle of weeds and swim to the outside. She knows if she thinks about it any longer she will not move, so in one desperate, sudden action she forces herself under the surface. The sensation of going beneath the water is more than she can stand. She loses her balance, falling through the twisted undergrowth, her feet sliding so that she disappears into the brackish blackness. She reacts as she has always feared she would, as she has always imagined so vividly in her nightmares. She inhales. The mouthful of water becomes a lungful in a soundless scream of terror. Tilda feels time stop. Her intellect tells her she must get up, must break the surface, must push up, grab something, find air. Her instinct tells her to fight and flail and clutch and claw. But the blackness is enticing, the silence seductive. And the cold, the bone-deep cold, has her in its tight embrace, numbing her will as well as her body.

I

★

SEREN

All is darkness. Blessed night. Freed from light and troubled vision, my thoughts are fed instead by the howling of the wind outside. The sound forms pictures in my mind, where I see the trees moving in the raging air. Willow and hazel pull at their roots as they dance. Birch and ash bend the knee to the mighty force from the skies. But the oak will not bow down. He stands stubborn and steady. Would sooner break than yield. My mind is like the willow; it flexes and springs. My heart is a knot of oak. Let them try to wound me. Let them try.

★

TILDA

Feet find firm ground, thudding into dry mud. Nike on hard earth. Breathe in. Breathe out. In on second left footfall. Out on second right. Lengthen stride, a couple of inches, no more. Pace, rhythm, run, step, the poetry of movement, of exertion.

Tilda loves to run. Tilda needs to run. Her style is loose, fluid, easy, but with power and purpose. And with every step she lets her mind overlay the beat with plump, juicy images—images she will gather together for when she returns home, a crop harvested from the amber autumn landscape through which she now runs.

All her best work has been created this way. Running charges her body and her mind. If she does not run, her thoughts become composted in her head, overheated and overcrowded, potentially fertile but unusable. Too much of a mass to be employed as separate artistic ideas. She turns off the woodland track and follows the slender path out of the trees and across the open fields.

Breathe, pace, breathe, pace. Heart strobing against ribs. Lungs efficient, trained, strong. Turf opening up, stretching out. The vista is uplifting. Lush, plush, velvet grass. Green is the color of life.

Her left foot hits a small stone and her mind is momentarily jolted out of its meditative state, her rhythm disrupted. Cold air stings the back of her throat. The day is cool but dry. The year is turning the corner away from summer, but the fertile rot of autumn has not yet taken hold of the landscape. The smell of fungi is just faintly detectable. The crunch of broken nutshells underfoot still only occasional. Another full moon will see shortening days and lengthening shadows.

Tilda's long legs stride over the meadow to the bordering hedge. She finds the narrow gap and squeezes through, her breath loud in her ears as she stoops to pass beneath the brambles. A squirrel dashes out and fluffs its way up the nearest trunk. Tilda picks a glossy blackberry and pops it in her mouth, then presses on, winding a now-familiar route between neglected hazel and blackthorn. At last she is in the open again, alongside the lake. A smile, as involuntary as a hiccup, curves her mouth. As on each occasion that she runs here she is reminded of how she is drawn to what she fears. Deep water is the nightmare of her childhood that she never grew out of. Nothing she can imagine would induce her to step off the path and break that silky surface. And yet she loves to run here, to be close, to be fascinated by the terror and the beauty of it. Laughing at her fear a little each time. Like the thrill of watching a horror movie. A reminder of what it means to be alive. And how close at hand death is. Any death. His death.

Mustn't think of it, not now. Mustn't falter. Quicker now. Up a gear. Legs and arms help each other. Calf muscles tightening, ignore that. Run, girl, run. Fleet. Fast. Foot sure. I see you, waiting water. I see you. One more mile. Turning for home.

Home. Though she forms the word in her head it is still hard to think of the cottage as anything other than the place where she lives. For, what is home? Surely more than a set of rooms, a roof, an address? Home suggests belonging. Suggests warmth, safety, companionship. Love. When Mat died, all those things died with him. So she returns to the cottage. It is the place where she lives now, has lived for a month, almost. It is the place where she must live. Where she will work. Where she will simply be. Home is too much to ask of it. For now.

She has not completely circled the lake today, but loops back, so that she passes St. Cynog's church and the Old School House a second time. The church is solid Norman, boxy and stout, built to withstand time and the damp air from the lake. Its graveyard is kempt and well-used, but even so there are some ancient tombstones which lean toward each other at angles that give away their age.

Like so many old men huddled in conversation after a few pints.

The Old School House is a building out of place. A nineteenth-century idea of rural perfection, with its mullioned windows, low eaves, and rustic charm. No longer a school, but the cozy home of an evidently proficient gardener. Tilda jogs on by, taking the footpath to the lane beyond. She crosses the narrow road that will be busy with visitors to the lake at weekends and leans into the steep slope to the cottage.

Ty Gwyn is a humble farmworker's cottage, positioned high on the hill and approached via a testing climb. It sits steady and serene, and ever-so-slightly smug, as if enjoying the view, and laughing just a little at the puffing people who struggle up to its blue front door. The whitewashed stone gleams in the autumn sunshine, sharp against the fading colors of the mountain pastures, while the slate roof is an exact match for the stone walls that mark the boundary of the garden. Breathing heavily, Tilda unlatches the wooden gate at the end of the bumpy track and secures it behind her against opportunist sheep. She reminds herself that one day she will enjoy tending the modest lawn and flower beds and recovering the neglected plants. One day. A path of uneven flagstones leads around the side of the little house to the back door, which she unlocks with the chunky key she keeps beneath a pot of thyme. The temperature inside is not noticeably warmer than out, but she is too warm from her run to mind. She raises the blinds to let the young day into the low-ceilinged room and places the filled kettle on the hot plate of the Rayburn stove. The aged beast heats so slowly it will take some time to boil. Already, in the few short weeks she has been here, she has formed habits. There is comfort to be had in the repetition of simple tasks. Reassurance to be found in ritual. Routine has a way of helping to make the new familiar, of filling the mind with purpose and, in doing so, leaving less room for unwelcome doubts and fears. She takes milk from the fridge and pours herself a glass to drink where she stands, leaning against the sink. She can feel her heart begin to steady after its exertion. The milk refreshes and chills her in equal measure. She glances at the kitchen clock and notices it has stopped.

Another dud battery. So much for value brands.

Tilda levers off her trainers and heads upstairs to the tiny bathroom. The shower is old and temperamental and coughs unpromisingly when she turns it on. She leaves the water on and pulls off her beanie and running clothes before deftly undoing the heavy plait that has restrained her hair. Steam begins to mist the mirror, so that her reflection is even more ghostly than usual. She wipes the glass and peers at the pale young woman who peers back at her. Swirls of vapor blur the image.

I could fade away entirely. It wouldn't require effort. Just grow a little fainter every day.

She steps into the shower and lets the hot water cascade over her. Her white-blond hair becomes slick, darkening to pewter. Her skin flushes. Now she is the most colored, the most opaque she will ever be. She should have come with instructions: To render visible, add warm water. Her mother once told her that when she had first held her baby daughter in her arms she doubted anything so fragile, so thin skinned, so seemingly insubstantial, could survive. But Tilda had shown her. Had grown tall and strong. Had proved her wrong. As in so many things.

By the time she has dressed, dried her hair so that it hangs straight and loose, a crystal curtain down her back, the day is properly awake. She takes her mug of tea and steps out onto the small patio of mossy flagstones beyond the front door. As always, the view is like a deep breath of pure oxygen.

This is why we bought this place. This.

The flat piece of garden extends only a few paces to the low stone wall that separates it from the dizzying drop to the valley below. The landscape falls away abruptly, so that Tilda is gazing down upon a thick copse of trees—still more green than gold— and beyond to the sweep of small fields that lay around the lake. The water is glassy and still this morning, undisturbed by any breeze or activity, save for the movements of the families of waterfowl that have made the place their home. Beyond the lake, the Brecon Beacons rise up, an ancient shield of mountains against the wild weather and people of the west. When she and Mat had discovered the cottage, had stood on this very spot for the first time, he had taken her hand in his and they had grinned at each other in silence. They had both known, in that instant, that this was the place they would start their married life together, would live, would work.

Except that fate had other plans for them.

Three rooks are startled by some unseen danger and fly from their perch, flapping and squawking. The sound is sharp and discordant and provokes in Tilda a fierce reaction. She is taken back to the moment of Mat's death with such brutal speed and vivid colors that she is forced to relive those heartbreaking seconds again. She is no longer in the garden beneath the September sunshine, but back in the car, Mat's car, on their way home from their honeymoon, rain lashing the windshield, watery lights of the motorway traffic flashing past. It was she who had been driving, she who had felt the pull on the steering wheel as the tire rapidly deflated, she who had slowed and halted on the hard shoulder. Mat had got out, walked around to examine the tire. She can see him now, in the cruel memory of her mind's eye, stooping to look in through the window of the driver's-side door. The rain, pouring onto Mat and the glass, has washed his features into a blur. He opens his mouth. He is speaking, trying to tell her something, but there is too much noise. She cannot hear him. He points, forward, and toward the edge of the road. She wipes the inside of the window with her hand, frowning to make him out, to make out what he is saying. And then, in a heartbeat, he is gone. Vanished. She has never been able to recall so much as the color of the truck that swept him away. She was told, later, that it had been empty, returning to the continent after a long haul, its driver not negligent, but not as vigilant as the speed and conditions required.

Tilda shakes her head, rubs her eyes, gasps against the pain of the vision, the renewed shock of the realization, the dragging weight of grief, all assailing her for the hundredth time.

Again. Again. And for how long? More than a year now and still every time as clear and as violent as the first. Will it never ease? Will it always be so unbearable?

She keeps her eyes closed for a moment longer. When she opens them the brightness of the sun makes her flinch. She tips the last of her tea into a pot of geraniums, turns on her heel, and heads back into the cottage. Once inside again she is reminded by the boxes in the narrow hallway, and in the sitting room, and indeed all over the house, that there is still unpacking to be done. She cannot imagine what she can own that fills so many boxes. She has not yet missed any of it, though soon she will be forced to search out a winter coat and some warmer bedding. The cottage is plenty big enough for her needs, but its rooms are small and cannot be used comfortably while the packing cases remain. Tilda knows it is a job she will not enjoy, but she will feel better for having done it.

Like a visit to the dentist, or filing your tax returns.

She can hear her father gently nagging her on both counts. Soon her parents will insist on visiting. To see she is all right. To make sure she has settled in. She must make sure every last book is unpacked by then, if her mother is not to shake her head and purse her lips.

Soon, but not quite yet. Today I begin work. Proper work.

The little barn attached to the cottage had been used as a garage for years before she and Mat became its owners. It had been a fairly simple matter to change the door—fitting in glass sliding ones to allow plenty of natural light—sweep it out and move in shelving, bins for clay and glazes, a Belfast sink, extra lighting, a small wood-burning stove and, of course, the kiln. Tilda regards the iron oven warily, wondering how long it will be before she is ready for a firing. In their old studio, before they had ever thought of moving out to Wales, so many times she and Mat had waited on tenterhooks for the thing to cool sufficiently to be safely opened, and to reveal the success—or otherwise—of the firing. At two thousand degrees Fahrenheit, the heat inside a potter's kiln would reduce a human hand to charred bones in a matter of seconds. Such terrifying temperatures are necessary to create the required chemical reactions within the glazes so that they are transformed from dull dust to colors of shimmering brilliance and mesmerizing intensity. Tilda is ceaselessly amazed by what transformations can occur amid that heat. The process of firing clay within such a domesticated dragon is a timeless and mysterious alchemy. Raw earth is slabbed from the ground, then worked and pounded, then teased and caressed, before being persuaded into forms to suit the craftsman's wishes. The piece is subjected to a biscuit firing, rendering it, as the name suggests, dry, brittle, and ready to receive its glaze. These magical powders mixed with water in a thousand variations—a pipkin more antimony oxide, a pinch less chrome, or a spoonful of cobalt to a measure of manganese—cling somberly to their given bodies, awaiting the crucial application of fire to bring about their chrysalis-to-butterfly moment. Every opening of the kiln door is an instant pregnant with expectation and hope, an occasion that will reveal the results of weeks of work and thought and art. It is a moment of exquisite agony every bit as intense as the heat inside the crucible itself.

Well, Mat, at least you are spared any more disastrous firings. I'll just have to face those on my own, won't I?

A part of Tilda believes it might, in fact, be easier. Easier not having to suffer Matt's disappointment as well as her own. She can recall all too well the occasions where they had both despaired of the wasted months of work when a glaze had failed to behave as it should, or a volatile piece exploded and wrecked the entire firing.

And now she needs to begin again. To find the pace and rhythm of her work, as sure-footedly as the pace and rhythm of her running. She rolls up her sleeves and takes a lump of earthenware clay from the green plastic bin beneath the sink. She drops the smooth, heavy clod onto the scrubbed wood of the bench and begins to knead it, letting the repetitive action of wedging the muddy substance steady her mind. Lifting and slamming the clay down with increasing force, she can feel the texture begin to change beneath her palms, the material begin to yield. Lift and slam. Lift and slam. Pummel, turn, scoop, lift and slam. Dull thuds of weight and effort growing louder with every focused, determined movement.

A Note From the Author

When writing *The Midnight Witch* I found myself in quite a dark and unsettling place, and I think the finished book reflects this. It is my dearest wish that readers will feel some of the same mystery and otherworldliness when they follow Lilith's story.

For me, part of the attraction of exploring the world of an ancient and powerful coven was to set it against the glamour and wealth of the upper classes in early-twentieth-century Britain. Not only did this set the darkness in stark relief to the glitter and frivolity of the aristocratic lifestyle of the time, but I felt it was symbolic of the way human nature can be so multifaceted.

Lilith is a witch who speaks to the dead, but she lives her public life in the light and privilege of her time and class.

She is beautiful, and surrounded by beautiful things, but she is a necromancer, who must deal with death and the dead in a very particular way.

She is a daughter, sister, and friend, and loves her family, but must put them second to her coven.

She is a young woman in love, but to be the lover of a Lazarus witch is a dangerous thing indeed.

Discussion questions follow

Discussion Questions

St. Martin's
Griffin

1. Who was your favorite character? Why?

2. Lilith had to make some hard choices regarding her family, her duty to the coven, and her love for Bram. Do you think she did the right thing? What might you have done differently in her situation?

3. Whose household would you rather have lived in, Lilith's or Mangan's?

4. Nicholas Stricklend was a very single-minded character. Do you think he was evil, or merely a man convinced what he was doing was right? Or both?

5. Who would you cast in the main roles of a film of *The Midnight Witch*?

6. The Lazarus Coven had a great responsibility to protect the Elixir and the Great Secret. Do you think they should have shared their knowledge of this gift to help people?

7. Lilith's life after the war was very different from the way she was brought up. In what ways do you think her life improved? How did these changes alter her relationship with Bram?